Grieving Daughters' Club

Endorsements

In a society and culture that shies away from dealing with painful emotions and grief, Andrea Bear's debut novel, *Grieving Daughters' Club*, offers a refreshing insight into how many women from varying backgrounds are able to come together and share their suffering in an authentic and candid manner.
—**Jeannie Ewing**, author, *From Grief to Grace: The Journey from Tragedy to Triumph*

Andrea Bear's novel, *Grieving Daughters' Club*, explores grief through a fictional but personal level via her character, Frankie, a woman whose mother passed away. Through Frankie's journey, the reader experiences the lows of loss countered by surprising interactions in an unlikely book discussion group that results in new friendships with heartwarming perspectives on life and loss.
—**Michelle Buckman**, award-winning author and editor.

Grieving Daughters' Club is a heartwarming story of love, friendship, loss, and personal transformation. Andrea Bear dives deep into the themes of mothers, daughters, and feminine friendship in a way that is sure to inspire you.
—**Danielle Bean**, author, *You Are Enough*

This novel is a beautiful story of grief, friendship, love, and hope. Andrea Bear's characters are poignant, heartfelt, relatable, and lovable. We all need the reminder that in grief, we do not walk alone. *Grieving Daughters' Club* will wrap you in warmth and offer much needed grief relief.
—**Brooke Taylor**, host of The Brooke Taylor Show

Andrea Bear's debut novel, *Grieving Daughters' Club*, gathers an eclectic group of characters dealing with challenging relationships, evolving friendships, and the struggle of grief. We come to know Frankie, Olivia, Scarlet, and the other members of the club as they discover the power of forgiveness and found community. It is an engaging tale of coming to terms with grief, an emotion that is often shunned by society in our desire to avoid pain and loss. The *Grieving Daughters' Club* will make you appreciate the women in your life that have shown up in the difficult hours.

—**Mary Lenaburg**, author, *Be Brave in the Scared and Be Bold in the Broken.*

Grieving Daughters' Club

ANDREA BEAR

A Christian Company
ElkLakePublishingInc.com

Copyright Notice

Grieving Daughters' Club

Cover Design: Melissa Solari, Derinda Babcock

Interior Design: Deb Haggerty

Editor(s): Sue A. Fairchild, Cristel Phelps, Deb Haggerty

PUBLISHED BY: Elk Lake Publishing, Inc., 35 Dogwood Drive, Plymouth, MA 02360, 2022

<u>Library Cataloging Data</u>

Names: Bear, Andrea (Andrea Bear)

Grieving Daughters' Club / Andrea Bear

394 p. 23cm × 15cm (9in × 6 in.)

ISBN-13: 978-1-64949-714-7 (paperback) | 978-1-64949-715-4 (hardcover) | 978-1-64949-716-1 (trade paperback) | 978-1-64949-717-8 (e-book)

Key Words: grief; book clubs; Catholic; wine; friendship; contemporary women; loss of parent, child, or spouse

Dedication

I dedicate this book in loving memory of my beloved mom, Debbie Kapina.

Mom, you were the first person to truly show me how to love, that forgiveness is powerful, and to always see the light amid the darkness. You inspired me in life and taught me even in death. Thank you for showing me what it means to truly have faith. You will always be in my heart. I love you, Mama.

Acknowledgments

There are so many people who influenced or helped me put this book together that it would be impossible to include everyone, but I do want to give recognition to those who helped specifically in the areas that helped advance the story.

First and foremost, I have to thank our Creator who guided me in my path of writing. This was not a path I ever considered or imagined, but it's amazing when you let God take charge of your life, he puts the right people in your path.

Courtney Vallejo, thank you for a chance encounter that August day. Your influence inspired me to take the first step toward my new journey in writing, which I never knew would lead me as far as it has.

I also want to thank my editors Michelle Buckman and Sue Fairchild who have taught me so much and encouraged me, but also gave honest and real advice. Thank you, Deb Haggerty, and the team at Elk Lake Publishing for taking a chance on me and bringing my story to where it is today.

A special thank you to Nick and Cristina Goucher as well as Cerissa Bear for your knowledge and explanation of police and medical terms so that details in my story were portrayed accurately.

I would also like to thank Maia Aguirre for encouraging me in my writing and listening to chapters as I read them over the phone while you were busy attending to things in your own life.

To Jonathan Collaco for your brutal honesty that I needed to hear to cover content and edits. As much as I didn't like it, I respect your feedback because it helped me grow as a writer.

I'd also like to thank my husband Kevin for all your support and for providing me the freedom to go down this crazy journey of writing that I so desperately needed to explore. Thank you for always being my supporter and my rock, and to my daughters Natalie, Emily, and Molly for loving and encouraging me. I know you have endured the storm of my grief, but you have also been with me along the way, and you have been my motivation to move forward.

And lastly a special thank you to the original Grieving Daughters' Club: Suzi Rosson, Sonny Tahkar, Melissa Solari, Felecia Benitez, Alicia Flores, Cassie Tahkar-Morse, April Rubio, and Lupe Graham. Thank you for allowing me to share parts of your stories. Your friendships have meant the world and hold a huge place in my heart. I hope that my readers will find a connection to one of you and help them in their own journeys.

Chapter 1

Grief never ends ... but it changes. It's a passage, not a
place to stay. Grief is not a sign of weakness, nor a lack
of faith. It is the price of love. —Elizabeth I

The smells of fresh basil and garlic permeated the house
as Frankie stirred the spaghetti sauce, her thoughts drifting
to her youngest daughter, Rena, who had begged her for
months to cook the special recipe. She skimmed over her
tattered cookbook, propped on a stand on the counter, and
reviewed the ingredients. Spaghetti was simple enough to
make, but the directions on how to make "Mimi's sauce"
pulled at Frankie's heartstrings. As she added the fresh
parsley and Italian seasoning, she thought back to the first
time her mother had taught her how to make the sauce,
finely chopping the onions and puréeing the celery and
carrots to conceal any "healthy" components.

"Don't forget to include fresh seasonings—that's
the key!" her mother, Barbara, would say, guiding
Frankie through the instructions. The recipe itself was
unassuming, but Frankie had loved calling her mother on
a whim to find out specific tools and techniques.

*Am I supposed to add stewed tomatoes or chopped
tomatoes?* She couldn't remember and the recipe didn't
specify.

She wiped away the tears welling in her eyes with the sleeve of her frayed sweater, another possession of her mother's.

I wish for just one moment I could hear her voice. She'd attempted the recipe several times over the past two years, but each time hesitation was met with sorrow and despair.

Tomatoes, parsley, basil, onion, Italian sausage. Something's missing. Frankie looked around her expansive kitchen island covered with the ingredients and supplies. Even using the inherited utensils—her mother's wooden spatula, cookbook, and beautiful lace apron—didn't complete her.

Lizzie, her ten-year-old daughter, walked into the kitchen and propped herself onto the barstool at the other end of the counter.

Frankie added some garlic salt and continued to stir the pot.

"Mom!"

She turned to see Lizzie's wide eyes locked on her. "What is it, hon? What do you need?" She wiped her eyes again.

"Are you ready to go shopping?"

"For what?"

Lizzie rolled her eyes. "For the party. It's next Saturday."

Frankie looked over her shoulder toward the kitchen desk. Sure enough, in large bold red letters, *Jeannie's 10th Birthday Party* was scrawled across the calendar. She shook her head. "We'll go next week before the party," she replied, hoping Lizzie would be fine with a later date.

Lizzie looked down at the floor. "But you promised we could go today."

"I did? Well, I, uh, have this sauce to make. I won't have time till later."

Lizzie furrowed her brows. "Okay, I guess if next week is easier." She crossed her arms on the counter. "Hey, is that Mimi's sauce?"

Frankie nodded.

"Tell me the story about the first time you made it for Dad. Mimi used to tell me and Rena and Candace that story, and I just loved it," begged Lizzie.

Frankie choked as she held back her tears. "Mimi" as her daughters had called her had been a great storyteller, and she knew how much her daughters missed the stories. She set down her wooden spoon and took a deep breath.

"Your dad and I had just started dating, and Mimi kept telling me the way to a man's heart was through his stomach. I wanted to impress him, so I invited him over for dinner one night to meet her and Papa and try out one of her special recipes. I was insistent that I make it myself." Lizzie smiled as she listened to Frankie reminisce. "The problem was it didn't turn out so well. I put in too much onion and garlic, and it tasted like a vampire's poison.

Knowing I might mess it up, your grandmother made a backup batch and pulled it out just in time. When your dad came for dinner he raved about how amazing 'my' spaghetti sauce was. Mimi beamed with pride and insisted he come over every Sunday for dinner, so I could make it for him. He eventually found out she'd made it instead of me, but by that time we were already engaged. Still, she would take the credit and tell everyone she was the reason your father fell in love with me."

Lizzie sighed and leaned back from the counter. "I love that story. Do you think you could teach me the sauce sometime?"

"I'm almost done with this one, but I think we could try again soon." She slowly turned up the heat, remembering she needed to bring the sauce to a boil. Her mother always said to "marry" the ingredients.

Lizzie frowned, conveying that was not the answer she was hoping for. "Well, could you tell me another story? A story about Mimi?"

Frankie turned away so Lizzie couldn't see her tears.

"Maybe another time. Why don't you make a list of gifts Jeannie might like?"

Lizzie huffed at her response. Frankie knew she was disappointing her. It wasn't intentional, but Lizzie didn't understand. How could she—she was just a child. Frankie needed all her strength to hold herself together. She took a deep breath, wiped her tears, and turned to place her arm on Lizzie's shoulder.

"Right now, I need to finish the sauce, but maybe later, I can tell you another story—you can decide which one."

Lizzie's brows clenched together as she crossed her arms. Instead of complaining more, she shuffled down the hallway.

Frankie yelled, "Hey, why don't we get a smoothie next week when we go shopping?" She hoped the idea would lighten Lizzie's mood.

Lizzie turned and looked at her from the other end of the hallway with the same scowled expression. "Yeah, sure, Mom. Sounds great." She disappeared around the corner of the hallway.

Frankie held the counter with both hands and took three deep breaths, trying to regain her composure. She had tried to cover her grief for her children's sake. She desperately wished Lizzie could comprehend the effort it took each day to make breakfast and lunch, let alone a special meal, all because she knew they needed her. Her hand shook as she reached for the tomato paste. *Let's*

4

pray this is the right ingredient. She was about to add a tablespoon when the phone rang.

Who could that be? Frankie had stopped putting in the effort to reciprocate friendships following her mother's death. After two years, the phone calls had dwindled.

She put down the spoon and walked into the living room to pick up the phone. Max insisted they keep a land line as he felt the girls were too young for their own cell phones. She reached for the portable phone and pressed the answer key. Her voice quivered as she placed her ear to the receiver. "Hello?"

A warm, robust voice came through the line. "Good evening! Is Frankie Waters home?"

"Speaking."

"Oh, wonderful! This is Bernadette Dalesandro from St. Seton Church. Most people call me Birdie. I'm calling ladies of the parish to join our upcoming book talk."

Frankie looked back toward the kitchen door, hoping the sauce wasn't burning. "Thanks, probably not this time. I'm not even sure what a book talk is."

Birdie chuckled. "Parishioners ask that a lot. It's similar to a book club except for its low commitment. I know how busy everyone gets these days."

"Thanks, but I'll pass."

Birdie seemed to ignore her reply. "Oh! And I almost forgot to tell you the most important part. The title of the book. It's a good one!"

Frankie didn't want to hear the title or keep talking to Birdie, nevertheless, she let her continue.

"It's called *Heaven's Entrance: An Encounter with Near-Death Experiences*, by Lloyd Rine."

"Did you say *death*?"

"Yes. It's about people who've gone to the other side and—"

Frankie hung up the phone. *Death and heaven*, two words she'd been trying to avoid without success. She crumbled to the couch, tears flowing, consumed with despair.

After a few minutes, she brushed away her tears and reached for the picture frame on the side table—a selfie of her and her mother sitting inside of Fizz's coffee shop on a random Saturday morning. She missed those ordinary moments sipping coffee and people watching. She traced over the silhouette of her mother's heart-shaped face. Pictures, lacy aprons, and recipes were only memories now.

"Frankie, the sauce is burning!" yelled her husband Max from the kitchen.

Frankie jumped up and dashed across the room to see blistering, oversized, red bubbles spraying onto the kitchen counter. She dodged the piping sauce as she turned down the heat and tried to stir what remained of the sauce, which had burned bits floating to the top.

Max grabbed a wet kitchen cloth and wiped down the front of the stove. "What happened?"

Frankie rubbed her splotchy, tear-stained face. "The phone rang."

"You're lucky I came in. This might not have ended well."

She lifted her shoulders. "Don't be so dramatic, Max. It's just a little burned sauce."

"This isn't the first time." He rinsed off the towel in the sink.

Frankie raised an eyebrow. "The first time? I've never burned our dinner before."

Max frowned as he turned to her. "This isn't the first time you've lost track of what you're doing."

She refocused on the sauce. "Don't be ridiculous."

"Frankie, it wouldn't hurt if you tried to make some changes, you know, about trying to move forward."

"You don't know what this is like."

"You're right, I don't. But you don't know what this is like for me, for the girls."

Frankie knew her despair had been hard for her family to endure. When her mother died, Frankie had removed herself from the world and even from her family. But Max had never before criticized her for it. He'd been very patient.

"I know how much you miss her. We all do."

He came up behind her, and she turned to bury her face in his chest as he tenderly wrapped his arms around her. She looked up into his brown eyes. "I never knew how much this could hurt."

Max took a long, deep breath. "I know you need her, but your family also needs you. Something needs to change."

"Dr. Jude says I'm making progress. I've been going for a few months now."

"I'm sure your therapist is great, but it might be good to take a new step. Get out of the house a bit. I don't want to come home to our house going up in flames."

She yanked the cloth from him and began scrubbing the counter, even the clean parts.

"I just figured it's been over two years and—"

She spun back around to cut him off. "Why do people feel the need to say that? Is there some special finish line that happens when the one-year mark hits? Now we've hit two and I'm just supposed to forget?"

"I didn't mean it that way."

"I know I have my moments, but I'm here, aren't I? I'm cooking dinner! Her dinner!"

"But you're not here. Your heart is somewhere else." Max ran a hand through his hair. "Remember the movie night you planned with the girls?"

Frankie remembered it all too well. Max had worked late and Candace, her thirteen-year-old, suggested they order pizza and make popcorn. *A girls' night,* she called it.

"What was wrong with the movie night?"

"Candace said you left and went into your room."

"I just needed a few moments to myself. I came back and watched the movie."

"Lizzie and Rena told me you just stared at the TV in a trance."

She shrugged. "Isn't that what you do when watching a movie?"

"When it's a comedy, you're supposed to laugh."

"I didn't realize how close you all paid attention."

Max shrugged this time. "It's hard not to see. You're different than you used to be."

She'd been sensing her family's concerns, but her husband's comments validated that feeling.

"What do you want from me? I can't go back and just rewind."

Max came close and squeezed her shoulders. "No, you can't but ..." He paused. "Listen, I don't have all the answers, Frankie. I just know you've got three girls who need you. Right now. Just consider it might be good to try something, anything, other than this." He kissed her forehead, then left the kitchen.

Frankie crossed her arms. She didn't want to put herself out there. What she wanted was to stay in the living room wrapped in her mother's sweater, embracing the photo in her cocoon of grief. Everyone expected her to move forward, to forget. He didn't understand. No one did.

She reached for the rag and continued to scrub the counter, wiping every crevice to remove the pain. She rubbed back and forth, pushing and tugging. The more grief and pain that came to the surface, the more intensely she cleaned. Frankie proceeded to continue aggressively in side-to-side motion until she caught sight of another picture, haunting her from the kitchen wall.

She gazed at last year's family Easter photo. Candace smiled awkwardly behind a mouth full of braces with her arms wrapped around Max, while Rena, only six years old at the time, stood in front wearing her pink paisley dress. Her dark brown curls enveloped her face as she smiled brightly looking down at the baby chicks in her hand. Lizzie, grinning from ear to ear, had her arms tightly wrapped around Frankie.

Everyone stood beaming in their Easter best, except for Frankie. Her eyes, hollow like an abandoned mine, were covered by a forced smile. She'd stared at this picture a thousand times and never noticed.

Shaking her head, she resumed wiping the counter, but her eyes kept moving back to the picture. Frankie continued this pattern until she had reached the end of the counter, and there was nowhere left to clean. She stood staring at the picture, then took a deep breath. Even if she wasn't ready for it, she knew it was time. She returned to the living room and called the last number on her caller ID.

"Hello?" answered the robust voice.

"Hi, Birdie. This is Frankie Waters. I'm sorry our conversation got, uh, cut off earlier. Can you tell me more about this book talk?"

Chapter 2

I came to realize that the commonalities of experiences far outweigh the differences. —Dr. Eben Alexander

Frankie fretted about the book talk all week, pacing around the house, cleaning, and dusting where no dirt existed just to expend her nervousness. "Old Frankie" would have been jovial and invited a few girls to join her, but "New Frankie" felt nervous and fearful. In the previous two years, the only real conversations she'd had were with her family and, occasionally, with her cousin Scarlet, who she assisted with her photography business to supplement income. Even conversations with Scarlet remained focused on business, never intimate or emotional. What if these ladies wanted to talk about feelings? Would she be ready to delve in? What if she didn't mesh with their personalities?

So many thoughts ran through her mind, she was tempted to forgo the whole situation. But each time she was ready to quit, the portrait of her daughters in their Easter dresses loomed in the back of her mind, and she would return to the beginning. "Low-level commitment." She said the mantra over and over to remind herself of her purpose.

Friday night finally arrived. She stared at herself in the mirror one last time, taming her crazy auburn curls and adding a touch of gloss to her lips. Then she took a deep breath and strode from the house, hollering a final goodbye to her husband and girls. She arrived an entire hour before the gathering even started and realized it would look bizarre to be so punctual. She circled the neighborhood a few times and even drove through a coffee drive-thru, killing some time by grabbing a latte. Ironically, the drive-thru had taken so long with customers ordering their "double- tall-complex-no-fun" mochas that by the time she had finally emerged from the line and picked up her order, it was close to 6:30. *So much for being early*.

As she pulled up to the address Birdie had given, she looked for something to tell her to go home. She started judging all the houses in the neighborhood. Birdie lived in a middle-class, well-to-do area that probably had homeowner associations to keep up the curb appeal. The only things distinguishing the houses from each other were the different flowers in the yard and the color of each home—tan, beige, and dark tan. Even with its continuity, Frankie couldn't find anything majorly annoying.

Enough stalling. She got out of her car and gradually walked toward the one-story beige-colored home. Cars sat all along the walkway. One car stood out to her—a metallic gold jaguar parked in front of Birdie's home with the license plate that read "LPRDLDY," which she guessed meant "Leopard Lady." She didn't know Birdie, but it didn't seem to be the style or expense she would attribute to a woman who ran a church ministry. What kind of women would be inside? She couldn't handle ladies who might judge her without knowing anything about her. She turned around and began walking back to her car until she heard a squeal of delight from behind.

"Frankie!" She spun around to see a familiar lady with champagne blonde hair calling her name in excitement. There was no escape now.

"Frankie? I didn't know you'd be a part of this group! Honey, how are you?" Lucile Durham, or Lucy, as everyone called her, walked down the driveway to meet her. The retired widow opened her arms to hug Frankie.

Frankie reluctantly reciprocated. "Hi, Lucy. I didn't know you'd be here either." And truth be told if she'd known, she might not have come. It wasn't that she didn't want to see Lucy, but it was more of a sting to see her. Lucy had been one of her mother's friends.

As Lucy held on, she furthered the hug with a big squeeze that was both heartbreaking and comforting all in one. When Lucy finally pulled back, she didn't let go, but rather held onto her arms and leaned back to stare at Frankie's face.

In Lucy's eyes, Frankie saw the reminder she had tried to avoid—Lucy, a woman the same age as her mother, was here. Her mother wasn't.

Friends had been a constant reminder that Frankie had tried to avoid. Now it was too late, and she would have to endure that reminder for at least six more weeks.

"I was coming out to check for Birdie, to see if anyone else was here, and lo and behold it's you! I haven't seen you since ... well, since the funeral. How ya been, honey?" Lucy asked, still half holding Frankie in her grasp with somber eyes.

Frankie had grown accustomed to the question, but it was never easy. She'd developed pre-rehearsed responses just so she wouldn't have to dig into the pain from within. "Just hanging in there."

In the months following her mother's death, there'd been plenty who tried to reach out and offer support. Frankie knew they meant well, but there wasn't anything they could truly do to take away the sadness. She had canceled one invitation after another, so much so that she'd offended a good number of people, but Lucy didn't appear to be swayed.

"I know I told you this at the funeral, but I'm sorry about your mom. I miss her still. She had the most memorable laugh." Lucy continued to keep her hands clutched around Frankie's elbows. "She was such a wonderful woman, and everyone loved her. She had a remarkable light about her."

Frankie was used to people offering variations of "I'm sorry" phrases by now. She never really got accustomed to hearing it, but after two years of "How are you doing?" and "It will get easier as time goes by," she numbed out and politely said "thank you" to avoid the constant conversation. She knew the book talk might discuss emotional topics, but that didn't mean she had to talk. She just needed a place to hang out.

"Thank you," Frankie said as she slowly pulled back and forced her emotions to remain in check.

"How's your father?"

Frankie lifted her quivering chin and replied. "Moving forward."

Lucy lifted her brows and let go of her arms. Frankie knew she'd gotten the message to end the discussion and immediately switched topics. "So, I should probably let you in on a little secret of mine. The main reason I joined this group is that they serve really good wine."

Frankie smirked at Lucy's confession.

"I mean, I'm here for the book and discussion too, but Birdie and her husband always buy top quality." She guided Frankie up the walk.

Somehow Lucy's admission lightened the mood as they drew closer to the house. "Oh, and you'll get to meet my neighbor Monica. You'll love her." They walked through the doorway and into the living room, where empty chairs and notepads were set up.

Frankie frowned. "Am I the first one here?"

"Oh, heavens no. We just like to do a little pre-gaming or 'pre-booking' before we get all serious," joked Lucy. She guided her toward the back of the house where noise began to echo.

Birdie's home was nicely decorated with burgundy throw pillows, antique furniture, and pictures of children spread across her mantel. A large hutch displayed wines and whiskeys from all over the world, which she assumed was what Lucy had been referring to when she'd said "pre-gaming." As Lucy guided her into an adjoining room, they entered the kitchen. As she'd promised, it was far from empty. Birdie's kitchen was quite expansive with chairs and counters and women spread throughout. Around the granite covered island, ladies hovered around the trays of cheeses and olives as they mingled and avidly poured glasses of wine and coffee. Frankie hadn't expected this to be so social or even so "spirited" considering it was a church group, but then again, she knew Catholic groups enjoyed a glass of wine or two.

Birdie stood across the room talking with two other women, but the minute she saw Frankie, she stopped and walked over to her. "Frankie?"

Frankie nodded.

"Oh, it's so good to finally meet you!" Without asking, she leaned in and gave her the heftiest hug, which was as jovial as her voice had been over the phone, and also more abrasive.

"Thanks." Frankie gasped, coming out of her grip. "It's good to finally meet you too." She heaved a sigh and smiled as she managed her first coherent sentence to Birdie.

"Would you like a glass of wine?"

"Uh, sure. I noticed your collection as I walked in."

"Oh that. The whiskey is my husband's, but I honestly only open stuff up when we have company. It's Lucy, here, who's the wine connoisseur."

Lucy tipped her glass toward Frankie as if reminding her about their conversation from earlier. Lucy had been known for taking wine trips and traveling to different vineyard regions of the world. She often said it was for business, but Frankie didn't actually know what Lucy did for a living.

"I guess I've been known to dabble here or there," Lucy said, winking at Frankie.

"You dabble?" prodded a tall, slender woman flashing a crooked smile as she approached them. "She's practically a sommelier with the number of times she's visited Napa. I should know, having to watch her house all the time." The woman nudged Lucy's side.

Lucy looked up and smiled, placing her hand on the woman's shoulder. "This is Monica, who I mentioned to you."

Monica reached out to shake Frankie's hand.

Frankie's eyes widened. Realizing she was in a room full of women who would want to talk with her, she faltered to lift her hand. She hadn't reacted quickly enough to the handshake and Monica noticed. Frankie felt her cheeks grow warm. She had been out of practice, and unlike Birdie and Lucy who had taken the heavy lead of introductions, Frankie felt awkward.

"Don't worry. I don't have cooties." Monica removed her hand and straightened her crisp-collared shirt.

Frankie felt overwhelmed by the rush of women around her. She'd been thrust into hugs and wine and small talk, all in such a short time.

"No, it's not you. I just—"

"Don't want to be here?" said Monica bluntly. "I could kind of tell from your frozen body language. No worries though. I get it. I got dragged here by Lucy *and* my mother. She thought it would be good for us to 'bond'," she said, holding her fingers up in mocking quotations.

Frankie offered a half smile, relieved to know she wasn't the only one with reservations. "I'm just trying to figure out what I'm doing here."

Lucy waved toward Frankie. "This is Frankie's first time at a book talk. Monica's too."

Frankie let out a sigh to ease her nerves. Monica twisted the string of pearls she was wearing around her pointer finger. She winked back at Frankie, and their relationship was off to a better start.

"My mother insisted this would be a place where she and I could connect and find new interests. She thinks I need an outlet. She's the one over there chatting it up with the olives." Monica pointed to a blonde-haired lady whose hairdo looked like it might not move if a tornado passed through. "Her name's Judith."

Judith was heavily engaged in a plate of cheeses and olives, unaware of Frankie or Monica's acknowledgment. Frankie guessed the woman to be in her late sixties, but she was dressed about twenty years younger yet incredibly tastefully with her cashmere sweater and leopard brown slacks. Even with her sophisticated decorum, her table manners didn't match her polished look. She stuffed one olive after another into her mouth.

A familiar voice rose from across the room. "Frankie?"

Frankie immediately recognized the petite redhead in an earthy, flowing sundress with flip-flops as Maisie Joyner, a bubbly and charismatic parent she knew through the girls' school. Maisie rushed over to her in a wisp of excitement. Frankie had just begun a friendship with her before her mother died, but then cut all contact as she had with everyone. Fortunately, Maisie was a bit of a free spirit, so she didn't seem to be the least bit upset.

"What are you doing here? I haven't seen you much around the school. It's cool though. Doing your own thing?" Maisie seemed genuinely happy to see her.

Frankie felt the knots ease in her stomach as Maisie talked. One thing she liked most was her low expectations. Maisie took away the need to appear to be more than she was.

"I'm still trying to figure that out, but I'm surprised I would find you in this type of group." To tell the truth, she was downright shocked to see Maisie. Frankie knew she was married to a Catholic but had never joined the church. Before her mother died, back when Frankie was active in her daughters' schools, Maisie had casually mentioned she'd attended various Christian denominations growing up, but nothing had ever "vibed."

"Yeah, my mother-in-law mentioned it, and you know, it looked pretty cool, and I'm like totally into learning about near-death experiences or any cosmic forces." She smiled. "But hey, now we'll get to see each other more!"

Frankie smiled back. She wouldn't prod any further, but one thing was for sure—there was no way she could be sad around Maisie.

"Excuse me, ladies," Birdie shouted over the din of conversations. "Why don't we assemble in the living room so we can get started."

Frankie followed Maisie and a dark-haired lady with a bright orange top toward the living room. Birdie plopped into an oversized recliner, while Frankie took a seat on the couch with only Maisie next to her. Monica and her mother, bearing a bottle of wine and a cheese plate, crossed the room to the extra chairs, with the brunette woman following them.

"Good evening, ladies!" Birdie exclaimed. "We have such a quaint group here this time. Normally we get a much, uh, more mature gathering of women."

Judith and Lucy both gave her the heightened eyebrow.

Birdie cleared her throat and continued. "But it looks like we have a bunch of 'youthful' faces tonight." Several women chuckled.

"My name is Birdie, and I've attended St. Seton parish for the past thirty-five years with my husband Raymond. I started doing these book talks a few years ago as a way to get to know other women in my parish. My kids are all grown, and this is a great way for me to be a part of my community," she said. "I used to run the Monday group, but I realized the ladies were all falling asleep. So, I decided to switch it up to Friday nights to make them a little livelier."

Frankie smirked at the thought of Birdie wanting more action from a book group. She imagined a bunch of blue-haired ladies complaining about the late start of 6:30. She couldn't imagine a Friday night group becoming unhinged.

"Let's start with a short prayer." She gestured to everyone to bow their heads, and Frankie followed suit, making the sign of the cross.

"Heavenly Father, we are here tonight to come together as a church community, to read, to share, and to grow closer to you. While our reasons may vary, we share a common goal—to know more about our eternal home. We ask that you bless us all along the way, and during these next six weeks, show us how all things are created for your glory. Help us to recognize you are with us on our journeys. In Jesus's name, we pray. Amen."

"Amen," everyone responded in sync.

Frankie contemplated the reference to a "journey." She wondered if this really would be a journey for her or just a roadblock, but it was too early to tell.

"So, let's take care of some housekeeping," said Birdie. "If you haven't already signed in, there's a sign-up sheet in the kitchen. Feel free to volunteer to bring a snack for any of the weeks that we're together. Also, any money owed for the supplies can be placed in the envelope on the coffee table. By the way, did everyone get a book?"

Frankie looked around and saw the stack of books on the coffee table, next to a manila envelope. Birdie signaled to Lucy who got up and passed one to each person, including Frankie. She'd slip some money in the envelope before the night was over. As she took the book, she looked over the cover and its title: *Heaven's Entrance*. Despite its slightly cheesy cover design with a golden gate and clouds seeping through the background, it didn't look like a horribly long read.

"There seems to be an extra copy. Are we missing someone?" Birdie scanned the group and glanced at her list. "Well, why don't we do introductions? Then I can figure out who's not here." She looked expectantly at a woman to her left. "Anyone care to start and share some special thing about themselves?"

Frankie noticed Monica's mother raised her hand very eagerly.

"Judith, go ahead," said Birdie.

"Hi, everyone. I'm Judith. Judith Raleigh." She turned a bit in her seat to face the group, very erect and poised. "I've been attending St. Seton's for a long time, and this is my third time in one of these groups. And Birdie's right—the Monday group always falls asleep."

Some of the ladies giggled. Now that she could get a better look, Frankie noticed Judith was the most polished of the ladies in the room. Her leopard scarf lay neatly over her shoulders. *That must be her sports car outside.*

"Why am I here? I love to read. I read mysteries, romance, biographies, cookbooks, even history books. And when I heard of the topic for this session, 'near-death experiences,' I thought to myself, 'Wow! What could be waiting for us on the other side?' There's never been a doubt there's a heaven, but that doesn't mean I'm not curious now. What's it like?" She sighed. "I lost my mom, Josephine Danette, over ten years ago, but not a day goes by that I don't wonder about her and what's happening. What's she doing? I've heard people say they have different experiences when they cross over, but I always wonder what she has experienced."

Frankie relaxed a touch, knowing she wasn't the only one who wondered. She too had looked up stories about heaven and near-death experiences just so she could feel somewhat connected to her mom but had never admitted to anyone how often she did this.

"So, I hope this book is going to give me answers. Plus, I like to share all this with my grandkids. They always think their gran has so much wisdom. Isn't that right, Monica?"

Monica smiled and rolled her eyes but didn't respond. Instead, she took the opportunity to introduce herself. "Hi. I'm Monica Stone. I'm thirty-six, and you've probably figured out that Judith is my mom." Judith looked at her with pride as she continued. "I don't know why I told you all my age. I guess I'm not sure what I should say."

"Just say what's on your mind," said Birdie. "Why are you here tonight?"

"Well, I'm not sure why I'm here, other than Mom wanted me to come along. She thinks I need to get out more."

"I thought we could spend the next few Friday nights together," Judith said. "There's nothing wrong with bonding."

Monica rolled her eyes again but continued. "Plus, I knew Lucy was going to be here, and she's my next-door neighbor, so it was great to hear I'd know a face."

"That's right. You mentioned that earlier," said Birdie. "It must be a joy being Lucy's neighbor."

"We're kind of like sisters."

"I'm her 'slightly' older, but fabulous, sister," joked Lucy, pretending to suck in her cheeks to look youthful.

Monica laughed at Lucy's expression. Ironically, Lucy and Judith were probably in the same age group, but it was her and Monica who appeared to have a strong friendship.

"Well then, if she's the 'slightly' older sister, that makes me thirty-five." Judith fluffed her hair.

"Mom, nobody believes you're thirty-five."

"Hush." Judith looked the other way, pretending to ignore Monica.

"Wait a minute," said Maisie as she looked at both women and pointed. "If you're thirty-six, how can you be thirty-five?"

A stifling silence settled over the room. Age was an issue most women knew not to go on about. Judith glared at Maisie as if she had asked an unforgivable question. Everyone waited for a response.

Judith cleared her throat. "Well, that's her problem." She crossed her legs and took a sip from her glass.

The room erupted in laughter as Judith smirked, and Monica became more annoyed. Maisie chuckled back as she realized Judith was not about to change her answer.

The moment was quite humorous, to say the least, but Frankie saw the annoyed expression on Birdie's face as the conversation got away from their actual purpose. She sat up straight and said, "Okay, fine. Judith's thirty-five and I'm a size ten. And can the 'slightly older but fabulous sister' introduce herself before someone else turns into a unicorn?"

"Lucy doesn't need an introduction after that," teased Monica.

Lucy blushed, but she conceded at Birdie's stink eye to move the introductions along.

"Well, everyone already knows that I'm fabulous." She winked at Monica. "So, let's see. I'm originally from Georgia, but I moved here to Tuleberg with my family when I was nineteen. You know, I travel a lot with my job and I've been all over the world, but I think what I like is these groups really center me. After my husband Don died five years ago, I knew I needed a connection with people. It was my church community"—she looked at Monica and Judith—"who kept me going."

Frankie remembered when Lucy lost Don. He had been so active in the community, everyone felt his loss. Unlike Frankie, Lucy hadn't isolated herself from the world. She appeared happy and involved.

Now there was more than just wine drawing Frankie to the group. So far, two people had already shared about their losses. She wondered if this was the criteria for joining the group, but she hoped she wouldn't have to talk about her own experience. Not yet anyway.

Frankie's attention returned to the conversation as Birdie moved things along.

"I love your perspective, Lucy. And you're right that we need to maintain those connections. Okay, we still have a few more people to meet."

Maisie perked up and signaled to Birdie that she wanted to be next. "Hi," she said as her soft red-bob danced around her face when she smiled. "My name's Marjorie Joyner, but it's a dreadful name so most people know me as Maisie. I like to help foster dogs, so my husband and I support animal shelters."

Frankie knew Maisie devoted herself to the shelter almost as a full-time job, on top of helping her husband's construction company.

"Hmm. What else about me?" She tapped her chin. "I'm not a big book reader, but my mother-in-law said I'd like attending because of the wine."

"I guess this group's getting a reputation," Judith chimed in as she lifted her glass.

Everyone laughed.

"But to be totally honest, I've wanted to form friendships with women where my children attended church and school. I figured this was a great way to meet people. My husband is Catholic, but he isn't super practicing. Still, I know it means a lot to my in-laws."

"There's no rule that says you have to be a Catholic to join this group," said Birdie.

"Oh, no. I think it's great. I'm still learning a lot, and if I listed all the different types of churches I've tried out, you'd flip."

"Thank you, Maisie, and I think those are great reasons," Birdie said.

Frankie thought it might be her turn next since she was next to Maisie, but the lady with the bright orange top seemed adamant to go next as she waved her hand in the air and scooted close to the edge of her seat.

"Hi. I'm Johnna Campos-Johnson," she said in a warm bubbly voice. Her deep mahogany skin radiated as she smiled, bringing a flicker of rosiness to her cheeks.

"Ooh, a modern girl," Judith said. "You kept your maiden name—progressive."

Johnna's cheeks brightened even further from the comment. "Well, actually, just like Maisie, I've altered my name a bit. You see, I hadn't expected to marry a man whose last name was so similar to my first name."

Frankie put it all together in her head. *Johnna Johnson.* The hyphenation made sense.

Judith covered her mouth as if she was choking on a chip once she figured it out. Monica nudged her mother to put her back in check.

"It's okay. You can laugh." Johnna continued to move her hands about in the air as she spoke. "I think it's hilarious. I was named after my dad, John, since I'm an only child ... he wanted a boy." She shrugged her shoulders and smiled. "I've always liked my name, but now that I'm married, being John twice just makes it confusing, so I broke it up."

Lucy winked at her. "Well, I think you are just double blessed by two men."

Her face brightened. "Gee, I never thought of it that way."

"And what brought you here tonight?" Birdie asked.

"I think my reason is much like everyone else's. I want to learn more and meet others." But then her smile dimmed. "Since I've already brought up my dad, I should also mention he's been battling skin cancer this past year, so I take care of him a lot. My mother mentioned I haven't done much for myself in a while and saw the announcement in the church bulletin, so I said I'd check it out. Plus I've always been fascinated with heaven." Despite the sad news, Frankie noticed Johnna kept the smile on her face.

Birdie nodded. "Thank you for being so willing to share that, Johnna, and we'll make sure to keep your dad in our prayers."

Hands clasped together, Johnna let out a sigh. "Thanks. I'll take as many prayers as I can get."

Frankie admired Johnna's ability to share so naturally. Her heart pounded as she considered what she should say. She was next. She had to say something, but what?

The doorbell rang, interrupting the discussion. An attractive brunette walked in without waiting for anyone to answer. She wore an oversized leather jacket and her purse synched tight to her hip—clearly younger than the current group of ladies assembled.

She pulled her dark curls out of her face and glanced around the room. "Is this the book talk group?"

Lucy waved her forward. "Come in, honey." The young girl closed the door behind her.

Birdie looked down at her list. "We were just making introductions. I'm guessing you must be Olivia Mazenod."

"Yep, that's me. Sorry, I'm late. I mixed up the numbers on the address." She scratched her head and clenched her purse tighter as she looked around the room making eye contact with some of the ladies. She had not moved past the front door area. Frankie wondered if this girl was having reservations about coming in as she had.

Birdie stood and stepped toward the new girl with a gentle grin. "Let me take your coat and help you get situated."

The girl pulled back and held her coat. "No! I mean, I'm a bit cold, so I'll keep my jacket." Then she stepped forward and took the empty spot on the sofa next to Frankie.

"Well, how about some wine?" Birdie asked.

"Uh, I don't drink, but I'd love some decaf coffee or a glass of water if you have any."

Birdie raised her brows. "Lucky for you I always make decaf in the evening." She nodded to Lucy who went into the kitchen.

Frankie scooted a couple inches over to make sure Olivia had enough room. She smiled gently at the young girl and then noticed a small mermaid sticker on Olivia's purse.

Frankie lowered her voice and said, "I like the mermaid sticker. My daughter Lizzie has them all over our house."

Olivia took a deep breath, and her shoulders relaxed. "Thanks, so does my daughter."

Frankie smiled back. Olivia seemed more at ease after the comment. Lucy returned with a tray filled with a mug, a pot of decaf coffee, and an assortment of cream and sugars. Lucy placed the mug on the coffee table and poured the piping hot decaf while Olivia added four sugar cubes.

Judith spoke up. "Why don't you tell us a little about yourself, Olivia? We were just doing introductions, telling each other what drew us here tonight."

Olivia looked around a little nervously as she stirred her coffee with a spoon. Frankie had dreaded her own introduction but was glad she didn't have all eyes drawn to her the way Olivia now had.

"Uh, there's not much to tell, I guess. I'm a single mom. My daughter, Cameron, is eleven."

"Oh, you're a young mom. Geez, you can't be older than twenty-four!" Judith exclaimed. "What are you doing here?"

Olivia blushed and stared at the floor.

Monica glared at her mother. "Mother!"

Lucy tried to smooth it over. "I think what she means to say is that you seem too young to want to hang out with an old group like us."

Judith smirked. "Speak for yourself. I'm thirty-five, remember? But still, I guess we're surprised that someone your age wants to chat with us on a Friday night."

Olivia fidgeted with her spoon clinking in her mug as she stirred. "I'm twenty-six, so yeah, I had my daughter kind of young."

Monica nodded. "I'm sorry for my mother's comment. You don't owe her an explanation. If it's any consolation, I was a young mom too. My daughter Regina is eighteen now."

Oliva smiled timidly and stared back, wide-eyed.

"It's okay. I moved here to Tuleberg about a year ago and I love books. I guess I just wanted to meet other women too. I don't really care what age everyone is."

Frankie was impressed with how Olivia handled herself. It must have been tough to answer questions to a room full of strangers, let alone acknowledge she was a young mother. Frankie sat up a little straighter in her chair knowing that her introduction was next, as Birdie motioned to her to finalize the introductions.

"Well honey, you're the last one. Don't hold your breath."

Frankie exhaled and started. "I'm Frankie Waters." Okay, that part was out, but what else should she say? She was grateful for Olivia's delay, but she hadn't really thought of what she wanted to share. Unlike Olivia, she wasn't as quick to cover up whatever secrets she meant to hold back. And tonight didn't seem the right time to tell them her whole story—that she felt like she was dying on the inside, saddened over the loss of her mom, and only attending to try to find her way back to life. She couldn't admit anything.

So instead, she plastered on a fake smile and said, "I'm looking forward to reading a new book about heaven." It sounded lame, but it was as good as she could come up with as she sank back on the sofa.

Almost intuitively, Lucy intervened. "I noticed there's a group of us that have lost loved ones." She glanced over at Frankie. "It almost seems coincidental we're all here to learn about heaven."

Frankie looked away, realizing Lucy knew her presence here was more than just about reading a book.

"Yeah, must be a coincidence," added Frankie, unable to hide from Lucy.

Judith leaned forward. "Seems like a coincidence, right? But there's no such thing as a coincidence." Judith stared around the room and her eyes ended on Frankie with intense seriousness. "When people just happen to talk about the same topics or just happen to have the same experiences, those aren't coincidences. There's a purpose for it. We're all here for a shared reason, so my guess is there's a bigger reason you're here too, Frankie."

Frankie sat in the ensuing silence repeating the phrase in her head. *There's no such thing as coincidence.* How could Judith know she was hiding something? She said nothing yet felt Judith could see everything about her.

"Even if there were no such thing as coincidences, there is such a thing as getting started," Birdie interjected and started pointing out the parts of the book that everyone needed to read.

But Frankie wasn't listening. She wondered if there really was a reason for her to attend. She knew coming to the book talk was an effort to work past her grief, but the introductions alone had been enough for her to wonder what she was getting into.

Birdie pointed to the section of the book that they were covering, then glanced around the room. "Since we haven't started the book yet, let's just begin with some icebreakers. What do you think heaven looks like?"

Chapter 3

The irony of grief is that the person you need to talk to the most is no longer there. —Unknown

That night when Frankie got home, the house was empty, but she found a note from Max on the kitchen counter. *Went to get ice cream. Should be back by 9:30.* It was already a quarter-past nine. Normally, Frankie would have loved the rare occasion of having the house to herself, but the quietness felt a little too consuming. If her family had been home, she would have had a good excuse not to read, but there was nothing else she had to do, so she might as well try to see if this book was worth reading. She had already pushed herself out of her omfort zone, so it made sense to go one step further.

She walked into the living room then sat in her favorite tan recliner. She opened the book and stared at the first page: *Chapter One. What's an NDE?*

Near-Death Experience, maybe? To her, this bit sounded like background information, which didn't really interest her, but she knew the group would discuss this chapter at their next meeting. She flipped through the pages, perusing the chapters until she came to the section about survivors of NDEs seeing a bright light.

So many questions about the moment of her mother's death had crossed her mind over and over. What had it been like for her mother at that moment where she entered the other side of the veil? What was she doing now? Had her mom seen Jesus face to face? Was anyone waiting for her when she arrived ... in heaven? So many questions. It was hard to sort through all the feelings. She wanted answers, but there was no one around to fill her insatiable quest to know. The biggest question—would she see her mom one day—was also the biggest unknown. The more she read about survivors seeing beautiful lights full of love and unblinding brightness, the more she wanted to know, and the more frustrated she became at the lack of firm answers.

Frankie put down the book, which wasn't helping assuage her feelings. Instead, anger rose inside her. "Was this the right move, joining a book club? Or talk? Or whatever they called it?" The ladies were nice and all, some a little more direct than others, but was she ready to go down this path? What other choice did she have? Did her family know she was trying? They expected her to be back to normal, but what was normal now that her mother was gone? And yet staring out the window or doing mindless tasks wasn't helping her get through this grief either.

A mixture of feelings felt like knotted ropes inside of her. One minute she sank with sadness, the next minute her soul blazed with anger and frustration, then she felt emptied of everything, like a deflated balloon. Her only constant was her frustration.

Low-level commitment. I don't have to read if I don't want to. I just need to show up to the meetings. Maybe just keeping to this small goal could serve as a sign of her progress. She put the book in the drawer of the side table next to her recliner and pulled out her cell phone. She needed a distraction with little emotion and lots of energy. She called her cousin Scarlet.

Scarlet Bedford was a blonde, high-strung, over-worked photographer with lots of high-profile clients in the Tuleberg area, but she never made time for hanging out with friends. Scarlet always stuck to business, which was a good way for Frankie to take her mind off things.

Frankie had worked for Scarlet off and on over the previous year to help supplement income with easy work she could do at her leisure. The extra income had helped with home finances too, since Frankie had quit her teacher's aide position to stay home. Working for Scarlet was a great alternative that gave her some freedom. But Scarlet's schedule had gotten busier, and she needed more than just Frankie's part-time assistance.

Scarlet picked up on the second ring and was very short with her. "Hey, what do you need? I have an early shoot for the children's hospital tomorrow morning."

Despite being younger, Scarlet had the mentality of an eighty-year-old, always sticking to early bedtimes. She came across as curt, especially since she didn't like talking on the phone, but Frankie never took it personally.

"Honestly, I was surprised you picked up, but I took a chance. I just wanted to see if you need help on any paperwork." Frankie paused. "Wait a minute, I thought you didn't like kids?"

"I never said I didn't like kids. I just don't want any of my own, and I try to avoid being around them."

"Do you remember the set of twins you made cry?"

"That's because I wasn't prepared, and all the more reason I need to get ready. Besides, this is different. I know for a fact the organizer for the gig is married to Mayor Hegland, and if this shoot goes well, I could be a photographer for other big events."

"You're so committed to your work. I wish you had time for other relationships that didn't just involve digital editing and proofs."

"Working *is* a committed relationship," argued Scarlet. "Besides I don't have to worry about attending to emotional needs or worrying about another person's life. Just refocusing my lens is enough commitment for me."

"Well, maybe you'll meet a single dad at the shoot tomorrow, and it'll change your mind."

Scarlet ignored Frankie's comment. "Hey, didn't you go to that book thing tonight?"

Frankie knew her cousin was being deliberately evasive. "Yeah, I'm not sure if I want to keep going though."

"Did they serve wine?"

"Actually, they did."

"Well, heck, stay for the wine at least. You can get a few drinks out of it."

"I did actually like some of the ladies in the group. I thought it was interesting that half of them had lost a parent or a spouse, though I probably wouldn't have joined if I'd known that."

"So, it's a grieving daughters' club?"

"A what?"

"You said you're reading a book about near-death experience and it's about grief, right?"

"It's not about grief, it's about NDEs," she said, using some of her new lingo from the book. "At least I don't think it's about grief." Frankie hadn't considered that maybe some of the woman had joined for the same reasons she had. None of them had actually said they were grieving, but then again, she hadn't either.

"Well, keep going for the wine and maybe you'll find out."

"Maybe you could come with me the next time I go?" Having Scarlet there would help her feel more comfortable, but she doubted her cousin would take the time from her busy schedule.

"Listen, no offense, but I don't have time. I barely have a free moment with what I'm doing right now. My business is just starting to get prospective clients, and at this rate, I still need to find an extra person to help with my billing and photo editing. But let me know how the wine is."

She knew Scarlet would probably decline, but she had to try. "Call me tomorrow after your shoot?"

"I will. Pray I don't lose my cool with sick kids. We're shooting a calendar with children from the hospital. I've got to get through twelve months, but man, will the exposure be worth it. By the way, I'll need you to help me send out the billing for last month's sessions. Can you do that on Monday?"

"Sure."

"Great. Gotta go. Night!" she hung up the phone before Frankie could even reply.

Scarlet's conversation hadn't helped much, other than to reinforce that wine was a common denominator. It wasn't a wine club. But was Scarlet right? Could others be dealing with grief too? The ladies seemed happy and social, while Frankie felt none of those things. But she knew everyone handled grief differently.

She glanced at the clock—9:35 p.m. Frankie figured Lizzie and Candace had talked their father into an oversized banana split. She looked around the living room. The silence was all too consuming. Maybe some television would help. She scanned the room for the remote, but it was nowhere in sight. Lizzie was notorious for hiding it from her sisters so she could be in charge of what they watched. The last thing Frankie wanted to do was rummage through the gray couch pillows to find it.

She had no one else she could call. The only comfort was the soft dim lights from her Victorian lamp that left her heavy-eyed. She didn't want to fall asleep—she wanted to talk with Max. He might convince her she was on the right track. With nothing left to distract her, she kicked up her feet to lounge back in the recliner. She took a deep breath and pulled the book from the drawer and decided to go back to chapter one. As she scrolled through the first few pages, her eyes began to get heavy and she had almost nodded off when the phone rang ...

She sprang straight up, wondering if Scarlet forgot to tell her about the invoices she needed to fill out too.

"Okay, I promise I'll get the invoices done," Frankie said half alert, trying to cut Scarlet off.

"Hi, Frankie."

"Oh!" Frankie said, surprised by this caller. "Hi, Mom."

"You didn't call me today. How was your book talk?"

"I'm sorry I got busy, but yeah, it was actually pretty good," said Frankie. "Still trying to figure out whether it's my thing or not."

Her mother's voice was soft and reassuring through the phone. "I'm sure you're going to be fine."

"Thanks, Momma. By the way, don't you have some appointments lined up tomorrow?"

"Do I?"

"I think so."

"Well, can you take me?"

Frankie smiled. "Sure, Momma. You know I always do."

"Your dad and I are watching a movie right now, but I can't remember it."

"You're watching a detective who discovered a murder that was fifty years old. You and dad love those dumb crime shows."

"Oh yes, you're right. I do. Was I supposed to ask you something?"

"Yes. You wanted to ask me when I'm going to bring the girls over."

"Oh, that's right. When?"

Frankie visualized the calendar and the week's plans in her head. "Maybe tomorrow, Momma. I know they have some weekend activities, so I'll try to figure out when I can get them there."

"Okay, because I miss seeing my girls."

"I know. They miss you too. I'll try to bring them over. And I'll bring you a coffee too," Frankie promised.

"Oh, okay. That sounds good. You know my drink, right?"

Frankie scratched her head. "Iced, sugar-free, vanilla soy latte with cinnamon on top."

"Is that my drink?"

"Yes, Momma, that's your drink."

"Okay, good."

"And remember that next week we have to go to the hospital so you can get your chemo treatment."

"Do I have to?"

"Yes, Momma. I'm keeping Thursday open just for you, remember?"

"I think I remember. Was there anything else I wanted to talk about?"

"No, I don't think so."

"Okay. Well, then, I'm going to hang up, honey."

"No, Momma. I still want to talk to you."

"Just call me, Frankie. I'll be home ..."

Frankie felt a moment of panic before feeling a gentle shake of her shoulder and her husband's voice as if calling from far away.

"Frankie. Frankie!"

She woke abruptly to see Max standing over her and gently shaking her shoulder.

"No. I still wanna talk. No. Stop!"

She looked around a little dazed for a moment before she grasped reality again. The sporadic dreams always seemed so real and always left her feeling even more unsettled. She tried to interpret the dream but didn't know what to make of it. Her mother had suffered memory loss, due to brain cancer, so her dream conversations often reflected those times.

Her husband helped her to her feet. "Go to bed, babe." He motioned her to the bedroom.

He had been so patient, for so long, so helpful in her struggles. On the days when she didn't want to talk and withdrew from the world, he let her be and do whatever she needed. She felt guilty a lot of the time for being so withdrawn, yet so grateful he allowed her to stay in her warm cocoon of sorrow. She knew he was hurting too, but it wasn't the same pain she felt. Hers was deeper, she was sure of it. No one could feel as forlorn as she did. When they finally reached their room, Max helped her to her side of the bed. Her thoughts were still disoriented, even though she was partially awake, but she prayed her mother would reappear in her dreams.

She slept soundly, and her mother didn't reappear. Disappointment set in as she longed to see her mother's face again. Instead, two big brown eyes stared at her as she awoke the next morning. Rena, her youngest daughter, stood next to Frankie's bed peering at her with great intensity. Frankie sometimes thought Rena could see shadows of her mother. She often found her playing in her room without any companions, having tea, or playing her dolls with Mimi. Her kindergarten teacher had even commented at one point that Rena talked about her grandmother daily.

"Morning, Momma," Rena whispered.

"Hi, sweetie."

"Are you sleeping, Momma?"

"Oh, no. I'm just getting up," she replied sweetly but half-sarcastically. Based on Rena's usual schedule, she guessed it was around 7:30 a.m.

"Oh, good. Can you turn on the cartoons for me, then?"

"You don't know how to turn on the TV?"

"I can't find the remote, and I just like when you're up with me while I watch them."

Frankie rubbed a thumb across her daughter's cheek. "Sure, Sissy. Just give me a second."

Frankie pushed back the covers and grabbed her robe while Rena waited patiently. Max gave out a ruffling snore as he rolled over on his side, unaware of their presence. When she was ready, she grabbed Rena's hand, then shuffled from her bedroom into the living room to turn on the TV. Despite her lack of effort the night before, she easily found the remote wedged between couch cushion seats blocked by a teddy bear with a note covered in tape that read.

Congratulations! You found the remote, but next time won't be so easy.

Frankie grinned as she imagined all the effort Lizzie must have taken to hide it. She turned on the television to Rena's favorite princess cartoon, keeping the volume to a low murmur as the rest of the house was still asleep. Fortunately, the living room was connected to the kitchen, allowing for an immediate beeline to the coffee pot, one of her regular routines of the morning. Frankie had a fondness for coffee as most tired mothers might, but each time she made a cup, she thought of the many coffee shops and memories she'd shared with her mom. They had frequented a few regular spots, one place in particular called Fizz. Back when her mom was healthy, they would sit for hours talking, ordering iced espresso drinks, and people watching for hours, making up stories about the unknown faces that walked by.

She heard the coffee pot percolating as it slowly filled the carafe. Having her morning cup always brought her back to these memories. Frankie still frequented coffee houses, but it felt different, and she rarely sat around as much as she did back then. She avoided Fizz altogether because the memories were too painful.

She poured from the pot of simmering coffee into her favorite blue mug and drowned it with cream. She turned to look out the kitchen window filled with potted flowers. Keeping her mind focused seemed harder these days. Her mind wandered to the book talk, the dream, and what kind of impression she was making as a saddened mother. It was too much to think about.

She hadn't called her father all week, but the connections when she did were spotty considering his proximity to the aurora borealis. Unlike her need to be a recluse, Frankie's father, Rudy, hadn't curled up from the world when his wife died. Promising her he would continue their love of travel, he had journeyed to Alaska to see the northern lights, one of the many destinations on his check list. Frankie's parents had a love of travel, but when the cancer got too aggressive the only places they could travel were the hour and half visit to San Francisco to see the neurooncologist.

Frankie pulled out her cell phone, surprised to see she'd missed a call from him. She plopped into one of the barstools along the kitchen island and played back the message he'd left.

"Francesca, I know its kind of early, but the sun hardly sets up here this time of year, so my sleep patterns are off, but you'll never guess what I saw today. A pod of orcas came up to our ship! Your mom would be ecstatic! I can't talk long, the tour is taking us to the Icy Straight Point so I need to get ready, but I wanted to let you know before I lost reception. Only a few more weeks and I'll get to see those beautiful lights. Tomorrow the ship docks at Juneau and I'll try to give you another call. Love you, Frankie Girl!"

Frankie smiled as she heard her father's high-spirited voice. Bittersweet emotions leaped over her heart knowing her father was moving onward, fulfilling her mother's wishes while she was struggling to walk forward with her own. She dialed the number back and, just as expected, the call went immediately to voicemail. "Hey Dad, hope you're having a great time with the orcas. Hope you're behaving for the tour guides and not going off on your own. Call me again when you get reception."

She hadn't told him about the book group. If she quit she wouldn't have to own the responsibility. And she didn't want to worry her father anymore than she had. Her conversations were always upbeat, to avoid letting him see her sorrow, unlike the sadness she openly displayed to Max and the girls. She continued in the silence, still in her uncomfortableness. She would try him again later or wait till he called through again.

She decided scrolling through social media might serve as a good distraction instead. Scarlet had already posted some early morning pics from her hospital shoot of little girls hugging teddy bears and young patients with firetrucks. So far no one in the photos looked like they were crying, and Scarlet seemed happy enough or else she wouldn't have posted anything.

She sipped her coffee slowly as she continued to scroll, seeing lots of summertime photos of friends and acquaintances sharing happy moments of vacations and weekend plans. Phrases like *#weareblessed, #familyfun,* or *#makingmemories* filled her feed. These types of posts annoyed her. *Don't they know not everyone is so perky and happy all the time?* Sure, people posted a variety of not-so-pleasant things—political topics, bad reviews of a restaurant, and even prayers for loved ones in life-threatening situations, but why were sad moments so limited? If someone did post a sad moment, it drew unnecessary attention, which Frankie felt made it worse. She knew these kinds of posts made people uncomfortable. But what if people were comfortable enough to talk about the hard stuff without trying to cover it up with warm fuzzies? Maybe, just maybe, it wouldn't be so hard. Still, most people liked to hide their despair.

Maybe her dad was hiding his and she didn't know it. Her neighbors across the street posted pictures of outdoor barbequing, but she thought they really should post pictures of law enforcement showing up to handle family arguments for the umpteenth time. *#copswerehereagain #yellingmatch.* Or the school librarian who posted images of family literacy day, when she should post about her lack of trust in her husband. *#familydisfunction #dealwithmyhusband.* Frankie's profile, instead of a family Christmas photo, would show her looking out the window in sadness with the hashtag *#dyinginside* or *#griefdreams.* But of course, if she did, she'd be met with sympathy and limited solution.

She had to get out of her head but, for whatever reason, she continued to scroll. She had just switched to the sales section of her news feed when a friend request came through from Monica, one of the ladies from the book talk. Frankie hesitated to respond. Maybe it was too soon to let this new person into her world, and yet she also thought about how rude and awkward it might be the following Friday if she didn't accept her friend request.

She hit the confirm button. Immediately, Monica responded by sending Frankie a private message.

> Hello, friend. This is Monica. Thanks for the friend add. I was hoping I could get your number so I could put you in a group message with the other women. I know that's surprising coming from me, but I told my mom if I'm going to be in this group, then I'm going to do a few things my way.

Frankie read the message and again hesitated, unsure what to say in reply. Saying yes was a definite commitment, but if she said no, she would certainly push out the world. Either decision felt uncomfortable. Still, she liked Monica, and she was the first to admit that being a part of the group was not her first choice.

She took a leap of faith and made a short reply.

> That's a great idea, Monica. My phone number and other contact info is attached.

A half hour later, she received a text from Monica. As promised, she had conveniently put everyone into a group text so they could easily communicate with each other. Frankie expected Monica to send a message about the book, but instead she texted:

> **MONICA:** I get these great messages on my desk calendar and wanted to share them with you girls from time to time.

She followed the message with a screenshot of a quote.

> Self-improvement does not come through self-effort. It comes from dependence on God. From faith in him. He allows us to make an effort, but it must be an effort made while depending on him, not effort apart from him.

Frankie hadn't expected to receive this kind of message, let alone from Monica.

She reread the quote and reflected on the words. *What an interesting thought.* Was her personal effort to get out of grief her own doing or was God helping her along? She didn't know the answer, but she knew she had to at least try to do her part.

Frankie's thoughts were interrupted by a buzzing sound outside the window. She got up from her barstool and returned to the window. Several bees circled the snapdragons in the flowerbox. Frankie's mom had loved bumblebees and would collect little tchotchkes of bees as decoration. She shook her head, wondering if the bee's presence was a sign.

As she finished pondering the quote and the bees, Lizzie strolled into the kitchen.

"Morning, Mom." She slapped her hand on her head. "Ugh, you found the remote. I thought I really had it this time!"

Frankie chuckled. "I'm sure the next one will be just as good. What are you doing up so early? Everyone else is still asleep."

"I got up to get ready for Jeannie's birthday party, remember? She's having it at the Jumpy House Emporium. I need to get ready."

Frankie had made a point to remember. "That's not till one o'clock. It's barely eight-thirty."

"I know, but we haven't bought a gift, and I wanna be super prepared and cute for the party." Lizzie stared at her with wide eyes, pleading. She loved shopping and surprises and parties and giving gifts.

Frankie sighed and tried to keep the irritation out of her voice. "Well, I think we've got a little bit of time, Lizzie. We'll go to the department store in a couple of hours—when it opens—and then you can pick something out."

Lizzie's smile vanished and she seemed to deflate. "Ugh. I guess."

"Why don't you read for a while?"

"I'd rather clean my room, Mom." Lizzie moaned dramatically as she walked into the living room to join Rena for cartoons.

Frankie topped off her cup of coffee and decided she'd had enough social media for one morning. This was the perfect time to do some writing in her journal. She went into the living room and pulled out a light blue, leather-bound book from the drawer on the side table. During the past year, she had written thoughts about life. Most of what she wrote had been bleak, sad hashtag moments, but journaling was an escape that surprisingly gave her comfort, and she didn't have to bestow the burden on anyone. This morning, however, she took a different approach. She copied the quote Monica had sent her. Something new. Frankie smiled—a genuine smile—as she looked at the words on the paper.

A few hours later, Frankie and Lizzie hopped into her Highlander and drove to the store. Frankie would have much rather picked up a gift card to give as a gift, but knowing her daughter loved looking through the aisles for the perfect present, she decided to indulge her. Frankie's mom had also been a shopper. As Lizzie shopped, Frankie's spirit lifted knowing that her mother would have enjoyed being there, and, therefore, she should make more of an effort to join Lizzie's excitement instead of thwarting it.

"Mom, they have cute scarves over here. Let's check them out!" Lizzie screeched as she pointed to a mountain of scarves on a sale rack in the middle of the accessories section.

As they sifted through plaids and colored prints, Frankie spotted her neighbor Mallory walking through the same aisle.

"Well, hello, Frankie," Mallory said. "What brings you out today?"

She smiled and offered the simplest of replies. "Lizzie's getting a gift for a party."

"I heard you signed up for that book club at St. Seton's."

Frankie shrugged. "Uh, yeah, I guess." *It's a book TALK and how the heck did she know I signed up?* Somehow, Mallory seemed to know everything about everybody. Frankie needed to cut the conversation short before the busybody tried to get more information out of her.

"I think it's great that you're getting involved. I've been wondering when you'd start coming out of your shell to get back on track with the world. You can't grieve forever, ya know." Mallory smiled, but her voice seemed laced with a mocking tone.

"Thanks for the great advice." Frankie gritted her teeth and grabbed Lizzie by the back of her shirt, stopping her in her tracks so they could move to another aisle.

"Mom, I'm not done here."

"I think I see some mini backpacks that might be more Jeannie's style."

Lizzie relented and followed her, leaving Mallory behind.

These were the moments Frankie hated. What did it matter if she were still grieving? Mallory didn't know how she felt. No one did. One thing she'd learned from Dr. Jude was that everyone handled grief differently. There wasn't a right or wrong way, and that gave her comfort. What it didn't do was explain to the world what she needed, nor did it block others from passing judgment.

By the time Frankie and Lizzie finished their shopping, it was close to party time. Lizzie settled on the mini backpack purse and a brightly colored gift bag and tissue to wrap it in. Frankie used her GPS to locate the Jumpy House Emporium, which the map showed as being located in an industrial part of town. Lizzie stuffed the backpack and tissue into the gift bag as they drove in the direction of the party. Frankie thought it odd the location was in the industrial district, but, then again, where else would hold massive indoor-inflatable bouncing forts? They moved into an older part of Tuleberg and were stopped by a railway crossing.

"Oh, the train cars! I can't wait to see how many are on this one. One, two, three, four ..." Lizzie began counting the freight cars that flew by.

Frankie gazed toward the frontage road lined with mom-and-pop businesses near the railway. There were rows of storefronts in an oversized parking lot—a car stereo installation shop, a welding shop, and even a printing company. From an angle, she noticed the start of second row of businesses directly behind the frontage stores. She imagined there must be other industrial warehouses out of view that carried further back in the massive lot. How many times a day did trains roar by, while businesses adapted to the bellowing sound, Frankie wondered.

"Twenty-six, twenty-seven, twenty-eight ..." Lizzie continued as Frankie curiously looked around trying to pass the time.

Suddenly, she caught sight of a familiar face coming out of the plastics and welding warehouse, through the narrow alleyway between the industrial buildings—Olivia from her book talk. The young girl exited the shop and proceeded to a beat up, little pickup truck just east of the building in a narrow line of cars along the building.

An older man followed Olivia to her car. They were too far away for Frankie to hear the conversation, but something about his pacing and clenched jaw showed Frankie the man was annoyed and irritated.

"Forty-nine, fifty, fifty-one, fifty-two ..."

Lizzie's voice became distant in the background as Frankie concentrated on the two. Olivia briskly walked toward her car before the man grabbed her wrists. She twisted her body away from him, but he held on, pinning her against the drivers door of the car with no way to escape. She wouldn't look him in the eye, but rather narrowed her view to the ground. The noise of the train muffled their voices, but Frankie could tell he was yelling in her face from the pulsing veins in his neck as he spoke. Yet, Olivia's body language told her that he wasn't a stranger. She quickly switched course and began caressing his arm almost unsuccessfully, trying to pacify him.

"Seventy-four, seventy-five, seventy-six ..." Lizzie continued from the back seat, more of a murmur now.

Olivia's caresses seemed to work temporarily as the man's shoulders relaxed and his tirade stopped. Then Olivia mumbled something, and he grabbed her wrists, tense again as if a switch had been thrown. Olivia tried to pull away and shouted, but her voice was drowned by the train. Frankie looked around the cars near her. *Did no one see this?* Many of the drivers faced the train crossing, oblivious to the scene that lay only less than a hundred yards away from them. Frankie turned back to see the man backhand Olivia across the face. Her limp body slid down the side of the car.

Frankie gasped, not believing what had just transpired. Olivia was now grabbing onto the car, trying to pull herself up with no help from the man. He stood over her smiling like a hunter who had just conquered his prey. Frankie needed to call the police. She needed to call Max. He worked for the police department. But she froze in place, unable to do anything but stare. Olivia had finally pulled herself up as the man stood there with his arms folded and his neck pulsing.

"Ninety-three, ninety-four. Mom! The train is done. You need to move the car!"

Cars behind her honked, urging her to move forward.

How did no one just see that? As she inched her car forward, she noticed tents set up for a large sale at the stereo shop. The tent and merchandise narrowed the view of the businesses and cars in the alley.

The horns made Olivia and the man turn to look at the crossing line and, at that moment, Olivia and Frankie's eyes locked. Frankie knew she'd been spotted.

Chapter 4

Blessed are they who mourn, for they will be comforted.—
Matthew 5:4

"Mom, what's the matter? You gotta move the car. You're holding up traffic!" shouted Lizzie as the horns continued to honk.

"Uh, sorry. I wasn't paying attention." Frankie pulled out of her shock quickly and put the car into gear to cross the rails.

So much had happened so quickly. Olivia had been hit. Frankie had been spotted. She hesitated to call the police, knowing she was a clear witness. What if the man found out her identity? Would he retaliate? Frankie couldn't turn the car around and didn't want to draw attention since Lizzie was with her. Should she even hesitate to call Max? Her husband was a seasoned police officer with the Tuleberg police department, and he'd probably advise her to let them take over. She reached for her phone but realized she had left it on the kitchen counter with her coffee cup. The horns kept honking as she continued to move forward. She hated herself for not doing anything.

A moment later they arrived at the Jumpy House Emporium. Frankie met with Jeannie's parents and dropped off Lizzie, promising she'd be back in a few hours when the party was over.

As she got back into her car, a crazy idea came over her. She was going back to the warehouse. Max would've discouraged such bravado, calling it irrational and dangerous, but Frankie didn't think this was the type of situation where she could play it safe. She had to do something and going back seemed the best course.

She drove around the bend, crossed over the tracks again, and past the warehouse. No one was outside, but Olivia's car was still there. Frankie's nerves were on edge, and she said a small prayer for protection. *Dear God, if I'm to check on this girl, I ask that you guide me the whole way as I have no idea what I'm doing. Please keep my guardian angel close. Amen.*

She pulled onto the frontage road, then down to the car stereo parking lot, across from the lot where Olivia's car was parked. Finding a shady area at the far end under a slightly overgrown bush, she could keep the entire alleyway in view. At least this time there wouldn't be any horns honking, and her car blended with other cars.

No one approached Olivia's old pickup as Frankie continued to watch, not sure what she was waiting for. Frankie still didn't have a plan beyond sitting in the parking lot. She waited and waited. No one came in or out of the warehouse. She waited almost thirty minutes, and still, no one came out. She hoped Olivia wouldn't be there beyond three hours. How would she explain to Lizzie if she were late? Let alone Max, who would think she was crazy for following a girl with a potential danger attached to her. She knew she'd confide in him at some point.

Another fifteen minutes passed, and she was about to give up when she saw some movement from the building. Olivia walked out of the warehouse. This time she was alone and looked more composed. She had on a pair of dark glasses. *Probably to cover up the bruise.*

As Frankie watched, Olivia looked around and pulled out her keys to get in her pickup. Frankie had not thought through her plan any further than seeing her come out, but as Olivia started her car, Frankie decided to follow her. She pulled slowly out of the parking spot and discretely followed the pickup, trying to avoid being noticed. The intensity built as she merged into traffic, trying to keep up with Olivia without being detected.

Olivia continued straight and soon drove out of the industrial region into a neighborhood called Westley Park, which was the complete opposite direction of where Frankie lived and, in certain respects, an opposite way of life. Max had told her time and time again to stay away from this part of town. Westley Park was definitely not the type of place where women should drive alone.

Still, Frankie continued to follow, staying five-car paces behind Olivia's truck. They drove past homes that gave "gated community" a whole new meaning—fences around each window and chained gates with loud aggressive dogs pacing the yards, ready to protect their area. Most of the homes had overgrown lawns or none at all. Frankie felt little love in this area as if it had lost hope long ago.

She continued to follow Olivia, assuming she hadn't been detected, until, all of a sudden, the younger woman turned a quick right and sped down the street. Frankie tried her best to follow. As she gained a bit of speed, she noticed Olivia turning down a busy street then into a gas station. Frankie wasn't sure what to do, but then noticed Olivia had leaped out of her truck and stood with folded arms glaring at Frankie.

Frankie pulled in next to the old pickup and turned off the ignition. Olivia obviously wasn't happy to see her. Her face froze with stoic emotion and her fingers tapped her arm in rhythmic cadence as Frankie got out of her car and approached.

"I knew something was up when I noticed your nice car in my not-so-nice neighborhood. Why are you following me?"

Frankie played with her keys in her hand, unsure how to start. "I saw ... I saw you back at the warehouse earlier today with that man."

Olivia glared at her. "What did you see?"

"Come on. You know what I saw. He was hurting you."

Olivia glanced around, then scowled at Frankie. "Follow me." Without another word, she got back into her truck.

Frankie did as she was told and returned to her car. She followed Olivia a few blocks just two streets off the main road. They stopped in front of a faded white house, paint chipping off much of the exterior, and patched up boards on the side of the house that looked deteriorated from the elements—a complete opposite to Birdie's cookie-cutter home with picturesque lawns and pristine features. A beautiful garden full of gladiolas, germaniums, and cactus roses redeemed the house—an oasis among the unkempt yards of the surrounding homes.

After parking and making sure to lock her car, Frankie followed Olivia up a cracked cement walkway to a covered porch, swept clean and brightened with a few potted flowers and succulents lining the steps.

The ripped screen door squealed on its hinges as Olivia swung it open and unlocked several deadbolts on the main door. She led the way inside, letting the screen door slam shut behind her. As Frankie stepped inside, once more causing the screen door to creak, she noticed the interior was antiquated but accommodating. A couch and a simple television set sat in an otherwise barren living room. On an old-fashioned fireplace mantel sat a picture of Olivia and what Frankie assumed was her daughter at an amusement park. A few more potted succulents sat along the walls and an orchid stood centered on the table connected to the adjoining kitchen. Frankie widened her eyes with surprise—it was the favored flower of her mother.

"Those are some beautiful flowers," she said.

"I love to garden when I can, and pots are easy to transport. You never know when you're going to move." Olivia shrugged. "It's not much but it's home." She motioned to Frankie to take a seat on her couch—a worn, floral love seat with lumpy couch cushions. The pattern had faded on parts of the fabric, but still looked clean. Frankie took a seat.

"Would you like something to drink? Maybe coffee? I only have decaf. Or maybe water?" The young lady deposited her car keys in a chipped glass bowl as she moved to a cupboard.

"Decaf is fine." Frankie wondered how many guests Olivia had over to her house. Or if she was the first.

Olivia walked into the adjoining kitchen, still in view of Frankie. She finally removed the sunglasses from her face, and Frankie could see the purple and blue shades on her cheekbone and surrounding her eye socket. Olivia hastily reached for the pot and began making the coffee. When the coffee began to perk, she returned to the living room. Frankie remained on the couch as Olivia stood next to the fireplace twitching her fingers. An awkward silence ensued before Olivia spoke again.

"Cammy, my daughter, isn't here. She's with her gymnastics coach."

Frankie pursed her lips and waited for Olivia to continue. She wasn't here to make small talk, but she knew this wouldn't be an easy conversation.

"Listen ... what you saw earlier today ..." Olivia fumbled for words. "That wasn't ... that wasn't anything." She stared up at the ceiling and ran her fingers through her hair. "It's not a big deal. We were having a disagreement and I said some things and ... and Travis ... Travis was just upset."

Frankie sighed, weighing her words. "Well, I'm no expert, but even when upset, a man shouldn't put his hands on a woman that way."

"He didn't mean to hit me. He's already apologized for it. We just didn't see eye to eye on things, that's all." Olivia walked backed over to the kitchen counter straightening out cups and coffee filters, a pile of mail, anything to keep her hands busy and to avoid eye contact with Frankie.

"What could you have said that was so horrible he had to throw 'disagreement' across your face?"

Olivia didn't respond. Instead, she played with her hair, sweeping the dark curls over her face although it did little to hide the bruise.

Frankie barely knew this girl. They had only met the day before and now she was sitting in her house demanding an explanation about her history. She took a deep breath and backpedaled. "Listen, it's not my business, and you don't owe me any explanation. I just know what I saw. No one deserves that, no matter what the conversation was about."

Olivia's eyes filled with tears and her lower lip trembled, but then she mashed her lips together and blinked the tears away.

Frankie softened her voice. "I know we barely know each other, but if you need to talk, I'm a good listener."

Olivia's gaze flickered from Frankie's face to the floor and back again for a fleeting moment before moving over to the nearest plant to inspect its leaves. "I filed the papers wrong in the office and it messed up an account. We would have lost a lot of money over my mistake. But it's all fixed now. I've made sure of it." She returned to the kitchenette and poured two cups of coffee not bothering to ask if Frankie wanted any cream or sugar.

Frankie could tell her explanation wasn't the truth, but she couldn't demand any justification from this woman she barely knew. She took the coffee and held it in her hands. One thing she'd learned from her husband was if he suspected that a criminal was telling a lie, he'd have them repeat the story or parts of the story over again. That usually pulled the truth out eventually.

"You work for him?"

"It's a good-paying job and it helps me and Cammy, so I can put food on the table and even have some extras." Her eyes welled with tears again and her bottom lip trembled. "I don't have to work two jobs, and Cammy can take gymnastics. He was just upset today. He's not always like that."

"Not always like that?" Frankie repeated. She suspected Olivia and this guy were far more than just boss and employee. "Are you … are you in a relationship with him?"

Olivia avoided Frankie's eyes and stared at the floor, her mouth a grim line.

Frankie frowned. "You're beautiful, smart, and you have so much to offer the world, why would you be in a relationship with someone who treats you that way?"

"It's not so simple, Frankie."

She knew she'd asked too much, but also knew the situation was obviously not simple. She hadn't imagined any of this to be anything but the opposite of simple. She knew she had to approach this subject with caution. She and Olivia were still strangers, hardly even acquaintances.

"Has he ever hit your daughter?"

Olivia put her coffee down on the kitchen table and locked hard eyes at Frankie. "No. He's never even met her. Listen, whatever you saw, I just need you to forget it, Frankie. I need you to forget it and move on. I know from your point of view it might not look like a good life, but it's the best one I've got, and if that means sacrificing so that my daughter is better off because of it, then so be it."

Frankie knew she was being more intrusive than she should be. Olivia didn't owe her an explanation, but there was something deep inside telling her not to let this go. She wanted to help. She hadn't felt anything other than grief for a long time, but this feeling of protection charged her like a lightning bolt and she couldn't turn away.

"I just think there's got to be another way. You can't put up with this."

"What else can I do, Frankie? I don't have an education. My father's in jail. My momma's dead. I don't have any family or anywhere else to go. It's just me and Cammy and ..." She hesitated and Frankie caught the slip-up.

"And who? Is there another person?"

"And Travis, and that's all."

"But I thought you said they had never met each other?"

Olivia gazed at the walls of her house trying to find a focus or distraction. "You don't know anything, Frankie. You don't know what my life is like, and you don't ..." She stumbled for a word. "You just don't know!"

Frankie knew she was walking into unchartered waters, but she'd gotten this much out of her, so she kept going with questions. Why would a young girl try to protect a man twice her age and be content with it? What could she have said that was so horrible for him to lash out?

Frankie got up from her seat and set her coffee next to Olivia's. "You're pregnant, aren't you, honey?" Frankie asked in an almost whisper.

Olivia turned and looked at her, her dark brown eyes filling with tears. Frankie had unlocked the mystery. Olivia walked past Frankie and collapsed onto her couch, burying her head in her hands.

"Oh, Olivia." Frankie sat down gently next to her without touching.

She watched without words as Olivia wept with anguish, a deep, pent-up cry like a locked-up bird who had struggled to escape from a rugged cage and was finally released, only to see the scars and tares of the cage. An unwanted pregnancy?—yet somehow, she sensed it wasn't. The situation made more sense now. She was reluctant to give up her jacket at the book talk, and she didn't drink wine or caffeine. She was covering up but not denying it. Frankie could now see the tiny curve of her belly exposed. She pulled Olivia to her, and her new friend fell sobbing onto her shoulder.

Olivia finally came up from her heavy sobs and wiped her face on the hem of her sleeve. "You know I'm kind of glad you figured it out. At least now, I don't have to keep this secret to myself anymore." She sat up and wiped the rest of her face. "It feels good to be able to share something I haven't been able to share with anyone."

Frankie nodded and kept rubbing her back.

"You know—he's married. He wants me to have an abortion. But I don't want to go through with it. I can't go through with it!"

"And if you were to go through with it, would that make things better?"

"I ... I don't know. I just don't know." Olivia worried her hands in her lap as fresh tears started to fall.

Frankie remained silent, letting her open the gates of her secrets.

"He doesn't want the burden of having a child. He said he'd pay for it, and he'd take care of me, but if I didn't go through with it, we'd be out on the streets, and he'd make my life miserable."

"That doesn't sound like love."

"Who said anything about love?" Olivia narrowed her eyes at Frankie. "I don't love him, but I love my daughter. And I'd do anything, and I mean anything, to make sure she is cared for. So, if that means to let men like Travis abuse me and take crummy jobs so that I can put food on the table for her, then I'll do it, but this … this is different."

"It's different because you already love this baby, don't you?" Frankie knew what it meant to be a mother. What it meant to feel those first stirrings of life inside.

"I've loved this baby from the moment I knew."

"Then why is this a problem?"

Olivia swiped again at the tears on her cheeks. "No one knows about us. This would ruin him."

Frankie scowled at her. "So only his life is important? Yours and the baby's aren't?"

"I've already said too much. You can't say anything, Frankie." Olivia looked at her with such wild eyes, but she couldn't promise.

"I wasn't planning on telling anyone. I just … I just care about you."

"No one cares about me, Frankie," Olivia said as she began to sob once more. "No one."

Frankie took a deep breath and pulled the younger woman close once more. "I don't pretend to have all the answers to your situation, Olivia. I don't even have all the answers for my own life sometimes, but what I do know is a beautiful girl with a beautiful soul doesn't deserve to be treated this way. And if there is any good in all of this, that child is part of it."

"But having another baby … that changes things. It will affect how we live."

"Well, if I've learned anything in my own life, change is inevitable. But who's to say you won't be affected without the baby?"

Olivia sank back into the sofa. "When my momma died, I was only three years old. And no one wanted me from that point on. I don't want my child to not be wanted, but I don't know another way out." Olivia pulled a box of tissues close and wiped her nose. "Do you know why I joined that silly women's group, Frankie? I wanted to know what heaven was like, and I thought if I went through with the abortion, I could know my baby would be okay. Maybe I could get some answers. I had to know that even if my soul was damned for my decisions, my baby wouldn't be."

"You don't need a women's group for that." Frankie squeezed Olivia's hands. "God is all about love. He loves us. Even if we don't love him back, he never stops loving us, and he hasn't stopped loving you."

Olivia shook her head. "I don't know much about heaven or God, but there's no way he could love me. Why has he turned his back on me all these years?"

Frankie said a quick, silent prayer for wisdom, then did her best to offer advice from her heart. "You know when my mom died, I lost my best friend, my focus on life. I could have easily said, 'God doesn't love me because he took her. Why am I going through this pain and loss?' But what I realized is God gave me the gift of knowing love through her. She was the most selfless and giving person I've ever known, and she always showed me God's love. She suffered for me when I suffered, she cried for me when I cried, she loved me unconditionally even when I didn't deserve it. I don't know why you've had a harder life compared to others, but I promise if you turn to God, especially in times like these, you'll see that love, Olivia."

"I'm still not sure about the whole God loving me thing, but it does sound like you had an amazing mom."

"I did. She was the best. But my guess is you're an amazing mom to Cammy too."

Olivia smiled.

"You might not have had the love as a child, but you have that love now."

Olivia looked down into her lap. "I know I love Cammy, and I love this baby, but there's nothing easy in that."

"Who said anything about being easy? Love is hard, but it's worth it. And if I could go through it all over again, because I was fortunate to know love, I would."

Olivia cried in Frankie's arms again for what seemed like a long time as she rocked her. As Frankie held her and empathized with Olivia's pain, a calm came over her. Their stories were so different. She couldn't understand or comprehend Olivia's life, but she understood the loneliness of not having anyone know what she was going through. She could understand the need for comfort. Frankie wanted to help her. The notion of being needed and offering comfort to someone rose in her. Even though Olivia had a heavy mess, it was a comfort to share that mess.

"You know, since we're sharing, I have to say it's nice knowing your true reasons for joining the book group. Truth be told, I didn't want to tell anyone either, but I feel like I could maybe share with you?"

Olivia nodded as she sat up and listened.

Frankie proceeded to tell her about her last two years and the new world she was attempting to create through the refuge of the book group. Her tense muscles relaxed as she shared her secrets with Olivia.

"You've been pretty blessed, Frankie, to have the love of a mother, to have the love of a big family. It's funny, you've been grieving a mother you've had your whole life, and I guess I've been grieving one I've never had."

"I guess we're both chasing something."

"Who knows when we'll catch it?" Olivia looked at Frankie and smiled. "Thanks."

"For what?"

"For following me."

"I'm probably the craziest person for doing that, but I'm glad I did." Frankie looked at her watch and realized the birthday party would be over soon. "Olivia, I've got to pick up my daughter, but I don't want to leave you like this."

"It's okay. I'll be all right." She shrugged. "I still don't know what I'm going do, but I feel a little lighter not having to carry it by myself anymore."

Frankie grinned and gave her a big, embracing hug. "No, you don't have to carry it alone."

Chapter 5

While we are mourning the loss of a friend, others are rejoicing to meet them behind the veil. —John Taylor

"Frankie, the shoot was exceptional! I didn't make any kids cry, and I even got booked for an upcoming auxiliary event," Scarlett bragged over the phone about her triumphant day. "Apparently the mom of Little Miss February is the head chair of the animal auxiliary in town. Mayor Hegland's wife recommended me for her upcoming event in a couple of weeks. It's a huge contact."

"That's great, Scarlet. I never doubted your skills."

Frankie was only half-listening as she folded a pile of towels in her laundry room. But it wasn't the pile of clothes or the sound of the washing machine rumbling that distracted her. Her thoughts were absorbed by her encounter with Olivia from earlier in the day. She kept wondering about Olivia's past. Who was Travis? And how did she ever get mixed up with someone like him? She thought about Olivia's confessions: being pregnant, not having parents, being on her own. She wondered what the world had given to her and what had been taken away. Her world certainly offered a different perspective from anything she'd ever known.

"The best part," Scarlet continued, "is that I liked the kids today. I can't believe it, because normally I never like kids."

"Mmhmm."

"Frankie?"

"Mmhmm, yeah?"

"Frankie, are you even listening?"

"Uh, yeah," she mumbled still deep in thought. "That's great. Good job, Scarlet."

"Frankie, what's your problem?"

"Uh ... er ... sorry. I'm just distracted today, that's all."

"What's going on? This isn't your normal distraction."

Frankie finished folding the last towel in her pile. "What do you mean?"

"Well, you're usually distracted, but I at least get some feedback from you beyond a single sentence. You haven't asked me about any of the pictures for the calendar or even if kids tried to bite me."

Frankie had promised Olivia she'd keep their discussion confidential, but she could still work toward helping her with her situation. Doing so didn't mean she couldn't seek advice without disclosing whom she was discussing. *Hypothetical advice.*

She took a deep breath as she contemplated how to broach the subject. "Have you ever been in a relationship that, well, uh, you just, you just knew was wrong, but you stayed because it made things convenient?"

Scarlet snorted. "Duh. That's pretty much every relationship I've been in, which is why I stopped dating. They always mooch and want me to take care of their finan—Wait! Are you and Max having problems?" she shrieked through the line.

"Max and I are fine."

"Are you sure? Because you're the only couple I know who still has their act together. If you go down, then there's no hope for humanity."

"Calm down, Scarlet," she replied, feeling a little honored that even Scarlet who loathed relationships valued what she and Max had. "I was just asking hypothetically." She reached into the washing machine to pull out the finished load and transfer the items to her dryer one by one. The smell of the fresh clean clothes always soothed her. But today, not even the lingering crispness of the bleach or the fabric softener could ease her worry.

"Hypothetically, huh?"

She turned the knob of the dryer to high, pushed the button, and quickly picked up the towels to leave the room before the rumbling sound of the dryer or Scarlet's disposition intensified. "It's just that … sometimes I see young girls in bad relationships, and I wonder if my girls will ever get caught up in that. There's so many who get caught in that trap—feeling as if there's no way out." Frankie was being partially truthful. She really did worry about her daughters and relationships, though hopefully, that time wasn't for a while. She didn't need Scarlet to dig further into her motives.

"Well, 'hypothetically,' I think sometimes girls just don't think they're worthy of anything better. Once someone has had a bad experience, they tend to expect the rest will all be like that."

"So, you don't think girls know they have better options?" Frankie balanced the phone with her shoulder and ear, and she placed the towels carefully into the hallway closet between shelves of sheets and blankets.

"Well, maybe they don't. Maybe they've never had anyone believe in them, or maybe they think they're being loved when really, they're being deceived. Maybe they think the world is cruel and a bad relationship is as close to love as they will ever get to the real thing."

Frankie could hear a slight shift in Scarlet's tone and realized the conversation wasn't completely "hypothetical" on either end. Scarlet's last relationship had proved to be a disaster. When her parents, Frankie's Uncle Jim and Aunt Debbie, had died ten years ago, Scarlet found comfort in Scott, a forty-five-year-old bartender. Being less than half his age, Scarlet had submerged herself into his world and blinded herself to his controlling nature and infidelity. He wasn't the type of guy Scarlet would have normally dated, but her youth, inexperience, and grief allowed him to manipulate her. Scarlet had been so enraptured by Scott she was willing to do or go anywhere to be with him. She gave him passwords to her bank account, and he blew through her inheritance. When the money dried up, so did their relationship, leaving Scarlet with just debt and heartache. Frankie had been there for her, but Scarlet had changed. She was hardened now. The only way she knew to move forward was to focus on herself and what she could depend on. She rebuilt herself by taking photographs and promising herself she would never get involved in a relationship again.

Scarlet affirmed Frankie's summation. "No relationships for me. I'd much rather be on my own without having to deal with that."

"Well, I guess I can just hope my girls know their value and there's someone out there worthy of them," Frankie said, trying to soften the conversation from sounding like an attack on Scarlet. She knew it was probably a moot point to continue further. "I'm glad your shoot went well today. I'll try to come in on Monday as promised to finish the books, so you don't get behind."

"Thanks. You've always been good at picking up the pieces."

Frankie placed the last towel on the bottom shelf next to a few lumpy ones she assumed Lizzie had tried to haphazardly put away. Scanning the closet and its array of imperfect folded towels and sheets made her think back to Olivia. Just like the towels, Frankie could reorganize but ultimately Olivia would have to be the one to sort things out. She would have to figure out her own arrangement whether Frankie liked it or not, but that didn't mean she couldn't at least help or guide her. She smoothed out the lumpy towels and closed the door. "I've decided I'm going to stick with the book group, at least for a little while longer to see how it goes."

"I told you wine is always a good reason."

Frankie chuckled. Even though she had no idea how to help Olivia, or even herself for that matter, she figured being a part of the group could at least serve as a distraction.

"I think it's more than just the wine, but it's good to have a new purpose."

***

The next Friday quickly rolled around, and Frankie arrived fifteen minutes early to the book talk. Instead of driving around as she had done the previous week, she figured it more practical to just go in. As she approached the front door, she saw a sign on the lawn that said, "Let yourself in." She opened the door, and just as the previous week, followed the voices coming from the kitchen. Birdie and Lucy stood in the kitchen, deep in conversation. Birdie was proudly holding a framed photo showing off her ten-year-old granddaughters along with her four-year-old grandson.

"You have twin granddaughters?" Lucy exclaimed as she admired the photo. "They're so beautiful."

"There's double to love. Little Mia and Molly. My grandson, Blaise, now he's quite the handful, but he's got a sweet side to him too."

"Darling. Just darling," said Lucy.

"Do you have any grandchildren, Lucy?"

"Oh, heavens, I wish I did, but I just wasn't blessed with grandchildren. My late husband and I couldn't have any children together."

Birdie rested a hand on her shoulder. "Oh, honey, I didn't realize. I'm sorry."

Frankie had known through her mom that Lucy didn't have any children of her own but didn't know the reason behind it.

"It's all right, dear. Besides, I make a fantastic auntie and spoil the heck out of Monica's children all the time."

"Hi, ladies," Frankie said. "I hope I'm not interrupting."

Birdie swept her into the room. "We were just looking at pictures."

"You're here a little early this week," said Birdie.

Frankie blushed.

"Do you want some wine?" asked Lucy. "It's my night to bring the treats, so I brought some wine from my last Napa trip."

Frankie grinned at the spread. Lucy had brought a lot more than wine. The table boasted a large charcuterie board filled with an array of cheeses and different meats coupled with crackers and fruits. Quite impressive. Maybe a little too grand for a women's group, but Frankie knew that Lucy loved to entertain and host whenever possible, even in someone else's home.

Lucy proceeded to show Frankie all the wines she had brought for the night and to give her a very notable description of how she acquired each one. Before Lucy's husband Don died, they had gone on wine excursions and visited France, Italy, and even up-and-coming regions of wineries in South Africa and Argentina. Now that Don was gone, she still traveled, but the wine excursions were more local. She frequented Napa Valley for a week here and there and also the Lodi appellation that had started to host popular labels.

"I'll take the Old Vine Zin," Frankie said.

Lucy picked up the bottle. "Perfect choice."

Monica and Judith entered, followed by a frazzled Johnna who plopped her purse onto a barstool by the island. "Let me tell you, it was by the grace of God that I was able to get here in one piece tonight."

Lucy waved at the wines. "Sounds like you've had a day, honey. You want some?"

"To be honest, I don't really like wine. I know everyone here drinks it, but I've always found it kind of bitter. I can barely chase Communion wine. But if you have anything that'll fix two doctors' appointments, a T-ball practice, and an hour-long-wait-phone-call with the insurance company, I might consider it."

"Moscato," Lucy encouraged. "It's sweeter." She poured a glassful and held it out to Johnna, then proceeded to get glasses for Monica and Judith, already knowing what they liked.

"Wow, this is quite the spread," Judith said. "Did you do this, Birdie?"

"No, it was all Lucy."

Johnna appeared stunned. "How am I going compete with this next week? I doubt I can put together something like this."

"Oh, honey, you don't have to do anything like this. I just had a few extra kinds of cheese and meats and pâté in my fridge and wanted to use them up," Lucy said nonchalantly as if everyone had extra pâté sitting in their fridge.

Maisie walked into the kitchen next. "Well, whatever you bring, make sure you have something gluten-free."

"Well, hello there, Maisie," Birdie said, walking over to her. "I didn't hear you come in."

"The door was slightly open and the sign said to come in, so I figured it was okay. Wow, this is quite the feast!" She dropped her satchel onto one of the barstools near Johnna's purse and poured herself a glass of Pinot Noir.

All eyes shifted to Maisie's outfit—a pair of pale green palazzo pants with a red-polka-dotted tube top and a fringy teal eternity scarf. Below her bobbed hair hung some leopard dangly earrings. Nothing about the combination coordinated, but somehow Maisie made it look spunky and tied together. Frankie imagined that if she had shown up in that kind of getup, the reaction would have been a lot more eye-bulging than eye-opening.

Maisie, completely unaware of the curious eyes, loaded a plate with hummus and olives.

"Well, that's an outfit," Judith said unabashedly as she grabbed some of the olives. "Where'd you get those earrings?"

Monica looked at her mother in horror. Judith didn't seem to have a filter.

"Oh." Maisie smiled and felt for the earrings, completely unaware that Judith was taking a full inventory of her. "I was at an endangered rescue event for African wildlife a few years back and bought these to help raise money for the animals."

The room went silent, and Frankie saw Monica tense, unsure whether to intervene or let the moment play out.

"I love them!" Judith exclaimed. "Anything with leopard makes a girl look classy."

Monica exhaled a huge sigh of relief.

"You mean faux leopard," added Maisie.

"Of course." Judith winked.

"You know, I bought some extra pairs to help raise money. I should bring you a pair."

"I'd love that. There's something about leopards that attracts attention. I'm always one for making a statement." She lifted her glass to toast with Maisie's.

Monica took a long sip of her drink. Frankie smiled in amusement.

"Why don't we start moving into the living room, girls," said Birdie, ushering them all into the adjoining room.

Frankie grinned. *Week two may prove to be entertaining.*

As they all took their seats, Birdie seemed to notice the empty chair. "Wait. Olivia's not here."

"Wasn't she late last week too?" Johnna asked.

Maisie shrugged. "I'm sure she'll be here soon."

Frankie hoped she hadn't scared Olivia off. Maybe their interactions earlier in the week made her rethink coming back, but she seemed responsive to the group text Monica had started. Frankie promised she wouldn't say anything, but she hoped her promise was good enough. If Olivia didn't show up, she would go by her house afterward and talk to her in person.

As the ladies assembled in the living room with their books and wine, Birdie carried out the charcuterie board and set it on the coffee table.

"So, what did you ladies think of the first two chapters?" asked Birdie. "Last week we left off with what we believe heaven looks like. What are your thoughts this week?"

Surprisingly, Frankie had gotten through the chapters with more success than she initially thought, even the parts about death and dying hadn't affected her like the first time she'd picked it up. But she still was on the fence about sharing with the group. Sharing with Olivia had been less scary compared to sharing with a whole group of women. Maybe she could handle sharing bits here and there, but she didn't know if it was still good to open up.

"Well," Judith began, "I was surprised about these first couple chapters. They were pretty deep. I mean deep!" She glanced at everyone's faces and smiled. "At first, I was thinking about the people who say near-death experiences are fake. I thought the same once—that everything we understood about healing had to be based on science. You know, like that scientist on page fifteen who had meningitis? Most of his brain stopped working, and he was out for days. He was an unbeliever who changed."

Johnna leaned forward, her eyes wide with interest. "What happened? I didn't get to finish my chapters."

"Well, apparently his brain stopped working, the part he always believed created the image or dream-like state where the NDE patients experience their, well, you know, their experience. After that, he didn't doubt anymore."

"His brain stopped working? That's crazy. Now I have to finish the reading." Johnna gasped in amazement.

Judith continued, "Apparently, he'd gone to the other side and met a relative, a lady who knew him and knew things about him, even though he'd never met her. It wasn't until he was out of his coma and a family member showed him a picture of the girl that he finally put it all together. I'm telling you, his testimony alone made me a believer."

Maisie nodded. "Well, I'm a believer in life after death. I remember my grandma came to me in my sleep one time, years after she died, and told me that my mother was going to remarry three times before she settled down." Maisie smirked. "And that's exactly what happened! At first, I didn't want to believe it, but Nana had been very descriptive about my mom's third husband having a tattoo with a heart and thorn and a scar in the middle of it, and when I met Phil, her current husband, sure enough, it was on his arm. The image all clicked, so I knew it had to be Nana coming in from the other side to give me a message. The only part I never understood was why it took my mother three times to marry, but after that, she converted and found Jesus."

Monica straightened up in her chair. "I know I'll come across as a cynic, but I just don't buy it. I mean, no offense, but couldn't it just be coincidental that she married a guy with a heart tattoo? Plus, that's not a near-death experience, but more like a dream encounter."

"I would've thought so too, but Phil's tattoo was very distinct, and the image I saw in my dream was identical to that one. Besides, how could he have a scar on the exact same spot? You can't typically find that on just anyone."

"There's no such thing as coincidence, remember," Judith said, pointing a finger in the air as if to scold everyone for even mentioning the word.

Monica rolled her eyes.

Lucy leaned forward. "Well, I have to admit that after what we've read so far, I went online and started listening to people's near-death experience testimonies. I think I have officially become an online video junkie. It's amazing what people will put on the internet. I saw a lady who choked on an apple and died and believed she saw her ex-husband standing at the gates of heaven holding the same apple!"

"Are you sure she was in heaven? It may have been a poisonous apple," joked Johnna, which made everyone chuckle.

Monica rolled her eyes. "You can't believe everything you see on those video sites. Half of them are trying to get subscribers. Besides, if any of my dead relatives came to me, I'd—"

Just then, Olivia came through the door.

All eyes glanced toward her, but Olivia immediately looked at Frankie. Her body stiffened, locked at the threshold. They hadn't seen each other since the day Frankie had followed her home.

Frankie gave her an easy smile to reassure her that her secrets were safe.

Birdie moved toward the door. "Well, hello. What took you so long to get here?"

Olivia's eyes flickered from Frankie to Birdie and back again before she held up a bottle of wine. "I brought some wine."

Lucy and Judith got up to meet her, took the bottle out of her hands, and began chatting about the label as they headed into the kitchen. Olivia crossed the room, took the empty seat across from Frankie, and pulled out her book and a pen. Like the previous week, she wore a long pair of stretch pants and a very baggy sweatshirt, covering the marks on her wrists that might or might not be there and, of course, the pregnancy. She had a heavier amount of makeup than the previous week, which Frankie guessed was due to the bruise left by Travis. Given that Olivia had brought wine, she worried she had gone through with the abortion, but when Lucy offered her a glass, she refused. Olivia timidly smiled at Frankie and she smiled back. She could tell something was wrong, though, and hoped Olivia would share.

"We should probably get back on track," Birdie said as she tried to corral the group.

Judith and Lucy finally settled down in their seats again, each with a fresh glass.

Maisie looked to Olivia. "Okay, to bring you up to speed, we just talked about getting signs or having dreams of loved ones from heaven, and about apples and the internet." She giggled.

"Sounds like quite the conversation," Olivia commented.

Lucy leaned forward. "Since we're still kind of on the topic, I have a new question. Do you think that getting messages from our loved ones is the same as being a mystic or having a prophecy?"

"Are you asking if we think our loved ones giving us a message in a dream is the same as getting a divine revelation from God?" asked Monica, looking puzzled.

"Well, yeah, I guess I am."

Frankie thought about the dream she'd had about her mom. Nothing about it felt like a message or even a sign. It didn't feel like a revelation from God. All she knew was that she missed the conversations she and her mom used to have. That was the only thing that gave her some comfort.

"Well, I don't know," remarked Johnna, "but seeing my aunt Millie tell me she was okay a month after she died and that it was okay for me to get engaged to my husband felt like a message."

"You know our last book talk was about Catholic mystics, and the amazing revelations foretold," said Birdie. "But I think that has to do more with God's will on a much bigger scope than maybe a dream from a relative who might try to warn us about taking a bad job or getting into a relationship."

Monica scowled. "I'm not sure I believe in any of that. No offense to anyone, but that stuff just doesn't happen in today's day and age. Foretold prophecies? I mean, I guess it could happen in like the 1300s or something, but today?"

"I don't know much about mystics or dreams either," said Maisie. "I'm still learning about all of this, but I believe we're all in the place we're meant to be. Even the bad moments or experiences lead us to the good things. And when there are signs in front of us, those are blessings. I don't know if it's a Christian idea, but I believe it."

Frankie thought back to the bumblebees she had seen the week before and the orchid on Olivia's table. Could those be signs from her mother?

"Actually, that's a very Christian thing," Birdie said. "First to bring up Monica's point—God still has many messengers. In our last book talk, we looked at St. Padre Pio."

Judith nodded. "That's right, we did."

"And secondly, God puts people into our lives in the right moments that we need them, especially in the hard moments. But I think most people are expecting some magical experience, a wind-blowing-your-hair moment, so we sometimes overlook the help when it's there."

Monica swirled the wine in her glass. "And that brings up another thing. If he can put the right people in our lives, why can't he take the bad ones out? I mean why does he allow bad things to happen? Don't you think those are done by God too?"

"Yeah, like cancer. Why does God give people cancer?" asked Johnna.

Everyone looked to Birdie as if she was the authority on all things godly, and she seemed up for the challenge. She sat up straight in her chair and rolled up her sleeves. "I'll try to simplify this as best as I can. I'm no expert but I know God's will isn't about harm. That doesn't come from him," she said, looking at each woman in the circle before moving on. "Nor does he create evil, but he may allow it to take place, and he may allow people to die or get cancer."

Johnna shrugged her shoulders at the statement. "Yet I know he works through all the bad stuff, and in the end, there's always good."

"That just seems complicated," replied Johnna.

Olivia looked over at Frankie and smiled. She felt her gaze and smiled back as they listened to Birdie.

"It's actually not as complicated as you think. Think about it. If he allowed his own son to suffer, then I imagine we are no different. That's the hardest suffering you can picture, and yet we all benefited from it. And I'll add to what Maisie said. I know every challenge in my life has always turned into a blessing in the end."

Monica and Johnna sat quietly as they thought about Birdie's revelation.

Frankie mulled it over too. Did God work good even in the difficult times? Her mother's cancer had been so difficult. She had seen the suffering, her mother's physical suffering, her own emotional suffering. Even after two years, Frankie hadn't felt any blessings. But she had never doubted God's plan.

"Olivia, you're awfully quiet tonight. What do you think about all this near-death, sign-seeing, blessing stuff?" asked Judith.

Olivia had slumped in her seat but straightened up. "Well, I guess. I don't know. I've always wondered what was on the other side if my momma was there." She bit on her bottom lip before she finished her sentence. "She died when I was really young, and I have very few memories of her. I've never had any of those dreams you're all talking about. I've never had many dreams period." She paused looking down in her lap. "The only blessing I've ever had is my daughter, and I'd do anything for her, and ..." There was a long pause as tears swelled in Olivia's eyes. Everyone watched and waited.

After a full minute had ticked by, the stillness in the room intensified. Frankie looked across the room and saw a bumblebee fly past the onlooking window. Her eyes widened and she knew. She straightened in her seat and took a deep breath to break the silence. "If I could add to what Olivia said about God's blessing and being able to see the good in the hard stuff, I have a bit of backstory I need to share. I know, last week, when we started, I said I was here to learn about heaven, and I still want to, but the real truth of it is that I've been in a fog these past two years, and I haven't known how to get out of it."

Olivia took a heavy breath and smiled with relief as Frankie took over.

"I still don't completely know how. I've been grieving my mother's death, and it's an emptiness the world doesn't see."

Lucy turned to look at her with a heartfelt smile as she stood from across the room.

Frankie continued. "A part of me died when my mom left. I felt all alone, but I knew I had to keep moving forward for my family, even if I didn't want to. But I haven't been doing a very good job of it. I guess the real reason I'm here is that I didn't care if this book talk was about how to take care of penguins in Antarctica. I just needed something to take me out of my funk. I would do anything for my family, but it never occurred to me till just this moment how big of a blessing I have. I've had them all along. If I hadn't had them, I couldn't've gotten through half of it. But I guess I stopped counting them as blessings because I was so focused on myself." She took a deep breath and exhaled with liberation. "I wonder how long that might've taken me to figure out if I hadn't come tonight."

Lucy came up and hugged her tightly. "You're absolutely right, Frankie. You are blessed."

Birdie nodded. "We're all blessed in this room. Losing someone you love is hard and it changes you. Losing anything is hard. Having cancer or having a struggle you didn't expect—both are tough, but I promise you that your blessings will be abundant."

"That's right, Birdie," added Lucy, smiling. "You know, I lost my husband five years ago, and I still think about him every day. I might not have wanted God to take him, but I never questioned once why he did it. Don brought so much love into my life, and that was my blessing. Now that he's gone, well ... I have new ones. If I hadn't had Monica and Judith to help me through that, it would've been a lot harder. They've been one of the biggest blessings to me. But no matter what struggles we have in this room, God will lead us to our blessings."

Olivia smiled as Frankie and Lucy shared their testimonies. No one prodded her to finish her story. Olivia's eyes were still teary, but she seemed to be less restless.

"Well, I'm still on the fence about all this near-death and God-letting-us-suffer business," Monica said as she leaned over to hug her mother. "But I do know you have been a blessing to me, Lucy, and you too, Mom."

Lucy wrapped her arms around her from behind.

Johnna put her book on the table. "You know, I know this is only our second meeting, but I feel like we've all known each other for a long time. I was racing to get here today because I've been juggling my dad's health and my kids' appointments. I'm trying to pull it all together all the time—his chemo treatments, managing my kids' after-school activities—and lately, I just haven't been good at anything. But when I came here tonight, I felt like I could let go of my worries for a few hours. Maybe that's my blessing right now."

Lucy nodded. "You know, God puts people into our lives to help us get through hard times. I truly believe it. I believe we're all here tonight because he's working on each of us."

"There's no such thing as coincidences!" Judith repeated with her hands up in the air.

"That's starting to be your mantra, Mother," said Monica, laughing.

Chapter 6

Grief does not define who we are. Grief is a doorway into
a new life.—Mary Lenaburg, author

At the end of the night, Frankie lingered to help Birdie
and Lucy clean up the mess and the charcuterie board,
which only had bits of scraps left by the time Judith
finished with it.

Olivia was still there, sitting on the couch, unmoved.
The night had ended but Frankie sensed she was in no
hurry to go home.

"You okay, Olivia?" Frankie asked.

"Uh, yeah," she said. "I'm just waiting for Cammy
since a friend took her to the movies tonight, and I have
about an hour before I need to pick her up."

Frankie had meant more her mental state and not her
physical state, but she let the moment pass.

"Would you like to come to my house for some coffee?
Decaf, that is? We can talk for a little while you wait for
Cammy?"

Olivia nodded. "I'd like that."

Both women said their goodbyes, and this time Olivia
followed Frankie to her home. As they drove toward her
house, Frankie thought about the breakthrough she'd
had that night. She hadn't expected to share anything,
but she knew Olivia needed help and, in an instant, she'd

been there to help her deflect. Maybe it had been the talk of divine intervention or the bumblebee and little hints of her mother that caused her to intervene. Whatever it was, it was more than a diversion. She genuinely felt she'd gained a new revelation. She'd taken her family for granted, rather than as a blessing. She needed them just as much as they needed her, but she hadn't realized it till tonight. Frankie felt a sense of release and liberation that she hadn't expected. Could this be the beginning of her healing? There was more to explore, and hopefully, this was a step in the right direction. She pulled into her driveway with Olivia pulling in behind.

"Wow, you have a great house," Olivia praised as she got out of her car and walked up the flagstone pathway.

Frankie could tell she was thinking of her own house. Unlike the cracks in the walkway to Olivia's home, Frankie's were intentional with tiny bricks paved together to create a cobbled appearance. Frankie's house was an older home, too, but unlike Olivia's, Frankie and her husband had not only maintained it but also continued to improve all its Victorian features.

They walked up the steps to the porch with white wrought iron chairs and built-in flower pots attached beneath the bay windows. A scalloped trim edged the border of the slate roof, which was supported by turret columns, giving the home a cozy impression.

Olivia followed Frankie into the house through the front door and into the kitchen.

"Is that your mom?" Olivia pointed to a picture hanging on the wall near their entryway.

Frankie nodded at the photo of her and her mom standing along the bay overlooking the Golden Gate Bridge.

"That was taken a year before her diagnosis. We had a girls' trip." *The last photo of Mom looking healthy.*

Olivia smiled as she touched the frame. Frankie peeked into the living room, where she discovered Candace and Lizzie watching TV next to a conked-out Rena. Max was nowhere to be found. *He must have dozed off in our room.*

"Girls, this is my friend Olivia."

Lizzie and Candace turned to wave hello as Olivia nodded back.

Back in the kitchen, Frankie pulled out some decaf coffee and prepared a pot. "Let's go back out to the front porch so we won't have any eavesdroppers."

Olivia agreed and followed her with the cream and sugar.

"We'll be out on the porch having some coffee," Frankie told the girls on their way past.

"Okay, Momma," said Lizzie with her brightest smile.

Olivia and Frankie each took a seat on one of the wrought iron chairs and sipped their coffees. A slight gust of wind gave off a light breeze. The moon was almost full, lighting up the night sky, and the night air was surprisingly cool for mid-July. Olivia dropped two sugar cubes into her coffee, while Frankie drowned hers with tons of cream and sugar. They sat for a moment in the silence, sipping and taking in the peacefulness of the evening without any uncomfortableness between them.

Olivia watched Frankie as she sipped her coffee. "Something seems to be on your mind, Frankie."

Frankie nodded. "You know, tonight was pretty amazing. I hadn't planned on sharing. I didn't want to share, but since I did, I don't feel so bottled up as I did before."

"I was grateful to you for jumping in."

"I know." Frankie felt like she hadn't smiled this much or this wide in a long time.

Olivia shrugged. "I wasn't ready to share much, it felt so uncomfortable, and, I guess, I don't want these ladies to have a bad opinion of me."

Ironic, since Frankie felt the opposite. For the past couple of years, she had shied away, but tonight she'd bared her soul, or at least what felt like a revelation.

She looked over at her new friend. "Do you think I have a bad opinion of you?"

"Well, no. I mean, I don't think so." Olivia fidgeted with her spoon, overly stirring her coffee. "To be honest, I don't know what you see in me."

Frankie glanced across the street at a neighboring yard where the branches of the birch trees swayed effortlessly with the night breeze. She looked back toward Olivia. "I see a girl who has so much good in her, even when bad things have happened around her."

The spoon clinked against the white ceramic mug as Olivia finally stopped stirring. "I'm not good, Frankie."

"Why do you say that?"

"If I were good, I wouldn't be questioning this pregnancy. I wouldn't have made choices that got me into this mess."

"We're all human, Olivia. We aren't meant to live perfect lives. We all make mistakes from time to time."

Olivia sat forward in her chair placing her mug on the wrought iron table between them. "But mistakes aren't always small ones. How do I go forward?"

Frankie fixed her gaze and examined Olivia. "First of all, a baby is never a mistake, no matter by what means it came to be, and secondly, how we choose to live with the consequences is what truly defines us."

Olivia turned her face toward the street as the light breeze caught a few strands of her hair. Frankie watched her as she closed her eyes momentarily.

Olivia placed her hands on the table and squared her shoulders together. "I was thinking about what Birdie said—that God works through the bad to get to the good. But I'm scared."

Frankie leaned forward and took her hand. "I know you are."

Tears flooded Olivia's eyes again. "I don't want to give up this baby, but if I don't sacrifice her, then I know I'll be sacrificing a lot of other things in my life too."

"Her?"

"Yes, it's a girl. I'm already twenty-six weeks."

Frankie hadn't realized she was already so far into her second trimester, her bump was so small. She suddenly understood why Olivia felt so distraught—time was a factor.

"Little girls are the best, aren't they?" Frankie said, thinking about her three blessings inside.

"They sure are. I don't know what I would do without my Cammy. I want her to have all the things I never had. After-school activities, friends to hang out with, nice clothes, a mother."

Frankie caught the last part and realized Olivia probably put so much attention into her daughter almost as reconciliation for the childhood she never had. "You'd really give her the world, wouldn't you?"

"If I could take away any pain in the world so she wouldn't have to experience it, I would."

"Well, that's not realistic."

"What do you mean?" Olivia frowned.

"If you didn't allow her to experience anything bad, she would never know how good she has it."

Olivia looked down into her mug. "I guess I've been trying to shelter her from being like me."

Frankie narrowed her eyes at her new friend. "I haven't met your daughter but, having three myself, I'm guessing she wants your happiness just as much as she wants her own." She held her breath for a second before continuing. "I know my girls have suffered these past couple of years, and they want nothing more than to see me happy. They couldn't care less if I had a million dollars. They just want their mom." Frankie knew her girls had been through just as much as she had. All the more reason for her to stay the course.

"You're probably right." Olivia shrugged. "Cammy's always wanting to check on me. She's always saying we don't need to spend this or buy that. It's so funny that our kids try to take care of us."

"Well, my guess is your daughter would be just fine with less if it meant her mom was happy." Frankie tapped her fingers on her mug as her thumb intertwined the handle. "I know I'm probably getting too involved, but I hope you haven't had any more 'encounters' with that Travis."

"Travis is still upset, but he hasn't touched me again, if you're wondering."

Frankie was relieved Olivia hadn't felt the wrath of Travis again, but for how long would his temper be diverted? She stared up at the moon. "Have you considered looking for a new job, Olivia? This can't be the only job in the world that you can do."

Her friend took a small sip of coffee then looked into her cup. "Who's going to hire a pregnant, non-skilled woman? Besides, most jobs don't pay much for a single mom. Face it, it's hopeless."

"I just can't see this as your only solution. There's got to be another way." Frankie scratched her head. Like a tiger trying to escape from a hunter's trap, she contemplated ways to help with her new friend's limited options.

Olivia's phone rang and she picked up, talking in a soft tone, but Frankie could hear parts of the conversation.

Cammy's movie was over, and her friend's parents were driving her home.

"Cammy," Olivia said, "I told you I would pick you up. I don't want the Nelsons seeing our house."

Frankie could see the embarrassment in her friend's eyes. "Why don't you have them drop her off here?" she whispered.

Olivia looked at Frankie with grateful eyes and quickly gestured to Frankie to mouth the address to her so she could relay it over the phone.

"I'm at a friend's house, honey, I'd much rather you get dropped off here. The address is …" Olivia wrapped up the conversation, then relayed that Cammy would be arriving in fifteen minutes.

Olivia sighed and closed her eyes as she leaned back in her chair. "I'm just not ready for people to see where we live. Well, besides you anyway."

"I'd say this is a nice turn of events. Now I get to meet her."

"Cam is such an amazing girl, Frankie." She opened her eyes again and stared up at the sky. "She's spunky, confident, and so smart. All the things I never was. I'm kind of excited you'll get to meet her too."

Frankie smiled. "She sounds like a remarkable girl."

"She's my life, the only family I've got. I was lucky if I stayed in one foster care family for more than a year or two."

"I knew you mentioned you didn't have a mom, but I didn't know the extent of it."

Olivia wrapped her hands around the back of her neck. "There's a lot to my past that I don't wanna share." She squinted her eyes. "It's too hard to relive. But let's just say that anything you can imagine that could happen to a kid, well … most of it has happened to me."

Frankie couldn't fathom the childhood that Olivia had endured, and it wasn't her place to pry into the specifics. She knew her life must have been horrific to go through, which made it clearer why Olivia wanted to abort—so Cammy would be better off. Olivia was obviously torn by the fact she would have to choose between her two children, born and unborn, to determine which one could thrive. But how could she choose one child over another? A defeating decision, for sure.

Just then, a Subaru pulled up to the house. Cammy popped out of the car and turned to thank her friend and her mom. "Thanks, Mrs. Nelson," Cammy said, then she closed the door and waved the car away. Olivia and Frankie walked down the porch to greet her.

"Hi, baby. Did you have a good night?" Olivia stroked her daughter's sandy-brown hair.

"Yeah, Momma. We had a lot of fun. The movie was amazing, and they even had mermaids swimming."

"That sounds like your kinda movie."

"I heard the word mermaids!" Lizzie said from the front doorway. "I was hungry then heard a door slam. I was sure hoping it was a delivery guy. I guess I'll settle for ice cream. Can I have some, Mom?"

Frankie playfully rolled her eyes. "Sure, Lizzie, but come out here. I want you to meet Olivia's daughter."

Lizzie skipped down the steps and stood next to her mother.

Frankie smiled at Olivia's daughter. "First, let me introduce myself, Cammy. I'm Frankie, and this is my daughter, Elizabeth. She goes by Lizzie."

"Nice to meet you." Cammy's sandy-brown ponytail swished as she extended her hand. "I'm Cameron, but everyone calls me Cammy. I think nicknames are so much cooler."

Lizzie smiled. "I totally agree. Elizabeth sounds so boring." She extended her hand as if the two were tiny adults having their own conversation.

"Your mom tells me you like mermaids," said Frankie. "So does Lizzie."

Cammy's eye's widened. "Yeah, there's nothing better. They're the perfect creature—half person, half fish. They can live in more than one world."

"That's what I always say!" exclaimed Lizzie "I have tons of mermaid decorations."

"Me too. I'm obsessed."

"Hey, do you wanna see my bedroom?"

Cammy turned to her mother and pulled on her arm. "Momma, can I?"

"And can she have ice cream too?" Lizzie chimed in, taking full advantage of the opportunity.

Frankie and Olivia both looked at each other. How could anyone deny their sweet faces?

Frankie nodded. "Sure, go ahead, as long as it's okay with Olivia."

Olivia grinned. "I'm fine with it."

The two young girls darted into the house.

"Well now, I think she feels right at home." Olivia and Frankie chuckled as they climbed the porch steps back to their seats. "This night has definitely been full of surprises."

"Surprises can be a good thing, don't you think? Especially when they aren't always planned out," Frankie said, resuming her gaze at the moon.

Olivia shrugged. "Lizzie seems very sweet."

"She loves without limitations," said Frankie. "She has a way of looking at the world with goodness."

"I wish I could see the world her way."

"Sometimes I wish I could see it like that too, believe me. I guess that's why I'm here to protect her, to keep her that way, so I know the world still has a little bit of light in it through her. She sees the good in the world and others. And if she can find it, then I know there's more out there."

Olivia cocked her head to one side then stared out into the night. "I hope one day I'll be able to see it like that too."

"I think whatever God has in store for you, he's already leading you to it." Frankie shifted and leaned forward. "When my mom died, and I couldn't focus on anything but my grief … couldn't find good in any circumstance, I was blessed to have Lizzie show me that light, even when I was in the dark. She knew everything would be okay, all my girls did. But it wasn't until the meeting tonight that I've finally started to see it. It's easy to take something for granted when it's there in front of you all along."

"You know, when Monica was talking tonight about God and whether he allows bad stuff to happen, I thought a lot about what I went through. For most of my life, I've had bad stuff happen. I got pregnant when I was fifteen."

Frankie sat still and listened, wondering about all the baggage Olivia carried with her, never sharing more than what she needed to.

"The first time I saw Cammy, I knew there had to be a God because he'd made this most precious creature, this beautiful child. I knew no matter what bad stuff I might've gone through, none of that mattered because it led me to her. Maybe you're right about that blessing stuff."

"I guess our kids help us see it. Maybe that's why God says in the Bible to become like children."

Olivia placed her hand over her belly, stroking it in motherly affection. Frankie smiled as the two sat and took in the summer night. Olivia's friendship had lightened her, and she realized the more she was around Olivia, the less saddened she felt.

Chapter 7

The best thing about the future is that it comes only one day at a time. —**Abraham Lincoln**

"Momma, I don't think I can." The little girl gripped the handles of her bicycle as the training wheels were taken off for the first time. The five-year-old wanted to ride a two-wheeler like all the kids in her class, but the training wheels gave her comfort in knowing she wouldn't fall.

"I'm scared," said the little girl, nervous as she looked at her bike with only two wheels and the possibility of the unknown awaiting her. "What if I fall?"

Her mother smiled down and gave a little nod. "I know you can do this if you set your mind to it." She never promised her she wouldn't fall but assured her it would still be okay.

Feeling the tiniest bit better by her mother's words, yet nervous and not wanting to let her mother down, the little girl swung her foot to straddle the bike. The wind blew the tassels on the bike handles, but the little girl's nerves were flying higher.

One step to push off, and she bravely moved forward. The wobbliness of the bike made her jerk with unsteadiness, and she panicked, dropping her feet to the ground in fear.

"You can do it," her mother encouraged. "Just keep trying."

The young girl, nervous but determined, looked straight ahead rather than down this time and pushed to the ground. At first, she wobbled a bit, but as she continued to pedal, the steadiness thrust her into movement. Pumping the pedals, one and then the other, she kept her balance, and, to her complete surprise, she was riding!

"You're doing it, Francesca. You're doing it all by yourself!" cried Frankie's mom. "I'm so proud of you!"

Frankie woke, then turned over and looked at the time on her nightstand. 8:33 a.m. Frankie felt a new sense of self-determination. Her dream had started with uncertainty, fear, but by the end, she was riding on her own. It was the first time she'd dreamed of herself as a child. The sadness she felt as an adult had been replaced by the comforts of her youth. Looking back to the previous night, she could only assume her interactions with the women had been the reason for this sense of confidence. Sharing with the women about her mom and her grief, being around Olivia, and confiding in each other's hardships, had affected her in a way she hadn't expected. She wasn't free from struggles of loss, but for the first time the ropes weren't cutting off her circulation—they seemed manageable. It was as if she had "taken the training wheels off" of her grief so she could learn to ride on her own—a little wobbly and uncertain, but she was doing it.

She headed down the stairs to the living room to grab her journal. As she turned on the coffee pot to wait for her first cup of the morning, she settled on the barstool and opened her journal to a blank page, eager to write a few words.

Last night was the first time I opened up to the ladies in my group. I hadn't even planned on it. It just happened. It's nice to not feel alone.

Frankie thought back to Birdie's lessons and Lucy's story of loss, to the feelings that Johnna held in the place that Frankie had been only a couple of years before. These women had experienced loss in their lives. Even Olivia had experienced loss, but hers was extended beyond death, to the loss of her innocence, childhood, family, and even trust. Yet the night left no judgment or competition. The women understood and recognized their pain in their own way. Being able to talk to Olivia, knowing there was still a chance for her life as a new mother, gave Frankie a sense of hope. Maybe her interference would help Olivia put things into perspective. If only she could get Olivia to end her ties with Travis.

Her writing was interrupted as Max entered the kitchen to get some coffee.

"Mornin'," he said, mid-yawn, as he walked to the cupboard for a coffee mug. His hair was matted from sleep, and he had on a pair of boxers and an old faded Cubs T-shirt that was snug in the mid-section.

"Morning, honey," she replied, then sipped her coffee.

"I didn't hear you come in last night from your book thing. Must have been an exciting night. What time did you go to sleep?"

"More like what time did you pass out?" she teased. "I got home, and you were nowhere to be found."

"The girls and I ordered some pizza and I got sucked into one of those mermaid shows Lizzie watches. I guess I passed out."

Frankie looked at him with arched eyebrows.

"Okay, I was watching that zombie Western series you don't like. I tucked away in our room to watch some back episodes." He smirked. "But I did fall asleep after the third show," he added, trying to convey some inkling of truth to his first statement.

She shook her head. "I still don't know what you see in those movies, but I guess we all have our vices."

"So, how was the group book thing? Feeling better about sticking it out?"

"The book talk?" Frankie corrected Max with a soft smile on her face. "Actually, it was a great evening." She relaxed back in her chair as she thought about her night and looked down at the notes she had recorded in her journal.

"That's good, babe." Max put down his coffee and came closer to wrap his arms around her waist. "I'm glad this is helping you."

"You know ..." She swirled around on the barstool and put her hands on his shoulders, comforted by his embrace. "I shared some stuff with the women last night, and it didn't feel weird like I was burdening them or anything."

He put his forehead to hers. "Good, get it off your chest."

Frankie appreciated his tendency to be short, simple, and straight to the point. Unlike her propensity to externalize her thoughts, Max was more of a thinker and processed his thoughts before saying anything. Much of what came out was terse in a compact container.

"I didn't expect those results," she admitted.

"That's good, babe." He rubbed her back slowly, which was his way of saying, *"I'm glad, and I miss you."*

Frankie appreciated Max's support of her belonging to the book talk. Even though he couldn't understand her grief process, she was glad he'd recognized she needed some comfort, which heartened her. He'd been a patient man, letting her do what she needed to, and that's what Frankie probably loved about him the most. In their sixteen years of marriage, he'd never suffocated her or argued about her feelings.

Still, she knew the past two years had been rough for him too. He missed his mother-in-law, but he missed his wife more. On the days she'd spent shut away in their bedroom with little communication, Max would arrive home from a shift to find her in the same place she'd been when he'd left. When she was up and moving, she was consumed with books or doing tasks on autopilot, always by herself—there but not. Alive and breathing but non-existent.

She knew he missed how close and intimate they used to be. She had allowed her grief to force its way onto everyone in the house. She'd known all along he was grieving for the woman he'd married, the bubbly vivacious person who was no longer there, and that he couldn't do anything to fix other than give her time, which he'd done. She'd wished she could turn back time, but grief had a stronger hold on her than any other force in the universe.

She hoped the glimmer of life she felt that evening would blossom and grow and fill her with life again.

"I guess I needed this group more than I realized," she said, leaning back now. "And it was surreal—the others shared too."

"Isn't that what you do at these women groups?"

"Yeah, but it was different this time. I felt connected. Last night one of the girls from the group came back to our house afterward for coffee."

"Oh?" Max smiled. "I didn't expect you to start establishing friendships so quickly. You haven't had someone over in a long time."

"Her name's Olivia. She has a daughter about Lizzie's age."

"A friend so soon. Tell me about her." He released her waist and stood back, eyebrows raised.

Then Frankie remembered. She hadn't told him about following Olivia home or seeing her with that man. She'd promised to keep it a secret for Olivia's sake, but Max was different. He wasn't a girlfriend or an acquaintance. She didn't want to lie or keep something from him, but it wasn't her secret to tell. And yet she hadn't told him about following Olivia home either. She figured if she could tell him only the parts he needed to know, then she wasn't being deceptive.

"She's a little younger than most of the women in our group. It's kind of surprising she even wants to be with us older women, but I guess we all have our reasons for going."

"Hmm, wonder what's her reason?" He turned slightly toward the coffee pot to top off his cup. Max was always thinking with a detective mind.

Frankie hesitated, trying to be cautious of spilling too much, but felt her body tense. "Who knows? I mean I guess these book groups make avid readers." She stared up at the ceiling, avoiding eye contact.

Max was quick to pick up on her body language. "Hmm. As you said, seems odd she's so young." He raised his mug to his lips and gazed at her. She knew he was prodding her for more information.

"Yeah, I know." She began to fidget with the pen that lay on her journal, clicking the top. Her nerves rose to the surface.

"Frankie ..."

Clicking the top of the pen fanatically, she stammered to answer. "Yeah, I guess she—"

"Francesca ..."

"What?" She put the pen down and looked at him, brows furrowed.

"I know when you're holding out. You're not exactly good at keeping things in. What's going on?"

Frankie considered what to say. She didn't want to hold back from Max, but she didn't want to divulge or break

Olivia's confidentiality. She knew Max wouldn't approve of starting a friendship with someone with so many hardships. She tried to tell him what she could without breaking her trust.

"This girl, Olivia, I really connected with her."

"Okay. And?"

"And what?" She rocked back and forth in her barstool, tapping her ankle in a nervous motion.

"You're just acting funny, that's all."

Realizing there was no way around the conversation, she stopped moving and decided to be as honest as she could without divulging too much. She let out a heavy breath and looked straight at Max. "She just told me some private stuff that I can't share. You know—girl's stuff."

"Girl's stuff, huh?"

Frankie knew Max, in his line of work, was skeptical about a lot of things, and he was even more skeptical when it came to his family. "I'm not sure exactly what I can share with you about her other than I know she doesn't have much family, and I know she's had some hard times. But I promised her I would keep her story private. It's not for me to tell."

Max leaned his six-foot, three-inch frame against the counter next to Frankie as he cupped his coffee. "Well, in my experience, when a person has a story they can't share, nothing good usually comes from it. The truth always comes out in the end. I just don't want you getting tangled up in anything."

She knew he was right, but she felt protective of Olivia. She continued to hope, with her guidance, everything would work out for the young girl. "I promise whatever her story is it won't affect me."

"That's a pie crust promise, Frankie. Easily made, easily broken. Just remember, you can't take on someone else's problems. I know from experience that people with struggles won't accept help unless they make the choice to do so on their own. And you, my dear wife, have the heart of a big Labrador puppy. You will stay devoted to whatever person or project no matter the outcome." He set down his coffee and stood upright. Then he put his hands on her shoulders and pivoted her to him.

"But this is the first time in a long time you've looked outside your grief, so maybe some good will come of it. Just promise me you'll be careful." He lifted her chin with his finger. "You haven't had anyone over in a while, and now you want to be friends with someone I can't even know much about. So just take it slow."

"Well, I may not be able to tell you, but that doesn't mean you won't find some clever way to investigate." She winked at him. "And by the way, I forgot to turn off the security cameras last night." She smiled.

Frankie knew Max could look on the security camera and easily look up her car plates to run any numbers if he wanted. She figured this was her way out of keeping secrets from Max, but also keeping her word to Olivia.

"There's always a good loophole, isn't there." He grinned widely.

"I don't know what you're talking about, Max Waters." She kissed his cheek and got off the barstool.

Simultaneously, Lizzie made her entrance into the kitchen. She walked over to the kitchen cabinets, stood on her tiptoes, and reached to open the top cabinet. "Good morning," she said, as she grabbed a box of cereal to pour herself a bowl. "Hey, Mom, that Cammy girl is so cool. Do you know she knows all the names of Ariel's sisters and even knows some of the songs of the sirens." Lizzie grinned as she added milk to the bowl. "Do you think we could have her over sometime again, Mama? Could we, please?"

Frankie looked at Max. "Cammy is Olivia's daughter. She came over last night too."

Max shook his head, then turned back to Lizzie. Frankie knew her cautious husband wanted to tell her, no, to sidestep any new friendships, but as usual, he couldn't resist his daughter's enthusiasm.

"Let's take a look at our schedule this week and see what's planned first," he told their daughter. "Then we can see if Cammy can come over." Frankie knew this was his way of putting on the brakes until he could assess the situation better.

"Thanks, Daddy. I'll even do extra chores!" Lizzie was always a negotiator when it came to friends or extra activities.

She took her bowl of cereal and headed to the living room.

Max turned to look at Frankie with raised eyebrows. "Extra chores?"

"Well, it looks like I'm not the only one who wants to get involved." Frankie crossed her arms.

"I just want your involvement with her to be one of caution, Frankie."

"I promise, babe, I won't put myself or this family in dangerous situations." She meant it too.

"So, what've you got planned today?" he asked.

"Nothing really. Probably just some home projects."

Max walked toward the box of cereal Lizzie had left out and returned it to the pantry and nodded. "Home projects. Got it." He repeated the phrase as if he already knew what that entailed. That she'd return to the same monotonous desolate routine she'd been doing for the past two years. She knew he would give her as much space as needed, even if it meant doing so would drive a wedge between them.

She thought of her father, who was probably taking a helicopter ride right now exploring an Alaskan glacier or kayaking a river along the freshwater salmon. She felt a surge to prove herself. To show Max she was moving forward.

"And ... and I'm thinking of calling Scarlet for lunch," she said, trying to add some kind of new activity. The cocoon of safety that grief offered would have to wait. She knew her family needed a small change, even if she had to force it again and again. Dr. Jude had said there was no timeline with grief, but her family needed some healing too, and their timeline wasn't as patient.

"Really?" Max turned toward her. "Are you sure you're up for that?"

She took a deep breath and lifted her chin. "Absolutely. I haven't done that in a while and it might be good to get out."

Max eyed her cautiously but didn't discard her statement. "Well, if you think you're up for it, call her up, babe."

Frankie took the cue and picked up her phone with shaking hands, almost as if to prove a point. She dialed Scarlet's number. She was ready. She had to be.

The phone rang for only a moment until Scarlet answered in a raspy voice. Before Frankie could change her mind, Scarlet cut her off. "That's so funny. I was just about to call you. Can I borrow that oversized crate from your house? I have an idea for a newborn shoot, and your crate would make the perfect accessory to the photo. "

"Sure, I guess. I could drop it off to you." This wasn't going the way she had planned.

"Okay, that's perfect. I'll be home all day."

Frankie stumbled to get the question out as Scarlet rambled on about the ideal baby shoot and unnecessary backdrops until finally she mustered up the courage to interrupt. "Actually, I called because, I was wondering ..."

She fidgeted for a second, then took another deep breath. "Maybe we could do lunch today?"

There was a long pause on the other end of the phone.

"Scarlet, are you there?" Frankie didn't know if she'd lost the connection.

Finally, she heard Scarlet's voice. "You want to go to lunch?"

"Uh, yeah. I think it'd be fun to meet and just have lunch together. We haven't done that in a long time." She wondered if Scarlet could hear the tremor in her voice. She could envision Scarlet staring at the phone, mouth hanging open in surprise. She started to have second thoughts. *Maybe this was too soon.*

"Scarlet? Are you still there?"

"First you join a book club—"

"Book talk," Frankie corrected.

"Whatever," said Scarlet. "And now you want to have lunch when I couldn't get you out of the house for these past two years? Who is this Frankie and where has she been hiding?"

"We don't have to go. It was just an idea," Frankie said in a grimacing low voice, trying to backpedal.

"No! We're going!" Scarlet nearly screamed into the phone. "I'm just trying to figure out where all of this is coming from."

Frankie noticed Max's eyebrows arch, looking puzzled, probably hearing the scream. Her chest pounded, unsure what to say. She took a deep breath. "I don't know. I just feel like... I haven't done anything with you except work stuff." She gulped. "Sometimes it's just nice spending time with you."

There was partial truth to the statement, even if she'd only initiated the contact because of Max. Scarlet had been her only female companion over the past couple years but even then, she had kept her at arm's length. She missed the "old times" with Scarlet, but there were painful moments that reminded her of her mother, and she hadn't been ready to embrace them. Even now she wasn't sure ... but she would try.

"Well, geez, we better make it a nice place, because I'm not sure how long I'll have you this way. Why don't we meet at Roux downtown at 12:30? My treat."

Frankie raked her hands through her hair. "That's pretty fancy." Was she ready for something so posh? She looked at Max whose eyes had never left hers. "I guess I could go for that, but what should I wear?" In the last two years, her attire had been made up of oversized sweatshirts and yoga pants. She would have to dig to see what was in her closet and still fit.

"On second thought, make it noon. I need to see this sooner. Make it your best," Scarlet replied and hung up.

"So ... lunch?" Max asked as he leaned over the counter.

"Yeah." Her hands continued to shake as she hung up the phone, but this time in full view. What had she just done? Maybe she could call Scarlet back and cancel, but as she considered this she saw the smile on Max's face. She knew she needed to try.

She turned toward him wide-eyed and lifted her chest in the air. "It's no big deal. Both of you act like I never want to go out for lunch." She sat on her hands to keep them from shaking.

"Well, it's just surprising, but a good kind of surprising." Max grinned. "Go enjoy your lunch with Scarlet."

Chapter 8

Even now, as broken as you may feel, you are still so strong. There's something to be said for how you hold yourself together and keep moving, even though you feel like shattering. Don't stop. This is your healing. It doesn't have to be pretty, or graceful. You just have to keep going.—Maxwell Diawuh

About two hours later, Frankie was going back and forth through her closet, scavenging for something to wear. She hadn't gone to lunch with anyone in so long, she was clueless to what Scarlet meant by "make it your best." Finally, after sifting through and piecing together some suitable shirts and pants, she decided on a powder-blue blazer and white shell top with a draped neck, which she paired with loose navy-blue Capri pants and a pair of strappy sandals. *It's only lunch with Scarlet.* She knew she was only trying to convince herself that it wasn't a night at the opera. Still, her nerves were pulsing as she thought about being out in the world—even more so that she might enjoy herself. Guilt gnawed in her gut. How could she be happy when she had felt so buried in depression for the past couple years? Was it okay to be happy? Did that mean she was getting over her mother? Did that mean she would just forget about her? She anxiously pulled all her accessories together and styled her hair. Surprisingly, it felt good to dress up for a change, but that's what bothered her the most.

Enduring social gatherings after her mom's death had been a struggle. Unlike her father, she'd avoided any place or event that breathed a small resemblance of her mother. But doing so left her remote from friends and acquaintances. Whispers of her mother permeated the town, from the coffee shop they used to frequent to the downtown shops close to the restaurant. For the first six months after her mother had died, Max had to do the shopping because a simple jar of tomato sauce would make Frankie break down and cry. She finally built up endurance to visit some stores, but not without effort.

Going to Roux would also be a struggle. She and her mom had talked about going there during her treatments, but never put the plan into action. Today would have its share of obstacles, no doubt, but as she kissed Max and prepared to leave, glimpses of her mother's face passed through her mind indicating everything would be okay. She exhaled a deep breath. She might not be fully ready, but it was time to try. She had pushed herself this far. She could take the next step.

Frankie arrived before Scarlet and checked into the chic and stylish restaurant called Roux. She could see why Scarlet frequented it so often. The building was older—probably built in the 1920s but retrofitted and modernized to fit current trends—and sat in the middle of downtown Tuleberg. The hostess guided her over the dark-stained wood floor toward a long row of white plush couches and distressed tables partitioned from the rest of the restaurant into the waiting area where she would sit and wait for Scarlet. Purple and white orchids graced each coffee table as people lounged with their cocktails in uniform rows. Over them hung repurposed mini-chandeliers from the high vaulted ceilings. She could hear the murmur of business deals and mergers from the bodies of dark suits she passed as the hostess seated her on a couch in the center of the room and handed her a menu. The place was beautiful and booming.

Frankie examined the menu, taking in the overpriced brussels sprouts and wedge salads. She imagined how her mother would have reacted to being there—she probably would have oohed and aahed over the food and immediately made friends with the waiters. She, like the old Frankie, had loved socializing and soaking up the energy of her surroundings.

She continued to create images of what lunch might have been like here with her mother. Her mom would have browsed through the selection of pasta and mispronounced the Italian-themed names while Frankie playfully scolded her for taking too long to speak to the waiter about each entrée. She closed her eyes and imagined her mother's smile after finally giving the waiter her order, but she'd have pointed out every entrée on nearby tables and wondered if she'd made the right decision. Frankie would laugh at her mother's indecisiveness, and they'd toast to an afternoon of brewed iced tea and small gossip.

Frankie opened her eyes and gazed at the vacant seat across from her. She put on her sunglasses to cover the tears dribbling down her cheeks. She would never get that extra girl time again. The *what-ifs* that would never take place.

She blotted her tears under her glasses, careful not to smear her mascara, and reminded herself she couldn't stay in that place of regret. Her need for *what-ifs* would never suffice. There was no point in looking at what she could no longer do. She could only focus on *what is*. She sat up in her chair and sniffled. She'd had many moments of happy times with her mother, for which she was truly grateful. They'd been to the spa right after her diagnosis, both wrapped in bath towels and green masks on their faces. Even as her mother's health deteriorated from the effects of cancer and chemo, the memory of their time together was something both would cherish. Frankie rubbed a small tissue under her nose and imagined her sorrow like a bruise on her knee that hurt but didn't prevent her from using her leg—painful, but she could endure it.

She flipped the menu over to glance at the other selections, but then spotted Scarlet from afar and immediately sat up. Scarlet's presence changed her focus. She had to pull herself together. She smoothed out her blazer as she watched Scarlet sway into the room with her white slacks, tucked-in collared print top, and gold stiletto heels. Her blonde hair flowed behind her shoulders, and the men in the room moved their heads with her cadence. She knew she was beautiful and liked to flaunt her attractiveness, but only enough to keep the gaze of men flocking to her from a distance. Her attention was fixed on Frankie as she strolled toward the sofa.

"Sorry, I'm a few minutes late. I had a client call me right before I got here. Have you put in for a table already?" She signaled to the bar waiter to take her drink order.

Frankie lifted her sunglasses from her eyes and pushed them back onto her hair like a headband, grateful her tears had dried and Scarlet was unaware of her emotional flash only a moment before. "Uh, no, I hadn't thought to."

"I'll let the waiter know we want to be seated when he takes my cocktail order." She snapped her fingers, expecting someone to get there faster. A young, stoic waiter arrived momentarily.

"Are you ladies dining for lunch or just for lounging in the white room today?"

Frankie guessed that was the name of the area where they were currently sitting.

"Lunch," Scarlet replied in a sweet but commanding voice, "and I'll have a dirty martini. How about you, Frankie?"

"Uh, I guess I'll have a gin and tonic?"

The waiter looked at Scarlet, tipped his head, and walked away as if he was used to her style.

"You must come here a lot, I'm guessing."

Her cousin dug neatly through her purse and pulled out her phone, a tube of lipstick, and a compact. "I bring my high-profile clients here to impress them. And to my studio, of course. Let's just say I can probably do more work in this restaurant than in others." She quickly typed a message then tucked her phone back into her purse. She certainly knew the type of client she was after.

Frankie looked around and realized everyone was either doing business or was there to be seen. Suddenly her eyes caught a tall, slender man with dark brown wavy hair glaring at Scarlet from the far end of the bar. He was fairly handsome but looked out of place, neither wanting to be seen nor doing a business deal.

"Do you know that guy?" asked Frankie. "He's staring right at you."

His dark black T-shirt with a distressed pair of jeans seemed far from the proper etiquette for this place and made him appear to be a more laid-back, coffee-establishment kind of guy.

Scarlet looked up from her compact as she finished reapplying a light shade of soft plum lipstick and smiled at the mysterious man. "Oh, that's Charles," she said with a playful smile. "He comes around here from time to time. I don't know why. It's definitely not his scene." His deep blue eyes stared at Scarlet as he tipped his glass to her.

Frankie chuckled. "Well, whatever his reason, he seems to enjoy the view. He's definitely into you."

Scarlet twisted her lips. "He works at the law firm down the street and comes over here for lunch sometimes, but he tends to mock places like this."

"You seem to know quite a bit about him." She could see Scarlet was embarrassed, which surprised her. Scarlet rarely seemed captivated by a man, nor did she stay with one for very long.

Snapping her compact shut, she turned her back to Charles and focused on Frankie. "We're not here to talk about him or even me. We're here to talk about you, so let's cut to the chase before I change my mind."

Frankie took the cue and changed the topic. "You know this is my first time coming to Roux. It's pretty impressive."

"I'm still shocked you wanted to meet. Is there a motive?" Scarlet asked.

What *was* she was doing here? She scratched her head as she thought about what had pushed her into so many new situations over the last two weeks. Yet she couldn't admit her fears or even her motivations to Scarlet, because she wasn't sympathetic to vulnerability. Instead, Frankie pushed forward with her biggest, bravest voice to sound as nonchalant as possible.

"No motive. I just thought it'd be nice to meet. Is there something wrong with just meeting for lunch?"

Scarlet eyeballed her dubiously. "Well … yes, if you're Francesca Waters, and you've been a zombie for over two years. I'm just trying to figure out where this change has come from all of a sudden."

Beyond Max, Frankie didn't know why she'd asked her cousin to lunch. She'd been doing a lot of things out of character. But her experience with the women the night before had made her feel cautiously daring, even valiant in ways she hadn't completely understood.

Frankie fidgeted with her gold bangles on her wrists. "I guess what it really comes down to is it's time to start living again." It was an honest confession, even if she didn't know how to proceed—even if it felt uncomfortable and scary.

Tucking her compact and lipstick in her purse, Scarlet leaned toward Frankie with large eyes. "This book club or grieving daughters' group or whatever it is has pushed you to do this?"

"Book talk," she corrected, "it's low-level commitment. And for your information it's not a grief group." She paused, realizing she didn't know how true or untrue her remarks were in terms of the intentions of the other women. "But to answer your question, I don't know. I just know that since I've been going, I've felt ... different. So, yeah, maybe they have had a small part in it."

Scarlet sat back and stretched her arms across the back of the chair. "Well, I don't care if they're a singing group or a knife-sharpening club, it's nice to see you trying to do things again, like washing your hair and going out to lunch."

Frankie threw her head back and chuckled at Scarlet's exaggeration.

"See? You're laughing and it's not even forced."

"I never stopped washing my hair."

"Yeah, but it's always frumpy. You finally have on clothes today that don't look like you're going to sleep or working out. You were starting to look a little 'hags-ville,' and, as your cousin, it's my job to tell you the truth." Scarlet put her right hand over her chest as if to make a pledge.

"The truth has never been a problem for you, Scarlet."
Frankie raised an eyebrow. "But you're right, I do need to
start taking some steps to care for myself."

"So, what's your plan?"

Frankie continued to toy with her bangles. "Well,
I don't have one. But I guess that's what scares me and
motivates me at the same time."

"In any case, I still want to meet those knife-sharpening-
book singers or whatever group you say you're in." They
both laughed.

"I'd like that," said Frankie. She smiled at Scarlet as
they sat quietly waiting for their table, enjoying this new
moment with her. She'd forgotten how much she enjoyed
just talking and laughing. Their drinks arrived, but the
waiter had brought Frankie an iced tea instead of her gin
and tonic. Scarlet pointed a finger to object, but Frankie
stopped her. She smiled into the sky, realizing she was
having her *what-if* moment. They toasted to the afternoon.

She took a sip of her iced tea and sighed. These little
moments were reminders that while her mother might not
be there in the physical sense, it didn't mean she wasn't
there in some form, another lesson she had learned from
the book talk. Maybe Max and Scarlet weren't the only
ones encouraging her to move forward, that these little
hints from heaven were ways of support to cheer her on.
Whatever the case, there was a reason she had made it
this far, and now she had to trust this new life she was
attempting to explore would lead her to healing. She and
Scarlet sat for a moment in silence until she noticed a
hand vigorously waving in the dining area. She turned to
Scarlet and raised her brow. "I think your wish is about to
come true."

She nodded to Scarlet to turn her head. Judith, from
the book talk, eagerly waved from one of the far dining

tables, motioning her and Scarlet to come over. Monica, much to her chagrin, waved in smaller motions, hoping her mother would stop.

"Who is that?" Scarlet asked, looking confused.

"Some knife-sharpening singers."

"Your book people? Looks like they want us to join them."

"We don't have to go over there," Frankie said to Scarlet.

Scarlet furrowed her brow. "I'm kind of intrigued. I've been wondering what kind of ladies go to these things. They seem fairly normal."

Frankie made an annoyed face as Scarlet kept observing them from afar.

"Besides it might give me some insight as to why you all of a sudden want to be social again. Come on. Get up."

Frankie shrugged as Scarlet tilted her head in a prodding motion. They picked up their drinks and Frankie took the lead through the restaurant toward Judith and Monica's table. They were seated toward the back of the restaurant in a partitioned platform with other tables that elevated their table a few steps. There were two empty seats, one next to Monica and the other Judith.

As they stepped up to the table, Judith stopped waving and stood to greet them. "Frankie, it's so great to see you." She reached out for a hug.

As usual, Judith was impeccably dressed in a leopard-print blouse, suede skirt, and a string of pearls tied in a knot in the middle. Her tan shoes coordinated with her purse. Frankie reached in to reciprocate the warm embrace.

"I didn't know you dined here. Who knew we'd meet again so soon?" remarked Monica as she moved in to give Frankie air kisses on both cheeks.

"Must be a coincidence," said Scarlet smirking as she stood behind Frankie.

Judith put her hands on her hips and gave Scarlet a reprimanding look. Frankie remembered the first night of the book talk when Judith quieted the room with her lecture about coincidences.

Judith shook her head at Scarlet. "There's no such thing as coincidences. Everything happens for a reason." She raised her right eyebrow. "There's probably even a reason why we're meeting today."

Scarlet crossed her arms, mystified by the comment.

"This is my cousin Scarlet Bedford," Frankie said, motioning to Scarlet. "She's a photographer."

Judith nodded. "I know you. I've seen your pictures in the local society magazines." She arched her eyebrow again. "Impressive."

Scarlet lit up, probably at the fact that someone recognized her for her work. She extended her hand to Judith. "Pleasure."

"Judith Stone and my daughter, Monica Raleigh." Judith stretched her hand to reciprocate Scarlet's. "I just might give you a call. My husband and I have been looking for a photographer for our upcoming wedding anniversary."

Scarlet's eyes widened, always looking for an opportunity to gain a new client.

It was Monica's turn to shake her hand, then she rolled her eyes at her mother. "It's very nice to meet you, Scarlet."

"Come sit with us for lunch," pleaded Judith.

"Oh, we couldn't impose on you," said Frankie.

"Please. We've only just started appetizers, and this will give me a chance to chat up your darling cousin."

Frankie noticed trays of marinated artichokes and calamari on the table. She turned toward Scarlet to

Grieving Daughter's Club

confirm if she was okay with the idea but before she could ask, Scarlet was already pulling a chair out by one of the empty seats and placing a napkin on her lap. Their time alone was over, but she didn't mind the new company. Judith, just like Scarlet, snapped for the maître d' and informed him the four would sit together.

"Where's Lucy today?" asked Frankie, as she sat next to Monica and the waiter came by to tuck a napkin in her lap.

"We might be neighbors, but we don't do everything together," muttered Monica.

"Who's Lucy?" Scarlet asked.

"Remember my mom's friend Lucile Durham?"

Scarlet scratched her chin. "Oh, I think I so. She was always helping your mom at church events."

"Yes, that's her. Monica and Judith know her too."

"Monica is peeved because Lucy is going to Napa for the weekend," replied Judith as she placed some calamari onto both Frankie and Scarlet's appetizer plate. "She wanted her to come to lunch with us today, but she's so committed to those Napa trips."

"I'm not upset. I'm just bummed. I don't understand why she can't reschedule. Besides, we have local wineries in this area, and it's not like it's a special occasion. She could go anytime. I even suggested I could go with her, but she said it was an exclusive tasting."

Judith patted her daughter's hand from across the table. "Well, you know she always brings you something when she comes back."

"I suppose." Monica picked at an artichoke with her fork.

"Speaking of wine, I heard your group likes to drink," Scarlet chimed in.

Monica's fork hit the plate. "You make it sound like we're a bunch of winos or something."

115

"Speak for yourself," said Judith, then tipped her wine glass filled with something white and bubbly. "I enjoy a good glass whether it's in our group or just by myself. Besides, Jesus had wine with his friends, and if it's good enough for him then it's good enough for me." She raised her glass to toast everyone.

Scarlet and Frankie chuckled as they raised their glasses.

"So, what's good here?" asked Frankie.

"Everything is good here," chimed in Scarlet and Judith simultaneously. They looked at each other and laughed.

"My mom comes here a lot for the desserts and appetizers." Monica had resumed her dissection of her artichoke.

"This is only the place that serves the best tiramisu in town, and since my husband can't have any types of desserts or salty foods with his health issues, I try to convince Monica to come here any chance I get."

Monica laughed. "Yeah, she calls it mother-daughter bonding time, but my dad knows she just wants to pig out."

The waiter arrived with a tray of pancetta basil crostini. "Are you ladies ready to order?" he asked.

"Mom has quite the appetite, if you haven't noticed."

Scarlet looked around at multiple plates of food before them, then eyed Judith's slender figure. "Ready to order? Where do you put it all?" exclaimed Scarlet.

"Give us a few more minutes." Judith dismissed the waiter with a polite smile and wave. "If I don't eat regularly, I get light-headed. You should try the bruschetta here, it's fabulous."

Frankie could see Scarlet was in awe, and yet totally entertained by Judith.

A light chirping began in Judith's purse. "Oh, pardon me." She rummaged in her expensive bag and pulled out her cell phone and looked at the screen. "I need to take this. It's your father. He's supposed to get his physical results from the doctor." She excused herself from the table and walked over to the lounge area to take the call.

"So, what's your story, Scarlet?" Monica asked.

Scarlet finished a bite of the calamari then wiped the corners of her mouth with her napkin. "Not much to tell. I work. I take a lot of photos. I work more. I go to sleep, then start all over again."

"Are you trying to earn money for something in particular?"

"Yeah, so I can keep taking Frankie here out to overpriced lunches," she joked.

Monica smirked. "Any kids?"

"No, no kids. Never married. Just work." It was Scarlet's turn to pick at her plate while Monica asked all the questions.

"Wow—no kids, no husband." Monica leaned back in her seat, assessing her. "If I had that freedom, I'd only work when I needed to. I'd be taking trips all over the world, left and right. My son, James, is eight and my daughter, Regina, just graduated this spring from high school. I have a few more years for James, but what I wouldn't give to have that freedom to throw caution to the wind and go wherever I wanted whenever I wanted." Monica looked up to the ceiling.

Frankie turned to Scarlet. "Taking a trip would be therapeutic for you."

Scarlet avoided eye contact and pulled out her phone instead. "Maybe if I were meeting a client. Otherwise, it seems pointless."

Frankie knew taking time for herself was a touchy subject for Scarlet, but she was glad Monica had pointed it out.

Judith returned and slid back in her seat and turned toward her daughter. "Your father's health looks pretty good. They found his blood pressure was a bit higher than normal, but they aren't really worried about it. A prescription should help him lower it, and he just needs to lay off the salt." She speared the last piece of prosciutto from the meat platter with her fork and wrapped it around fresh mozzarella.

"Well, I guess that rule doesn't apply to you. You'd kill him with all the things you eat," Monica said, a hint of sarcasm in her tone.

"I can look out for his interests without giving up my favorite things," Judith replied as she added some butter and salt to the top of her baguette. "Let's change the topic. I want to talk about how come you didn't sign up with Frankie for our group, Scarlet."

Scarlet looked up from her phone and scowled. "I don't do social gatherings unless it's work-related. No offense— it's just not my cup of tea."

"Well, maybe it could be your cup of wine?" Judith smiled.

Scarlet grinned back. "Frankie keeps me up-to-date with your group and what you're doing. She can fill me in. Plus, I think it's more therapy for her."

"We were just talking about how much freedom she has," Monica said filling her mother in on the conversation. "No kids, not married. You could carve out a little time for us, couldn't you?"

"I don't have time for that stuff. But you girls seem like normal people. Honestly, I expected you guys to be some sad, depressed group. Either that or overly judgmental religious women."

Frankie stared at her, open-mouthed. *Is she trying to give a dig back to Monica or is she totally clueless?*

"I guess that's the stigma of church groups, isn't it?" admitted Judith. "If only you knew how much we support each other."

Monica smirked as she stretched her arm behind the back of Frankie's chair. "I expected the same thing, but it's kind of grown on me." She winked at Frankie, seemingly unbothered by the remark. Frankie sighed, relieved they hadn't taken offense to Scarlet's brazen, unfiltered mouth.

Scarlet speared another bite of calamari. "But, whatever you're doing, keep doing it. Frankie seems to be awakened by it."

Frankie smiled at her cousin. Despite Scarlet's inability to admit the group might be beneficial, she appreciated Scarlet's awareness of her own needs.

Monica sipped her drink, then spoke. "I didn't think being in a women's group with my mom would be that interesting, but to be honest I've enjoyed spending time with her. These ladies see her in a way I haven't, and it's amazing what you learn when you mix up your company from time to time."

Judith looked over at Monica, a smile playing across her face. "We do have a lovely group of people, don't we?"

Frankie loved the relationship Judith and Monica shared. One moment sarcastic and critical, the next fearless and supportive. She thought back to her mother and how they had teased each other. They had been each other's best critics and biggest cheerleaders. A single tear trickled down her cheek.

Monica noticed and reached out to lightly touch Frankie's hand. "Everything okay? Our group's good but nothing to cry about."

Frankie smiled, trying to hold back more tears from forming. "It's just … it's just nice to see mothers and daughters spending time together."

"I don't usually have a choice in the matter," joked Monica. "She drags me to everything. It's painful."

Scarlet's neck reddened as she tapped her fork on her plate. "Okay, timeout." She pushed her plate away. "It's getting too mushy for me."

Knowing her cousin's limits, Frankie wiped her tear and spoke. "Scarlet doesn't do mushy very well."

Judith grabbed another hunk of bread. "Why not? Everyone needs a little mush once in a while. Seriously, Scarlet, you should join us."

Scarlet crossed her arms. "Like Frankie said, mush isn't really my thing. Work and schedule, that's my thing. Besides, don't you guys sit around talking about feelings and stuff?"

Judith put down her bread and turned to look at Scarlet. An ordinary person might have been offended at this point in the meal by Scarlet's blatancy, but Judith didn't seem fazed at all.

"You know, you remind me a lot of myself—young, fabulous, overly attractive. I guess I'm still many of those things. But I was also ambitious and power-driven, strictly business, and I liked having things a certain way. That combination can backfire though." Judith squinted at Scarlet. "I bet you're not very spontaneous, are you?"

Scarlet didn't answer but turned to Frankie and cocked an eyebrow.

"You probably go to bed at the same time every night, go to the same restaurants, and have all your clothes organized by color." Judith pointed her fork at Scarlet now. "You don't like to go out of your comfort zone, do you?"

"Having structure isn't a bad thing, Mom," Monica replied. "Leave her alone. We barely know her."

"But it means you don't trust easily," Judith said, determined.

Scarlet still didn't reply.

Judith put down her fork and wiped her hands on her linen napkin. "I want to share a Bible passage that someone shared with me a long time ago, and it's made all the difference in the world. 'Delight yourself in the Lord, and he will give you the desires of your heart. Commit your way to the Lord, trust in him, and he will act. He will bring forth your righteousness as the light, and your justice as the noonday.' That's Psalm thirty-seven, verses four to six."

Judith had quoted one of Frankie's mother's favorite passages. It almost seemed too perfect, like her mother was sending another message. But what was more notable was Scarlet. Her eyes had grown dark, as if she'd throw butter knives across the table into Judith's baguette. A long silence ensued at the table.

"She's pretty straightforward, isn't she?" Scarlet said, looking to Monica for some answers.

"She's never been one to hold back."

Judith continued unfazed by their exchange. "I bet if you trust more, you'll see your world in a completely new way."

Scarlet puckered her brow but sat quiet for a moment. Frankie didn't think this would end well, and Scarlet would get up and leave and give her a piece of her mind later.

Finally, Scarlet spoke staring straight into Judith's eyes. "So, wait. You're trying to tell me that if I pray and trust more, Jesus will give me more clients?"

Frankie exhaled a heavy sigh. The point had completely gone over her cousin's head.

"I kind of like it. Okay, what else have you got?"

Judith threw her hands in the air and burst into laughter, then leaned over to hug Scarlet. "You're more like me than you even know, but it's a good place to start."

Scarlet smiled and squeezed her back. As Judith unlocked from their embrace, she stared at Scarlet. "Just know I'm expecting you to show up one day to our group. If you ever decide you just want to come for a glass of wine, and not the 'therapy stuff,' we'll be here."

Scarlet gave a quick nod. "Deal."

Frankie settled more comfortably in her seat and enjoyed the rest of the visit. When Scarlet insisted on picking up the tab, Monica and Judith were very appreciative, but Frankie knew Scarlet was looking at it as a business lunch write-off and a way to entice new clients. Either way, everyone was happy.

As they finished their goodbyes to Judith and Monica and left the restaurant, Scarlet put her hand on Frankie's arm. "Well, I can see what you like in them. They're nice. Are the others like them? They don't seem too grief-stricken."

"I already told you it's not a grief group, but as Judith said, we do share our experiences. I think you might like it if you came just once."

"Nah, still not my cup of tea or wine." She winked. "But I'm glad it's giving me my cousin back, whatever they're doing with you."

"You know, Monica's right. You're young, single, no kids. What's stopping you from taking a vacation? It would be good for you to get away sometime."

"Really, Frankie, you too? You know I can't do that." She clenched her purse on her shoulder. "Who would I get to help me run the studio? If I leave, then other studios will get the better clients in town."

"You could always schedule your clients for a different week."

Scarlet rolled her eyes and turned her body away from Frankie. "I just don't think it's smart. I'm getting a lot of big names right now, and I need to be available at any moment."

Frankie knew it was an excuse, but for what she didn't know. She had to tread lightly. "I just don't want you to burn out, Scarlet, that's all."

"I know you've been taking time off from the world, Frankie, but for me, it's what keeps me going. I've never felt so good. I'm good at what I do."

"But you can't take on so much. Even with my small help, it's still too much for you."

Scarlet crossed her arms. "I admit, I'm a little behind with the billing and editing, but I'm working on it."

Frankie still wasn't convinced.

"I was thinking I might even like to expand, you know. Hire some assistants to help me out."

Suddenly, Frankie had a lightbulb moment. *Olivia.* "Hey, what if I said I had someone in mind that could help you? Her name's Olivia, she's from the book talk, she would work flexible hours, and she's looking for a job." She blurted it out so quickly Scarlet had to take a step back.

"Try to breathe between words, Frankie," said Scarlet. "I'd have to meet her, but can she talk to customers and deal with a person like me?"

Frankie didn't know all of Olivia's qualifications, but if she could deal with a man like Travis, she imagined a strong businesswoman wasn't anything she couldn't handle. "I think she could handle a lot of intense personalities if that's what you mean." Scarlet scowled her brows, unconvinced. " And ... she's also a pretty good novice photographer." She didn't know how true the last part was, but she thought back to the photo in Olivia's home of her and her daughter Cammy and figured it was worth mentioning.

Scarlet pursed her lips. "Hmm, I guess meeting Monica and Judith weren't too bad." She leaned up against the railing outside of Roux that partitioned outdoor seating from the sidewalk. Frankie watched her as she stood silent in her thoughts. At last she turned toward Frankie. "What the heck. Let's do it!" She smirked. "See. I can be spontaneous."

"Will you consider possibly taking a vacation too?"

"Taking your word about a hire is one thing, but vacations ... I'll consider it, but I can't say I'll do it."

"Fair enough. One thing at a time." Frankie grinned.

Chapter 9

I command you: be strong and steadfast! Do not fear
nor be dismayed, for the LORD, your God, is with you
wherever you go.—Joshua 1:9

Frankie called Olivia early the next morning to tell her
the good news. She'd already arranged a meeting time for
Scarlet and Olivia so they could get a feel for each other,
but Scarlet had pretty much confirmed it was a go.

"Wow! Uh, that's great, Frankie. You didn't have to do
that," Olivia said with an unenthusiastic voice.

"This'll solve your problem. You don't have to worry
about being supported by Travis and you can have the
baby. Isn't it great? You don't have to choose anymore."

"That's so generous of you."

Her monotone reaction mystified Frankie. "I thought
you'd be happy, Olivia. My cousin is willing to hire you,
hands down, sight unseen."

A long pause ensued on the other end of the line. Then
Olivia let out an exasperated sigh. "Don't get me wrong,
Frankie. I'm grateful for what you've done. It's just that ...
it's not that simple."

"Yes, actually, it's very simple. You won't have to worry
about being on the streets, and Cammy can continue
gymnastics. Your baby can be born, and you can move

forward with your life. Where is that complicated?" She waited for Olivia to respond.

"It's not just about getting a new job. Travis ... he ... he doesn't want the baby." Frankie could hear the desperation in her voice. "Even if I completely broke it off with him and leave him, he's still gonna press for me to have an abortion. Remember, he already has a life and a family. If word got out he had another baby with another woman around town, it would ruin his life and career."

Rage rose in Frankie's chest. "So, you're willing to kill your child for the sake of his reputation? Has he threatened you?"

"He's never said anything in particular, but I know him. He won't let this go easily."

"If he so much as ..." Frankie paused, at a loss for words, and gritted her teeth.

"He's a powerful businessman. He's got connections in this town, and he's not going to just let this go." Olivia's voice cracked on the other end of the phone. "I want this baby, so bad I can't even tell you. But I feel like either way I'm gonna have to pay for it, one way or another. I always lose in the end."

Frankie's temper cooled to an ember as she listened to the contrite words. She knew Olivia's situation wasn't an easy one. But unlike Olivia, she hadn't lost that fire. She knew there had to be a flicker of light, and she hoped she could be that for her new friend.

"Listen, just meet me Monday morning at Clement's coffee shop. If you're still a no by the end, I'll drop it."

Olivia reluctantly agreed, and Frankie hung up the phone.

Why couldn't Olivia listen to reason? How could she prioritize Travis over her own child? But Frankie knew Olivia had no one. Her decisions had always been about survival, her own survival. And a man like Travis would make her feel as if her life didn't matter. She felt sad for Olivia, that her fear of Travis had caused her to even consider this. She remembered in her own counseling sessions a phrase that Dr. Jude had pointed out. *Fear is a liar.* Fear could convince even rational people to do the most irrational things. She had to find a way to convince Olivia not to let fear lead her decisions, but she knew it would be a hard stretch.

Candace entered the room, interrupting her thoughts. "Hey, Momma. What time are we going to church this morning?"

"I suppose around 10:30. Why? What's up?"

"Well, there's this dance at the end of the summer, sort of a back-to-school thing, on Friday." She paused and took a breath. "I'd like to get a new outfit to wear. Half of my clothes don't fit me anymore, and I need new jeans for the dance."

Frankie nodded. Candace was right. She'd had a growth spurt and everything in her closet looked like she was preparing for the next flood. But jeans? "Don't they wear dresses to a dance?"

"No, not my friends. Everyone wears jeans now. And it's a sports-theme dance anyway."

Frankie glanced at the time. "Hmm. Okay. I guess we can go shopping after church."

"Who were you talking to on the phone just now, Momma?"

Living in a house with five people didn't always offer moments of privacy, but Frankie obliged. "That's my new friend, Olivia. Do you remember that young girl who Lizzie was playing with on Friday night? Her mom."

"Oh, she seemed really nice."

"I'm hoping she'll take a job with Auntie Scarlet." Even though Scarlet and Frankie were cousins, the girls called her auntie.

"Yeah, I know Auntie Scarlet could use some help. Does she need a new job? She doesn't have one already?"

"Well, Sissy, Olivia lives a hard life. She's been on her own and getting this job might help her get to a place where she can feel safe and learn new skills. You know, a fresh start."

Candace looked at her and frowned. "What do you mean?"

"You girls have been blessed to be raised in a house with a mom and dad and safety. Olivia hasn't had that."

"She doesn't have a mom and dad?"

"It's not for me to tell her whole story, but she didn't grow up with what you have here."

"Wow, that's really sad. So, Cammy doesn't have grandparents either? I don't know what I would do if I didn't have you guys and if I hadn't had Mimi and Papa. I feel bad for her."

Frankie looked at Candace. "First of all, don't feel bad about having a big family, and second of all you weren't lucky—you were blessed. I was blessed to have your mimi and papa as parents. When you feel sad about it, look at it as a blessing. Because that means you got to experience love, and love is a powerful thing." Frankie watched her daughter absorb her words and try to make sense of it.

She decided it was the perfect moment to share with Candace something that had been on her mind for some time. "I've been meaning to tell you for a while how proud I am of you for always stepping in and helping around here since Mimi died. I know I haven't been myself these past couple years, and that hasn't been easy on you or anyone in our family."

Candace stared at the floor.

"I don't know if I'll ever be that same person I was before. A part of me left when Mimi died." Frankie drew in a deep breath. "But I know I haven't stopped loving you and our family. And that's what keeps me going."

"It's okay, Momma. I know how much you miss Mimi. I miss her too, but as you said, we were blessed, so of course, it's going to hurt."

Frankie had taken close to two years to see the connection of the blessings that came after her mother's death. She gazed at Candace with true admiration as she'd managed to grasp the concept within a few short moments.

"Candace Grace Waters, how did I get so blessed to be your mom?"

Frankie pulled Candace close and caressed her hair.

She returned her love to her mother with a long, heartfelt hug.

Rena walked in. "Are you doing a group hug without me?"

Both Candace and Frankie laughed. Rena seemed to have a special gift for knowing when people were hugging and jumped right in the middle.

"Get in here," said Candace, and the three of them embraced in a group hug.

"Lizzie, Dad! It's group hug time!"

Frankie and Candace giggled. They knew how much Rena loved family hugs. Lizzie scurried in, and Max joined them straight from the bathroom with his face half shaved.

As they all embraced each other in a squished and loving embrace, Frankie had to admit she loved these group hugs just as much as Rena.

As they started to depart, Lizzie yelled, "Did someone say something about shopping later?"

As usual, the church parking lot was full of cars with people already inside waiting for Mass to begin. St. Elizabeth Ann Seton's was one of the bigger parishes in the Tuleberg area and could hold more than nine hundred people at one Mass service.

The building, a contemporary design with large pillars and Pentagon-style seating, boasted traditional stained-glass windows and stations of the cross. Despite the blazing July heat and regular vacationing of parishioners in the summer months, the church was surprisingly full. The Waters took a seat toward the front in their normal area. Rena liked to sit close so she could see what the priest and others on the altar were doing. This proved to be helpful since the location positioned the family close to the air conditioning unit.

Because the pews were arranged in a half-pentagon design with the altar in the center, Frankie could virtually see almost everyone in the church from her seat. She noticed that many of the women from her book talk were here. Birdie sat on the opposite side next to her husband fanning herself while in prayer. Judith sat with Monica, along with some others—possibly other family—Frankie hadn't met. Johnna was seated in the back, in the east corner, by herself.

The choir led the opening procession as they sang the hymn of St. Francis, "Make Me a Channel of Your Peace." Frankie felt a feeling of peace as she listened to the choir belt out the beautiful song. Rena tried her best to follow in the missalette, sometimes making up the words she couldn't read.

As Frankie glanced around observing the congregation, she noticed everyone seemed a little more agitated as the heat outside sweltered its way into the church. Little old ladies with veils bowed in prayer with grimaced looks on their faces as young children climbed the pews trying to avoid the heat, only intensifying their body temperature. Others nodded off to stay cool. Even with the heat, Frankie smiled as she saw Father Gabriel process in for the start of the Mass, patting his balding forehead with a tissue. Despite his obvious discomfort, his smile and attention to his parishioners felt welcoming.

After the Gospel, Father walked toward the center of the altar to face the congregation. He patted his face again as he tried to stay cool. "What if today was your last day on earth? How would you spend it?"

Immediately a few bodies sat up in their pews. His remark had taken them back, even while he continued to smile so sweetly. Frankie found their reactions amusing as she watched some ladies wave their fans more vigorously. Father Gabriel had a way of drawing people's attention.

"If it was your last day, would you spend it on a vacation or would you spend the day talking to and forgiving your enemy? Would you spend all your money on a fancy meal or help feed the poor? Today in the Gospel, Jesus essentially asks this to his disciples when he gives the Sermon on the Mount. He asks them to take a look at themselves, which is what we need to consider as well."

Father Gabriel smiled again as he fixed his eyes back to the crowd. "How do you live each day and what do you value? Is your goal to have a perfect life or is your goal to enter the kingdom of heaven? If it's the latter then when do you start working on this? It's easy to think that heaven is far off in the future, and we've got plenty of time to help, to offer our time. But we find that these tasks get pushed to the back when we prioritize arbitrary things as more important."

Frankie looked around as parishioners lifted their chins eagerly, taking in his sermon.

"It's easy to justify that you can start helping when you have more money, more time, but what if today was your last? Would you be ready for Jesus? Jesus isn't looking for wealth or accomplishment. He is looking for the meek, the merciful, those who in their weakness seek to find him. How can you, today, make yourself ready for him? What do you need to do to show him you're ready for heaven today?"

Father Gabriel continued with his sermon, but Frankie mulled over those words. *What if today was my last? How have I been using my time?* She took a pen and a piece of paper out of her purse, shoved her purse back under the pew, and wrote down the words. *How have I been using my time?* Looking at the words she realized she'd been so focused on the past that she hadn't looked at the present. She'd only been focused on the loss.

She didn't think Father Gabriel was speaking specifically to her, telling her to get over her grief. Her therapist had confirmed it was important to grieve and feel the effects of her relationship. "You need to feel it in order to heal it." But Dr. Jude had said that when the time was right—whenever that would be—she would know. Maybe God was looking for her meekness here. The words of the sermon felt like the crisp, cool morning air despite the blazing heat—a wake-up call. Now was the time to start doing things. She clenched the piece of paper in her hands. The words created a blueprint without instructions, but at least now she had the foundation.

After Mass, Lizzie and Rena ran to grab donuts the church gave out each Sunday near the front steps of the plaza at the hospitality table. Max stopped to talk to a few familiar male faces, probably counting down to the beginning of the football season and comparing fantasy leagues. As Candace and Frankie walked toward Max, Frankie looked down and realized she didn't have her purse, only the paper still clenched in her hand.

Frankie tapped Candace's arm. "I need to go back inside. I forgot something."

"Okay. Hurry. It's hot," said Candace, as she walked toward the awnings for some shade.

"Take your time, honey," Max yelled with his back turned.

She returned to the cool mahogany pews, leaned under, and found her purse where she'd left it. As she stood, she noticed Johnna still sitting in her spot, eyes closed and rosary beads clenched in hand. Frankie wondered why she was alone but imagined she didn't get too many quiet moments like this. In some respects, Johnna's world was parallel to what Frankie's had been only a few years earlier—rushing from one appointment to the next, juggling multiple schedules. She admired Johnna for taking this time for prayer. She left her undisturbed.

She stepped back outside to the stifling heat and walked right into Judith and Monica.

"Well, it looks like we keep running into each other," exclaimed Judith as she grabbed Frankie and brought her in for an immense hug. "We need to start planning this."

"Mom, we go to the same church, we're bound to run into each other." Monica leaned in to give an air kiss. "Sorry. This heat's too much for contact."

"I'm just saying it's nice to see you three days in a row. By the way, this is my husband Salvador. Sal, this is Frankie, one of the girls from the book group."

"Nice to meet you." Frankie stuck out her hand. Suddenly she had an image of Judith eating a whole plate of salty foods and wondered if Sal knew how many meals she'd had without his knowledge.

"Nice to meet you, indeed," replied Sal, reaching out to shake Frankie's hand.

Judith's husband was tall, with a lean athletic build. He wore a light blue, collared golf-shirt that contrasted with his tan skin. Frankie was surprised at how trim he was despite Judith's report from his doctor only the day before about his blood pressure and salt intake. She'd imagined a short, beer bellied, out-of-shape man, but then again Judith ate like a hungry football team and still kept a trim physique.

"My wife says she loves this group and can't wait to go each week."

Frankie nodded. "It's a pretty special group of ladies."

Then Monica gestured to the tall, hunched over man standing next to Sal. "This is my Gerard and our kids, Regina and James." Gerard gave a slight smile but kept his head down as he stuck out his hand to shake. Frankie thought him an opposite match next to Monica's erect and bold nature, traits clearly inherited from her father. She continued down the line and met her daughter Regina, a beautiful, vibrant, younger version of her mother with long dark curls and no resemblance to Gerard. Little James had the same slump as his father but Monica's smile.

Frankie gazed at the group. "It's great to finally meet your family."

Suddenly, Rena and Lizzie popped up with donut icing on their faces. "Hi, Momma. Want a bite?"

Frankie dodged the sticky fingers as Lizzie attempted to shove a donut in her face. "Um, no thanks, Liz. Did you get a napkin?"

"Oh, we don't need one. That's what dresses are for," replied Rena.

Judith chuckled, then took a pack of tissues out of her purse and handed it to Frankie.

Rena stuck a half-chewed maple bar in front of Judith's face. "Would you like some, ma'am?"

"Oh, no. I don't eat that stuff." Judith looked at her husband out of the corner of her eye, pretending to be appalled by the donut. Monica leered at her reaction.

"Pardon their appearance but these are my two youngest, Elizabeth and Rena." Frankie quickly tried to wipe the glaze off Rena's face, but the heat and the stickiness made it worse.

"Call me Lizzie," she said as she stuck out her gooey hand. Rena followed her big sister and did the same.

"You can pass on the handshake," said Frankie, ushering the girls toward the bathroom. "Lizzie, take your sister to the bathroom and both of you wash up."

"But, Mom!"

"Go now, please."

Lizzie huffed and reluctantly went to the bathroom. Rena, being her little shadow, huffed too, but followed.

Sal looked at his granddaughter Regina. "Come on, Gigi. Let's go get dirty in some chocolate bars since the maple is taken. Maybe they even have a raspberry-filled one. Those really get everywhere."

"Salvador?" Judith called.

"I'm not going to eat one, but that doesn't mean my grandkids can't. It's not Roux, but it's still good." He winked at Frankie as he grabbed Regina's and James's hands and scurried toward the donut table.

"Well, I guess he's onto us," proclaimed Judith.

"On to us?" Monica arched her brows at her mother and turned toward her husband. "Gerard, go over with them to make sure they don't get into too much trouble."

Gerard said nothing but docilely walked over to supervise.

"It was great to have lunch with you and your cousin yesterday," Monica said, turning back to Frankie and her mother. "She seems like a sweet girl." Frankie was surprised Monica would refer to Scarlet as sweet. That wasn't the usual description one would give about her cousin, but she was relieved that Monica and Judith could handle strong women and hadn't been miffed at Scarlet's direct nature.

"Oh, I adored meeting Scarlet!" Judith exclaimed. "Such a young sassy version of myself. You know, I have the perfect young man I want her to meet."

"Mom, stop trying to fix up every single person you come across. Maybe she wants to be single."

"You never know if love could happen. It's like Father Gabe said, this could be your last day. You don't want to die not finding the right person."

"I don't think that's what he was referring to, Mom. Besides, let the lady determine her own destiny." Monica half-whispered to Frankie, "You know, she's going to use that line about the last day of your life for at least a good month or until Father Gabriel has different material."

Frankie laughed at the thought. "I wouldn't worry about Scarlet. She can find dates, but she doesn't want to take the time with them."

"If I can't set her up, then you tell her I want her to come to the next book talk, even if she doesn't read," declared Judith, placing her hand on her hip.

Frankie took the church bulletin that was wedged in her purse and fanned it over her face to keep cool. "I'm pretty sure she'll say no, but either way, I'll see her tomorrow and deliver the message." Frankie wanted to tell the mother-daughter duo about the meeting with Olivia and Scarlet, but felt it was too soon.

"You okay, Frankie?" Monica picked up her worry just like she had the day before, fanning the bulletin faster.

Frankie was unsure what to say until Judith spotted Johnna coming out of the church.

"What a nice surprise that we all picked the same Mass this morning."

"Why are you ladies standing out in this awful heat?" Johnna said, fanning herself just like Frankie with her bulletin.

"Yes, why are we standing out here? I'm starting to melt," proclaimed Monica.

"Let's move under the awning—it's shadier," suggested Frankie as she saw her husband start to beckon her over to leave.

"Have you been in the church this whole time?" Judith asked Johnna as they walked toward the shade.

"I pray my rosary after Mass when I can," Johnna said. "My dad has some checkups in San Francisco, so I try to get some extra prayers in before big trips."

Frankie remembered from the talk that Johnna had an excessive amount of responsibility. She sympathized as she remembered the days of one appointment after another with her mom.

Candace and Max waved their hands signaling to Frankie from afar they were ready to head out. She had wanted to talk longer and comfort Johnna, but she knew now might not be the right time.

"Ladies, I've got to leave, but please keep us posted, Johnna, and lots of prayers your way," Frankie said as she reached out to give her a hug.

"Thanks. Will do," Johnna replied.

She gave Judith and Monica hugs as she said her goodbyes.

"You okay, babe?" Max asked as they walked to their car.

"Yeah. It's just hard to see other people going through struggles. I sometimes feel like I'm going through the same emotions over and over again when someone is experiencing what I experienced."

"I think you become a better person for it, Frankie. You understand them." Max placed his hand on the lower part of her back.

Frankie gave him a half smile. The sadness she took in from Johnna's look was now replaced with empathy and understanding. She'd been oblivious of hardships before her mother's death. Now, the awareness could not be taken for granted. Frankie heard a small vibration come from her phone in her purse. She pulled out her phone to see a missed call followed by a notification of a text message both from her father.

> **DAD:** We seem to miss each other. I guess texting is easier. Hanging out in Juneau today. Oh, how I wish your mom could have seen this. I'll try to call again or text.

"Who's that?" asked Max.

"Dad texted me. We haven't been able to have a phone conversation since he's been in Alaska, the reception or our timing has been off."

"Tell Rudy hi and I hope he doesn't see any grizzly bears," joked Max.

Her dad had been trying to make up for lost time. Even though he was having a great trip, Frankie knew he wished he had gone when her mother was alive. The last two years, he had spent visiting, Italy, Ireland, Brazil, all the places her mother would have wanted to go if she was still alive. Now they were a bunch of what-ifs he was trying to carry out. Maybe his grief was deeper than Frankie realized. He was living in the past too. She knew she had to be more present. She quickly texted her father back.

FRANKIE: Enjoy your time in Juneau. Don't worry if we don't connect. We will when you get back. Just be present in the moment. And avoid grizzly bears.

Frankie dropped off Max and Rena at home, then drove herself and her two other girls to the department store for Candace's outfit.

Frankie spent the rest of the afternoon shopping with her girls, watching them try on outfits and browse for bracelets. She continued to think about Father Gabriel's message. She had to be present. Her time was now, and she had to spend her time with purpose.

Chapter 10

We are all travelers on this great adventure of life, and I am forever grateful to have been able to share this journey.—Dr. Mary Neal

Monday morning, Frankie arrived at Clement's coffee shop an hour early. She planned to convince Olivia to take the job, but still needed to figure out how to do that without endangering her. She needed to rehearse her strategy. She'd brought her journal along so she could record any thoughts she might find helpful.

As she stood in line for her order, she recognized Johnna's familiar dark-haired silhouette two people in front of her. "Johnna!"

Johnna turned around. "Oh, Frankie!" A big warm smile crossed her face as she let the customer in between them cut in front of her, then reached out and gave Frankie a big hug. Johnna's hugs were like being wrapped in a batch of laundry warm from the dryer. Frankie felt bad about leaving after seeing her at Mass, so this made for a good reprieve. "What are you doing here?"

Frankie fidgeted with her journal in hand. She hadn't considered the publicness of her meeting with Olivia when she'd made the appointment, but she couldn't tell Johnna about it. She wondered briefly if she'd told Olivia to go to Scarlet's studio instead, but that probably would have been too intimidating. Frankie hoped Johnna would be long gone by the time Olivia arrived.

"I'm meeting my cousin in a while," Frankie said, "so I thought I would do some journaling before she got here." She stuck as close to the truth as she could, leaving out the Olivia part. "Today's another big appointment for your dad, right?"

Johnna nodded. "I just dropped off my kids at school and coordinated with the sitter. Everything is set. Now I'm in need of a little caffeine boost before I get on the road to take him."

"Sounds like a big day."

"It's a lot of driving and then waiting, but I brought my book with me so I can catch up in the waiting room." She glanced at her watch. "I'm going to try to read this week, I promise. Sometimes, the week flies by, and I just can't get it all done, but I like coming for the conversation."

Frankie placed a hand on Johnna's arm. "Isn't that the point of our book talk? It's okay if you don't get all the reading done—just do what you can. I think you put a lot of pressure on yourself to be everything for everyone. I used to do that too."

"You're probably right, but I have to make sure it gets done sometimes."

Frankie nodded. "And it will get done. Trust me, it all gets done. If I can give you any advice, enjoy these drives with your dad. I used to take them with my mom, and I can look back now at all the memories created. We would count trucks passing on the freeway, find fun new restaurants, and do almost anything to make the trips to San Francisco less about hospital and more about quality time together."

"You're right. I do get caught up in the job of it all."

"Just remember to look at it as an experience rather than a task."

"Thanks, Frankie. I know you get it. The other night, when you shared about your mom, it helped me a lot. Sometimes this journey feels lonely."

It hadn't occurred to Frankie that her sharing at the meeting might benefit someone else. "I just want you to know if you need help with anything, picking up kids or helping out in anyway, I'm happy to."

Johnna winced at the comment. "We'll see."

Frankie sensed Johnna had the same intense pride as she once had when juggling her mother's medical schedule. "Someone once told me, 'If you deny others the ability to help, then you're denying them the ability to serve God.' I know that when my mom was sick, I never took anyone's help, but when someone did something for me, I always appreciated it. I never wanted to admit how much it helped me," confessed Frankie.

Johnna looked at her with grateful eyes. "Thanks, Frankie. I feel like I'm looking in the mirror sometimes with what you're saying."

Frankie pushed a piece of hair behind her ear and smiled. She felt the warmness of her mother wrap around her in that moment.

"Will I see you this Friday?" Johnna asked.

"I'll be there. But first, I have to drop off my daughter Candace. She has a junior high dance on Friday. I doubt she'll want me to stay and chaperone." She chuckled.

"Oh, I remember those days," said Johnna, looking up at the ceiling. "Everything is so special, new and real and … awkward."

They both laughed.

As they approached the counter, the cashier had two cups of coffee already prepped and in a carrier with Johnna's name on them. Apparently, she had called ahead. She was so efficient, always on top of things.

Johnna turned, ready to leave, then paused and turned back to Frankie. "There is actually something I'd like help with. I have been wanting to get my dad some special succulents for his garden just to cheer him up, but with his appointments and my crazy schedule I haven't had the chance. Do you think you could help me look for a good nursery? I probably wouldn't have asked anyone, but since you know what all of this is like, I don't feel like it's such a huge favor to ask."

Frankie didn't know the first thing about plants or gardening, but Johnna had made a big effort to ask for help so she couldn't tell her no. "Of course, let me see what I can come up with."

"Thanks, Frankie. I'm glad we ran into each other this morning."

As Johnna left the coffee shop, Frankie felt at peace. She hadn't imagined her admission could be cathartic for others. She beamed with joy as she placed her order—a triple latte with almond milk and a berry scone. She was just about to hunt for an open spot when out of the corner of her eye she noticed the guy at Roux who'd winked at Scarlet. *Kevin? Chris? No. Charles is what Scarlet called him.* He was in the corner sitting under the hanging plants having a pour-over coffee, a more appropriate setting than where she had first seen him. He waited for the water to drip through the liner and funnel attached to the top of his cup and didn't seem to notice Frankie, but he wouldn't really know her anyway. He was working on his laptop and seemed eager to get something done. As before, his overall appearance seemed out of proportion. He was very well dressed in a blue pin-striped blazer and yellow tie. Ironically, this time he seemed overdressed for the location. Scarlet mentioned he was an attorney, so perhaps he was working on a case.

As Frankie waited for her order, she continued to scan the room for an open table. The place was full, and, as fate would have it, the only table open was next to Charles. *How convenient.* She picked up her order and took the table. Even though she hadn't met him directly, curiosity prompted her to speak.

"Good morning. Charles, right?" she said in a timid voice.

The young man's piercing blue eyes contacted hers, and he offered a friendly but questioning grin.

"Good morning."

"My cousin is Scarlet Bedford. I was with her the other day at Roux, and she mentioned you."

"Oh, good morning." Recognition slowly dawned on him. "Oh! You were the lady sitting with her." The mention of Scarlet sent another grin across his face.

"Yes, I'm Frankie Waters. Scarlet never mentioned how you two know each other."

"Well ..." He closed his laptop, then stretched his arms leisurely and took his time finishing the sentence. "I've worked with her on some of the commercial photos she's done. I do a lot of legal contracts. She's very talented at what she does, and she's also done some shoots for the firm."

"As far as I know," Frankie said, "she's the best. I sometimes wish she took a little time for herself, though. She's always so busy."

Charles nodded. "I used to be as busy as her, if not busier. I practiced corporate law years ago. One day, I realized I didn't like working for things I no longer believed in or spending hours on cases I no longer felt ethical about. But she'll figure out being busy isn't always as productive as we think it is."

"Well, she keeps moving faster and faster. I hope she figures it out sooner than later. You might be a good influence on her." Frankie broke a piece off her scone and popped it in her mouth.

"She plays hardball, but that's what I like about her." He smirked. "Fortunately, I'm a great catcher."

"So, what are you doing here today? It's a big change from Roux."

He laughed a deep husky laugh that warmed up the room. "Yes, I suppose it is." He stretched out his arms again. "Roux isn't really my style, but they have the best martini in this town." He glanced around Clement's shop and smiled as his eyes settled on the homegrown plants in the window. "This is definitely more my scene. I have a lot of freedom in the firm and decided to come over for a cup and to work on some small projects. It's just nice to get away and ... be."

Frankie thought his response seemed pretty unusual considering lawyers were typically known to be knee-deep in work with long hours. *Maybe he's slow on clients.*

"Well, I'm meeting Scarlet in a while, so if you're still here, you can always join in on the conversation." She really didn't mean it but thought she should be polite.

"Oh, that's not her style. I'm sure you know that," he said, waving his hand.

Frankie was amazed he knew Scarlet was not a person who liked to go deep about her personal life. He also seemed to know she wasn't an easy catch, and he was perfectly fine with that.

He stood then and placed his laptop into his computer bag. "It was nice meeting you, Cousin Frankie," he said, offering her a smile.

She smiled back. "Nice to meet you too, Lawyer Charles."

Before he walked away, he bent down to tell Frankie a final thought. "By the way, let her know that the marigolds are in full bloom right now." He picked up his computer bag and coffee and walked out of the shop.

"Marigolds?"

Frankie opened her journal and took a few more bites of her scone. She returned to her thoughts, trying to come up with an action plan to convince Olivia to take the job, but nothing surfaced. A few minutes later, Olivia walked into the coffee shop wearing a striped shirt and a short-length jean jacket—showing just a bit of her baby bump. Frankie thought the outfit made her look very stylish, but then again, everything a twenty-something-year-old wore looked stylish and darling to her, a far contrast to her middle-aged-looking khaki puffer vest and yoga pants.

Frankie closed her journal and went up to the register to pay for Olivia's coffee.

"You don't have to pay. I'm capable of paying for my own things."

"I know," Frankie replied, "but I figured I dragged you down here, and if I can't convince you to work for Scarlet, at least you get a free cup of coffee. Besides, I have to put in her order too."

Olivia grimaced but ordered a decaf Chai latte. Frankie ordered Scarlet a regular coffee black with three sugars. They sat down at the table where Frankie had her things.

"My daughter Lizzie has been asking nonstop about Cammy and is hoping she can come over and hang out again. They hit if off really well."

Olivia's faced contorted, as if she struggled to enjoy the conversation. "Too well. Cammy really enjoyed herself at your house." She looked down at the ground avoiding eye contact. "Apparently, they've started a mermaid club."

Frankie smiled at the thought. "Of course, they did."

"Listen, Frankie," Olivia said, cutting the small talk. "I still don't know if this … this job is a good idea. I mean,

I feel like I'm dragging you into my problems, and, well, I don't know if you want to go down this road with me. Why do you care so much? I mean, you hardly know me."

Frankie put her elbows on the table and stared across at Olivia. "I need to be honest with you. I know these past two years, I haven't felt like myself at all. I don't honestly know why I care so much or what I'm doing." She raked her hands through her hair. "I don't know why I'm going down this road either. I'm probably crazy, but what I do know is you need a chance. You deserve to have your own life, not one that someone has dictated, but a life for you and Cammy and—"

Just then, Scarlet arrived with her glasses on top of her head and her camera slung over her shoulder. She plopped down next to Frankie and did a once-over on Olivia, then picked up the coffee Frankie had bought for her. "Thanks, Cuz." She sipped her coffee then turned to face Olivia. "You're Olivia, right?"

Olivia didn't seem fazed by Scarlet's abruptness. "That's what my birth certificate tells me, but you know never know with hospital mix-ups."

Unamused, Scarlet proceeded. "So, I'm looking for an assistant who can keep track of my client base and do some light computer work. Downloading and saving images. If you can do billing too, that would be helpful. If that sounds interesting to you, you've got the job."

"Do you have a set list of hours you would need from an assistant?"

"Most of the stuff can be done at your own time or when I need you. I work whenever the client needs me or when I'm inspired to take new tasks, but I would expect you to work as often as possible."

Olivia crossed her arms. "I'm just not sure if it would work."

Scarlet took another sip of her coffee and flung her glasses to the table. "Listen, I don't have time for 'I'm not sure.' You either want it or you don't." She glided her finger around the top of the coffee cup. "Frankie here helps when she can, but I don't do 'maybes' or 'I'm not sure.' She's given me her word on you. So, if you're in, you're in. If you're not, I need to move on."

"I think what she's saying," Frankie began, but Scarlet railroaded her involvement by holding up a hand.

"You're either in or you're out. It's not half empty or half full. Pregnant or not pregnant. There's no in-between with me."

Frankie grimaced. Scarlet obviously didn't know that Olivia was pregnant. Nevertheless, the analogy hit home.

Olivia sat up straight and said, "Actually, I am pregnant. Can I still get the job?"

Scarlet looked toward her belly. "Will it interfere with your ability to download files and work on a computer?"

"It shouldn't," said Olivia.

"Good. Then I'll see you tomorrow at my studio, so we can start training. Gotta go, Cuz. I have a new shoot at eleven o'clock. The mayor wants me to shoot the pics down at the new courthouse."

As Scarlet picked up her coffee and glasses and proceeded to head out, Frankie remembered the message from Charles.

"Wait! I forgot to tell you—" She scrambled to remember the message relayed to her only an hour before. "'The marigolds are in full bloom right now.'"

Scarlet stopped and turned back to the table. "Huh?"

"A message I was asked to pass onto you."

Her cousin grinned. "I may need to make a pit stop before I go to the courthouse." Without another word, she turned and headed out the door.

Olivia stared wide-eyed at Frankie. "Wow. Did that just happen? I guess I'm working for Scarlet now. Scarlet ... what's her last name?"

"Bedford."

"Scarlet Bedford." She stared a moment, still awestruck.

"So, you came here this morning still determined that this wasn't going to work. What just happened that changed your mind?"

"I guess ... I just ... I don't know." She smoothed her dark curls to the side of her face. "Her abruptness made me realize this is my life and my baby's life too. She decided about me without knowing me. You both took a chance on me. You didn't even think twice, and here I am. I guess I want to be that self-assured too. I'm tired of living in fear, tired of depending on men to tell me I'm worth something."

Frankie grinned and leaned across the table to touch Olivia's hand. "I'm really glad you made that decision, Olivia. I know you've got more decisions to make, but this is a step on the right path. I promise, you made the right decision."

Olivia squeezed her hand back. "I admire Scarlet. She knows what she wants and goes for it. I'm still worried about Travis, but I can't let that fear control me."

"Fear can be deceiving."

"I just wish I had a little more time."

"Well, I don't know how much more time you're going to have. That baby is definitely showing. But whatever you say to him, just know that you're not alone."

Olivia turned toward Frankie and squeezed her hand again. "I don't know what I'm going to say either, but for now"—she picked up her cup of Chai—"I'm just going to enjoy my tea and think about photos."

Chapter 11

What is impossible for human beings is possible for
God. —Luke 18:27

The next day, Frankie paced her house, eager to know
how the "first day" had gone for Olivia and for Scarlet.
She'd tried hard not to intervene and spent most of the day
pulling weeds in the front yard, scrubbing the bathroom
tub, and any other mind-numbing task to take away her
need to drive over to the studio to spy on both of them.

Frankie knew Olivia would have to face Travis at some
point too, but she couldn't imagine how the scene would
play out. From the way she'd described him, Olivia seemed
incredibly fearful of his reaction. Hopefully, working for
Scarlet would help create a clean break, but only time
would tell.

Finally, around six-thirty, she couldn't take it any
longer and picked up the phone.

She dialed Scarlet first, but her phone went straight to
voicemail. Eager to get some answers, she quickly dialed
Olivia. Before Olivia had completed her "hello," Frankie
interjected, "So how did the first day go?"

"Uh, Frankie, is that you?"

"Sorry, let me start over. Hi, Olivia. Yes, it's Frankie.
How was your first day?"

"Uh, hi. I guess it went okay."

"Just okay?" Frankie moved to the edge of her chair.

Olivia sighed. "Well, you're right. She's definitely intense, but I think I stayed up on everything she showed me."

"Like what?"

"Well, to start, she showed me around the studio, but was adamant I not leave a mess wherever I worked. But then she showed me the storage room, which was in total disorder with samples and proofs from past weddings lying around and told me I'd have to figure out how to keep them organized."

Frankie knew this was Scarlet's way of testing Olivia but didn't want to give the secret away. "She can be a little contradictory at times, but I'm sure you'll figure out a system that works. Did she show you any of the digital files?"

"Yeah, that computer system looks complicated, but I'm sure I'll get the hang of it."

Frankie knew that Scarlet already opening up computer files to Olivia was a good sign. "So, what do you think?"

"It's only my first day, Frankie."

"I know. I'm just excited for you. It's a big step, a change."

Olivia's voice sounded calm over the phone, but Frankie could swear she detected a hint of giddiness. "She's supposed to show me some of the billing tomorrow, and she said she'd tell me about a 'code word' she uses, but I wasn't totally sure what that was all about."

Frankie knew Scarlet must have been impressed if she was willing to mention the "code word," which was more of a phrase than just one word that Scarlet used if ever she needed some kind of decoy or an alert. If she said, "As my father used to say," followed by a particular message or simple statement, it meant Olivia would need to come up with some kind of distraction. Frankie had done this a few times on the occasion an irate client tried to get Scarlet to lower her price or when a sleazy customer tried to hit on her.

"I'll let her explain that, but that's a great sign she trusts you. Sounds like you had a terrific first day."

"Yeah, I think I did have a good one."

Frankie could sense Olivia felt pleased with the progress, even though she wouldn't divulge more. Suddenly her voice changed to a serious tone.

"Frankie."

"Yes?"

There was a long pause before she continued. "I don't know if there's a way to repay you for all your kindness, but I'm grateful to you."

Frankie grinned. "You don't have to do anything. That's what friends do, Olivia. They help each other." She had called her a friend. She was no longer just a face from the book talk. Frankie cared about this woman. "The fact that you're going to get away from that jerk is all the thanks I need."

"It isn't just a simple 'anything,' Frankie. It's a big deal to me."

She recognized Olivia's sense of propriety and knew she felt indebted, even if Frankie didn't expect anything in return. But what could Olivia do for her? All of sudden an idea came to Frankie.

"Actually, there is something I need help with."

"What? Anything."

"Well, I ran into Johnna the same day we were at the coffee shop. She wants some unique succulents for her dad's garden and asked for my help. I didn't want to admit I know nothing about plants. I can barely keep a cactus alive. Do you think you could help me find some for her? Like those pretty ones you had at your house? It would mean a lot to me, and I know it would mean a lot to Johnna too."

"I think I can definitely help with that." Frankie noticed Olivia's voice now had a bit of excitement in it. "In fact, I can put some really beautiful arrangements together. When do you need them?"

Frankie was pleased she could extend a form of repayment even though it wasn't necessary.

"I know it's pretty soon. Maybe in about a week or so?" Just as she was about to discuss the details, Frankie noticed a call coming through—Scarlet calling her back.

"Uhm, hey, I've got a call coming through that I need to take, but I'll let you know really soon when I need them."

"Uh, er, okay."

Frankie didn't want to tell her it was Scarlet, but she also didn't want to be rude by cutting her off so abruptly.

"Olivia."

"Yes?"

"I just know things are looking up for you."

"Thanks, Frankie."

She smiled as she hung up and switched the lines. So far everything was turning positive, and she hoped Scarlet's sentiments matched.

"Hey, there," Frankie said in a chipper voice.

"Hey, yourself."

"How did the first day go?" Frankie fought to keep any indication that she'd talked to Olivia only moments before out of her voice.

"Well for starters, she showed up."

"Oh no, that bad?" Maybe Olivia didn't have an accurate read on things. Frankie wondered if her hopes were higher than Scarlet's. This could be devastating.

Then Scarlet laughed. "I'm just kidding. She did better than I expected."

Frankie breathed a large sigh of relief. "Don't scare me like that!"

Scarlet laughed again. "I knew you couldn't wait to find out. I just wanted to mess with you. My guess is you've already called her too." Scarlet knew her too well. "She's actually a fast learner. She picked up everything from downloading images to our system of keeping client photos separate. I even showed her the back room with all the storage and the mess of old proofs. That in itself is enough to scare someone away, and she didn't seem fazed at all."

Frankie was relieved that Scarlet's impression harmonized with Olivia's. "Well, it sounds like she's the perfect fit."

"Time always tells, but for a first day I'd rate her an eight."

"Why not a nine or ten?"

"Because there's always room for improvement in anything."

Frankie smiled. She knew Scarlet could never admit her true satisfaction. "So did you give her my desk and let her make it her own?"

"I told her she could keep her things in the drawer, but I still expect you to help out when I need you, Frankie."

"You know I'll help wherever I can, but I want Olivia to feel comfortable there too."

"She asked to put her daughter's picture on the desk. It's a decent photo, so I don't mind."

"Maybe she has an eye for photography."

"Don't push it, Frankie, it's only her first day."

"I know. I'm just happy it's worked out for her, for you."

"If I haven't scared her off, she'll be back tomorrow to learn the billing system. She's a lot more organized than I am, so that's a plus, but I didn't tell her that."

"Nobody has to know your weaknesses," teased Frankie. "Oh, since we're talking about my book talk members, Judith was asking about you again. She really wants you to come next Friday. I've told her you're not interested a hundred times, but she's relentless."

Scarlet chuckled. "Yeah, still not interested, but when she's ready for that family photo shoot, I'm ready. You know, you've really met some cool people from this book talk."

Frankie smiled. She didn't know what to make of all the feelings she was having, but she agreed she had met some wonderful women.

★★★

The week quickly rolled by. On Friday, Frankie looked back over her journal entries from the week and the progress she'd made. While she hadn't finished all the readings from the book, she had managed to make spaghetti without the assistance of the fire department, and even Max commented she'd seemed less withdrawn. But she was more pleased with Olivia and Scarlet's working arrangement. It had solved a sundry of problems—Olivia's financial and emotional freedom from Travis, and Scarlet's ability to organize and manage her busy schedule. Although Scarlet might not have admitted it openly, Frankie was certain she would gain more than just an assistant, but time would tell.

She was the first to arrive at Birdie's, but unlike the previous weeks, she felt less concerned with time. As she leaned over the kitchen counter to pour herself a glass of wine, she mulled over how much had changed since the first book talk and how important the meetings had come to be in her life.

Shortly after, Johnna strode in, hands full of juggling her book and dessert. "Am I late?"

"No, you're right on time," Birdie replied as she and Frankie pulled plates and glasses out of the kitchen cabinets.

"It was such a hectic week, I fell a little behind on my reading." Johnna struggled as she placed a large metal container onto the counter without dropping her book and purse. "With Dad's appointments and my kids' activities, I'm just glad I could make it tonight. And I came through with the dessert. Carrot cake!" She waved a hand over the cream cheese frosted cake.

Birdie took the cake out of the container. "Well, you're here now, honey, and I'm sure you'll catch up in the discussion."

Maisie, covered from head to toe with dog hair, walked in a few moments behind Johnna. "Hi, guys. The door was open, so I let myself in. Do you mind if I change my clothes before we get started? I just left the animal shelter, and I didn't have time to go home. I hope you don't mind."

"Aaaah aaaah choo! Of course ... aaah choo!" Birdie motioned Maisie toward the bathroom.

Frankie grabbed a tissue for Birdie. "Allergies?"

"Oh, just a little. I wish I could have a dog, but the hair is just too much." She wiped her face. "You think I could ask her to leave her clothes in her car, so I don't have a wheezing attack for the rest of the night?"

Frankie smirked. "Good idea."

The doorbell rang, and Birdie went to answer it and also get some fresh air. As Lucy, Monica, and Judith walked into the kitchen, Frankie noticed Monica scowl at her mother, who had quickly found a place to sit at the counter.

157

"Well, hi, everyone," Lucy said with an overly exaggerated smile as she walked cautiously behind Monica.

"Hey there." Frankie smiled back as she sliced the carrot cake and plated a few pieces.

A mist of tension circled around Monica as she walked past her mother to the opposite end of the counter. She silently poured herself a glass of merlot and looked down at her book.

"Is she okay?" Frankie whispered to Lucy, looking over her shoulder.

"We're getting closer to the countdown before Regina leaves for school, so she's a little bit of a basket case right now and doesn't want to admit it," Lucy whispered back.

"Oh, I see," said Frankie.

"She doesn't really want to be here tonight," Judith added, clearly not caring if her voice was too loud. "She wants to spend every waking moment with Regina, but I encouraged her to be here. I told her when Regina leaves, she's going to need a new outlet, so she's a little mad at me. But I know she'll get over it."

Monica turned her back to her mother and pretended even harder to be engrossed in her book.

Judith looked at Frankie. "She says I can't relate because she never left home, so I don't get it. Maybe I don't, but she's behaving like a baby." She stabbed a fork into her slice of cake.

"Frankie and Johnna," Lucy said, "would you help me get some more bottles of wine out of my car, so they don't get hot?"

Frankie and Johnna stood and followed her out as they passed Birdie coming back into the kitchen. Frankie didn't have the heart to tell her what she was walking into.

As they got to the car, Lucy opened the trunk to reveal three cases of wine from her last trip to Napa and a few Lodi wines. She pulled out a couple bottles.

"Wow, that's a lot of wine," exclaimed Frankie.

Lucy blushed. "I don't drink it all. Well, maybe some of it, but the rest I give away."

"Won't it spoil back here?" asked Johnna.

Lucy smiled and arched an eyebrow. "I had my back trunk retrofitted a couple years ago so it would always be the perfect temperature. 'Wine-ty degrees Fahrenheit'," she joked. "You wouldn't believe how much wine I gift away."

Frankie looked bewildered. "So are we taking this all in?"

"Oh, heavens no. I just needed to get you girls out of the crossfire."

"Poor Birdie's left to her own defenses," joked Johnna.

"I figured that was the real reason," Frankie said.

Lucy handed two bottles of sauvignon blanc to Johnna. "So why is Monica so upset with Judith?"

Lucy took a deep breath as she handed her a third bottle. "Judith's trying to be supportive of Regina. She's eighteen, ready for college, and Judith thinks it'll be healthy for her to stretch her wings. Monica's a very devoted mom, but Regina's having second thoughts about leaving and Judith thinks it's because Monica has guilted her into staying. You know they're a very tight-knit family."

"But Monica's not alone," said Frankie.

Lucy shook her head as reached into a different case and pulled out two bottles of Tempranillo and handed them to Frankie. "You and I know that, but Monica has put so much time and energy into her, she's kind of grieving in her own way that Regina is moving on without her."

Johnna looked to the ground. "That must be hard for Monica."

"Yes, she's going through a rough time, but I think tonight will be good for her. She needed to get out." Lucy closed the trunk of her car and gave it an extra press. "And it's good for Regina too, to see that her mom will be okay. Time has a way of working these things out." She winked at Frankie as they strolled back up the walk path.

Frankie understood that feeling of pre-grief. She had mourned her mother's loss long before anticipating the inevitable. But Monica's situation was different. Her daughter was living, and Monica was grieving the end of a chapter. But was it really any different?

Frankie walked with bottles in hand behind the two, pondering Lucy's statement. *Time has a way of working things out.* Time really was a tricky thing. Only a few weeks before, she was sitting at home staring into a dark corner of her room on a Friday night and now she was joined with social women, Napa vintage wine, and carrot cake. Maybe Lucy was right. Maybe time would help Judith and Monica. She furrowed her brow still contemplating the final answer as they entered the living room.

Maisie came out of the bathroom and left her clothes on the back porch before she and Birdie moved into the living room with their pieces of cake. Birdie still was wiping her nose but seemed less concerned about her allergies than she had been in the kitchen. Judith and Monica still sat at opposite ends of the kitchen counter.

"Johnna, did you make this cake from scratch? It tastes fabulous," Judith commented just before taking another bite.

"It's nothing fancy like last week's spread, but it's a family recipe. My mother actually made it for me, to help me out."

"Well, it looks fabulous. I can't wait to try it," exclaimed Lucy.

"Thank goodness for mothers helping out," Judith said in a terse tone directed at Monica as she picked up her plate and walked into the living room.

Lucy looked frazzled as she glanced between Monica and Judith's retreating back, but Johnna came to the rescue and helped extinguish the situation.

"Come on," Johnna said, putting out her hand to Monica. "Let's go pretend we read the chapters together. I didn't finish mine again."

Monica smiled wryly, grabbed her book, and Johnna's hand. Frankie followed behind them with the cake platter. Olivia had also arrived just as they were getting started.

"Well, honey, you made it. Do you want some wine?" offered Lucy.

"No, but I'll take a big piece of that cake. It looks delicious."

Frankie made eye contact with Olivia and smiled. None of the ladies knew about her pregnancy yet, and Frankie wondered when she would come clean.

"Here, I can help." Olivia approached and cut a huge piece—almost a quarter of the cake—then dug in to take a bite.

Maisie's eyes grew wide. "That's a nice hunk of cake there."

Olivia shrugged. "I'm so hungry and carrots sound so appetizing. I just can't get enough of them."

Frankie smirked.

"That's one way to get your vegetables," Birdie said as she bit into her own piece of cake.

Johnna walked up to get her slice from Frankie. "Wow, you're right, that's a big piece of cake. My kind of girl!"

Olivia shoveled bite after bite into her mouth.

"By the way, Frankie, were you ever able to find some succulents?" asked Johnna.

"Actually," she said looking over at Olivia. "Olivia here is pretty handy at getting some beautiful arrangements together, and I've asked her to help."

Olivia finished her chewing and spoke up. "Uh, yeah, I guess I am pretty good at flowers. I love gardening whenever I can. I used to work for a nursery a while back. I'm sure I could get something special for you."

"That would be awesome. My dad's appointment is coming up next week and I want to surprise him. He hasn't been feeling so great with all the chemo and the treatments, so I think this will be just the thing to lift his spirits. We've got to go for his final treatment soon, and this will be like a celebratory surprise. Can I pick them up at your house?"

"No!" Olivia quickly replied, bits of cake spilling from her lips. "I mean, why don't I bring them to you? I live so far out … you wouldn't want to travel all that way."

"What about if I deliver them to you, Johnna," Frankie said. "And I can add some small touches, like a little gnome in the pot or a stick with a dragonfly? Just a little extra something? Olivia and I can work out the details." Frankie winked at Olivia, and she saw her let out a sigh of relief.

Birdie clapped her hands. "Okay, girls, it's time to start."

Frankie and Olivia sat next to each other, and Johnna joined them on the couch. When everyone was settled in, Frankie noticed Monica was still sulking, but not as intensely as when she had first arrived.

"Well, I admit," Johnna said, throwing her hands up in the air. "I'm behind again this week on the readings. Can someone please fill me in on what I missed?"

"This week's chapter focused on out-of-body experiences," Maisie explained. "Can you believe what people see when they have an NDE? I can only imagine what that must be like. I think my favorite story was the lady who had a kidney transplant and saw the doctor listening to rock music while he was operating. Her children and family were in the next room and were crying for her to pull through."

Monica let go of her gloomy mood long enough to chime in. "Wouldn't that be a common response if a relative was having surgery? Wouldn't you be crying? How can we be sure those who have so called NDEs can actually see what's happening?"

Frankie sighed. Maybe book talk wasn't good for her after all. Monica was going to be a killjoy tonight, and she'd wanted a more uplifting night.

"I know it's true," said Lucy, turning her body toward Monica as she sat down to jump into the conversation. "Once my friend Gari had a ruptured appendix. While the doctors were taking it out, he ended up coding for five minutes before they could revive him, and he says he floated out of his body and saw everything. The whole operating room and all."

The other ladies looked at her in disbelief, mouths agape and forks akimbo.

Monica scowled. "How do you know he was telling the truth?"

"Well, he defined all the procedures the doctors were using, and he even described the conversation his ex-wife was having in the next room while the procedure was taking place."

Monica and Maisie looked at each other with wide eyes.

Lucy pushed her last bite of cake around on her plate and said, "She was complaining to her sister how she might have maxed out her secret credit card on her last shopping spree. Apparently too many purses and watches exceeded her credit limit."

"Hey, there's nothing wrong with accessories," Judith chimed in with a smile.

Lucy smiled back. "Apparently she was worried about her husband finding out, especially now that he would be out of work from the surgery, but Gari heard the whole conversation."

"Wait, let's rewind. Why would his ex-wife be at the hospital?" Maisie asked.

"Well, they *were* married when he had the appendectomy," Lucy said, emphasizing the "were." "After he healed, he finally called her out on what she was doing but didn't tell her how he knew. Well, something made her suspicious, since she knew it couldn't have been her sister. The ex-sister-in-law and Gari weren't very fond of each other, so his knowing came as a total shock. At first, she didn't believe him, because he kept saying he had 'divine intervention.' This caused a major ruckus in their marriage. He started to dig deeper and found she had been hiding *all* sorts of secrets. She had a separate bank account she'd been putting money in on the side."

The ladies in the group were all wide-eyed now, especially Olivia and Maisie, who giggled at Lucy's dramatization.

Monica leaned forward. "Huh. It takes an out-of-body experience to find out your wife's not very trustworthy? He sounds like the really stupid one. Who's so blind that they don't know the person they're married to? I would have wanted a divorce too."

Maisie laughed. "I wonder what he would've found out if he'd gone all the way to heaven?"

Lucy replied, "Well, that's just it. Gari's a very pious man and didn't want a divorce. He wanted to work through it, but his wife felt she couldn't trust him anymore, even though she was the one who wanted to break it off. But that's a whole other story. The point is, I know it's real."

"Well," Maisie said, "if my mother had had an out-of-body experience at least one time in her five marriages she might have saved herself the trouble and held off on at least a few husbands. I sometimes think that's why I was always distrusting of relationships when I was younger, and why I like dogs so much."

"You might have a point," Monica said. "What people say and what they're really like aren't always the same thing."

"Well, it might not have worked for Gari, but no relationship is perfect. You can't stop trusting just because some people are dishonest," added Judith.

Monica curled her lip and turned to look at her mother. "Not everyone has what you and Dad have."

Judith sat forward in her chair and placed her cake on the table. "What your father and I have was not built overnight." She looked Monica straight in the eye. "We have to work at it and be willing to admit when we're wrong and to have mutual respect for each other."

Frankie sensed somehow the conversation was no longer about Judith and Sal.

"Are you implying that I don't trust?" Monica moved to the edge of her seat and scowled at her mother.

"I'm not implying anything. I'm simply saying that one bad apple doesn't throw out all relationships. Being in a union means having vulnerability and respect. Gari's wife kept things from him, but he viewed it as an even partnership. I would imagine he would have let his wife buy anything if she'd been open with him."

Lucy lifted her finger to interject. "Well, actually—"

Monica's reply to her mother cut her off. "Gari's the fool to open his heart too much."

"Maybe if more people saw things like Gari, the world would be a better place," Judith replied.

"Only to be abandoned and betrayed!" Monica got up from her chair and stormed into the kitchen.

Maisie and Birdie looked at each other in astonishment.

"What the heck just happened?" asked Birdie.

Judith shrugged. "When something bothers Monica, she doesn't know how to cope very well. Excuse me for a moment." Judith rose with tears in her eyes and walked in the direction of the bathroom.

Frankie turned to look at the group. "Would it be wrong to think this has something to do with Regina?"

Lucy sighed as she turned to look at the rest of the ladies in the room. "I think it has everything to do with her and maybe even a little more. Regina's leaving for college is more than just empty-nest syndrome. It's affecting Monica's identity."

Everyone leaned forward as Lucy continued.

"Monica got pregnant her junior year of high school, and she did the only thing she thought was right and married Kenny, her high school sweetheart. But in doing that, she was forced to grow up too quickly. She traded dances and football games for diapers and bottles."

Olivia sighed. "I know how tough that can be."

"She was willing to do it for the sake of her little family. She even dropped out of high school and got her GED, so she could stay home. But right before Regina turned a year old, she discovered Kenny had been cheating on her. She was devastated. She tried to stay in the relationship for her daughter, but the cheating continued. Judith encouraged her to annul the marriage. Monica knew she had her family to lean on, but the whole experience changed her trust."

"So, Monica's not a grump—she's just guarded," said Olivia.

Lucy nodded. "Very guarded. She has a high wall, and it wasn't till she met Gerard years later that the wall started to break down."

Johnna tilted her head as she scratched her chin. "He seems a bit boring and predictable, at least from what I saw at church last Sunday."

Lucy leaned forward as to make sure her voice didn't carry into the next room. "But he's safe. She knows he'll never betray her." Johnna and Maisie looked at each other in disbelief as Lucy continued. "Now that Regina is grown and about to go off to college, Monica has to think about herself. Somewhere between Regina's elementary years, driving her to ballet classes, and serving on every PTA-type committee, she submerged herself in her daughter so much she forgot who she was."

"But wouldn't this be a good time to start thinking of herself?" Birdie asked.

"I don't think she sees it that way. It's been the two of them for so long, long before Gerard came into the picture. She still has James at home, of course, but it's different. Regina represents everything she's been through. Even when she got accepted to Hillsdale College, Monica felt like she'd accomplished something for herself, as if it was her own award." Lucy looked to the floor. "Except she won't be going along, she'll stay behind ... again."

Frankie hugged her book to her chest.. "So, she feels left behind." She understood that feeling, the acknowledgment that life would be different as loved ones moved forward. Her mother moved forward into her eternal life, while Regina would move forward into her adult life. "Excuse me for a minute." Frankie got up from the couch and walked into the kitchen to find Monica.

She found her sitting on a barstool wiping her face with her sweater sleeve. "Did my mother send you in here to give me a lecture too? I should just get over everything?"

"Actually, my advice is for you not to get over it."

Monica looked up at Frankie with arched brows as she continued to wipe her face.

Frankie took the barstool next to Monica. "I don't think you ever really get over anything when it comes to love."

"I probably look like a fool to everyone, don't I?"

"I think love sometimes makes you do things you wouldn't do otherwise, but no, not a fool."

"Thanks, Frankie." Monica smiled through her sniffles. "For what?"

"For not trying to change my mind about anything."

Frankie handed her a dessert napkin from the counter. "I'm no expert, but if there's one thing I've learned in the past couple years, it's that feelings are valid. Sometimes you have to feel it in order to heal it."

Monica blew her nose then took another napkin to wipe her mascara. "I think I'm ready to go back in, even if I look like a huge mess."

Frankie smiled and rubbed her arm. "I think that's what I like about this group the most. Being a mess is acceptable."

Monica giggled and then hopped down off the stool. As they proceeded into the living room, they caught Birdie in mid-conversation.

"My point is, if hadn't left my driver's license at home that day I wouldn't have had to go to the DMV, and I would have never met my Raymond. Best speeding ticket of my life."

Johnna cocked her head to one side and gazed at Birdie. "You know, I never thought about it like that. I've always prided myself at being cautious. It's safer that way."

Frankie looked at Monica, unsure what they had walked into.

Maisie clapped her hands together. "Well, that's just it! Misfortunes can be blessings in disguise. Look at all the dogs I rescue. These poor animals have been through some hard times. But they're given an opportunity to be with new owners. It sucks what they've had to go through, but they wouldn't be in the loving homes they have now if they hadn't."

Frankie looked at Monica out of the corner of her eye. She seemed to be holding her breath, but slowly released it and relaxed her shoulders. Frankie squeezed her hand to reassure her.

Judith slowly came out of the bathroom and stood behind Frankie and Monica. She said nothing but rather placed her hand on the small of Monica's back and rubbed. Monica stayed quiet too, but she half smiled at her mother, and her shoulders relaxed. Frankie thought it interesting how they had made up without any words spoken.

Maisie continued, "So, I guess what I'm trying to say is those hard situations make for the better. Most of these animals shouldn't trust anyone, and I've seen some tough cases, but dogs are much better at reopening their hearts than humans."

Olivia cleared her throat, and the ladies looked toward her.

"Did you want to say something, honey?" asked Lucy.

"Well, it's not about dogs or speeding tickets, but I guess you could say, since everyone is so open tonight, it fits into the category of misfortunes turning into blessings." She took a deep breath. "I have some news to share."

Everyone turned toward Olivia as she fidgeted with her fork. "First, I haven't really been honest with all of you about my background. It's a lot, and honestly I don't know if we have enough hours in the night to share it all."

"But you don't owe us an explanation. You share here what makes you comfortable," said Birdie.

"Well, that's just it. I haven't been comfortable because I haven't been able to be honest. You see I've always felt I was never good enough."

Monica perked up—giving her attention to Olivia.

"I've always felt that I needed a man's attention to make me feel valuable, and it's caused me to make some decisions I'm not really proud of. But recently someone reminded me I am worth more because I'm a child of God." She looked at Frankie. "And well, I want you to know if you haven't already figured it out ... I'm pregnant. I'm expecting the first of November."

Everyone gasped at the news and seemed unsure of what to say or how to respond.

Judith smiled. "I thought you were a little bumpy."

Olivia giggled at the comment. "I'm not sure if I'm totally brave enough to tell you my whole story, but I have to say that I struggled a lot with whether or not I should keep this baby. I considered selfish reasons, in fact every reason imaginable, except the one that probably was the most important. But hearing you all talk tonight, I guess I realized that even with the hard stuff maybe this will turn out all right in the end."

Birdie nodded. "If God is in charge, which he is, it always turns out right in the end."

"That's what I'm hoping for." Olivia beamed a big smile and shrugged. "I just know that there's a reason bigger than me."

Frankie walked over and hugged her new friend, proud of her for opening up to the group.

"Aren't you scared, Olivia?" Monica asked.

"Yes! I'm terrified. I don't have any family, but Cammy and I have gotten by before, and this time I know I have more support. God will see me through this. He has to."

Judith walked over and placed her hand on her shoulder. "You know we're all here for you, Olivia. Any advice you need, any support. Besides, it'll be nice to have a baby to snuggle. Remember there's no such thing as a coincidence. I know there's a purpose behind it."

"Do you have everything you need to take care of the baby?" asked Lucy.

"Well, Frankie's cousin, Scarlet, has hired me on as an assistant in her photography studio, and she's been super flexible with hours, so that's gonna help me a ton."

Frankie squeezed her hand.

"I can even work with the baby in the studio after she's born."

"A girl? You know it's a girl? What a blessing!" Lucy exclaimed.

Frankie guessed Lucy was already planning a baby shower in her head.

Birdie slapped a hand on her knee. "You see how good God is? Just when you think nothing will work out, God is there. He's so good."

A small tear trickled down Monica's cheek. Frankie watched as the message slowly penetrated her rough exterior.

Judith looked at Monica and turned toward the room. "You know what I think we need?"

Lucy looked at her. "Wine?"

"No, we need a good dance."

"A dance?" Monica frowned at her mother.

"Yes, let's seize the moment. Let's celebrate a new life, new moments of moving forward and trusting that God is going to see us through it all." She moved toward the middle of the room and started swaying with her cha cha heals wedged into the carpet.

Birdie sauntered over to an old 45 rpm record player in her living room. Frankie remembered her telling the group her husband was a collector of old vintage records.

She shuffled through a stack of LPs and put an early '6os album on the player. The ladies twirled each other around the living room, laughing, joking, cracking up with laughter. Olivia danced in the middle, while Frankie twirled her around. Judith showed Johnna how to do the Twist, a dance move popular when she was in high school, while Lucy clasped Monica's hand in hers, swaying with her to keep her mood light. Birdie clapped her hands as Maisie twirled around the room, jumping from partner to partner holding a remote control in her hand to represent a fictitious microphone while she lip-synched the song.

The room filled with laughter as the ladies released some of the tension and the worries they had brought with them that night.

As the song ended, Frankie collapsed on the couch and watched Monica embrace her mother. Judith smiled as she hugged her daughter tight.

"One day, my darling, you will see what a mother's love will make you do."

Chapter 12

Only people who are capable of loving strongly can also suffer great sorrow, but this same necessity of loving serves to counteract their grief and heals them.—Leo Tolstoy

Dancing with the ladies and seeing how much change she'd experienced in the past couple weeks kept inviting Frankie's boldness. She decided it was time to be brave and do something she had been putting off for the last two years. On Monday morning, she woke and drove to her mother's favorite coffee shop, Fizz—the one they had always gone to together. She hadn't set foot in the store since her mother's passing. Each time she had tried, it had been too painful to even think about. Today, she decided she finally had to face her sorrow.

Frankie walked in and saw the manager, Leah, behind the counter, busying herself with tasks of putting out extra cups and checking the supplies for more syrups and coffee beans. Leah had always been kind to Frankie and her mother, and even attended her mom's funeral and donated coffee for the gathering afterward. Leah was a kind lady who didn't say much, but her actions always showed genuine care and concern.

The table where Frankie and her mother used to sit was empty, despite the place being a little busier than usual. Frankie remembered countless visits where she and her mom had sat there to have their morning coffee. Her mom would have her cheese Danish and her sugar-free vanilla soy latte. Frankie would criticize her, saying a sugar-free drink wasn't going to cancel out the cheese Danish, but her mother would ignore her and continue to eat her breakfast.

She remembered the occasions where the girls would tag along too. When Rena was a baby, her mother would hold her granddaughter and show her off to any passersby who would stop to listen, showing how proud she was of her grandbabies. Frankie thought about the many conversations they'd had at that table. Her mother always wanted to plan holiday celebrations and a new menu. Frankie would listen to her ideas, agreeing or disagreeing on what should be served.

As Frankie got closer to the front of the line, her emotions were running high, but she felt she had come this far and didn't want to back down. She didn't recognize the cashier, a young kid with blue spiky hair. Why would she? This was a coffee shop like any other, and new people would be hired. Life would continue to go on whether Frankie was there or not. As she approached the front of the line, Leah looked up and saw Frankie, immediately stopping what she was doing to come take her order.

"I've got this order, Petey," said Leah, nudging the young cashier aside. Leah's soft smile and warm eyes greeted Frankie. "I'm so glad to see you."

Frankie swallowed hard and tried to muster up words without crying. "It's really good to see you too, Leah. I haven't been here for a while. It's just too hard." She could barely get the words out.

"I know it is, but you're here today." Leah didn't say anything about being sorry for her loss or ask how was she doing, but simply acknowledged Frankie's sorrow.

"Do you want your usual?"

Frankie smiled. Of course Leah would remember. "Sure, that would be great."

Leah grabbed a cup and wrote on it with a sharpie. "It's on me today. I'm glad to see you back."

Frankie thanked Leah for her hospitality and reached around the counter to give her a hug. Leah smiled and went back to her regular tasks. Frankie felt gratitude she'd kept it simple and didn't make this moment a big deal.

Next, she walked over to the blue-scratched table where she and her mother had sat for so many conversations— so many trivial moments in their life that now seemed like the most important ones. She sat down and looked around the bright room with mix-matched chairs at each table, just taking in the moment.

She felt a breeze as the door opened with customers going in and out. A distinct scent of freesia and tuberose lingered in the air as a customer walked by. Frankie recognized the scent immediately as her mother's perfume. Perhaps she was imagining things, but the lower notes of peony and vetiver followed. Her mother's perfume was a distinct fragrance that was hard to come by.

In that moment, Frankie let her tears come out like a jar of glass marbles rolling and scattering on the ground. Her heart ached an uncontrollable ache, something she had tried to stifle for a while, but now let free. She would never have knowingly chosen such a public place to cry, but her need to let the tears flow felt stronger than her discretion. Still, she put on her sunglasses, not because of her own embarrassment but for the sake of customers walking by, so she wouldn't draw attention.

Leah delivered her usual—an iced latte with an extra shot and a ham breakfast sandwich—and, to Frankie's surprise, also brought over her mom's sugar-free vanilla soy latte and the cheese Danish. Frankie looked at Leah, startled by the order. It hadn't occurred to her what she meant by usual. In that moment, she realized the enormity of not being the only person who felt sadness over her mother's death. She stood to hug Leah, and the two embraced without any words. Frankie broke down even harder as Leah held her, not caring who saw them.

When the two finally let go and the marble-like tears slowed, Leah spoke. "Your mother was a special lady, but I think you already know that."

Frankie nodded in agreement. "Thank you, Leah. This was really helpful this morning."

"Just know that your usual will always be ready if you ever want to come in again."

"Thanks. I might try to come in more often. What should I do with my mom's order?" Frankie considered the extra coffee and pastry.

"What would your mom have done?"

Frankie smiled. "I know exactly what she would have done."

Leah's eyes' twinkled at Frankie as she went back to her task pulling espresso shots and filling coffee orders. Frankie picked up her order and left the coffee shop to drive to her next stop.

She hadn't been to her mom's gravesite in a while and decided it was time to pay her mom a visit. She drove to St. Anne's Catholic Cemetery and through the rows of old historic tombs that dated back to the late 1800s when Tuleberg had first been built. There were rows of tall headstones with angels and large crucifixes. Some of the wording had faded, and some tombstones were covered with dirt. Time had eroded the stones.

She drove toward the section where there appeared to be the newer plots and found the area where they had laid her mother to rest. After parking off to the side of the drive, she grabbed the coffee shop orders and walked through the rows of newly placed headstones. The place looked fuller than the year before as more people had made their transition into their heavenly home. She looked for the familiar gravestone and saw it from afar where it had been placed many months before. Frankie's maiden name, Vochazer, could be seen from far away.

She walked up to the headstone, cleared out some dried flowers, and put her mom's drink and Danish on the side marble panel. Frankie knelt down then on the grass and simply absorbed the silence as she sipped her coffee. The sun warmed her back, despite the slight chill of the morning breeze as she had coffee once more with her mother. She sat in the quiet and stared at the picture of her mom and dad together, embracing, that had been attached to the stone. There was a reserved space for information about her dad for when his time would come, and Frankie looked at the Bible verse they had selected on the headstone.

> They that hope in the LORD will renew their strength, they will soar on eagles' wings. They will run and not grow weary, walk and not grow faint. Isaiah 40:31

She read the words over and over. She and her dad had picked that verse knowing her mother liked it. She thought about the words and what they meant in that moment. She hadn't lost hope. She had always had hope but hadn't had the strength. Would God renew her? The past two years had been arduous—loss, rediscovery, lack of direction and purpose. Her mother had moved on to eternity, and she wasn't coming back. It was time for Frankie to move on too. This didn't mean she would forget her or that grief wouldn't sometimes catch up with her, but she hadn't died. Frankie had more life to live, and it was time to start living more of it. What that looked like, she still wasn't sure, but she would put one foot forward and then the other. Not because she had to, but because she realized it was her time to refocus on her family and life.

As Frankie looked around the cemetery again, she saw other headstones adorned with flowers and candles. Some had little tchotchkes with football flags or mementos of the loved ones who'd passed on. She loved the oversized Betty Boop ceramic doll someone had brought to their loved one, not far from her mom's plot. She smiled knowing that others found ways to honor their memories.

As she continued to sip her coffee, she noticed a familiar face across the lawn—Lucy.

Her friend from the book talk dusted away dirt from a small gravesite, then scrubbed the headstone with a brush she'd dipped into a bucket. Then she squeezed water from a rag and wiped around the worn lettering.

Frankie was surprised to see her there. For some reason she didn't know if Lucy would want to be discovered, so she stepped behind a large angel statue and watched from afar, wondering who the stone belonged to. Frankie knew Lucy's husband had been cremated and she kept his remains in an urn, but she didn't know who else Lucy might visit at the cemetery.

Frankie saw Lucy move to the next stone and continue in the same manner. She watched as Lucy washed each headstone, one by one, scrubbing between the etchings with loving care.

Suddenly Lucy stopped and looked up, right in Frankie's direction.

Frankie dodged behind the angel, unsure if Lucy had seen her. There was no crime in watching, but Frankie felt as if she were invading a private moment.

She waited a few minutes before looking again, worried she might be spying on what she didn't know. Suddenly, Frankie realized she was being foolish, it was childish to hide behind a statue. Obviously, whatever Lucy was doing or who she was caring for wasn't a mystery. She was out in public. Frankie reappeared and decided she would go up to Lucy.

When she came out from behind the statue, though, Lucy was gone.

Chapter 13

All your ways may be straight in your own eyes, but it is the LORD who weighs hearts.—Proverbs 21:2

Frankie didn't know what to make of Lucy's presence at the graveyard. It seemed very mysterious, some might even say secretive, but she didn't seem the scheming type. Maybe her actions were simply her doing a good deed? Whatever the reason, Frankie considered whether it would be wise to approach her at the next book talk meet up.

When Frankie returned home, she walked into the kitchen and glanced at the calendar. The next day was Johnna's dad's appointment, and she had promised she would get the succulents to her. She called Olivia to see if she could pick them up and surprise Johnna a day early, especially since she knew Olivia had the day off from Scarlet's. The phone rang and rang then finally went to voice message. *Weird.* She called her again about fifteen minutes later—still no answer. She texted her instead.

FRANKIE: Can I swing by right now to pick up the succulents? I want to drop them off to Johnna before she goes to her dad's appointment.

Frankie was sure Johnna's dad would love the succulents—so hearty and fresh—after so many doctor appointments. She didn't have a green thumb, but she knew these were easy plants to take care of. She looked down as a text arrived back from Olivia.

OLIVIA: Now is not a good time.

Frankie thought the response vague. Usually, Olivia's texts were a little more forthcoming. She replied back.

FRANKIE*:* Can I come by later? I want to get them to her a little earlier so she can enjoy them before her appointment instead of after.

OLIVIA*:* Today's not a good day. Will have to wait.

Little alarms went off inside Frankie's head, but she couldn't explain why. The more interactions she had with Olivia, the more protective she felt. She put the phone down and began aggressively scrubbing the kitchen sink.

Candace walked into the kitchen and headed for the refrigerator. "What's the matter, Mom?" she asked as she grabbed a yogurt from the shelf.

"Nothing. Why do you think something's the matter?"

"You tend to clean when something's bothering you."

"I just need to get those succulents to Johnna by tomorrow and thought maybe I could get them from Olivia tonight, but I guess she's busy. She's not answering her phone." She walked to the toaster and started dusting all the crumbs from under the machine.

"Why don't you drive by her house then?"

Frankie stopped her dusting, pleasantly surprised at the thought. "Well, maybe I could. If she's not home, then at least I've tried."

As Frankie drove toward Olivia's house, she passed through the bleakness of the neighborhood and hoped Olivia could soon move from this scary, dark environment. When she finally arrived at the house, she noticed Olivia's car wasn't there. A flicker of light in the living room caught her attention, so she parked and went to the door. As she drew closer, she could hear the TV on inside. Someone had to be home. She knocked on the door.

The window sheers jostled, and she recognized the silhouette of Cammy behind the curtains. A moment later, Olivia's daughter opened the door and grinned at Frankie.

"Hi, Cammy."

"Hi, Mrs. Waters."

"Is your mom here?"

Cammy leaned on the door jamb. "No. She's working right now."

Olivia hadn't told her daughter the full truth. Frankie wondered why but decided to not give Cammy any indication she knew differently. She peeked inside their home. "Looks like you guys have a lot of boxes."

"Yeah, Momma and I are moving soon. She found a new place that's closer to her new job."

"Oh, that's good." Frankie was relieved that Olivia had plans to get out of this forsaken area.

"I'm glad too," said Cammy, now picking at her nail polish. "There's a lot of people that walk around here at night, and I don't really like it."

Frankie didn't like seeing Cammy by herself in this neighborhood. It was still daylight, but who knew when Olivia would be home?

"Do you want to come over and stay at our house till your mom gets off work? We can text her. Do you know what time she'll be off?" Frankie tried to act relaxed, but something didn't feel right.

"Uhm, that would be great, Mrs. Waters. I know she should be done by 7:30."

Frankie glanced at her watch. It was only 3:30. "Well, that gives you enough time to come over and have dinner with us and have some visit time with Lizzie."

Cammy smiled then turned, snapped off the TV, and grabbed her bag. Frankie didn't know how she would explain to Olivia that she'd stopped at her house and picked up her daughter, but she just knew she couldn't let Cammy stay by herself. As she started a text, she came as close as to the truth without sounding snoopy.

FRANKIE: I came by to see if you were home just in case you might have had Johnna's plants. Cammy was home by herself, and I've asked her to have dinner with us. She's with me now.

There was no immediate answer. Frankie's first thought was that Olivia would think she was overstepping by taking Cammy, but she couldn't leave her in that neighborhood by herself. She started wondering what else Cammy was exposed to on a daily basis. *What kind of person doesn't text back immediately if their daughter has been taken out of her home?* Frankie was creating scenarios in her head about Cammy staying home by herself as she drove in the direction of her house. She really hoped Olivia had a plausible explanation.

Twenty minutes later, Olivia replied.

OLIVIA: Let her know I'll pick her up around 7:30.

What could she be doing? She knew for sure that Olivia wasn't working that night, at least not for Scarlet. *What could she be hiding? Why hadn't she just come clean about the whole thing? Why was she still working for Travis?*

Around 7:30, Frankie watched as Olivia pulled into her driveway. She'd been thinking about all the things she wanted to say to Olivia about her welfare, about her safety. She felt the need to let her know how unsafe her lifestyle and neighborhood was for Cammy, but she kept a stone face as she opened the door.

Olivia walked in all smiles and cheerful. "Hi, Frankie. Is Cammy with Lizzie?"

"Yes, they're in the back room." Frankie hesitated, thrown off by how bubbly Olivia acted.

"Oh, by the way, I have those succulents in my car. I'll have Cammy bring them in. Cam! We need to go!" she called out.

Frankie stared at her. "Where have you been?"

Olivia didn't make eye contact with Frankie and acted as if she hadn't heard the question. "You know what? I'll grab the succulents out of my car. Cam! Come on, it's getting late," she yelled again.

Frankie walked out of the house, hot on Olivia's heels. "I know you didn't work for Scarlet today."

Olivia pretended she hadn't heard Frankie's comments again.

As she was about to say something more, Cammy came bounding from the house. "Thanks again, Mrs. Waters."

Frankie didn't want to worry or scare Cammy, so she simply stared wordlessly at Olivia.

"Oh, wow, look at the succulents. Are these the ones you got from your job, Mom? Did you get attacked by the weeds again?"

Frankie frowned then looked at Olivia's wrists, which were badly bruised. The damage had clearly not been done by weeds. Olivia didn't reply to Cammy's comment, but rather tried to cover up by turning her wrist out of sight, unsuccessfully as the mark wrapped around. Frankie waited for Olivia to reply but she didn't, so she took the box out of Olivia's hand and handed it to Lizzie, who had followed Cammy from the house.

"Lizzie, take these and put them on the back porch for me. Cammy, will you help her?"

Cammy looked back at her mother, who silently nodded. The girls took the boxes and walked away.

Frankie stared at Olivia. "Do you want to tell me what's going on? Why your daughter was home by herself in a dangerous neighborhood? And why you have marks on your wrist that clearly aren't from weeds? Are you still working for Travis?"

"As a matter of fact …" Olivia began but faltered. She crossed her arms and stared at Frankie. "What's it to you, Frankie? Do you think that just because you saw me get hit one time and because I'm knocked up that you can come in and rescue me? Does that somehow give you the right to go to my house whenever you feel like it? How dare you pick up my daughter and act like you have some kind of say over my life."

"Woah. Wait. I picked up your daughter because she was by herself. Your neighborhood is not the safest place for a ten-year-old girl to be alone."

"So, you think you're a better mom than me? I'm sorry I haven't had it so great like you. I've had to do the best with what I can." Tears rose in her eyes.

"That's not what I meant," Frankie backtracked. "It isn't safe. It's …" She stumbled for the right words. "I just worry about you, Olivia."

"Why? You don't even know me." Olivia threw her hands up in the air.

"I care about you." Frankie didn't know why she cared. She didn't understand it herself, but she felt a need to reach out to protect this woman.

"Do you? Or are you just finding a project to mask your own grief?"

The cold blow hit Frankie hard. Olivia crossed her arms over her chest again. "You know, it's typical, another person trying to control me, except this time it's not a guy. Who'd of thought?"

Frankie felt like she'd been punched in the gut. "I wasn't trying to control you. I just … I just worry about you." Her voice lowered. "I didn't realize there was something wrong with that."

Olivia chewed on her lower lip and pushed her flip flop into the grass at her feet. "No one asked you to interfere with my life. Thank you for helping me get a job with Scarlet, but as far as the rest of it goes, just stay out of it. I'm begging you to stay out of it."

"I–I'm sorry, Olivia. I just—"

Just then the girls returned from their errand. Olivia uncrossed her arms, flipped on a smile, then turned and walked around the car as if nothing had happened.

After Olivia and Cammy had driven off, Frankie stood in the doorway feeling defeated. She had thought her actions were out of concern, not out of nosiness. Maybe she'd been blinded by intention, but she didn't see the effects backfiring, at least not this strongly. Maybe Olivia was right. Maybe she was trying to mask her own grief by focusing on Olivia's problems. She barely knew her or the struggles she'd been through. But even if there was some truth to Olivia's accusation, Frankie knew she cared about Olivia deeply. Her concern was more than just grief.

The interaction between her and Olivia created a vortex of sadness. She'd been right to hide away these last two years. Relationships just caused more hurt and pain. She thought back to Max's cautionary discussion only a couple weeks prior. Had the book talk even been worth joining? Maybe she'd entered back into friendships too soon.

As she stood staring out at the dark, she wanted more than ever to pick up the phone and call the one person she could never talk to again. Her mother would have known what to say or would have least offered a place of retreat.

But there was no one to talk to now. She had to figure this out on her own.

She closed the door, leaned against it a moment, then forced herself to find her daughters.

Candace and Lizzie were in the kitchen digging through the freezer.

"Momma, you seem sad," said Lizzie, putting a pint of rocky road on the countertop.

"I'm okay, girls." She faked a smile.

"Mom, we know sad. We've seen it a lot in this house. What's wrong?" said Candace.

Frankie leaned on the kitchen island and looked at her daughters. She had never considered confiding in them. That wasn't the way it was supposed to be. She certainly couldn't talk about Olivia and how she had overstepped her boundaries. Those were adult matters. However, she could talk to them about some aspects of things happening around her. So, she took a leap of faith and, without including names, opened up to them.

"Do you ever feel like maybe you try to do the right thing and maybe you've stepped too far? I feel like sometimes I don't know what is too far." She couldn't believe she was asking advice from her daughters.

"What do you mean?" asked Lizzie, using a spoon to scoop ice cream directly from the container into her mouth.

"Well, when you know something is good for someone, but it's not really your place to interfere." Frankie moved to retrieve a few bowls, then removed the spoon from Lizzie's mouth.

Lizzie looked puzzled, but Candace stepped in.

"Mom, remember in school last year, when we were getting homework on Fridays, and you used to make us get it all done on Friday right after school instead of waiting till Sunday night?"

"Yeah."

"I really hated doing it, and I was mad at you because I looked forward to Fridays. I hated that you couldn't just let us decide when we did our homework and well, don't be mad, but back in April I lied to you about my history report and told you that I finished it all at school so I could go over to Hailey's house on Friday to spend the night. When Sunday night hit, I completely forgot about it and I was up till, like, 1:30 in the morning trying to finish my work. I never wanted to admit that you were right about getting it done early."

"Yeah, that was the project you got a B on," Lizzie said with a smirk.

"Shut up, Lizzie!" Candace jabbed her sister with her elbow. Seeing Frankie's raised eyebrow, she continued. "Well, after that night, I realized I never wanted to go through that again. My point is, you were just doing what was best for us even if we couldn't see it ourselves. You knew it would be harder later."

"I never knew that," said Frankie, scooping herself some rocky road. "Is that why you didn't make a big deal about your B? Did you think you deserved it?" She wasn't mad at Candace, but definitely surprised she had snuck this detail passed her. Still, she was glad Candace had learned something. Maybe Olivia had to go through this on her own to realize she was struggling. But Olivia also didn't have someone there to remind her that everything would be okay.

Candace piled a bit of ice cream into her bowl before saying, "As much as I hate to admit it, Mom, don't stop making us do our homework."

Don't stop.

"Yeah, but that doesn't mean I'm looking forward to it," said Lizzie. "I'm already dreading having my Friday afternoons taken up by homework again in the fall."

Candace and Frankie laughed as Lizzie made a face.

"Well, as much as I don't like hearing about all the devious behaviors behind my back, I'm glad at least you learned something from it."

Frankie put the homework issue aside and looked at her girls, their faces full of sweet ice cream. "You girls teach me something every day. And I'm grateful you are mature enough to recognize the right path. I'm pretty darn lucky to have you."

Candace moved around the counter and hugged her, a twinkle shining in her eye, the same expression Frankie's mother would have made. "We're pretty darn lucky to have you too, Mama."

Lizzie nodded in agreement.

"Now, pass the carton of strawberry ice cream over here before Rena gets a whiff of what we're doing and shows up to eat the rest."

Don't stop. Maybe it wasn't Frankie's place to butt into Olivia's life, but that didn't mean her intrusiveness couldn't be indirect. Frankie looked up to the sky and smiled. She didn't have to stop praying for her.

Chapter 14

We all stumble in many ways.—**James 3:2a (NIV)**

On Friday, as Frankie prepared the girls for the start of school, she realized the entire week had passed without Olivia speaking to her. She hadn't called or answered any of her texts. Yet, she'd been so busy with the girls, she hadn't really focused on anything else. She hadn't even read the chapters for the book talk. Frankie wanted to follow through since she felt it validated her reasons for being there, but her day was filled with last-minute school shopping and laying out class supplies, so she decided to settle for secondhand commentary.

That evening, after a busy day of chores and errands, she looked over the chapter title before heading out the door. "Regrets can be Re-gets." *Hmmm funny title.* She figured Birdie or Lucy would cue her in to what it meant. As she drove toward Birdie's house, she realized they were in the fourth week of the book talk, already past the halfway mark. So, much had happened in the short time. She felt drawn to more than just the readings though. Four weeks ago, she could barely lift her head off her pillow, let alone think about socializing. Now she was going to lunch, delivering plants, finding jobs, and visiting coffee shops she had avoided for the last two years. Life was far different than before her mom's death, yet now she was starting to see life resurface in a new way. She was figuring things out, but were the changes in her life contingent on the book talk? Would this brave new person come to an end in two weeks? These women had helped her more than they knew, but would they stick around? Whether or not she continued to keep the friendships, she knew they had helped her work her way back into the world. For that, she was thankful.

She wondered if Olivia would be at the book talk tonight. Even though they hadn't ended on good terms, she still believed she'd made the right choice to check on her friend and her daughter. She'd been worried sick about what Oliva was doing and how she was managing, but Frankie knew she had to let Olivia figure a few things out on her own. That was the hard part—not being able to check in. Her daughters had assured her—without directly knowing—that she had done the right thing, even if it hadn't felt like the right thing. She would continue to pray for Olivia's safekeeping.

As she pulled up to Birdie's house, there was no sign of Olivia's car and Frankie knew it was likely she wouldn't come tonight. She just hoped the ladies didn't ask her any questions.

Frankie had brought a nicer bottle of wine—a cabernet from the "twenty dollars and up" shelf at the grocery story—to thank Birdie for hosting. Tonight was just as good a time as any to indulge, and she figured, rather than wait till the last session, this would be a nice night to enjoy it. Birdie opened the wine graciously and poured glasses both for Frankie and herself.

Maisie was slicing up pieces of organic agave flourless chocolate cake with a pumpkin seed and chia topping for everyone, which Frankie decided looked about as appetizing as it sounded. She took a piece to be nice but poured a little extra wine in her glass too. She might need some more to wash down the dry cake. Thank goodness she'd splurged on the good wine.

Monica sat at the kitchen counter, scrapping the chia seeds off her cake, while Judith flicked pieces away too when no one was watching. They seemed to have made up from the week before, but it was evident Monica was still a bit emotional about her daughter leaving soon. Still, she seemed in better spirits.

Johnna, on the other hand, sat on the floor in the living room legs under the coffee table, eating her cake and drinking her wine by herself. Her eyes stayed focused on the coffee table as if deep in thought, only pausing to take a bite of her cake and large gulps from her glass. Something was bothering her, but it didn't appear to be the cake. Unlike earlier in the week, when she had met Johnna to drop off the succulents, her appearance had changed. She had gone from an ironed, crisp-collared shirt and styled hair to a floppy bun on her head, wrinkled pants, and a stained sweatshirt. Dark circles hung under her eyes, and Frankie could tell exhaustion had set in.

As Frankie turned the corner to the living room, she came face to face with Lucy coming out of the bathroom. She hadn't seen Lucy since the day at the cemetery. Lucy said nothing but wiggled her nose as she walked silently into the living room. Frankie left it alone. She'd had enough encounters for the week and wasn't going to inquire any further. If Lucy wanted to discuss anything, she would.

Birdie yelled out from the living room. "Come on, everyone. Let's get started!"

Judith took a seat behind Johnna. "Where's Olivia? We can't start without her."

Maisie frowned. "Yeah, I was really hoping she would try some of my cake. I made it from scratch. All the ingredients are organic."

"Lucky girl," Judith whispered to Johnna.

Johnna giggled, and Monica glared at her mom from across the room.

"It feels a bit empty without her tonight," said Lucy.

"I know, like something is missing. I wonder why she didn't come?" said Monica.

Frankie stayed silent, listening to the ladies' speculations.

"She called me earlier today," Birdie replied. "She has some big job with Frankie's cousin on Sunday, so she's skipping. Something about a lot of prep and animals?"

Lucy looked at her, wide-eyed. "Oh, I wonder if that's the auxiliary event?"

"Oh! My husband and I will be there. We're part of the board." Maisie squealed with delight. "It's at the animal estuary. They've held it for years to help rescued animals. It's an amazing event."

"You bet your baboon's butt it's an amazing event," Judith chimed in. "Everyone says they're there because of the animals, but people really go to see all the big names of high society that go."

"That's a pretty big gig to be photographing, Frankie. Your cousin is going to get so many clients shooting that event," Monica added. "By the way, how's Olivia working out with your cousin?"

Frankie choked on a chia seed. She didn't know anything about the event. "Uhm, I haven't seen her. But I guess she's handling everything okay."

"Well, I'm sure you'll see Olivia before I do," said Johnna, as she shoved another piece of cake onto her fork. "Please tell her thank you for getting the succulents.

I don't know where she got them, but they were a big hit with my dad. He wants to put more in his garden." She washed down the last bite of her cake with the rest of her wine.

"I'm going to the auxiliary on Sunday, so I'll look for her and tell her," Lucy said.

Monica nodded. "You're so sweet. You are always looking to take care of everyone."

Lucy smiled at her friend.

"Well, I don't know about succulents or animal auxiliaries, but being top grandma this week has worn me out," exclaimed Birdie as she stretched her legs out and rested her head back on her couch. "I had to house sit my grandchildren for three days while my daughter was at a conference, and as much as I love them, it's been a grueling week! Let's have some more wine tonight, girls."

"Already done. You don't have to tell me twice." Johnna poured another glass from the bottle in front of her—her third.

"Well, it's unfortunate Olivia's missing tonight. We're discussing how people return from their NDEs and talk about all their regrets. It's kind of like a life review," Judith explained.

"Well, look who did their readings," said Monica with a sneer.

"Hey, I can stay on top of the readings too, you know," Judith replied with her nose in the air. "It just so happens this was a very interesting chapter. If you had read them, you would know too. Anyway," she added as she turned to the others, "the author, was talking about how NDE patients have regrets sometimes when they return after their experience. They start worrying about their future. Some even have a life review on the other side and get to see all the things they did before they crossed over. I guess most of them say God shows the information in a loving, non-judgmental way. But somehow they return with a better attitude on how they want to spend their life."

Maisie glanced around at the group. "Why do you suppose it takes so much for a person to realize they need to change some things in life?"

Lucy shifted uncomfortably in her seat.

"I know," Judith replied. "Because if more people had that self-realization before waiting until the end, they'd limit a lot of foolishness."

Lucy was about to say something, but Birdie interrupted.

"Well, that's just it. People don't have realizations because they feel like they're going to live forever, that there's always more time, another tomorrow, and by that point too much time has passed. Besides if we knew everything ahead of time, wouldn't we try to control how life looked after that? And that's not exactly learning from our mistakes or even free will if we already know what the outcome is."

"I never thought of it that way," said Monica.

"When my daughter was young," Birdie said, "I was never good at living in the moment. I always thought each stage was difficult. When she was a baby, it was the crying and the midnight feedings. When she was a toddler, it was the terrible-twos and the house being a mess. When she was a teenager, I always looked at the negative attitudes of 'teenagedom.' I always wanted each phase to end, only to see that the next one had its own share of problems."

"I think that's normal for a lot of moms," said Frankie.

Birdie sat slumped in her chair. "But I dwelled on what I didn't do right instead of what I did well. I dwelled on those moments of 'imperfection' so much that I failed to look at them as moments of 'pure perfection.' My daughter never knew that because I kept it inside. I could have seen a sleeping baby with precious love, or a busy toddler curious at the world, or even a teenage daughter growing into a beautiful woman. Instead, I chose to look at the bad. I focused on waiting for the next chapter to begin instead of what was right in front of me."

Birdie used a tissue to wipe away a tear. "Now she's grown, and she's so busy, the only time I get to see her now is through watching my grandkids. And I can't tell you how much I loved being with them this week. At least with them, I feel like I have been given a second chance." She blew her nose.

"Well, I'm no expert, but maybe we're supposed to go through those regrets," said Maisie. "You might not be as devoted of a grandma if you hadn't made a few mom mistakes along the way."

Frankie thought she had a valid point.

"So, just like the chapter, I feel like our regrets give us something to look forward to, but in a different way." Maisie pulled a pillow up to her chest. "Besides, you can't bargain with what should've happened. You'll never be happy with the answer."

"If I've learned anything, it's that time is very precious," Birdie said as she wiped her nose. "We can't take anything for granted. Even the bad moments are important. My grandkids and I have a special bond, and maybe not being in the moment with my daughter has made me want to be more in the moment with my grandkids."

Frankie could see the love shining from Birdie as she spoke of her family.

Lucy looked like she wanted to say something again but stayed silent.

"We're always searching for something bigger and better," said Maisie hugging the pillow tighter, "but we don't learn anything till we mess it up. Kind of like this cake."

Everyone stared at her, surprised, until Maisie looked around then burst into laughter. The rest of the group followed. "I know it's awful. I just couldn't help watching you all eat it!"

Birdie threw her tissues at Maisie as she playfully blocked them with the pillow.

"Oh, thank God," Judith exclaimed, as she scraped the remainders of her cake onto Monica's plate. "I was praying this wasn't your normal cuisine. I was ready to go over to your house and make some food for your husband, poor man!"

"You should have seen the look on your face, Judith." Maisie chuckled.

Judith also threw her napkin at her, and everyone started laughing, especially Judith. They were cracking up so hard, it took a while for anyone to notice Johnna had started crying. Cake crumbs fell from her mouth with every sob. Maisie looked over and hushed everyone. Then they gathered close as Johnna made small whimpering sounds.

"Honey, are you okay?" asked Frankie, a little grossed out by the cake and drool coming out of her mouth, but still concerned.

The group quieted down to hear her reply.

"Tomorrow's my dad's follow-up appointment and, well, even though we're going through this crazy rollercoaster of doctors, and I've hated it ..." She paused. "I sometimes think this has led me to spend more time with him." She choked back a sob and said, "I love being with him." She let out another heavy sob. "But now I realize maybe I'm not spending enough time with my family."

Judith wrapped Johnna in a hug from behind. Their friend had been carrying far too much regret and worry.

Her ability to want to always do the right thing and "do everything" for everyone had caught up with her. Frankie knew the feeling. She remembered those thoughts: *Am I doing everything right? Am I getting it all straight? Do I spend enough time with my mom but neglect my kids and husband? Should I pull back and take more time with my family?* Frankie saw that Johnna didn't want to have any regrets.

"You can't do it all," said Frankie, touching her friend's hand. "That's too much for one person to handle."

"And you're not supposed to," Monica added.

Johnna's voice slurred from the wine as she continued. "I'm sthooo wooorried about his appointment tomorrow."

"Honey, I think you've been holding this in for too long." Lucy reached out to hold her hand. "It isn't healthy. You need to let it out."

"I don't know what's right."

"Johnna," Frankie proceeded slowly, "You're already doing the right thing. You love your family. That's all you need to do to make it right. That doesn't make this path easier. But it's what it's supposed to be." Frankie knew it wasn't the answer Johnna was looking for, but it was the truth. She couldn't do any more than she already had. If there was a person who did everything for their family and was one hundred percent devoted, it was Johnna. Yet, here she was thinking she wasn't doing enough.

"I need another drink," she said, holding her glass in the air with a very unsteady and wobbly hand, expecting someone to fill it.

"Honey, you might want to slow down and not drink anymore," said Birdie.

"I'm terfectly pine," Johnna said, mixing her letters around. She tried to prop herself up on the coffee table as she tried to stand, but her legs buckled.

Maisie swooped in to push her back onto the couch. "Uh, I think you need to sit."

Johnna burped in her face. "Why does your couch feel like it's moving? Are we on a boat?"

"Could be the chocolate cake?" said Judith.

Maisie giggled. "Don't give my cake that much credit."

"I think you need to rest." Birdie helped Johnna lie down on the couch as she continued to weep and sway.

"Well, this night has definitely been an interesting one," said Lucy.

Judith's phone rang, and she stepped aside to answer it.

Maisie pulled out her phone too. "We should probably call Johnna's husband to pick her up. She's in no condition to drive."

"I don't think she'd want us to call him," Frankie said. "I know she's a proud woman, and this is not her normal approach to things. She'd be upset if her family had to pick her up."

"You're right. I guess we're going to have to drive her. Maybe someone could follow in her—"

Judith screamed and dropped her phone. Monica and Lucy rushed to see what was wrong.

Monica put her arms around her mother. "What's the matter, Mama? Talk to me."

Judith clenched her hand over her mouth and couldn't get the words out. Finally, her news came out with great intensity. "We need to leave, Monica. We need to leave now!"

"Okay, Mama, we can leave, but what's the matter?"

"Your dad isn't breathing," she wailed. "We need to get to the hospital now!"

"Oh my gosh." Monica's face went white.

"Now!" Judith screamed in a blood curdling cry.

Monica composed herself, quickly grabbed her mother's purse, and pulled her from the room. The ladies moved out of the way while Lucy went with them to drive.

Poor Judith, her nerves must have been on edge. And Monica! Who knows what's going through her mind.

The room was silent after they left. Finally, Birdie turned to everyone remaining. "What we need to do right now is put it in someone else's hands. That's what we need to do."

Maisie, Birdie, and Frankie gathered around Johnna, who was now completely passed out, and bowed their heads.

Birdie started, "Dear Lord, these are the moments where we have to put our trust in you. If we've learned anything tonight, it's that all is in your hands. We pray for the healing of Judith's husband and Monica's father. Please Lord, if it be your will, help him through this and help Monica and Judith stay strong. And if you could also sober up this girl here on the couch pretty fast, that would be awfully helpful too. In Jesus's name we pray. Amen."

After the prayer, it seemed evident the night was over. Frankie offered to take Johnna home, and Maisie followed, driving Johnna's car. She said she would catch a ride back to Birdie's. Frankie noticed Judith had left her pashmina scarf, which was a pretty shade of soft brown. She took it and figured she would reach out to Judith later when the dust had settled.

Birdie said she'd put everyone in contact once she found out the situation with Judith's husband. The night had ended on a completely unexpected turn of events with more than anyone had anticipated. Frankie surprisingly felt calm through the whole thing, which was not her usual nature, but knew Birdie was right—she had to put her trust in something much greater. For all of them, the situation was truly out of their hands.

Chapter 15

What does love look like? It has the hands to help others. It has the feet to hasten to the poor and needy. It has eyes to see misery and want. It has the ears to hear the sighs and sorrows of men. That is what love looks like.—St. Augustine

Saturday morning, Frankie received a text from Johnna.

JOHNNA: Sorry for my behavior last night. I don't know how that happened. Please forgive me.

FRANKIE: No worries, girl. It happens to the best of us.

JOHNNA: How's everything w Judith? Too ashamed to call her.

FRANKIE: Haven't heard anything. Wasn't sure if u knew.

JOHNNA: My hubs clued me in this morning.

Johnna's husband had questioned why they had driven her home, and why they'd delivered his wife completely wasted and smelling like a sewer. Frankie had softened the blow by telling him first about Judith and Monica, but he seemed more interested that Johnna had thrown up in Frankie's car and had pumpkin seeds in her hair. He took the news rather well and laughed with a raspy voice. Apparently, he'd never seen his wife so disheveled.

He offered to pay for the cleaning of Frankie's car, but she declined.

FRANKIE: You have nothing to be ashamed about.

JOHNNA: Sorry about your car.

Frankie knew Johnna felt embarrassed by what had happened, but she couldn't fault her for her behavior. She remembered times when she felt out of control dealing with the responsibility of sick parents and family. Crazy moments were bound to sneak up. Frankie also remembered being in the thick of doctors' appointments and trying to balance her home life. She'd had a complete breakdown once and screamed at her whole family so loudly the neighbors closed their windows against her shouting. If Johnna got drunk, which was not her ordinary behavior, Frankie wouldn't judge her in how she dealt with her sorrows. People did funny things when they were at their breaking point.

FRANKIE: You're just being human. I get it. Would probably do the same. Anyway, Monica will let us know all the details.

She wanted to shift back to the condition of Judith's husband.

JOHNNA: Thanks for getting it. I knew you wouldn't judge me.

FRANKIE: It stays here.

Frankie knew Johnna was a proud woman who liked to keep appearances, but keeping her feelings and emotions in check were even more important to her. She knew feeling comfortable enough sharing what she'd had was a big deal for Johnna.

JOHNNA: Well, I'm off 2 the doctor with dad. It's a local visit. Prayers for good news. TTYL.

Johnna had picked right back up from before, business as usual.

FRANKIE: Prayers.

Frankie put the phone down and started the morning coffee, reflecting on the night before. The evening had started off with good wine and great company, but horrible cake. Somehow it had ended with hospitals and hangovers. And yet Frankie had somehow managed to come out of all of it unfazed. Maybe she was used to the feelings that had come with struggle during moments of trauma and even grief. She had experienced so much in the last few years that when chaos happened around her, she became the voice of reason and the place of safety for others. Maybe there was something to this grief after all. It wasn't something she would ever force others to experience, but, somehow, she had survived it. Johnna, seeing that, had looked to her for support, which gave her the sense that she was healing. She could pass her knowledge on to others.

Her thoughts were interrupted by the phone ringing. She wondered if it was news about Judith's husband.

"Hey," Scarlet greeted her. "I can't get into the system, and I need you to send me your password so I can give it to Olivia."

"Good morning, Scarlet."

She heard Scarlet blow out a breath. "Sorry. Hi. I'm just in a hurry to check on some of my accounts from the old computer and it's locked me out of my system. You know I hate computers." Scarlet had updated her billing system over the summer but hadn't transferred all of her old records over to the new program. Luckily, Frankie still had access to it.

Frankie chuckled under her breath. "Yeah, I'll text it to you right after we hang up." Then she thought of Olivia who hadn't been returning her calls or texts. "How's everything working out with Olivia?"

"Actually, really good. She's picking things up pretty quickly." Frankie could hear relief in her cousin's voice. "I've been able to get most of my billing up-to-date and now I'm having her send out emails to existing clients to schedule for the holiday sessions. Even though Christmas is still five months away, you can never be overly prepared."

Frankie sighed, relieved to hear how well the merge between the two was going. Olivia was a great help to Scarlet, and it sounded like they had a natural flow with each other. Better yet, Scarlet could no longer use work as an excuse for everything. And while Scarlet wouldn't admit it, Frankie knew she enjoyed having another female around with whom she could connect. Women didn't often take to her because she didn't show that warm, nurturing side. Her all-business approach to life tended to be off-putting for a lot of people. Leave it to her, though, to already be thinking about more projects.

"Hey, I also need a backup of the pictures from last year's wedding season. Olivia is going to make me a photo collage to show some guests. Do you still have that?"

"Yeah, it's on the drive, but I also have a flash drive of it around here somewhere."

"Good. Swing it by to me this afternoon?" She stated it as more of a command than a question.

"Sure, I can. Uh, wait. Why don't we meet at the coffee shop? I'm already planning on stopping by there, and it'll be easy to do two things at once." She didn't want to tell Scarlet about the episode with Olivia the other night, and she didn't know if Olivia was ready to see her. She figured it would be better for Olivia to come around on her own time. This way she wouldn't give her anymore reason to think she was prying into her affairs.

"That's fine, but I can't stay super long. We've got a huge gig, and I just know this is going to blow up my career. I may even need to hire a second assistant."

"Yeah, I heard about the auxiliary. You never cease to amaze me, Scarlet Bedford. Well, uh, tell Olivia hi for me and that we missed her at the book talk last night." She figured that might be a good way to get the dialog going without pushing things too far.

"I will when she gets back. She had to run off this morning to take care of some errands. Something about tying up loose ends. Not really sure. She had already finished all the billing, so I didn't care. She really is amazing at getting so much done at one time," Scarlet added. "Gotta go. A client just walked in the door. Later. Bye."

Frankie knew that "taking care of errands" probably meant Olivia was trying to either slowly pull away from Travis's grasp or was still in it. Frankie worried about Olivia being pressured further by that man to abort the baby. Getting a new job was one thing, but trying to detach from a man who didn't take change too well was another. She just hoped that whatever Olivia was doing, she was safe.

Frankie looked up from her coffee as Candace walked into the kitchen.

"Good morning, Mama."

"Hi, babe," she said, snapping out of her thoughts.

Candace leaned in to give her mother a hug—a rarity now that she was a teenager and focusing on friends and social activities. The school year, and its busy schedule, was quickly approaching. Frankie took in the hug and smelled her daughter's hair. Candace would always be her baby, no matter her age, and this baby was already a few inches taller than her.

Frankie smiled up at her. "How did you suddenly become bigger than me?"

"That's what you getting for feeding us—we keep growing," joked Candace as she pulled out of her mom's hug and seemed to tower over her. She had definitely had a growth spurt over the summer and was already measuring in at five-foot-nine compared to Frankie's five-foot-six. She was certainly a tall eighth grader.

"Mom, I got a text from Lanie last night that our student council is supposed to meet today to get the posters ready for school. Can you give me a ride? It should only take about an hour and a half."

"What time?"

"Like 10:30 or something."

"Sure, that's fine. Are you meeting at the school?"

"No, we're meeting at Lanie's house."

"You sure it's just posters?" She eyed her teenage daughter.

"Mom! Of course! We're just making posters. But it would be cool if I could hang out there for a little bit. I haven't seen Lanie all summer."

Frankie had been in such a funk this past year, Candace hadn't really been involved in many social events. She figured she deserved to spend moments like this with her friends, and Candace rarely asked for things.

"Sure, that's fine but—" Her reply was interrupted by the text she had been waiting for from Lucy.

> **Lucy:** Hi, everyone. This is Judith's message that I'm sharing on her behalf.

A screenshot of Judith's message popped up.

Sorry for the fast leave. Sal is okay, but he passed out because of low blood sugar. His kidneys are all messed up too, so they're going to keep him for a few more days for observation. Thank you, ladies, for your prayers and concern. Despite all of this, I know my faith is strong. Please pray for my granddaughter as she was very upset about the whole thing. By the way, does anyone have my scarf?

Frankie looked up from her text. "Poor thing."

"What's wrong, Mama?" Candace put down her spoon and yogurt on the counter.

"My friend's husband passed out last night, and her granddaughter witnessed the whole thing."

"Wow, that's awful. I don't know if I could handle that either."

Frankie thought how rough it must have been for Regina to see that happen and wondered how Monica was handling it. She imagined the Raleigh-Stone family all disheveled after the night they'd had. Still, she was glad to know that Judith kept true to her faith and believed everything would turn out okay. Her family needed that strong example of faith to hold them up. She kept thinking about what Judith had said before—that there was no such thing as a coincidence.

Frankie decided to text her directly.

FRANKIE: Hi, Judith. I have your scarf and I'll keep it till we see each other, unless you need it earlier. Glad to hear Sal is doing okay.

JUDITH: Thanks, Frankie. Actually, could you bring it to the hospital? It's my mother's, and I could use her support right now.

Frankie wasn't surprised at Judith's need to have her scarf so immediately. She understood how much sentimental objects of loved ones meant. She had worn her mother's watch for close to a year, even though it no longer worked, just so she could feel close to her.

> FRANKIE: Of course. I'm dropping off my daughter at her friend's in a while, and I'll swing it by. Would you like some coffee or anything?
>
> JUDITH: No, just the scarf.
>
> FRANKIE: OK

She put her phone down and reached for another sip of coffee. Again, she felt calm, which surprised her. She wondered what this new feeling of strength was and how it had transformed her within the last twenty-four hours.

She still feared the idea of having to walk through the hospital and the range of emotions it might bring, so a moment of peace felt like a blessed reprieve.

★★★

About an hour and half later, Frankie and Candace pulled out of the driveway and headed toward the hospital. After dropping off Candace at Lanie's house, she pulled into the St. Dominic's hospital parking lot a short time later. She saw Judith's car with the LPRDLDY license plate toward the front of the lot. She could only imagine how exhausted Judith must be.

The hospital hallways dispirited Frankie with memories of countless times she had to be there when her mom had a complication with her medication or some relapse.

She took a deep breath as she turned the corner to the East Wing and saw Monica sitting outside a waiting room. Monica stood, clutching a tissue, her eyes dark and wide with surprise. "Frankie, what are you doing here?"

"Your mom texted me to bring her scarf."

The darkness circled her eyes, and her face was pale with exhaustion. "Why would my mom want her scarf? She has tons of them."

"She said it was her mother's."

"Hmm. I don't think it is. She bought it on the sale rack last week at the mall. I'm guessing she wanted you here. Probably just an excuse to get you to come sit with me."

Frankie figured even if Judith didn't really care about the scarf, she must have some important reason for wanting her there. "We've all been keeping you guys in our prayers. How's your dad?"

"Well ..." Monica scrunched her tissue tighter in her hand and wiped her nose. "My dad is doing better than we thought. I was worried he was having a stroke or something. Turns out his kidneys have been acting up, but mostly his diabetes. They're going to give him dialysis. Whatever reason he passed out has a lot to do with that. They still have to run more tests and rule out infections, but at least he's stable now, and they've said that he's responding well to all the basic treatments. You know, going to the bathroom and eating and drinking, so it's nothing concerning."

Frankie was relieved that Monica's family hadn't had to endure the worst, but there was still a lot of uncertainty about the future.

"How's your mom doing?"

"She's still pretty emotional, but you know my mother—she's naturally going to be that way. As hard as this is, she's going to make it through. It's Regina I'm worried about. She won't leave my father's side."

"I'm so sorry, Monica." Frankie rubbed her friend's shoulder, unsure what to do or say.

"They were watching baseball on TV when it happened. She'd gone to the kitchen to get some drinks, and when she came back, she found him on the floor." Monica wiped under her eyes. "Now Regina is considering not going to school. She's so worried about her papa that she doesn't want to leave him."

"Oh dear." Frankie kept rubbing her friend's arm.

"Her nerves are so shaken. She's worried about me too—about me being by myself. It's funny, because twenty-four hours ago, I wanted her to stay." Monica cradled herself with her arms. "But she shouldn't be trying to take on the family worries. I'm just so confused."

Frankie wasn't surprised by the family's indecision after all the discussion and heartache that had taken place. "I know this is a hard time for all of you. But have you talked to your daughter?"

"I haven't had the chance. I know she's concerned about me, but I realize now she can't stay, no matter what." Her voice changed to a soft whisper. "I just don't know how to let go."

Frankie lifted Monica's chin up to make eye contact. "You're right, it's her time to go. It's a change for both of you. You have to remember it's not her job to fill your life. You have to find new avenues for yourself. One of them may be taking care of your father."

Monica pursed her lips, wiped her eyes, and looked at her with desperation. "Do you think everything will be okay, Frankie?"

"To be honest, I can't answer that. But I do know she's expecting you to know what to do next. So, whatever you tell her, you tell her with love. Don't tell her what *you* need. Tell her what *she* needs."

Judith and Regina walked around the corner then, both looking like they'd been hit by a train. Judith had on one of Regina's new college sweatshirts and her hair had been pulled into a high, disheveled bun. She had dark circles around her eyes. Regina looked even worse. She'd obviously been crying to the point her eyes were heavily bloodshot.

Judith approached and wrapped Frankie in a hug. "Thank you for bringing my scarf. It's an old family heirloom."

"Mom, I told her you bought it last week."

"Oh, I must have gotten it mixed up with the one at home. Besides, Regina is cold." She turned to her granddaughter. "Here, babe, you wrap yourself in it." She motioned to wrap the scarf around her granddaughter, then turned back to Frankie. "Come with me. I need a coffee at the nurse's station."

Monica stared at her mother, open-mouthed. "Doesn't Dad need us in there with him?"

"No," Judith replied. "We were kicked out so he can get some rest. Come on, Frankie, let's go see if they have anything free too."

Frankie glanced at Monica, indicating she needed to have her conversation with Regina sooner rather than later, and this was the perfect opportunity.

"I would love some coffee." Frankie followed Judith, understanding now why Judith wanted her to be there.

"How is that darling cousin of yours?" Judith asked as the two walked down the hall.

At the corner, Judith pulled on Frankie to stop, then glanced back down the hall. Monica was motioning to her daughter to come in for a hug, and Regina walked into her mother's arms. Frankie and Judith watched from afar as the two exchanged words they couldn't hear, only see. Mother consoled daughter as she sobbed, Monica holding her until she came up for air. When the two finally separated, Regina and Monica walked down the hallway hand-in-hand in the direction of Frankie and Judith.

"I think that's our cue to return," remarked Judith.

Regina walked up to her grandmother, puffy-eyed, and gave her a hug.

"I think I'm going to back to the house, Nonni. Mom said she'll ride back with you."

Monica push a strand of her daughter's hair away from her shoulder. "You need to go home and get some sleep. You're leaving in just a few days and have a lot to get done. Papa will expect a full report of your dorm room and what classes you're taking. It will give him something to look forward to."

Regina leaned into her mother. "I love you, Mom."

"I love you more than you'll ever know, Regina." Monica gave her daughter's shoulders a squeeze. "Now go home and let Gerard and James know I'll be home soon. I'm going to take your grandma home, so she doesn't fall asleep at the wheel."

"Do what she says, sweet pea." Judith caressed her cheek before she left.

Regina walked down the hallway as Monica stayed and watched her daughter disappear around the bend.

"Did you say everything you wanted to say to her?" Frankie asked.

"No, but everything she needed to hear." Monica swiped at her nose with her tissue. "You know, it wasn't till today that I realized, if I had let her stay, I would be doing the same thing all over again."

"What do you mean?"

"This whole time, I thought I was raising her, but she's been raising me. I thought my life was over when I became a young mom. I thought everything I did was a sacrifice, but I confused that with resentment. I didn't realize until now that sacrifice isn't about giving up something at all, it's about love."

Judith reached out to hold Monica's hand. "If you didn't love her so much, it wouldn't be so hard to raise her or so hard to let her go."

Monica offered a small smile. "We've been a team for so long, but today she helped me realize who I'm supposed to be."

Judith rubbed her daughter's back. "She'll always be a part of your team."

Monica turned to her mother. "Thanks, Mom."

Frankie sighed and smiled. Judith had known Monica wouldn't have had the guts to have the conversation if the time hadn't been just right, but, somehow, Judith knew the right time didn't have to be right, it just had to happen.

Frankie quickly excused herself and let Monica and Judith console each other.

As Frankie stepped away, Monica collapsed into her mother's arms and sobbed so hard she couldn't control it.

Frankie didn't say anything. She just smiled at Judith then walked away.

As she drove home, Frankie realized she should be happy for Monica having made the right choice. She realized, looking back, her own mother had made sacrifices too. That's what mothers did for daughters. Judith had done that for Monica, and now Monica was doing it for Regina, which left Frankie wondering what God would ask of her.

As she drove in the direction of her home she noticed a bumblebee buzzing inside her car. She smiled, realizing it was a sign that her mother had been there to guide her. She rolled down the window to let the bee escape. Perhaps God had already presented her with her sacrifice—to set aside her grief for the good of her own daughters.

Chapter 16

If there ever comes a day where we can't be together, keep me in your heart, I'll stay there forever.—Winnie the Pooh

Rather than going home, Frankie drove to the coffee shop, where she thought she might write in her journal. A lot of thoughts were going through her mind, and this was the peace she needed to be able to recollect them and write them down.

The morning had been an eventful but cathartic one. Judith's husband was on the mend, Monica had made the right decision to support Regina despite her pain, and Frankie had taken a closer step in her own healing. Yet, the argument with Olivia still weighed heavy on her heart. Would she be able to reconcile? She could have easily driven over to Scarlet's and dropped off the flash drive, but helping Monica face her fears wasn't the same as facing her own with Olivia. Even though she'd left a million messages earlier in the week, seeing her would be so much harder. She would eventually talk with her, but it didn't have to be this morning. She arrived at the coffee shop, ordered her coffee, then found a cozy corner at the end of the high-top counter connected to the barista station. It felt good to just get out and be, without any rhyme or reason. In the past few weeks, she'd made major progress in terms of feeling somewhat human again.

She closed her eyes a moment, took a deep, cleansing breath, then looked at her surroundings. She noticed the café was busy with people going about their day. Many faces weren't thinking about grief, sadness, or even progress. Her grief wasn't something others could experience with her. The reality was life would continue no matter if she felt pain or sadness. She wrote her thoughts down in her journal. The more she wrote, the more her pain transferred to the pages, helping her repair the heavy wounds. This time she included her progress in what she wrote. She jotted some notes about the book talk women and the help they provided. Whether or not their help was intentional, she was grateful to God for their intrusion.

By the time Frankie came up from her writing, five pages of thoughts, emotions, and feelings had poured out from her heart. She felt a little lighter. Just as she was beginning the sixth page, she looked down at her phone and noticed some missed texts.

The first was from Judith.

> **JUDITH**: Thank you for this morning. Sometimes a mother can only get her message across by speaking it through another voice. BTW Can I have your address? I have something I want to drop off to thank you.

The second text was from Scarlet.

> **SCARLET**: Hey, when can I get my flash drive?

She looked down at her phone and realized it was 1:30 p.m. She had completely forgotten about Scarlet.

Frankie quickly replied to Judith's text with a bland response and her address, and then turned her attention to Scarlet. She hoped her cousin hadn't thought she'd blown her off.

> **FRANKIE**: I'm here at Clement's. Can you come and meet me?
>
> **SCARLET**: Why can't you just drop off the flash drive here?

This time her avoidance of the studio wasn't about Olivia. Frankie wasn't ready to give up the bliss of her surroundings.

> **FRANKIE**: Just come meet me. I'll buy you a coffee and a pastry.
>
> **SCARLET**: Only if you get me the largest French roast they have.
>
> **FRANKIE**: Deal.

Frankie figured it was a fair trade. She hopped out of her seat and got back in line. A break would be good for Scarlet too. Frankie knew if she dropped off the flash drive, Scarlet would be consumed by work and simply dismiss her.

By the time she placed the order and returned to her seat, Scarlet had arrived at the café.

"Why in the world did we have to meet here?" Scarlet asked with a sullen face as she came in and dumped her bag on the counter next to Frankie. "The studio isn't that far and, honestly, I don't really have time for this today."

"I'm sorry I didn't see your text." Frankie passed her the coffee and freshly heated cranberry-orange muffin. "But sometimes, it's nice to get outside."

"Well, you picked a heck of a day to need my company. I have one of the biggest events tomorrow, and Olivia and I are getting everything squared away."

"Listen, I know you're busy, but you're always busy," said Frankie, trying to sound reasonable. "Can't you sacrifice like ten minutes here? You've always been on top of your game, and I highly doubt ten minutes will throw you off."

Scarlet spoke through gritted teeth. "Fine." She pasted on a fake smile. "How's the weather?"

"Seriously?"

"Well, we can talk about work and how I need to get back?"

Frankie smirked at Scarlet's sarcasm. "I don't really want to talk about your business. Not that it isn't great. I thought, just maybe, we could talk about something else."

"Well, what else is there to talk about? I don't really have time for this, Frankie. We should be productive."

"Scarlet, I'm starting to realize that not everything is about work. And not everything is about sadness either. There has to be a middle ground somewhere. I'm accustomed to feeling sad all the time, and you're accustomed to feeling nothing. But we can't be like that all the time. Today, I revisited some of that sadness, but I realized by letting myself experience those emotions, I could get through it. I don't want to be sad all the time. Writing out my feelings helps me understand how I can deal with my grief. So, I've decided we're going to sit here once a week. You're not going to talk about work, and I'm not going to talk about my grief about my mom's death. It's not healthy for either of us to focus so much on one thing. Even if by talking means we are forced into sharing food recipes or talking about the weeds in my yard, that's what we're going to do."

"Well, I like talking about work—it gives me purpose. There's nothing wrong with working, Frankie. And of all days, this is one I need to prioritize with work."

"No, there isn't anything wrong about work or talking about work, but when your work consumes your life, it's not healthy either. Besides, I know your doctors have said your blood pressure is high, and, if you don't take breaks once in a while, you'll collapse or have heart issues. Isn't that why you hired Olivia, so you could get some help?"

Scarlet picked at the top of her muffin. "I hired her so I could stay on top of my work and get more clients, not because I want a vacation. That was your idea."

"Well, just humor me for today, will you? I need this." Frankie took a sip of her drink as she waited for Scarlet's response.

Scarlet gritted her teeth. "Fine, I guess, but just so you know, this isn't very productive."

Scarlet stared into her coffee and fidgeted with the wooden stirrer. They sat for a while saying nothing as they drank their coffee. Frankie realized if it was this hard to talk about something other than her grief or Scarlet's business then her point was all the more proven—they both needed to get a life.

Frankie finally started. "So, did you think of something to talk about?"

"No, not really, except some clients I need to call."

"Remember, we need to think of something else besides our standard go-to topics." A smirk played across Frankie's face. "I've got it. How's that guy you're seeing? Charles?"

Scarlet scowled. "Really, Frankie?"

"Well, I was just curious, you know. He seems nice, and he's very into you. Did you know I ran into him here at the coffee shop the day you hired Olivia?"

Scarlet tapped her fingers across the counter. "Well, I figured you had spoken or something considering the 'marigolds are in bloom' comment," she said mockingly.

"Yeah, what was that about anyway?" Frankie had been curious from the moment he'd said it.

Scarlet straightened up in her chair and looked away from Frankie. "Yeah, uh ... It's just code for he wants to me to do another photoshoot."

Frankie crossed her arms. "I'm not buying it."

Scarlet took a deep breath and locked eyes with Frankie. "He brings me flowers, sometimes, to—"

"That's really sweet, Scarlet! He brings you flowers to ... wait, what?"

Scarlet took fidgeted on her barstool, twisting in her seat. "He brings me flowers to put on my parents' gravesite whenever he goes to visit his mom at the cemetery."

Frankie had no idea Scarlet visited her parents' grave. Her parents had died in a tragic boating accident almost ten years earlier. She rarely ever brought it up.

Scarlet pushed the food away and let out a deep sigh. "About three years ago, I met Charles when I was visiting their gravesite. I knew everyone would go to the cemetery on their anniversary, and I didn't want to be bothered by other visitors, so I decided to go the next day instead." She tilted her head down toward her lap and put her hands between her legs. "When I showed up, I fell into such a sorrowful stupor from seeing all the flowers from everyone that it ... it broke me down.

He was only a few sites over and started talking to me. His mom had died the day after my parents, so it was interesting I should see him there that day." She closed her eyes and lifted her chin. "He saw me crying, and he handed me a marigold to put on their headstone. He said something about his mom wouldn't have wanted someone to cry if she were alive. He started talking to me about other things and got my mind off the whole ... issue."

Scarlet looked up but diverted her eyes from Frankie. "I was pretty grateful for that. Every time I visited my parents from that point, I found a marigold on their headstone." Scarlet paused and smiled looking in the direction of her muffin. "Eventually I found notes asking if I wanted to hang out and get some flowers together. Well, one thing led to another, and now we still see each other from time to time."

Frankie's mouth dropped. She hadn't expected such an admission. She reached out to touch Scarlet's hand, but her cousin pulled away. "I had no idea you even still went to visit your parents."

"Well, I don't tell anyone because honestly I don't want to talk about it. These past two years have been really rough on you, Frankie, and it's made me think about my own mom and dad so much. But why would I want to talk about something that's so painful? All it does is make me sad." She sat up right in her seat. "Anyway, Charles and I are just friends, but he wants more. I don't have time for anything."

"I'm sorry, Scarlet. I didn't know. I thought you guys met working on some professional projects."

Scarlet shrugged. "That's what Charles says to cover for me. He knows I don't like to talk about it to anyone. And he's not totally off. I have worked with his firm on some projects, photographing all the boring lawyers."

"Oh, wow. I didn't realize that. I'm sorry you've been sad about your parents though. I didn't know. You never talk about them."

Scarlet arched her eyebrows. "Yeah, well, you're not the only person in the world who's lost a parent or a loved one, for that matter. Aunt Barbara lost a brother and a sister-in-law, but I lost everything."

Frankie hadn't thought Scarlet to be the emotional type since she never talked about stuff like this.

"I'm sorry, Scarlet. I wish I had known. I would have been there for you. I wish I had been a better cousin. I just assumed everyone grieved the same way, so I didn't recognize yours."

Scarlet interlocked her fingers together. "I don't talk about it because it hurts too much, and the last thing I want to do, Frankie, is feel. So, I'm sorry I'm not like you, all mushy and sensitive and stuff. I'm not that way. I just can't be, okay?"

Frankie wasn't sure what to say. She certainly hadn't expected to have this deep conversation. In fact, this was actually the opposite of what she wanted. She tried to flip the conversation to something lighter, something more in Scarlet's comfort zone.

She reached out and touched her cousin's hand, and this time Scarlet didn't pull away. "Why don't we talk about pictures. I want you to take our family photo this fall for our Christmas card."

Scarlet squeezed her hand back and the corners of her mouth relaxed. "Thanks, Frankie, I'd like that."

She knew that was the extent of small talk Scarlet would be able to handle. Maybe it was good for them to end their visit for the day. They could practice small talk another time. Just as she was reaching for the flash drive in her purse to tell Scarlet she could flee to the safety of her studio, Johnna trudged into the coffee shop. Frankie felt surprised to see her. Johnna still had heavy bags around her eyes from the night of wine and bad cake, but it wasn't a hangover that she noticed. Something in her demeanor seemed off. Her jubilant smile that she normally carried was replaced with a firm line of her lips and vacant eyes.

When she spotted Frankie, she stuck her hands in her pockets and dragged her feet in Frankie's direction instead of going to the front for her order.

"Well, hey, pretty surprising running into you here. Don't you have an appointment for your dad?" Frankie asked.

Johnna's head hung low. "Hey," was all she replied.

Frankie motioned toward Scarlet. "This is my cousin Scarlet."

Johnna put out her hand and limply shook Scarlet's. This was definitely not the happy, overly affection Johnna she knew. Even Scarlet eyed her warily.

Maybe it was the hangover. "Feeling better from yesterday? Are you on your way to your dad's appointment?" she repeated.

Johnna looked at Frankie with hollow eyes as she stood next to the barstool. "I just came from there, actually." Her lower lip quivered. "Turns out dad's cancer returned and ... and it's spread to his pancreas, so there's not much they can do." She took a deep breath and swiped away at her tears. "I'm just here to get my coffee before I head over to my parents' house. I've already had my share of booze for the week."

Frankie gasped in disbelief and reached for her hand. "Oh, Johnna, I'm so sorry. But I thought everything was going so well?"

"I guess we were too optimistic, and he doesn't want treatment. He's tired," she added. "He's decided it's time."

Chapter 17

Let nothing disturb you, nothing frighten you, all things
are passing, God is unchanging. Patience gains all;
nothing is lacking to those who have God: God alone is
sufficient.—Theresa of Avila

"Oh, my friend." Frankie stood and wrapped her arms
around Johnna.

Frankie could feel herself juddering with indecision.
She knew being the child of a parent with a "death
sentence" was dreadful, and yet all her experience on the
subject had not prepared her to be a supportive friend.
She understood everything Johnna was going through,
but how could she tell her in a comforting way that grief
was hard? How could she articulate it would be okay when
she knew there was more pain to come? She couldn't offer
comfort because hidden below lay a layer of suffering.
She decided to give her the most honest advice she could
think of instead.

"It's okay to not be okay."

"Huh?" Johnna looked up with heavy eyes.

"It's okay to not be all right with all of this."

Johnna straightened her shoulders and pulled away
from their embrace. Frankie knew that no matter what
advice she gave, Johnna would feel an obligation to be
brave.

As she wiped her bloodshot eyes with a tissue, she muttered, "Well, my dad has accepted it. He says he's tired of doctors and appointments. He just wants to live the remainder of his life however God gives it to him."

Frankie offered Johnna her full attention, despite the jab she felt in the back from Scarlet who obviously just wanted to take her flash drive and flee.

"Well, at least now he doesn't have to worry anymore about his blood sugar or hiding candy bars from my mom," Johnna said, trying to make a light joke. "He's actually pretty relaxed about the whole thing." Johnna scowled as she tried to discuss her dad's decision as if they were having an ordinary conversation, but Frankie could see the hurt in her eyes. "He wants to pick out his own casket and says we better not bury him in a solid oak. He says that maple wood is the only way to go."

The more she talked, the more tears continued to seep out. Frankie could see her ruse of trying to play it light was failing.

As Frankie caressed her friend's shoulder, she could sense Scarlet becoming more fidgety behind her. She nudged Frankie's leg to get her attention. Frankie knew her cousin was uncomfortable, but her uneasiness had reached a new level. Frankie felt torn. On one end she looked at her grieving friend on the verge of a breakdown and, on the other, her cousin who was about to lose her marbles if the tone didn't change. Frankie knew she needed to be the conciliating voice.

She placed her other hand on Scarlet's knee but stayed turned to Johnna. "Then, that's exactly what you let him do. You let him pick out his coffin, you let him eat candy bars, you let him spend his time however he wants to spend it. That's a beautiful gift you can give him. And you'll be able to honor him the way he wants."

Both Johnna and Scarlet simultaneously took a slow breath. Frankie's words seem to relax them both, but the moment didn't last. Scarlet tried to lift Frankie's fingers off her knee then bent to grab the flash drive, but she leaned back too far on the bar stool. She reached for some kind of support, but her fingers slipped from the edge of the countertop and her legs went soaring over her head, kicking Frankie's coffee mug to the floor, shattering it into pieces and spraying coffee everywhere.

Johnna and Frankie turned swiftly to look at Scarlet, who now sat on the ground with coffee and mug remnants surrounding her.

"Uh, I've got to go!" she stammered and shot up without the flash drive before Frankie could even speak. She darted past some of the customers, knocking shoulders with the barista cleaning a table close by before she headed out the door.

Frankie knew the entire meeting had been way more than Scarlet could handle, and she'd have to go over and deliver the flash drive and see her, but right now she needed to be with Johnna.

Her grieving friend dropped to the ground, hastily picking up pieces of broken mug and scrubbing the floor with her tattered tissue.

"Johnna, leave it." Frankie pleaded.

"No! I need to clean up this mess," she snapped. She reached out to the closest table and grabbed wads of napkins out of the dispenser to try to mop up the coffee and scattered mug residuals. Frankie watched as Johnna bent on her knees scrubbing and wiping with intensity.

"I need to fix this ... I need to fix this," she muttered as she cried. She scoured the ground forcefully until Frankie saw blood oozing from her hand.

"Johnna, you're bleeding."

Johnna lifted her hands. Napkins and mug pieces dropped and re-scattered over the floor. Frankie pulled her off the ground and motioned her to the table a few feet away, while one of the baristas rushed over and picked up the mess.

Johnna continued to sob as her finger bled. Frankie took some napkins to put pressure on it.

"I can't clean this up, Frankie. I can't clean this up." She moaned.

They both knew she was no longer talking about the broken coffee mug. Johnna continued to weep and couldn't stop. Frankie didn't care about the other patrons looking at them. She knew her friend was broken, and she needed to comfort her.

"This isn't your mess to clean," she whispered as she held her close.

After a few minutes, Johnna wiped her eyes and looked at her. "Why, Frankie? Why does God make this so hard for us? I've been trying so hard. I've been doing everything right."

Frankie rubbed small circles on her back as she talked.

"I just don't think God's listening to me anymore. I'm starting to hate him." She gasped at the honesty of her words, then shook her head. "How can my dad be okay with this, and I can't accept it? What have I done wrong? Why can't we try something else to make him better? I just don't know how much more I can take." She looked at Frankie with searching eyes.

There were so many feelings swelling in Frankie she didn't know how to proceed, so just like before, she spoke from the heart and experience. "You haven't done anything wrong. In fact, you've done everything right." She took a hold of Johnna and held the uninjured hand. "I guess when we know it's our time, there's nothing anyone can do to make it right."

Johnna frowned at her response.

"If your dad is okay with this, well, you have to respect that. It's not too often we can be comfortable or even accept our own mortality."

Johnna fell into sobs again, muttering her thoughts. "But why did God decide to make my dad sick? Why couldn't he have picked someone else to get sick? Why him, why now?"

Frankie spoke slowly and softly. "I used to think God only gives us what we can handle, but the truth of it is, the world gives us more, but he allows it so we can lean on him. I wish I had all the answers for you, Johnna, but I don't. I'm guessing God knows your dad has done all he needed to do here."

"Well, it's not fair," she said, crossing her arms. "We need him. I don't think he's done here."

Frankie recalled the experience with her own mom on her deathbed and knew it didn't matter what she thought. Her mom's time was her mom's, whether she'd been ready to accept it or not. This was God's plan not hers. The hardest part was accepting. Truth be told, some days had been a little harder to accept, but she had never doubted God's plan even if she didn't understand it. She just knew she had to keep moving forward.

Her thoughts returned to Johnna as a barista handed Frankie some gauze and bandages. She let up on the hand to wrap the other.

"When my mom died, I sometimes regretted I didn't do more things with her. I didn't create memories because I was too consumed with tasks—cleaning bed pans and administering medicine. I knew it was going to happen eventually, but I was so focused on making her better, I didn't consider she might not actually get better." Johnna listened as Frankie continued to wrap her hand. "I regret all that wasted time. I wished I had used it better, but then one day when Candace fell off her bike, and I tended to her bruises, I realized everything I was doing to care for her, I had learned from my mom."

Johnna sat quietly listening, her sobs now gone.

"It dawned on me the time hadn't been wasted, it was just a different kind of time. My mom taught me to care for her, and I was passing that on to my daughter. She taught me how to be a mother. She taught me how to love."

Johnna sat up and sniffed back some of her tears as she listened to Frankie.

"Your dad loves you, and he knows what an amazing daughter you are. Your dad might not have forever, but you've given him so much love in his life and he to you. So, maybe that's God's plan, to teach us what love is."

Johnna examined her now wrapped finger then stood. "You're right, Frankie." She reached over to hug her friend. "I knew there was a reason I needed to stop here. As Judith would say, there's no such thing as coincidences."

When Johnna left, Frankie turned back to her original spot to see the mess had been cleaned up. She gathered her things and walked out to her car. She still needed to pick up Candace, so she headed in her direction. She'd had a more emotional and tragic morning than expected, and somehow, through all of it, she had remained calm and had even become a voice of strength and wisdom. Her interactions today showed that life could change quickly and without warning—and it didn't just happen to her. Other people were experiencing grief in their own ways too. Maybe the last two years hadn't been a waste. Her suffering had helped these ladies with their own. Her path was starting to have a direction.

Chapter 18

Sometimes the only way the good Lord can get into some people's hearts is to break them.—Venerable Archbishop Fulton J. Sheen

Bolting out of the café had been a clear sign Scarlet wasn't ready to deal with emotionally charged moments. After picking up Candace, Frankie thought about Scarlet's reaction and how she would proceed. Learning about Johnna's dad had been a cumbersome and heavy happenstance, even more than Frankie herself had expected. Naturally the news had thrown Scarlet over the edge. Frankie had to tread lightly with these types of matters, and yet she still hadn't followed through with the flash drive Scarlet so eagerly came to seek out. *What would be the least emotional, unengaging approach?* She would send her a text.

> **FRANKIE:** I have your flash drive. Max can bring it over if you absolutely need it. If not, I will bring it Monday.

Scarlet's one word text back—*Monday*—confirmed Frankie's suspicions that her cousin needed some space. She'd resort, for now, to finding other means to take care of her work. Scarlet always had a backup plan.

As Frankie and Candace arrived home, Max met them at the door. "Hi, girls."

Candace high-fived her dad as she walked in. "Lanie and I got five posters made for the first week of school, and I even completed the agenda for our first student council meeting for next week."

"Sounds productive for Lanie's house," joked Max.

"I mean we hung out, but it was all business first. Don't worry. I always make sure the job gets done." Candace walked past him and down the hallway, leaving Frankie and Max at the door.

Max looked down at his wife with a somber frown. She knew how tired she looked. She glided into his arms and breathed in the scent of his warmth. Max's embrace helped soothe away an emotional yet cathartic day.

"This is quite the hug." Max smiled as he pulled back slightly but kept Frankie in his tender grasp.

She looked up at him with sanguine eyes. She didn't need to tell him about her morning with Judith and Monica or the events that unfolded with Scarlet and Johnna. She just needed him to hold her. His embrace somehow centered her. She knew he would always be there for her.

"You're my blessing," she said.

He grinned as he smoothed her hair. "You seem tired."

"Let's just say today was a day full of perspective." She tilted her head back and looked up at the ceiling, letting out a long sigh. "But I'm learning God is definitely in charge." She kissed the top of his nose and tossed her purse on the side table near their entryway.

"He always is," said Max, following Frankie into the living room. "Oh, by the way." Max turned around and pulled an envelope from the drawer of the entryway table. "A lady with leopard-print pants and a college sweatshirt came by and left this for you." He handed her the envelope. "She said it was to thank you for dropping off the family heirloom. What's that about?"

Frankie smirked as she thought of Judith meeting her husband.

"She also said she wouldn't be able to use it since she'd be at the hospital the next couple days, and you might put it to better use."

Frankie opened the envelope and saw two tickets inside with a note attached. She traced her fingers over the embossed calligraphy.

The Tuleberg Domestic and Wildlife Animal Protection Society cordially invite you to The 14th Annual Auxiliary Luncheon and Auction: A Garden Affair All proceeds benefit the animals of the Lamech Grove Zoo.

Attached to the tickets was a note from Judith.

Frankie,
Thought you might want to take your husband to this. They serve really good appetizers and for $200 a ticket I can't see these going to waste. Plus, there's no one else who deserves this more than you.—Love, JR

Frankie closed her eyes as she placed the letter and tickets over her chest.

"What is it?"

She held the invite and note out to her husband. "It's tickets to the event Scarlet's photographing tomorrow."

Max glanced over the tickets and the note. "You know, it's been a while since we've gone out and done anything together. Might be fun." He pulled her close once more.

Frankie frowned. "I don't know. It seems like a lot of fancy people and I—"

"Don't want to run into Olivia?"

Frankie's eyes widened. "How'd you know about Olivia?"

"I live in this house too, Frankie. I can hear from other rooms when you talk to the girls."

He had heard their conversation over ice cream and put the pieces together. A natural detective. Yet he hadn't said anything about Olivia, and even now he wasn't prodding to find out more information.

Frankie held the envelope near her heart. She knew if she went, she was bound to run into Olivia, and she'd promised herself she would give Scarlet some space.

"I'm sure it's so big we probably won't see her," Max said as if he could read Frankie's thoughts. "Besides this might be just the push we need to get out of the house and be together." He snagged the tickets and dangled them in front of her. "We wouldn't want these babies to go to waste."

Frankie wasn't sure this was the moment to come out of her shell. She thought about how angry Scarlet might be with her and about her fear of running into Olivia. But then she saw the eagerness in Max's face.

"I guess we could check it out for a while, but I thought you hated these things."

"I don't care where we go. I just want to spend time with my wife." Max wrapped his arms around her waist. "And we don't have to stay the whole time. Maybe afterward we could check out that new brewery downtown near Scarlet's studio?"

"Now I see your real motives." Frankie chuckled. "But where will we find a sitter by tomorrow?"

Max turned his head toward the hallway as a smile came over his face. "I think Candace is old enough to have her first babysitting job."

★★★

The next day, Frankie scavenged through her closet, pushing through hanger after hanger, trying to find some "appropriate" attire. She knew the luncheon would be a very high-end affair with bigwigs from all over the state. Lucy had mentioned it was an "A-list" event, but now that she was attending, she understood why Scarlet had been so intense at their meeting. Her pictures would be published in the *Tuleberg Society Magazine*, showcasing everyone's attire and status. Frankie felt less than equipped to attend such an event.

The tickets mentioned it was a garden-party theme, so she assumed there'd be lots of attendees with dressy cocktail apparel and oversized derby hats. She didn't own anything of the sort. She continued rifling toward the back of her closet, searching through her options, until she stumbled on a pastel floral dress she'd worn to a friend's wedding a few years back. She decided it would suffice and quickly matched it with the same sandals she'd worn to lunch with Scarlet. She added a diamond-crusted cross necklace that had belonged to her mother. As she fidgeted with her skirt, eyeing the back from the reflection in the mirror, she considered how many times her wardrobe had involved something other than her sweatshirts and grief-stricken yoga pants in the past few weeks. If she kept this up, she was going to have to start shopping for more clothes.

After she and Max—who had settled for some khaki dress slacks, a tan polo shirt, and a simple but elegant dark blazer—had gone over the "do and don't" list with Candace, provided her with the emergency contacts, and picked up a pizza for the girls, they headed toward the event.

As they pulled into the entrance to the Lamech Zoo, Frankie proceeded to straighten her dress for the umpteenth time. She pulled her compact out of her purse and did a quick look over.

"Does this dress look okay? Ugh, my hair looks horrible. You know, maybe this is a mistake ..."

Max parked the car and turned his adoring gaze to her. "I know you've been pushing yourself out of your comfort zone so much these past few weeks, and I just want you to know how amazing you are."

"So, why don't I feel amazing right now?"

"Most amazing people don't know they're amazing."

Frankie turned to Max with shaky hands. "I'm sorry you've had to deal with all the changes in me. I know I've put you through so much."

His eyes sparkled. "You don't need to apologize, Frankie, but promise me you'll allow yourself to enjoy the afternoon."

Frankie bit her bottom lip. "I can't promise that, but I'll try."

Max came around to open her door, and he reached for her hand as she got out of the car. Together, they walked toward the entrance.

Lamech Zoo had been transformed from a children's zoo into a garden oasis, and the place buzzed with people and animals. The grounds were covered with ivy and lush plants from every corner. Topiaries and ivy-covered lattice walls had been brought in to direct guests to key events for the auxiliary but still allowed for exploring other exhibits.

As they checked in and received their programs, Frankie noticed a row of banquet-style covered tables to the right of the entrance promoting various local agencies. Out of the corner of her eye, she spotted Maisie's beautiful red hair. Her new friend was passing out flyers and looked up to meet Frankie's gaze. She had on an A-line scoop-neck, mint-colored chiffon cocktail dress that cascaded to her knees. Frankie grinned, delighted to see her, as Maisie strolled over and gave her a hug.

"Frankie, why didn't you tell me you were coming? I didn't know you had tickets." Maisie waved her hand toward the next guest passing in her direction with a flyer of cute German Shepherd dogs and tabby cats.

Frankie smiled. "I didn't either till yesterday. Judith gave me hers."

"How's she doing? And her husband, Sal?"

"He'll be in the hospital a few more days to monitor his kidneys, but it looks like he'll be okay."

"Ugh, I'm glad it wasn't anything worse." She turned and stopped an older woman wearing an oversized blue-feathered hat and placed a flyer in her hand. "Adopt a pet today!" she said to the woman as she passed. The lady raised her eyebrow at Maisie and walked right by, but Maisie appeared unfazed and jumped right back into her conversation with Frankie.

Frankie stifled a laugh. "And what are you doing here?"

"Don't you remember, silly? I'm a board member for the group that puts this shindig on."

Frankie thought back to the night of the book talk. "Oh, that's right."

"I couldn't care less about all the glitz of these parties, but it warms my heart that the money helps keep the zoo going. "Want to adopt a pet?" She shoved a flyer advertising the local animal shelter into Frankie's hand.

Frankie looked at Max. "Not today, but I'll keep it in mind if we decide to add a four-legged friend to the family."

Maisie shrugged her shoulders and kept passing out flyers to others.

"By the way, this is my husband Max."

Max extended his hand to Maisie, who, in turn, handed him a flyer and smiled. "Pleasure to meet you."

Frankie tucked the flyer into her program as she turned her attention to the event. "Looks like you have a lot of big names here," said Frankie as she continued to inspect the program and the sponsors. "Joyner Construction, Kensington Industries, Perino Steel, Thompson & Clark Law Firm ..."

Maisie shook her head. "Yeah, that's how it all works, credit for doing something that should be done out of the kindness of your heart. But as long as the animals are all taken care of, that's what matters most to me."

Frankie smiled at Maisie's veracity.

"My husband, Auggie, is here helping me, and we're running the booth on dog adoptions from the local shelter. But it's not much of a job, no one seems to be adopting. Hey, why don't you come meet him?"

Frankie and Max walked with Maisie to the table where a sandy-brown-haired man with ruddy skin surrounded by stacks of flyers on the table was looking down at his phone, watching a football game.

Maisie scowled as she came close to the table. "Auggie, you're supposed to be handing out flyers."

"I'm just taking a break to check the score. No harm in that." Auggie looked back at his phone more focused on the next play.

"Stand up and meet my friend. This is Frankie from our book talk."

Maisie's husband smiled and stood up quickly to shake Frankie and Max's hand, but then went back to looking down at his phone. Maisie huffed as she put her hands on her hips. She was about to scold him when Max cut her off.

"Is that the preseason game you're watching?" Max leaned over Frankie's shoulder to catch a glimpse of the small screen.

Auggie lifted his brow, and a hint of life flashed across his face. "Yeah, I'm waiting for the score to tie up. I've got money on this game."

Max pulled up the empty chair to sit down next to Auggie, and the two men zoned out as they stared at the phone.

Frankie laughed. "An escaped tiger could be loose on the grounds, and they'd be oblivious."

Maisie shook her head and laughed. How could she object now that Max sat side by side with Auggie? She smiled and picked up more flyers from the table. "So, have you seen Olivia yet?"

Frankie frowned. "No, we just got here."

"She came by a few moments ago with your cousin Scarlet, who I finally got to meet. Anyway, your cousin had Olivia practice on us by taking some pictures. She might be new at photography, but that was one of the best pictures of me and Auggie. I don't think we've had a picture of just the two of us without kids since we got married."

Frankie was happy to hear Scarlet trusted Olivia enough to snap photos, but a sadness came over her to be left out of the loop.

"How did Olivia look?" Frankie inquired.

"She was super nervous, but I told her to think of these guests as animals in the food chain with better accessories." Maisie laughed.

Frankie wondered what would happen when they finally saw each other. She felt like eons had gone by since they'd spoken, and Olivia still wasn't responding to her calls. She had to prepare for a rejection, to be ignored if their paths crossed, which was highly likely.

"And how was Scarlet?"

Maisie smirked and crossed her arms. "She's a funny one, that cousin of yours. She was very sweet, except I couldn't understand why she kept referring to our group as more normal than she expected."

Frankie tilted her head back and laughed. "That sounds like Scarlet. Trust me, in her own weird way, that's a compliment."

"Well, all I know is the board is super pleased with her. I have a feeling they'll want to hire her for next year."

"I'm sure she's up for it. She's always looking for ways to fill her schedule."

"I was going to tell her to make sure she got a picture of the auction prizes, but Mayor Hegland whisked her away before I could."

"What direction did they go?" Frankie wanted to stay out of her sight.

"Well, Scarlet went toward the lemurs, but she told Olivia to go to the butterfly and bird estuaries and walk around and snap any woman with huge feathers in their hat. Naturally, Olivia seemed scared to go out on her own. So, I told her to compliment anyone before she took a photo and remind them certain pictures would go into the society magazine." Maisie rolled her eyes. "Everybody loves flattery. And that seemed to ease her nerves a bit. Hey! Why don't we go try to find her?"

Maisie didn't know the situation between her and Olivia. "I, uh, I don't want to bother her while she's working. I know how important it is for her to feel independent."

"Well, at least let's go explore. Come on, just for a few minutes," pleaded Maisie as she looked around at the guests dodging her hand full of flyers. "And I don't think you're going to peel those two away for a while."

Frankie turned to see Max and Auggie gabbing about the game they were watching on the phone. Max thrust his fist into the air, cheering on his team. She grinned at Maisie as they linked arms and strolled toward one of the walk paths.

The zoo had little trails that branched off into animal exhibits, which made it confusing to figure out where a person might end up. Frankie didn't really care so long as they didn't run into Olivia. As they walked through each exhibit, a large sign indicated a sponsor who'd graciously donated to the event. They walked past the chimpanzees and other exotic breeds. Frankie looked down at the signs with different species—*Spider monkey, capuchin, and squirrel monkeys sponsored by Perino Steel.*

They finally made their way to the sprawled-out lawn of the petting area where most of the trails connected. Normally the area would have been covered with small goats and approachable sheep, but tonight the area was bordered with large, round tables covered with elaborate sprays of peacock and parrot feathers.

In front of the petting barn sat an oversized stage surrounded by large ivy lattices and speakers that had been brought in just for the occasion. The auction tables were partitioned off by lattices to the left of the stage for any onlookers eager to bid. Frankie noticed an unusually large crowd of women standing near the tables observing some of the items. More unusual was the fact that they all seemed to be wearing outlandish hats, some made of feathers, a few that looked like tea pots, and others with an assortment of whatever kind of oddity could be attached to one's head. Chuckling at how ridiculous they looked, she and Maisie moved on till they found a tapas bar to the left where they stopped to get a drink and snack. She took a glass of wine from the server and surveyed the small bites in front of her.

This must be those expensive appetizers Judith was talking about.

As she bit into a large shrimp, she noticed a familiar face appear—her nosy neighbor Mallory.

"Well, Frankie, isn't this a treat. First, I see you shopping and now you're out on the town. I hear your book talk is going fabulous. Quite a change in the last two years."

Frankie gulped down the shrimp. Their last encounter had left Frankie feeling annoyed and frustrated as the nosy woman had prodded about her personal life and degree of grief. She wasn't as annoyed to see her this time, but something told her Mallory wasn't simply stopping by to see how she was doing.

"Nice to see you too," Frankie said in a cordial tone. "This is my friend Maisie."

Maisie put out her hand to shake, but Mallory limply reciprocated and quickly turned her attention back to Frankie.

"I can't believe how many people are here this afternoon. It's just crawling with more people than last year. A lot I don't recognize."

"So, you come every year?" asked Frankie.

Mallory's eyes surveyed the crowd as she fanned herself with her program. "It's definitely a who's who place to meet and be seen. And there's always someone to be seen with."

Frankie realized Mallory wasn't here for the animals or the appetizers.

"I've been trying to get the attention of that photographer Scarlet Bedford, but her phone lines are booked up, and her secretary keeps giving me the run-around."

"Oh! We know her!" exclaimed Maisie. "That's Frankie's—"

Frankie elbowed Maisie in the stomach. Mallory didn't need to know any more about her life or her family.

"Err, uh, she's my photographer. I know her because she's photographed my family for years," Frankie quickly said.

"Well, then this really is a treat. I knew there was a reason to come over and talk to you. How did you get her as 'your' photographer?"

Frankie raised her eyebrow at Mallory. What did it matter? She felt annoyed that Mallory thought she wasn't capable of hiring a high quality photographer. She wasn't about to tell her they had spent every Christmas and Easter together since they were kids. She would be honest, but she wasn't going to divulge any new information. She was about to tell her she was a preferred client, but Mallory continued.

"Her name is all the buzz, and I've been wanting to get hold of her for my son's wedding, but I just can't seem to lock her down. My soon-to-be daughter-in-law, Eliza, wants whatever is the best. Apparently Scarlet is the best. But I've heard she's already booked into next year. Do you think you could put in a good word for me since we're such dear neighbors?"

Frankie took a long drink from her glass before replying. Mallory wasn't the least bit interested in neighborly affection, but Frankie knew she would continue to prod and snoop around if she didn't at least say something. "I'll make a point to mention your name, although I can't make any promises."

"Oh, wonderful, Frankie. You're such a gem. From what I've heard she takes referrals as top priority."

"Uh, I'm not sure how she picks her clients." Truthfully, she didn't. She just knew the heavier Scarlet's calendar, the happier she was. "I imagine she'd pick them based on when she's available." Frankie didn't know where she was going with this.

"Well, from what I've heard, she jumps from one big name to another. First, it's the Thompson and Clark firm, then the children's hospital, and now the mayor."

Frankie scratched her head. "Thompson and Clark—where have I heard that name before?"

"Charles Thompson," said Maisie. "He's one of the biggest sponsors here."

"Charles? Scarlet's Charles? I thought he was just an attorney. I didn't realize he owned his own firm."

Mallory looked Frankie up and down. "You know him too? Well, I didn't realize you had such high connections in this town, Frankie."

"I only know him a little. But why does it matter?"

Mallory tilted her head back in laughter. "Oh, Frankie. I guess you really have been out of the loop these past couple years. His firm is the top in Tuleberg. He has a lot of lawyers under him, so he practically doesn't have to work. He's also the most eligible bachelor in Tuleberg. Since you know him, maybe you can also put in a word about my daughter."

Frankie tried to cover the sour look of disgust on her face. Mallory only saw people as a way to climb the social ladder, and apparently, her children were her key to moving forward.

"Well," Frankie replied, crossing her arms, "I don't think it's possible. Besides, I believe Scarlet and Charles are interested in each other." *So much for not giving away new information.*

Mallory crossed her arms and giggled. "You're just too cute, Frankie."

"What are you talking about?"

Mallory looked Frankie straight in the eye. "No offense to Scarlet, but word has it she's so frigid around men their teeth chatter. I guess that's why she's so booked—to keep them away. Besides, Charles just doesn't seem like her type. This is just between us, of course."

Frankie tightly crumpled her napkin in her hand. How could Mallory be so insensitive? She had no idea the kind of person Scarlet was or the pain she'd endured. She wanted to tell Mallory to shove it where the sun didn't shine, but instead she straightened her shoulders and looked her in the eye.

"Come to think of it, I've heard Scarlet's so busy, I don't think I can mention you. She's booked up for almost two years and my guess is she's only making exceptions for A-listers. Sorry, maybe next time."

Chapter 19

It is great wisdom to know how to be silent and to look at neither the remarks, nor the deeds, nor the lives of others.—St. John of the Cross.

Frankie walked away with Maisie in tow as Mallory stood with her mouth open and fan halted.

"Frankie, I can't believe you just did that," said Maisie, giving her a broad smile.

"I can't either, but Father Gabriel will have plenty to hear at the confessional on Monday. I just couldn't let her talk about Scarlet like that."

As they walked toward the center of the grounds, Maisie pointed when she spotted another familiar face. "Hey, look! There's Lucy."

They slowed as Lucy approached wearing a small chapeau-style hat with twisted blue feathers and gold leaves. "Hi, girls. I can only stay for a moment. Collette Kensington is trying to steal my bid for an item in the auction. It's an all-inclusive ski trip to Aspen with lodging at the Perino Estate, and if I turn my head for even a moment, she's going to scribble out my name. Nevertheless, I was hoping to run into you girls, especially you, Frankie. Judith mentioned you might be here."

"I'm surprised she gave me her tickets."

"Why wouldn't she? You were able to get through to Monica, something neither she nor I could do. Sometimes you just need an alternative perspective." She winked at Frankie. "And speaking of book talk members, I just saw Olivia. She's charming the pants off the guests around here."

Maisie grinned. "Sounds like she got hold of her nerves then."

Lucy nodded, the blue feathers on her hat bobbing. "I'd say she's holding up just splendidly. I was talking to some of the women in my group, and they mentioned I just *had* to check out the photographer for *Tuleberg Society Magazine*. Who knew it was our Olivia they were talking about? I think I'll let them know that she's my personal photographer." She nudged Frankie with a smirk. "That always makes the women start to claw at each other."

"She's figured these ladies out really quickly. Quite the brown-noser." Maisie chuckled. "Now that's talent."

"I think she just wants to make Scarlet pleased more than anything," Lucy said. "It's such a blessing your cousin gave her a job, and now she has a new apartment. I'm sure she has you to thank for all that, Frankie."

Frankie felt dumbfounded by all the news but pretended to be in the know, as the women had no idea she and Olivia were on the outs. "Yes, she's really figuring things out for herself."

"Well, no one has everything figured out, but she did mention something about tying up loose ends. I didn't know what she was referring to, but I'm happy to know things are moving in the right direction for her."

Lucy continued, unaware of Frankie's downward gaze. "And I just can't wait till that baby gets here. I've already planned the baby shower, which is going to be magnificent. We need some good news after all the hospital visits."

Lucy touched Frankie's arm. "I heard about Johnna's dad from Olivia. I can only imagine what she's going through."

Scarlet must have told Olivia.

"Well, I'd better head back." Lucy looked toward the large group of heavy-hatted women she'd arrived with. "I can already feel Collette is up to something. You girls should stay for the auction. It's going to be amazing." She took a few steps, then turned back to them. "By the way, I donated a case of the Chenin blanc from my last trip. It's right next to the photo session your cousin donated." Lucy waved and headed back to the group.

Maisie turned to Frankie. "Why don't we go check out all those overpriced auction items?"

Lucy's group moved toward their seats as Frankie and Maisie perused the tables and looked at the many prizes on display—an annual membership to the Tuleberg Yacht club, an Egyptian mud wrap and one-hour hot rock massage, and a diamond-encrusted peacock broach were just three of many elaborate items. Frankie looked at all the lavish things she could never afford and saw Lucy's case of wine and Scarlet's studio session. Sure enough, Collette had crossed out Lucy's name. Scarlet's item had a few takers, including Mallory's name freshly scribbled in.

As Maisie and Frankie circled the table to watch someone bid on a private chef lesson, Maisie exclaimed, "Oh, look! There's your cousin now. She's with the mayor and the Perinos." Maisie pointed to Scarlet near the ivy-covered gazebo. She was snapping some pictures of Mayor Hegland with a man in a suit and a woman wearing a derby hat.

Frankie quickly plopped her sunglasses over her eyes and stepped close to the oversized canvas Scarlet had displayed for her auction prize. They hadn't talked since the café, and she knew Scarlet would be all business today.

Frankie watched from afar as Mayor Hegland thanked Scarlet and left with the unknown woman in the derby hat. But the man in the suit lingered behind to speak to her cousin. Frankie noticed that her face went from smiles to scowling eyebrows. A wave of chills passed over Frankie's spine. She watched as Scarlet took a step away from the man. She mumbled something and turned, but the man quickly grabbed her arm. As he turned, Frankie saw his face and immediately recognized him.

"Travis," Frankie blurted. *What was he doing here? And why was he talking to Scarlet?*

"Oh, you know Travis Perino?" Maisie said, a hint of scorn in her tone.

Travis was the *Travis Perino of Perino Steel? Olivia's Travis? No wonder she'd been so secretive about everything.*

Frankie felt a rush of emotions come over her as she hesitated to respond. "Uh, no. I just know of him. I saw the sign back near the monkey display. Wait! Do you know him?" She turned to Maisie with wide eyes.

Maisie left out a snort. "Unfortunately. Perino Steel is one of the biggest steel companies in the area. They supply all of the raw material for commercial developments and skyscrapers. Auggie's been working with them for years, but this past year, Calvin Perino, Travis's father, retired, so now Travis has taken over. Let's just say he has a different professionalism than his father, and from the looks of it, he's trying some of it out on your cousin."

Frankie's pulse began to race. She couldn't believe the man who had taken advantage of Olivia was now standing inches away from her beloved cousin. She screamed inside. She wanted to walk over and wail in his face, but she knew a public attack, especially at the auxiliary, would end in disaster.

Frankie watched as Scarlet put on a fake smile and yanked her arm back from Travis's grasp, then walked toward the gazebo. *Good girl, Scarlet!* Frankie knew Scarlet could handle herself. Whatever she said had left him with a heavy scowl. He crumbled up his program in a tight fist and threw it on the ground. His wife walked over and mumbled something with a disapproving smirk.

Then Frankie remembered. *Olivia's here too. What if she sees Travis?* Frankie didn't know what would happen if they crossed paths. She didn't know much about him, other than his general lack of respect for women, but she couldn't imagine him to be pleasant.

"You know it's really sad that guys like that have—" *Beep, beep.* Maisie looked down at her phone. "Auggie's texting me. Someone wants to adopt a dog. We should probably head back."

Uneasiness shot through Frankie's veins, but she tried unsuccessfully to appear collected as she fidgeted with her program, overly waving it like a fan. "Actually, I'm going to stay here for a bit. I, uh, want to see if there are any more bidders on Scarlet's auction prize."

"All right." Maisie touched her arm before leaving. "Hey, are you okay, honey? You seem a little tense."

"Uh, yeah, I'm fine." She waved her paper fan more vigorously than before. "But could you tell Max to come this direction. I didn't bring my phone."

Maisie looked her up and down before leaving. "Yeah, no problem. Are you sure you're okay?"

Frankie waved a hand, but never took her eyes off her cousin. "Just fine, just fine."

Maisie left as Frankie continued to spy on Scarlet behind the oversized table canvas. She would need to tell Scarlet about Travis for Olivia's sake, but she'd promised herself she wouldn't intervene. Was it the right time to put all the puzzle pieces together for everyone? Before she could discern her next move, Scarlet began to stride toward the auction tables. Without thinking, Frankie impulsively cowered behind the other auction bidders to stay out of sight. The canvas wasn't big enough to conceal her so where could she go? She noticed the large ivy-covered lattice next to the stage and darted behind it before Scarlet could see her.

This is so foolish! What am I hiding from?

The move was an impetuous one, but if she came out now, she would definitely appear as if she'd been snooping. She saw a small gap in the ivy that allowed her to see the whole scope of the auction and close enough to see Scarlet as she veered toward her auction prize. Her cousin looked at the bid sheet and heaved a heavy sigh. Frankie could tell it wasn't the bidder prices that bothered her. The scowl on her face expressed she was holding something back. Was it being hit on by Travis? Or the experience at the café the day before? Frankie knew Scarlet was juggling so much on her plate. The more people connected to Scarlet in higher society, the more was at stake for her career. Whatever the case, Frankie watched as Scarlet stiffened and straightened the auction pages in her clipboard as Charles Thompson approached.

"Worried you aren't getting enough bids on your sheet today?" he joked.

"Actually, I was taking an inventory. Whoever doesn't win, I planned to contact them and offer them a special package."

"Always looking for a new business opportunity. I like it, although I hardly doubt you'll need to solicit any more business." Charles laughed a big hearty laugh like he had in the café. "Here, I brought you a glass of water to keep you refreshed."

"Thanks." Scarlet took the glass but didn't drink it, rather rubbed her index finger around the edge.

Frankie could tell whatever was bothering her before had reemerged, but she was trying to cover it up.

"So, how's the job coming along?" Charles asked.

She took a heavy breath. "Pretty good, but I need to make sure I cover a few more people as well as photograph some of the animals."

"Is there really a difference?" he jested.

Scarlet rolled her eyes. "Well, some are definitely more in heat than others."

"I guess I'll have to keep closer tabs on you. I knew these businessmen would be hitting on you sooner or later."

Scarlet stiffened. "I can take care of myself, thank you." She turned her back to him.

Charles put his hands in the air but stepped back, giving Scarlet her space. Frankie wondered just how much Scarlet had told him about her past and how much she had already let him in. Whatever the case, Frankie sensed he was patient enough to stick around. She continued to look through the ivy, hoping they would move away so she could escape. How much longer would she be stuck here?

"I should probably go and mingle with the guests." Charles turned to leave, but Scarlet spun around quickly to respond.

"Well, wait. I need to get your photo. They want pictures of all the sponsors." She put the glass of water and clipboard on the table and pulled a folded list and pen from her pocket, then marked off his name.

He grinned widely. "I guess there is something I can help you with."

Scarlet smirked back, quickly changing the filter settings on the camera as she raised the viewfinder to her eye. He stood with his chest high as he looked toward the camera, protruding dimples accentuating his smile, and his sapphire-blue eyes gazing straight through the lens.

Scarlet lowered the camera and sifted through the pictures on the monitor. "Okay, I think I got some good ones."

Charles stepped closer as she toyed with the camera. "Well, what about you?"

"What about me?" Scarlet looked up at him and scowled.

Charles held out his hand and smiled. "Doesn't the photographer need her photo taken too?"

"For what? I don't attend these things. I work them."

"Well, from a 'business standpoint' it would make sense to have your picture in the *Tuleberg Society Magazine* so you're recognizable. You know, for more clients."

Scarlet's eyes lit up. "That's actually a really good idea."

Frankie noticed how the mention of business relaxed Scarlet. Her cousin took the camera sling off and handed it to him. Their fingers grazed and a slight blush came across her face. Charles smiled back as his fingers lingered a few more seconds.

"I think you need to stand here next to the ivy." He motioned in that direction.

Scarlet moved toward the lattice, closer to where Frankie had been hiding, muddling part of her view. Frankie held her breath as the two walked closer to her hiding spot. If she was to be discovered now, she would need more than time or space to reconcile with Scarlet.

Charles positioned his right eye into the viewfinder.

"You need to adjust the settings," said Scarlet, reaching out to grab the camera.

Charles pulled it just out of her reach. "Hey, I'm not the great Scarlet Bedford, but I think I know how to use a camera." Scarlet smirked as he turned the dial and stared down the iris of the lens. "Wait, there is one more thing."

He strode toward Scarlet and lifted his hand to smooth away a piece of hair out of her face, gently brushing against her cheek. "Perfect." He grinned down at her as he returned to his position.

Frankie saw Scarlet blush a deep hue of crimson. She quickly placed her right hand on her hip, a tried-and-true pose Frankie knew she used on clients when she couldn't figure out what to do with their stance. It was evident she wasn't accustomed to being on the opposite side of the camera.

Charles hunched over the camera again to look into the viewfinder and hit the shutter button.

"Does it look okay?" Scarlet asked, fidgeting with her fingers.

Charles repositioned the camera again and snapped a few more, and again returned to look at the monitor.

"Lovely," he softly whispered.

Scarlet gulped as Charles straightened his arched back and walked toward her to return the camera. When she reached for the camera, he didn't let go. Instead, he pulled her close.

"I hope I'm, uh, able to get a few of these pictures? That is … the ones you took?" He lowered his chin and stared into Scarlet's brown eyes.

Scarlet's breath became irregular, but Frankie noticed she tried to keep her professional demeanor. "You'll have to wait, just like everyone else."

"I'll wait as long as it takes," he whispered back.

Scarlet gulped again as her hands folded over his and they both held the camera for a moment, sharing an intimate touch. Charles leaned in nearer to her.

She raised her chin as Charles moved in closer.

"Scarlet?"

"Yes?" Her lips quivered only inches away from his.

"I think your camera partner is headed this way."

Chapter 20

Have patience with all things, but first of all yourselves.—
St. Francis de Sales

Scarlet flushed and pulled away as she saw Olivia walking across the lawn. Charles smiled and let go of the camera.

"I should probably go," he whispered.

She reached back for his hand and turned to him. "Wait, where are you going?"

"You're not the only one who has to take care of business here."

"Maybe I could have a few pictures ready for you early." She looked down at the ground. "Maybe even some of the ones you took. "

Charles's grin grew wide, accenting his dimples. "I'd love that."

"I could have them ready for you later?"

"Like I said, however long it takes," he said reinforcing he would not hurry her. He turned to walk away as Olivia passed by, heading toward Scarlet.

"I've been looking for you. I got some photos of the butterfly and bird estuaries. I hope they look okay."

"Uh, what?" Scarlet asked in a dreamy tone, now fanning herself with her folded paper.

Olivia handed her the camera. "I got all the shots like you asked, but I also went around and took some candid ones of people and even the bigger animals, like the koalas and panda bears."

Scarlet shook herself out of the daze and took the camera Olivia held out and began sifting through the images.

The moment Frankie had been dreading and silently praying for had arrived, but her view was still clouded by the ivy trellis. She spotted another opening just a foot above that would require her to stand on her tip toes. *Why am I doing this?*

Deep down, Frankie knew the answer. Unlike the grief of death, abandonment was worse. She missed Olivia's friendship. Her pregnant belly had grown even in the short couple of weeks and her skin glowed. Hiding behind the lattice was not the way she had hoped to see her. She felt like a chicken for hiding, and yet she was more like a fox, sneaky in her approach. Whatever the case, she remained silent and hidden, convinced that her presence would be more detrimental.

Scarlet sorted through the pictures. "Wow, are you sure you've never had any experience before? These look pretty good."

Olivia flushed and pulled her dark curls out of her face. "I just imagined what the animals would look like if they were in the wild and zoomed in."

"Well, this has definitely cut down some of the coverage I need. You've saved me a ton of time."

"I just want it to go perfectly for you, especially for all that you've done for me."

Scarlet frowned. "I've already told you, stop thanking me."

"But you really don't know how much this has helped me, helped Cammy."

"Well, it's Frankie you should thank."

Olivia looked down at the ground at the mention of Frankie's name.

"Everything okay with you two?"

Frankie's ears perked up. She would finally get some answers, even it came at the cost of snooping.

Olivia's chin dropped as she continued to stare blankly at the ground. "There's just some things that need to be squared away."

Frankie saw the scowl in her eyebrows, a clear indication that Olivia was still upset with her. She held her breath as Olivia continued.

"Well, I don't know if I'm ready to see her just yet. But that's not important right now. What is important is being here, to help."

She isn't ready to see me.

Frankie's suspicions had been confirmed. Olivia still held a grudge for her intrusion. Pain pulled at her heart. There seemed little hope for reconciling, and yet Olivia didn't deny she *would* talk to her again, she just wasn't ready now. Tears trickled down Frankie's cheeks, and she quickly swiped them away.

"Well, whatever is going on, just know Frankie always has your best interests at heart, even if it involves being uncomfortable."

The remark lightened the pull at Frankie's heart, but only some. After all, Scarlet was family.

"At first, I thought it was her intrusion, but it's something more. It's …" Olivia paused.

Had she heard the words correctly? If she wasn't bothered by her intrusion, then what? *Finish the sentence, Olivia!*

Frankie stepped higher onto the lattice hoping to get a better view to see why she'd stopped.

Olivia's glowing skin turned pale. "Uh, Scarlet, I, uh, I need to go. I'm not feeling so good."

"Right now? But this is the time I need you most. They're going to give their speeches soon and then the auction will start."

Olivia held the table looking for a place to move. "I just, I just don't feel very good. I think I need to leave. You know, pregnancy nausea."

Frankie saw in the near distance, something evil had been lurking and now had reemerged. Travis had spotted them and was walking toward her.

Olivia's breathing grew heavy as she paced back and forth. Before she could do anything, Travis had found his way to the auction, spreading his stance to block her from escaping.

"Well, I see that good help is hard to find these days when you need to hire a knocked-up lady as your assistant."

"Do you know this jerk, Olivia?" Scarlet asked, arms crossed.

Travis licked his lips and stared her up and down. "Let's just say I've used her services." He put his hand in his belt loop and turned toward Olivia. "But I have to say, I'm disappointed you're never at the shop when I need you."

"I don't work for you anymore, Travis. It's over," Olivia said, cowering behind Scarlet.

Travis roared with laughter. "That's for me to determine. I'll tell you when it's over."

Frankie saw the disdain in Scarlet's face and knew she was not about to let someone intimidate her. Scarlet squared her shoulders and stepped toward Travis. "I think she's made it very clear that she's not interested. Get lost."

Ignoring her, the hulk of a man stepped around Scarlet and tried to grab Olivia's arm. "Your kind doesn't belong here." As she sidestepped his grasp, he pointed to her belly. "And I already told you to get rid of that thing."

Scarlet looked down at Olivia's belly and then back at Travis. Frankie could see her cousin's rage build as she made the connection. Like a mama bear protecting her cub, Scarlet stepped between the pair.

"Like I said, if you don't leave, I'll call security and be forced to make a scene."

Travis sneered at her again. "You already caused a scene for me and my wife, and I make it an issue when my wife gets involved."

Scarlet puffed up her chest. "Then you should work on fidelity instead of prowling around here like some heated baboon. I'm sure your wife would appreciate that."

"My wife couldn't care less about my fidelity. She just wants to keep up appearances. If you hadn't been so smug, you wouldn't have drawn attention."

Frankie couldn't believe what she was hearing—Travis accusing Scarlet for his own behavior. *What a narcissist!*

He stepped and snarled into Scarlet's face. "Let's say we settle this now, and I won't have to make your life a living hell. We can find a corner of the zoo and express our animal instincts, and I won't ruin your photography career. Deal?"

Scarlet narrowed her eyes at him, hands trembling. "Are you blackmailing me?"

He sneered. "Let's call it a favor for a favor."

Frankie could see the darkness within him. He viewed women as meat, thrown into the lion's den, only to be preyed upon. She decided this was enough. She couldn't hide anymore, even if it meant appearing as if she'd been spying on them. She stepped off the trellis onto the ground ready to come out, but before she could even come around the bend, Scarlet had acted by grabbing the glass of water Charles had left on the table.

"I think it's time for pigs to clean up and get out of the mud pile." She threw the water onto Travis's face.

Frankie froze next to the trellis as a wave of fear rushed through her.

Travis's eyes swelled with rage as he shook off the water. "You tramp!"

Olivia crouched on the ground and covered her face as Scarlet stood over her.

Frankie needed to get Max, to get help. She knew Travis's strength and rage was stronger than hers or even Scarlet's combined. All she could do was pray Travis wouldn't react. She watched as he stepped closer to her cousin, wiping the water from his face with his meaty hand.

He pulled Scarlet's wrist and yanked her close to him. "You're going to be punished for this."

She yanked her arm back from his grasp, but unfortunately couldn't get free herself of his tight grip. "You're a pathetic example of a man," she spat.

The veins in his neck bulged as he kept his hands on Scarlet's wrists. She screeched and Travis lightened up only enough to avoid drawing the attention of bystanders, but kept his hand firmly locked around her arm. Frankie feared he might break her wrist, but Travis seemed more of a calculated man. Such a public display would cause too much attention. Frankie took a deep breath to regain her composure and stepped forward, ready to intervene, just as Max emerged from the crowd and strode up to the conflict.

She watched in amazement as her husband reached for Travis's arm and pulled it behind him in a half nelson.

Travis let go of Scarlet's arm and began to struggle in Max's heavy grasp.

"Is this man bothering you, Scarlet?" Max asked.

Travis struggled to get out of her husband's hold. "Who the hell are you?"

Max lifted out his badge with his free hand and pushed it into Travis's face. "Officer Maxwell Waters of the Tuleberg Police Department."

Scarlet fell to the ground next to Olivia and cradled her bruised wrists as onlookers began to gather, observing Max's handling of Travis.

Scarlet looked up from the ground. "Max, what are you doing here?"

"That's not important right now. What matters is whether this guy is assaulting you."

Travis snickered in a low voice. "I was only trying to teach these girls a lesson, but apparently they just aren't trainable."

The words made Frankie's fingers clench. She tried to reach Scarlet, but now onlookers had gathered around Max and Travis forming a circle and blocking her ability to get through to her cousin and her friend.

Max ignored Travis. "You have the right to press charges, Scarlet, since his hand was on you."

Scarlet looked around at the crowd watching. The moment couldn't have been more public. Her body shook, but she kept her chin high and erect. "Let his wife deal with his bad manners."

Max tugged at Travis's arm, then released him, making him stumble to the ground in front of two ladies with heavily feathered hats. His slicked-back hair flopped into his face as he scrambled to regain his stance.

"Let this be a warning," cautioned Max.

"Did you say your name is Waters?" Travis asked as he looked around at the crowd that had gathered. "Might be a good name to mention the next time I see Captain Gonzaga."

Max straightened up and glared at Travis, unfazed. "You come near these girls again, you'll have me to deal with."

"Is that a threat? I would hate to have to call and complain about the out-of-uniform officer misusing his badge off duty."

Max jerked his body toward Travis in a flinching motion. Travis recoiled, then turned into the crowd. Frankie saw the crazy in his eyes that said this altercation wouldn't be the end.

Almost in perfect timing, the microphones blared from the stage on the other side of the grounds with Mayor Hegland's voice. The onlookers started to disperse toward the stage, allowing Frankie to push through. Scarlet sat with her arms around Olivia, who was shaking inconsolably. Max began to help them slowly to their feet.

Scarlet turned and glared at Max. "What are you doing here?"

"I was looking for Frankie when I spotted you with that jerk. Something about him told me he was trouble."

"Frankie? Frankie's here too? She didn't say anything about coming today." Instantly Scarlet looked up and saw Frankie walk forward. "What are you doing here?"

Max turned to his wife. "Babe, where have you been?"

Frankie paused, then made eye contact with Olivia. "I was trying to get through to you, but the crowds started to form and I—"

"I didn't know you'd even be here today," exclaimed Scarlet.

"Yeah, it was kind of a last-minute thing," said Max.

"Judith gave me her tickets," said Frankie.

Scarlet smiled and breathed a small sigh. "I guess it doesn't really matter. I'm just glad you're here now."

Frankie looked at Scarlet's wrists. "Are you okay? Are you hurt?"

"He definitely has a tight grip, but I'll manage."

Frankie looked down at Olivia still enveloped in Scarlet's embrace. Olivia stared back at her and then looked away without a word.

"Are you sure you don't want to press charges against that creep?" asked Max.

Scarlet shook her head. "I just want to forget about this and wrap up this job." She turned toward Olivia. "I think it's time we were done. I can finish this on my own. I'll let the directors know I have some high shots for the magazine and then we'll roll."

Olivia came out of her stupor and looked at Scarlet, sniffing back some of her tears. "Won't that affect your contract?"

"Money isn't everything if you lose yourself as a result of it."

Frankie smiled, proud of Scarlet's declaration.

Tears ran down Olivia's face as she cradled her belly. "He won't let this go, Scarlet. I know he won't."

Scarlet squeezed her hands. "I won't let him get near you, Olivia. I promise."

Frankie took a deep breath and stepped toward the pair. "And I won't either."

Olivia raised her dark brown eyes toward Frankie and smiled weakly but didn't turn away. "Thanks."

Almost instantly Frankie felt a surge of peace envelope her. One word and look had told her all she needed.

"You're not alone," added Max, "and if he continues to bother you, you need to file a restraining order. You have enough evidence today."

Olivia shook her head and rose from her crouching position. "But ... but he's so powerful. He has ways around things."

"There's enough witnesses here who would probably speak out against him," added Max.

Olivia blew out a breath as if to say she knew it was far from over, but for the moment she agreed it was time to go. She carefully bent down to pick up the photography equipment, but Frankie reached down faster. She knew Olivia's fears would continue, but she felt assured that this time she would be more receptive to help. Their small interaction confirmed reconciliation was in the future, and this time Frankie would not take the forceful approach.

As they started to walk away from the auction, Mallory came running toward Frankie. "What just happened here? I heard someone say there was a giant fight, then I looked over and saw you come out from behind that lattice. I imagine you saw and heard everything from where you were."

Within a moment Frankie's uncertainties had returned. Everyone now knew she'd been hiding.

Scarlet's eyes widened. "Were you really behind there?"

"Uhm, I uh—"

"Yes, she was. She could be a key witness for you against that man who just tried to hurt you. Travis Perino, right? I saw the whole thing too," exclaimed Mallory.

A pit grew in Frankie's stomach. She had been exposed. She didn't know if Mallory did it out of retaliation from blowing her off or if she was so desperate to have "the best" she would go to any length to get Scarlet's attention. Regardless, Frankie now looked like the predator of Scarlet's vulnerability.

Mallory stuck her hand out as if to try and shake but Scarlet was not receptive. "Hi, my name's Mallory.

Mallory Kingsly. It's a pleasure. By the way, I was actually wondering if—"

Scarlet ignored Mallory and glared at Frankie. "Were you listening to me?"

"I was trying to, I mean I was …" Frankie fumbled for words. This was becoming more of a nightmare than she'd expected.

In a split second, Scarlet's face reddened. The embers of the previous twenty-four hours ignited. "You mean to tell me you were there the whole time? When I was with Charles? When I … And with Travis? You heard everything, and you did nothing?"

"It wasn't … it wasn't like that. I was trying to stay out of your way and then I tried to help but I …"

Olivia looked in her direction, and their eyes met, but she stayed silent then returned her subdued eyes toward the ground.

"Get her out of my sight, Max!" Scarlet shrieked, then turned to Mallory. "And whoever you are, thank you, but go away!"

"Ugh! Well!" Mallory stepped back from Scarlet. "I guess my helpfulness just isn't appreciated. To think Scarlet Bedford is what everyone has been raving about. I think I'll go use Summerland Photography for all my future needs."

Scarlet was unfazed as Mallory marched off toward the direction of Mayor Hegland.

Frankie looked at Scarlet, who now had her back turned to her. "Scarlet, I'm sorry."

"Don't tell me you're sorry." She whipped around. "How could you stay there and spy on me and watch us and then pretend to be so helpful? I don't want to hear anything from you, Francesca Waters."

"Come on, Frankie. Let's go." Max pulled lightly on her arm.

Frankie wanted to tell her cousin it had all been just a mistake, an accidental encounter, but Scarlet was done.

Max finally led her away from the chaos, but before they reached the end of the open grounds, she peered over her shoulder. Olivia remained in the same place, standing silently, looking very fragile.

Frankie felt her heart fragment, not from the embarrassment of Mallory or even the yelling from Scarlet, but from the silence of Olivia. Her moment of reconciliation had fled as quickly as it had been given.

Frankie turned to her husband with heavy eyes. "Take me by the studio, Max."

"Why do you want to go there?"

"I need to drop off the flash drive. If I'm truly going to get out of the way, then I need to get it over with."

Chapter 21

God has not forgotten you. At the exact right time, He will make a way, where there seems to be no way.—Unknown

As they drove away, Frankie leaned back on the headrest of the car and glared out the window, consumed in her own thoughts. Trying to heal only caused more heartache and suffering. She would never reconcile with Olivia. And now Scarlet, furious and humiliated, would probably cut her off too. Here was another moment when she wished she could call her mom. Her mom would've known what to say or at least how to comfort her. The whole experience of attending the book talk, putting herself out there, now felt like a mistake. She felt like she was going backward rather than forward. What was God trying to show her in all this humiliation and pain?

As Frankie continued to stare out the window in her own pity, Max placed his hand on her knee, rubbing as he drove.

"I'm not going to ask you what you were doing behind the lattice. I'm not even going to ask about Mallory Kingsly. What I want to know is what are you hiding from?"

"Huh?" Frankie turned from the window to look at her husband. "You just said you weren't going to ask me that."

"I said I wouldn't ask why you were behind the lattice. There's something bigger you're trying to run from, and you've been trying to escape from it for a while."

Frankie didn't know the answer to his question. She thought about the last few years and how much easier it would have been if her mother hadn't died, if she had just continued on, if Scarlet could just be more sentimental, if all this went away.

She sighed. "This last month has pushed me to do a lot of things that I now regret."

"You mean like spending time with your daughters? Meeting some new people who've made your face light up? I bet you regret visiting your mom's gravesite and going to your special coffee shop after two years?"

Frankie crossed her arms and turned toward the door. Listening to Max point out all the positives didn't help her sense of misery. "Well, I guess I'm focused on the harder parts."

"Nobody ever said this was going to be easy, Frankie, but don't think the choices you've recently made are mistakes."

"I just know I feel worse now than I did before I joined that book club."

"Do you?"

"Well, not about everything. But I know Scarlet will never forgive me and Olivia ... well, forget it."

Max slowed the car as they approached an intersection and the yellow traffic light turned into red. "Nobody likes to feel pain, Frankie."

"But I've been working on that the past few weeks. I'm putting in the effort, and see what happens?"

Max pulled his hand from her knee and reached to lower the sun visor. Inside the shade was a clasped medal of St. Michael. He then reached in his shirt and pulled out the medallion he wore around his neck. Another medal of the archangel.

"You know, in my job, I come in contact with all sorts of people, but do you know one thing they all have in common?"

Frankie lifted her head for a moment to answer. "Crime?"

He turned to her and arched an eyebrow. "None of them like to endure pain. In fact most of the people I meet on patrol try everything in their power to escape it, transfer it, control it, or retaliate against it."

"So, you're comparing me to a criminal now?" She crossed her arms and slumped in her seat.

Max took a deep breath as he turned his eyes back to the road. "I'm trying to point out we're all trying to escape some kind of suffering. But the reality is life will always be hard. Sometimes, we get to choose our hard, and sometimes, we don't." Max rubbed his necklace medallion between two fingers. "I keep this St. Michael medal on to remind me my battles aren't over. I'm going to face new challenges every day. Some will be really hard and others I don't always have control over. But what gets me through is you, the girls, and knowing I've got some powerful warriors on the other side of the veil."

Frankie looked down at her lap. "I can't let go of the feeling I ruined their lives. I wanted to help, I wanted to be there for them, but everything I did was wrong."

"Nobody's faulting you for your intentions, Frankie, but I guess you haven't figured out yet who's in charge."

What did he mean by that? Weren't her good intentions enough?

"Don't you think I want to rescue each person I meet, to help every single person who crosses my path?" Max asked. "If I've learned anything in my years of policework it's that God's plan is bigger than mine or any of the people I come in contact with. I can't take away their suffering.

They have to figure out when to stop hiding from whatever it is that haunts them."

Frankie thought about her conversations over the past few weeks. Birdie's regret, Monica's mourning over her daughter's next chapter, Johnna's acknowledgment of her dad, and even Olivia's acceptance of another child. She had supported them with their dilemmas and even used her own agony to helped them gain perspective, but she hadn't made the even bigger connection.

Frankie turned fully toward Max. "I guess that's why you've been so patient these past couple years, isn't it?"

Max smiled at her. "I couldn't prevent your heartache, Frankie. You had to go through it on your own. Even though I miss Barbara, I know God still has a plan for me. And you. Us."

Frankie placed her hand on his lap, and he put his hand over hers. Max was right. As much as she had suffered, she realized God was in charge, and he would see her through this. But she had to stop putting conditions on her suffering. She had to stop putting conditions on how it would all turn out, even if it meant other heartache to come. She realized more than ever the person she needed to serve the most was not her husband, her cousin, her family, or even the ladies from the book talk. She needed to serve God. He would decide from there where she went.

"But one thing's clear," Max said, interrupting her thoughts. "You've become more patient with our girls, you love deeper, and, yes, you burn spaghetti sauce and hide behind lattices from time to time, but you're quicker to forgive."

Frankie chuckled through her tears. When had her husband gotten so smart. She looked out the window again to see they were nearing the studio. She directed Max to pull to the back parking lot.

"Do you want me to go in with you?"

"No. I'll just be a few minutes." She kissed his hand and placed it back in his lap.

Frankie pulled out the keys from her purse to the studio and let herself in the back door. She raced to the alarm pad at the opposite end of the hallway, bypassing the storeroom, to turn off the code. As she punched in the numbers, she noticed the coffee station out of the corner of her eye. Normally Scarlet would take sugar straight from the box, leaving a trail of sugar and coffee spilled across the top. But today the station had been wiped clean. It felt strange to be back in the studio after avoiding the place for so long. She glanced in the mirror hung in the hallway. Her eyes were heavy from the tears and weariness of the afternoon. As she wiped the excessive mascara around her eyes, the reflection strategically gave her an angular view of the loft from the narrow hallway.

She turned around to see frames that had been previously stacked on the floor now hanging neatly on the walls. Business cards and brochures used for advertisement had been neatly separated and laid out in containers on the coffee table instead of falling out of their half-opened boxes from the printers.

Frankie realized Olivia had not only managed to help Scarlet organize but had also created a warmth and hominess to the studio. Frankie walked to the two desks sitting side by side where Scarlet's computer was situated. A picture of Cammy and Olivia graced one desk. Smiling, she touched the edges before picking up a pen and oversized notepad to write Scarlet a note.

> Scarlet,
> I should have dropped this off from the beginning rather than trying to hide from my mistakes. The place looks great. I hope one day you can forgive me.
> Frankie.

She folded the note, taped it to the flash drive, and laid it on the desk, knowing Scarlet would find it there. As she headed back down the hallway, she passed by the storeroom and something else caught her eye. What had once been a disheveled mess of client photos scattered on the floor now housed neatly filed picture boxes. The holiday props had been sorted and rearranged onto separate shelves. Screen shades and backdrops had been rolled up neatly or layered instead of being crumpled up in an oversized box. Even the desk that housed security monitors to view the front loft and her mini safe was no longer blocked by boxes and props. Instead, a chair was placed in front and the desk was usable. Within a short period, Olivia had managed to help Scarlet make sense of her surroundings. Seeing the transformation made Frankie realize their unlikely partnership had been needed.

As she admired the backroom, she was interrupted by the sound of the front door chime, followed by the sound of jiggling keys. Frankie hadn't expected Scarlet to be at the studio today, at least not for a while. The last thing she needed was another encounter. If she could wait to see what Scarlet was doing, she could make a dash for the back door. Until then, she slipped behind the oversized wooden pumpkin from the harvest shoot. Apparently snooping and being caught was a reoccurring theme in her life now.

"Funny, I thought I turned the alarm on when I left," said Scarlet. "There should be some spoons in the drawer below the coffee pot."

"I saw them the other day when I was cleaning," Olivia replied. "Should I get some bowls too?"

"No, we only need spoons. Besides, you may be pregnant but I'm not sharing my cherry-chocolate chunk with anyone. The cartons are in the back of the freezer."

Olivia giggled. "I guess the rocky road is just for me."

Frankie remained super quiet, standing behind the pumpkin. She could see Olivia getting the spoons from the drawer and then returning to the loft. Frankie saw her reappear on the video cameras with Scarlet lounging on the oversized couches typically used for clients.

"Wow, I should have grabbed the spoons. Your feet are swollen like sausages."

"One of the blessings of pregnancy."

"I don't know much about that, but I'm guessing you should put your feet up. Today was probably a hard day for you."

Frankie gasped at Scarlet's comment. Even she knew the mention of what had happened at the event was still a touchy subject.

Olivia replied, "I'm really sorry about earlier. I'm sure you figured out by now who the father is."

Scarlet dug into her carton of ice cream. "Listen, it's not my place to tell you right from wrong, and I don't know your back story, but I know enough to know you don't need a man like that who treats you like garbage."

"It's too bad it's taken me so long to figure that out." Olivia scooped a hunk of ice cream into her mouth.

Scarlet laughed. "Isn't that life? Taking so long to figure things out?"

"But I'm worried this isn't the end of it."

"What do you mean?"

"Travis doesn't just walk away from things. He makes a point to get revenge, to retaliate. He was humiliated today, and when his ego is bruised, he makes a point to attack."

Scarlet's voice lowered as she contemplated Olivia's statement. "I can't deny he's a bit creepy."

"His ego is too big to be broken down. I'm just sorry you had to come to my defense."

"Well, it wasn't just yours. He tried to hit on me earlier today too."

"What?"

Scarlet shuddered as she scooped a bit more of ice cream onto a spoon. "Yeah, he's a regular Casanova."

"That makes sense now why he approached us."

"What do you mean?"

"He would have ignored me in such a public place, but he was trying to get at you, to antagonize you."

"Why would he do that?"

"Because you rejected him. He likes the hunt."

Scarlet shook her head. "What a sadistic man."

"That's a nice way of saying it." Olivia stirred her tub of ice cream. "On a similar note, I never finished telling you why I haven't called Frankie back."

"You don't need to."

Frankie could hear the anger in Scarlet's voice. Dually deserved as here she was again, spying on them.

Olivia stared into her ice cream. "I know you're upset about earlier today, and rightfully so. For a long time, I was mad at Frankie too."

"It wasn't right for her to snoop on me." Scarlet stabbed at her ice cream with her spoon.

"I'm sure that was hard for you."

"She can be the most prying, the most meddling cousin, always wanting to help and 'talk' and get involved. You know sometimes it's really annoying."

"And yet, somehow," Olivia's voice softened, "she's exactly what we all need."

Scarlet turned toward Olivia and arched her brows. "So, what does this have to do with Travis?"

Olivia took a deep breath. "You see, the real reason I haven't called her back is because she was right about everything. I knew I needed to stop seeing Travis, but I believed I needed him or someone like him. When Frankie set up this job interview with you, I was scared to get away from him, that he might do something. And on the other end, I wasn't used to someone actually caring about me like she does. We had some words, and I haven't had the courage to tell her. No one ever took an interest in me who didn't want something in return. Truth be told ... it frightened me."

Emotions swelled inside of Frankie as she listened to Olivia tell Scarlet about the succulents, picking up Cammy without permission, and about their fight.

"It doesn't make it okay for her to pry into my affairs, but I guess my pride and fear got in the way."

"I guess you're right." Scarlet shrugged. "But that's the irritating part—knowing she really has our best interest at heart. Why does she have to be so mothering sometimes?"

Frankie felt the pieces of her heart slowly mend together. Olivia didn't hate her—she wanted Frankie to be proud of her.

"Ya know, I never had a mother figure in my life, and I guess if I could describe one, it'd be Frankie." Olivia rubbed her belly and sighed. "I've owed her an apology."

Tears swelled in Frankie's eyes. She owed her an even bigger one.

"I didn't want to talk to her until I knew he was out of my life, until I could give her something to be worthy of, to show her I didn't need anyone, but I miss her."

Scarlet put down her tub of ice cream. "I think I was more upset at her today because it's hard for me to talk about things that bother me. And I know she saw me ... for me." She wiped her hands on a napkin. "But I know she's always there for me. These last couple of years have been hard on her, her losing her mom. Trust me, I get that part. I actually admire her for trying to deal with her problems. I always try to avoid mine."

"I know exactly what you mean," said Olivia. "I guess you and I have a lot in common, except the single mom part."

They both laughed.

"But Travis is something serious," Olivia said, coming back to her serious tone. "And I'm worried there's no turning back now that you're his target. He works to control me, and he'll try to control you if he can. He knows who Frankie's husband is. He'll try to manipulate him, your business, your family. This isn't the end."

Scarlet sat up and looked at Olivia. "Hey, you can't get rid of me or Frankie. Even if Travis wasn't involved, you're stuck with us. Besides, he isn't the only powerful guy in town. You aren't alone in this."

"That's what I'm afraid of."

Scarlet smiled and placed a hand on Olivia's arm. "I think you underestimate the Waters and the Bedfords. We're very resourceful."

Olivia smiled then grasped her stomach. "The baby must like this ice cream." She got up slowly from the couch and held the small of her back. "I should probably touch up before I grab Cammy. I don't want her to see me tear-stained from earlier."

"You can grab anything from my makeup bag. It's on my desk."

"Thanks." Olivia grabbed a lipstick with a gold container and a compact. "Hey, there's a note on your desk, taped to a flash drive. I don't remember this being here before."

Scarlet got up from the couch to check the note as Olivia proceeded to the bathroom in the hallway. Frankie wanted to run now more than ever, but she couldn't repeat her performance from earlier.

Once Olivia goes into the bathroom, I can sneak out. Scarlet will think the noise is Olivia.

As Olivia walked into the restroom, Frankie crept out behind the pumpkin. She was ready to bolt but the front door chimed again, and her gut told her Scarlet had not opened the door. And then a silence ensued. Frankie couldn't even hear Scarlet moving around. A chill came over her. Something was off.

Suddenly, a new, deeper, almost huskier voice surfaced.

"Just wondering where I can redeem this auction prize I purchased?"

Frankie stiffened as she realized Travis had entered the building.

Chapter 22

Though the mountains fall away and the hills be shaken,
My love shall never fall away from you. —Isaiah 54:10

A cold sensation lingered over Frankie's body as she heard Travis's voice. He must have followed Scarlet back to the studio. Olivia was right, there were no lengths he wouldn't go to get what he wanted. If what she said was true, this wouldn't be the end. Frankie realized the only way to get him out of the picture would be to catch him in the act.

Think! Think, quick! Panic set in her bones as she tried to figure out a plan.

Scarlet's face grew pale as she turned to see the salacious Travis circling around her. Her body stiffened, but her eyes stayed cool as if she had everything under control.

"You know, you don't come very cheap. I had to pay a lot of money for you," he said, biting his lower lip as his eyes danced up and down her body. "Apparently, you're highly sought after in this town. So, I expect to get a full session."

Scarlet replied in a quivering but stern manner. "Our store is closed. You'll need to leave."

Travis tsked. "Is that how you treat a paying customer?"

As Scarlet stood with trembling hands, Frankie turned on the recording feature of the security cameras. She peered at the side monitor which viewed the back lot. Max sat casually in the car, unaware of what was happening only a few yards away. She could easily sprint out the door but, if she darted now, Travis would know. Would he leave Scarlet alone after this or, even worse, retaliate on Olivia?

She decided to text Max. He'd be able to come to the rescue. *Ugh! The phone!* She had left it in the car, not expecting to be more than a few minutes in the studio. Max would eventually wonder why she was taking so long, but what to do in the meantime? Her best bet was to draw Olivia's attention as she left the bathroom. She'd have to warn her without Travis knowing.

Frankie ducked into the hallway under the mirror to wait, careful not to be noticed from the loft.

From the mirror, she saw Scarlet move away from Travis as he continued to circle. Without reacting too hastily, Scarlet leaned against the desk and reached for the phone and her container of mace, which was disguised as a tube of lipstick. Frankie heard a clicking sound and then feet shuffling. Travis had pinned Scarlet on the desk, blocking her from being able to reach the phone. Scarlet turned her face away from Travis toward the hallway. She spotted Frankie and her eyes grew wide.

His left arm blocked her from moving off the desk.

"I don't think you'll have much success calling anyone. Besides, I've bought so many cops in this town, you'll hardly find one to go against me except that Waters guy, and he won't be around much longer." He sneered as he pulled out a gun from his pocket, aiming it loosely in her direction.

Scarlet moved her gaze back to Travis and relaxed her shoulders. She forced her fingers to linger over his chest. "Don't be so quick to judge, Travis. Actually, I was streaming some music. Like you said, you're a paying customer. Shouldn't I set the mood for my clients?" She tilted her head back to expose her neck. "I wouldn't want my reputation in this town ruined, now would I?" Her hand gently crossed the tube of lipstick, vigilant not to attract Travis as she turned on the digital radio. Prudently caressing his neck with her other hand, she leaned toward him. His arms started to relax, and she turned him so that he faced away from the direction of the hallway. The move worked. He wrapped his arms around her waist and kissed her neck, as she continued to unnaturally rub her fingers through his hair. Frankie locked eyes with Scarlet again and pointed to the bathroom with a "hang loose" gesture, signaling she would use Olivia's phone.

Scarlet moved her hand from Travis's hair to gently open the tube of lipstick and then froze. Instead of mace, she'd grabbed just an ordinary tube of lipstick. She tossed the container onto the couch. Travis, engulfed in her bodice, didn't notice. Scarlet signaled to Frankie with her pointer finger and thumb.

She wants me to get the gun in the safe.

Scarlet signaled again with her fingers—seven, one, four, seven— She was cut short as Travis pulled her hands down and jerked her over to the high-top table. Frankie would have to figure out the code to the safe on her own. She just hoped she could do so in time.

The bathroom handle jiggled, and Frankie was quick to hold the door with her foot to cut off the noise. Olivia gasped, surprised to see her crouched on the ground.

"Shhh." Frankie silently motioned to the image in the hallway mirror.

Olivia's eyes bulged as she spotted Travis fondling Scarlet, her blouse now removed as he continued to ravage her. She clutched her stomach. Frankie carefully pulled her down on the ground.

"What's going on? How did you get here?" whispered Olivia.

"No time to explain. I need your phone to text Max."

Olivia's hands trembled as she handed over the phone. Frankie quickly punched in the numbers and then a message.

> **OLIVIA:** Max, this is Frankie, Olivia Scarlet 10-75, 240. Travis.

Frankie was thankful Max had taught her the code for "assault, call for back up."

She handed the phone back to Olivia.

"If he replies, tell him I've got the gun from the safe. Keep yourself hidden till I come back."

Frankie crawled down the hallway, keeping low. When she reached the safe, she punched in the numbers 7-1-4-7 ... Something wasn't working. She had missed the last digit. What could it be? She looked at the security camera pointed at the back lot. Max was still relaxing in the car, unfazed. *He hasn't looked at his phone. Come on Max, look down!* Suddenly she heard a low squeal and Travis's voice.

"I'm sure this means more to you than it does to me."

She glanced at the monitor. Scarlet and Travis had moved out of view. *Where are they?* Suddenly they reappeared with Travis holding a gun to Scarlet's head. Olivia was walking in their direction.

"Did you think I was dumb enough to think you were alone? As if I didn't notice the ice cream containers?" He grasped Scarlet's wrist so she couldn't step away. He turned the gun toward Olivia's stomach and stared back at Scarlet.

"Do you even know who you're dealing with? At least she knows better. She'll do whatever I tell her. I don't think you know your place yet." Scarlet's eyes blistered with tears as Travis waved his gun around like a magic wand.

"Finish undressing!" He repointed the gun back at Scarlet. Her hands shook and tears streamed down her face as she unbuttoned her pants.

Olivia trembled as she stared at the floor, her shoulders hunched and quivering.

Travis quickly began to unbuckle his belt strap, repositioning the gun at Olivia as he grabbed Scarlet and pushed her on top of the oversized table.

"No!" Olivia yelled, walking toward Travis.

"No?" He chuckled. "Who are you to tell me no?"

Olivia stopped shaking and stared into his cold, dead eyes. "You can have me as many times as you want, but not her!"

"No, Olivia!" shrieked Scarlet, struggling from underneath him.

Travis's eyes widened. "Don't worry. You'll get what's coming to you." He struck Scarlet across the face, knocking her off the table. She hit her head on the corner bar seat, then Travis kicked her body aside as he reached for Olivia.

He threw her onto the table. Olivia lay quiet as if she knew this routine a million times over. Frankie hurriedly tried to figure out the code of the safe. 7-1-4-7-5? 7-1-4-7-6? Nothing seemed to work as she anxiously prayed to get it open.

Please God, please help me! She looked back into the backlot monitor. Sure enough, Max had finally seen the message and was out of the car, probably trying to sneak in somewhere. If they could just hold on, help was on the way. She continued to punch away at the safe, trying to find the combination. Finally, she punched in 7-1-4-7-3 and the door popped open. Of course! July 14, 1973, Scarlet's parents' wedding anniversary. As she scrambled to open the safe, she heard another shriek from the room. Scarlet had sprayed Travis in the face with her mace lipstick tube. She must have grabbed the wrong lipstick before.

Travis released his hands as he scrambled to wipe his eyes, blinded by the mace. Scarlet, somewhat unsteady, lifted herself up from the ground and lunged toward him, knocking the gun out of his hand. He flailed, his hands in the air, but managed to touch Scarlet and pulled her arm behind her. She yelped in pain. His strength was no match for her. She screamed a bloodcurdling cry, but she kept moving and jerking her body with whatever strength she had. In a split second, he located her neck and grabbed her throat tightly, silencing her in her struggle.

Suddenly a blast of gunfire filled the room, and Travis stopped midmotion.

Frankie looked to see Olivia holding her hand up in the air—she'd fired Travis's gun into the ceiling.

Travis turned to look at her, still holding Scarlet in his grasp.

Olivia pointed the gun at him. "You let her go, Travis Perino. You don't need her. You came for me."

Travis looked at her with crazy eyes and laughed. He shuffled his feet, but kept Scarlet's limp body in his grasp and proceeded to pull her in front of him as a human shield. "You won't shoot me. You can't do anything on your own. You're nothing."

Tears streamed down Olivia's face as she pointed the gun at him. "No. You're the one who can't do anything on your own."

Meanwhile, Frankie opened the safe and instantly spotted the gun in the top corner, already loaded. Just as she reached for it, a second shot rang out.

Travis dropped Scarlet and rushed at Olivia, trying to grab the gun out of her hands. He twisted her wrist. She thrashed back, trying to keep the weapon from his powerful grip, but the gun fired again. Frankie screamed as Olivia fell to the ground.

Fire burned through Frankie's veins as she grabbed the 38-special out of the safe. She sprinted into the loft and aimed the barrel toward Travis's forehead. She cocked the gun.

He winced and squinted at her, trying to make out her face. She could hear sirens in the distance as loud bangs came from the front of the studio.

"Step away from her. Hands in the air where I can see them!"

Travis hissed at Frankie. "You think I haven't been in this situation before?"

Max broke the door lock and saw Frankie with the gun pointed at Travis. She beamed at her husband and then stared back at Travis.

"I guess you're slow at figuring out who's in charge too."

Chapter 23

It takes a minute to find a special person, an hour to appreciate them, and a day to love them, but it takes an entire lifetime to forget them.—Unknown

"Keep him cuffed. Don't let his wounds make you feel sorry for him," said Detective Kevin McKinley as he signaled the rookie officer transferring Travis into the ambulance. Frankie smiled at Max's former partner, who had made the special trip as backup.

Travis jerked around in his handcuffs, still trying to wipe the mace from his cheeks and yelling to anyone who would listen. "You can't prove a thing! My lawyers will handle this. What's your name?"

Officer McKinley glared at the rookie officer. "You do the job right. We're keeping this clean. Take him to the emergency department and put him in the holding area for criminals. They can treat him there."

The rookie nodded and directed the ambulance staff as Travis was hoisted into the vehicle and cuffed to the metal bars.

"Thanks for coming over here, Kevin," said Max as the two locked hands in a warm shake.

"When I heard the call on the radar and heard your name, I made it my priority to take the call. Besides, nothing makes me happier than knowing that snake will finally pay for his mistakes. He's been trying to manipulate our force for years. But what I want to know is"—he turned toward Frankie—"are you okay? You just witnessed quite an ordeal."

Kevin was right. The events of the day were starting to take their toll. She felt a heaviness in her chest. The fear for Olivia's and Scarlet's lives hung on her now, waiting to see if they would survive this ordeal. Both had been rushed by ambulance to St. Dominic's Hospital, and Frankie had not been able to get close to them with the rush of medics and police officers flooding the scene. As she stood outside the studio, Max draped his arm across her shoulder with her fingers locked in his hand. She knew there was more to come. Certainly, a trial, medical treatments, and the uncertainty of the future.

Frankie gave an exasperated sigh. "I'm surviving for now, but it's Scarlet and Olivia I'm worried about. They were taken away so quickly." So much had changed in the past few hours. She needed now more than ever to be strong. Her eyes grew weary as she clung to Max for support.

"We were lucky to arrive when we did. A injured pregnant woman has its own set of complications, but fortunately I got word the EMT was able to rush Olivia into emergency surgery in record time. As far as your cousin is concerned, she has a lot of bruising and several broken bones, but her vitals are stable."

Frankie burrowed into Max's arms.

"I know this is hard for you, Frankie," said Kevin, "but I'll need to get a statement."

"What else do you need to know?" she asked. "You already know he's a psychopath. I showed you the tape."

"Regardless, we'll need to keep the records as clean as can be. Perino is known for manipulating the court system."

Being the wife of a cop, Frankie knew testifying was key, but she felt emotionally drained from the day's events, her thoughts consumed with Olivia and Scarlet's welfare.

"You'll probably need a few statements from guests at the auxiliary too," said Max as if to take a small load of pressure off her. "I can contact Auggie and Maisie to see if they can help with that."

Kevin nodded. "Good idea, I'll need as many witnesses as possible. By the way, that was good thinking on your part to hit record on the camera, Frankie."

The comment soothed her, especially knowing Olivia and Scarlet had taken the more physical brunt of the ordeal.

"I know this is hard, but let's try to move forward and get this over with." Kevin gestured to a nearby officer holding paper and pen, ready to take her statement.

Frankie looked around. "But someone needs to go to the hospital. I need to know how Olivia and my cousin are doing."

Just then, Charles walked up. "Scarlet's in the hospital?"

Kevin held up a hand to stop him. "Sir, this is a crime scene. Do you have authority to be here?"

"I'm Charles Thompson. I own this building and most of the buildings on this section of the street. What's going on here?"

Detective McKinley looked at him and then at Frankie.

"He's okay, Kevin." Frankie turned to Charles. "It's a lot to take in."

"What's going on with Scarlet?"

Detective McKinley looked him up and down. "Let me know when you're ready, Frankie, but it needs to be soon. I need to head over to the hospital to deal with Perino."

He left to talk to another officer, who was placing caution tape around the front of the studio door.

Charles scratched his head. "Travis Perino? What's he got to do with this?"

Frankie took a deep breath before starting. "Everything. He's the reason Scarlet's in the hospital." She proceeded to give Charles a quick rundown—everything from Olivia's pregnancy, Frankie's unintentional snooping at the auxiliary, and Travis following them back to the studio. As Charles listened, his elbows pulled close to his body and both hands curled into firm fists, jaw clenched with anger.

"That slime ball! I should have known. I should have stayed with her." He kicked the side of the building. "I could have stopped this."

She placed her hand on his arm, trying to calm his rage. "I don't think you could have. He would have found another way."

Charles hunched down, looking pale.

She could see he felt as helpless as she did. "But you can help now by staying at the hospital until I get there."

Charles nodded. "I'll do whatever it takes for her."

She grinned. "I know you will." Knowing someone cared as much as she did gave her a small reprieve of peace.

Max nudged her.

"Oh, I forgot. This is my husband, Max, and this is Charles, Scarlet's, uh, somewhat unofficial boyfriend."

Charles's face reddened as he reached out to shake her husband's hand. Max smiled but tightened up on his grip as if to say he looked at Scarlet as his own daughter.

"That reminds me, I think it's time we check on the girls. They don't know any of this has happened."

Max was right. The girls were unaware of all that had transpired. Frankie thought of Olivia's daughter, Cammy and started to hyperventilate. Max rubbed her back as if already knowing what had crossed her mind.

"I spoke with Detective McKinley," Max said, using Kevin's official title. "They contacted Cammy's gymnastic coach to let her know what's happened. I told him Cammy was a family friend, and he's coordinated with social services that she can stay with us until Olivia is better."

Frankie looked at her husband in disbelief. "Are you sure, Max?"

"Remember when I told you to not get too involved a while back? Well, I think we're past that point. Besides, the girls miss her, and she'll need that extra support right now."

Frankie squeezed Max. She would get through this, and with the grace of God, everything would be okay.

★★★

Three hours later, the police officers finally left the studio with testimony and evidence obtained and the front door to the studio boarded up. Max had gone home to inform the girls and Frankie had proceeded to the hospital. Outside of St. Dominic's emergency department, Frankie moved through the crowd as quickly as she could, shuffling past patients waiting to be seen and news reporters standing around trying to get the story. The news about the break-in had spread quickly across Tuleberg, and news stations now stood outside the hospital trying to get in for interviews. She could hear comments from the press as she walked toward the emergency room's door.

"It's not so hard to believe that Travis would do something like this," said a reporter from Channel 8 to her camera guy.

The camera operator looked up from his camera. "Yeah, he's had a reputation in this town for a while—cheap women and a bad temper."

"There were so many people at the auxiliary, it won't be tough to convince a jury."

"We need to get an interview with Scarlet, but they say she's pretty beat up, can't talk. Her jaw is broken or something."

"The other girl, what's her name?"

"Olivia. Yeah, my insider tip said she's pregnant, and they're delivering the baby. Shot in the stomach. Just hope the kid makes it."

"That's risky, but it makes for a good story."

"I just wish we could get closer," said the young reporter.

Frankie teared up at how coldly the reporters talked about Scarlet and Olivia. She hoped most of it wasn't true.

She spotted Detective McKinley on the other end of the crowd near the emergency department doorway. She scurried through the crowd, past the cameras, to meet him.

Kevin took her inside, away from the crowd, and into a private waiting area.

"Well, let's start with the good news." He gestured toward a chair. "I'm telling you this friend to a friend, as I know the doctors will talk to you later. Your cousin is doing better than originally expected. She broke her arm and a couple or ribs, and they admitted her to a room. She's pretty bruised, but she's going to make it."

Frankie heaved a sigh of relief. "Is her jaw broken?"

"No? Why?"

"Someone ... Nothing. I just wasn't sure of the severity." She sighed, thankful that the reporters were wrong.

"Well, he had a hard grip around her neck, so she probably can't say much right now. Olivia on the other hand ..." Kevin paused.

Frankie clenched the arms of her chair.

"It doesn't look good, I'm afraid."

"Oh, dear Jesus." Frankie's hands went to her mouth as she choked back a sob.

"She's still in surgery. Fortunately, the bullet didn't hit her child, but it penetrated her left side. It's too early to tell, but there's a good chance it's affected some of her organs, and she lost a lot of blood. They're hoping to contain the wound and give her a transfusion, but—"

"So, what does this mean in terms of her baby?"

"They have to control the bleeding first, Frankie. I'm not sure what's going on with the baby just yet, but if they don't control her blood levels, well ..." Kevin scratched his head, trying to find the right words. "It might not be a good outcome for either of them."

Frankie crumbled and buried her head in her hands. Olivia had sacrificed herself for Scarlet. Her heart sank as she absorbed the news.

Kevin grabbed Frankie's hand. "Listen, I don't know much more other than they're trying to stabilize her and the baby. But what I do know is prayers would be a great idea right now."

She placed her elbows on her knees and looked at the ground. "Can I have a few minutes to myself, Kevin?"

Kevin nodded and got up to leave. "I'll just be outside."

Frankie fell to her knees, weeping.

Max was right, there would be more suffering along the way. If this was part of God's plan, she had to accept it. What she wanted to know was how much more. Why did God entrust her with all this pain and sorrow? She offered up her pain, her agony. Looking up at the ceiling she made the sign of the cross.

Lord Jesus, I can only hope some good will come from this. I've been praying to you my whole life. I've tried to make sense of loss these past couple of years. But now I need you the most. My husband says you have a bigger plan, and while I can't see it, I need to know you're there for Scarlet, for Olivia, her child ... and ... and for me. I place my sorrow at the foot of your cross.

Her cheeks shone with tears as she surrendered to him with her arms in the air. *My heart aches, Lord, but now more than ever, I will put my trust in you.*

Frankie knelt a few minutes longer, weeping in prayer. When she lifted her head and the tears dried from her cheeks, she saw Kevin standing outside with his head bent down. She was not alone in prayer. She got up and wiped her eyes with tissues from the box on the waiting room table.

As she opened the door, Kevin stiffened his posture then blessed himself. Frankie gave him a hug.

"You can probably go visit Scarlet. She'll want to know you're here. They haven't disclosed her room on account of the press, but I know where she is. That Charles guy is there too. I'm sure he'd like to see you."

Kevin took her past the emergency department and into the side entrance, to the general hallways of the hospital. The hallways were crowded with patients, which may have been normal, but everything would have been far less tense if the press weren't hovering around making everyone a little jumpy.

Frankie followed Kevin down the hall to a second extension of the building and then took the elevator to the second floor, where Kevin said Scarlet's room would be.

"Thanks for all your help." Frankie gave Kevin a big bear-like hug and got off the elevator. As she turned the corner, she saw Charles standing in a doorway.

His eyes were heavy, but he smiled when he saw Frankie. "Hey, there."

"Hi, Charles. How is she?"

He took a long breath. "She's beat up pretty bad. I can't lie to you. It's not an easy sight."

Frankie felt like heavy rocks were sitting in her gut as she listened.

"She's a fighter, so I know she's going to be okay. But if you hadn't been there, it might have been worse." Charles eyes dropped down as he tugged at the back of his neck. "I just wish I could have stopped this or that I'd arrived sooner."

For the first time, Frankie recognized her unintentional intrusiveness as a blessing.

"I'm guessing she's going to need lots of help in the next few months, so you'll get your chance."

"I want to do more for her," he said in a low voice, "if only she'll let me."

Frankie knew he was in love with Scarlet. She grabbed his hand and looked him squarely in his eyes. "Something tells me she's going to be more receptive to receiving your help."

He gave her a half smile. "I should give you some private time to see her. Besides, I've got to call the firm and start putting together a good legal team." He smiled and walked toward the elevator.

As Frankie entered Scarlet's dimly lit room, the mauve-colored walls gave her a feeling of peace and eased her anxiety. She noticed there were two beds, but only the far left was occupied. A pale curtain divided the beds and hid Scarlet from view. Frankie peered around the curtain and stared at the tip of her cousin's toes snug under the blanket. As her gaze moved farther up, she saw the evil that had been taken out on Scarlet's body. Deep purple bruises spread all over her arms slightly covered by a body cast that ran from her stomach up her torso keeping her locked in a still position. Worse was Scarlet's face. Her left side was a deep shade of purple that spilled over her cheek to the tops of her temple, like an ink jar leaving a stain across her cheek. An ace bandage was secured around her neck. Her eyes emulated swollen pillows clamped to her eye sockets. Her body had been through a tornado of wickedness, tossed around in the eye of the storm, and now she lay like a broken doll, fragmented into pieces.

Frankie sat in the visitor chair by her bed and watched her sleep.

As she waited, she leaned her head back, listening to the silence. No arguing came from her mouth, no strong opinions about work. Frankie thought of the times Scarlet had been so curt and direct. It hadn't occurred to her until this very moment how much she needed and depended on that roughness. Scarlet had been there for her during the darkness, trying to keep Frankie involved, giving her work to do. Maybe not in the soft, tender way she'd needed, but in her own way, with her own devotion and tenacity. She had needed Scarlet's determination to push through, and now she would have to be that person for her. Her eyes became heavy, and Frankie drifted off to sleep.

Chapter 24

Let us love, since that is what our hearts were made for.—St. Therese of Lisieux

Several hours later, Frankie woke to a vibrating sound coming from her purse. The silent buzzing came to an end before she pulled it out. She'd missed about five calls from Max. Early morning light cast a halo around the edge of the blinds as Frankie tiptoed out of the room. Scarlet remained still, most likely from the all the sedatives and drugs helping her numb the pain.

Outside the room, she saw Charles snoozing in the waiting area. She ventured further down the hallway to call Max.

After one ring, Max picked up. "Frankie?"

Frankie thought he sounded frazzled, anxious.

"Hi, babe. I guess I dozed off. I'm sorry I didn't call you sooner."

"It's okay," he said, his voice changing to a more relieved tone. "I figured. How's Scarlet?"

"She's pretty bruised up, but thank God she's going to make it."

"And Olivia?"

"I'm heading to the nurses' station after our call. I haven't heard anything just yet. How are the girls? And Cammy?"

"The girls are okay, just sad to hear about Scarlet and Olivia. Cammy's gymnastic coach brought her over late last night and broke the news. She's pretty emotional. I didn't know what to tell her, but you'd be amazed how the girls stepped in and have been really supportive. They've taught Cammy some of their prayers."

Frankie's eyes welled with tears. She wished she could have been there with them. "Let's hope their prayers come through."

"Frankie?" Max whispered. "I know you feel a huge obligation, but just know you're not alone in this."

In a pragmatic sense, she knew she wasn't alone, but the feeling of regret and the burden of knowing Scarlet and Olivia had been so severely injured sat on her stomach like an anvil. If Olivia didn't make it through, how would she live with the fact that maybe she could have jumped in sooner? Or even worse, how would she tell Cammy her mother hadn't survived? Her pondering came to an end as Max was interrupted by a mumbling background sound.

"Someone here wants to talk to you."

"Hi, Mamma."

Frankie felt a surge of pride at hearing Candace's voice. She cleared her throat before responding. "Hi, sweetie."

"Mamma, we heard the news. I'm really sorry about Auntie Scarlet and Cammy's mom. Cammy's been pretty sad, but I don't want you to worry about anything here. The girls and I are going to be here for her and for anything else you need."

Frankie's heart swelled. "I guess Dad and I were right about you becoming more responsible. How did you grow up so quickly?"

Candace sighed. "I've been watching you guys for a long time, you know."

Frankie beamed with pride. "I guess you have. I sure love you girls."

"I know, and we love you too, Mamma."

Max came back on. "She's one amazing girl, isn't she?"

"Pretty amazing."

"She and Lizzie want to help in any way they can. No matter what the outcome is, I think you're going to need it."

Frankie didn't want to think of outcomes, at least not bad ones. "Let's wait and see how Olivia is first, and then, we can go from there."

Max paused. "Just remember this time is different. Don't shut them out. They need you."

Frankie didn't like hearing his admonishment. She knew he was referring to how she'd handled the last two years with her grief.

"Listen, I've got to go check on Olivia, but tell Candace that when I go to Scarlet's house, maybe she and the girls can help me grab some of her things for the hospital."

"I think they'll be up for the task," Max said in a hopeful tone.

As Frankie ended the call, she considered how much her daughters must have watched her grieve over the last two years, and yet how much they still wanted to help her in their own way. Max was right, she needed to keep the door open for them.

As she walked toward the nurses' station thinking about her family, she turned the corner and barely missed colliding with Lucy, Monica, and Judith.

Monica gaped at her. "Frankie?"

"Frankie! What a surprise!" exclaimed Judith as she covered her in an embrace.

"What are you doing here? But more importantly why are you still in your clothes from the auxiliary?" Lucy asked. Before she could answer, Judith cut her off.

"Oh, I'm so glad you took the tickets. Lucy was just about to fill us in. Did you like the appetizers? Did they serve burrata or mozzarella? Any old vine zins?"

Monica put her hands up in a timeout. "Mom, give her a chance to speak."

Frankie smoothed out her hair, realizing she'd been asleep for several hours.

"Well, I never made it home from the auxiliary. I have some bad news."

Lucy gasped. "The rumors are true?"

"What rumors? Will someone explain to me?" exclaimed Judith.

"The news reporters downstairs said someone was shot inside the auxiliary after hours," said Lucy.

Frankie took a deep breath. "No one was shot at the auxiliary. I wouldn't believe everything you hear from the reporters outside." She looked at Judith with somber eyes. "But yes, someone was shot."

The ladies' jaws gaped as Frankie disclosed the past day's events. Monica clutched at her chest as Frankie revealed Olivia's fight to save Scarlet and the gunshot.

"I can't believe it. Our Olivia?" asked Judith.

"The worst part of it, he's the father of her baby." Frankie could finally tell someone. The news would now be out in the open.

Lucy clenched her fist as if she were going to hit the wall. "So, that's the jerk who wanted her to have an abortion and now all of this?"

"Well, where is she?" Monica asked. "She's going to need our help."

"She was in surgery last time I checked," Frankie said. "I was just on my way to get an update."

Lucy put an arm around Frankie. "We're going with you."

Frankie glanced around at them. "But wait, weren't you heading somewhere?"

"Lucy came by to rescue me from hospital food breakfast. I can only handle so much, but I think this is more important," said Judith.

Frankie squeezed Judith's hand as the four walked to the nurses' station looking for the head charge nurse or someone to answer questions. All the chairs at the desks were empty.

Lucy sighed. "When you need someone, they're never here."

"Where are these nurses?" Judith intentionally raised her voice, hoping to get someone's attention.

Finally, a middle-aged, dark-haired woman with a purple smock, wearing a badge that said RN, came to the center of the nurses' station and glared at Judith. "May I help you?"

"Can you tell us anything about Olivia Mazenod?"

"I can only tell family. Are you next of kin?"

Lucy looked at her sternly and said, "She's my family."

The nurse eyeballed her up and down. "And you're not with the press? We've had a dozen people say they're family."

"My husband is Officer Waters, and Olivia is part of our family," Frankie told her.

The nurse ignored Frankie's remarks but looked down at her computer.

Lucy fumed. "Hey! When I say she's family, she's family. Besides, who do you think is going to pay her medical bills today?"

The nurse looked at her, a little taken back. She left her station and walked to another room about two doors down the hallway. The nurse mumbled something to an unknown voice, then returned to meet the ladies once more.

"She got out of surgery two hours ago. She's been rolled over to ICU. I can't tell you anything else, as it's up to her doctors, but only two can go back and see her."

Lucy looked at Frankie. "You come with me."

Chapter 25

Come to me, all *you* who labor and are burdened, and I will give you rest."—Matthew 11:28

The nurse gave them sticker name badges before allowing them into the Intensive Care Unit. "Go directly to room 233," she said without looking at them.

They walked the long hallway from the nurses' station, navigating through corridors in search of the room. Frankie felt as if she were walking on an escalator in the wrong direction, never going forward but constantly moving. Thoughts flitted through her mind about Scarlet and Olivia. Scarlet would be okay—she would heal, she had family to rely on—but Olivia was different. What would she look like? Frankie still didn't know the extent of her injuries. Had the baby survived? There were so many unknowns. Finally, they arrived at her room. As Lucy reached for the doorknob, she looked at Frankie.

"Honey-girl, you okay?"

Seeing Scarlet had been a walk in the park compared to this situation. What would Frankie say? Would Olivia even be able to talk? They had barely a moment to speak in the loft and now she would see her in all her vulnerability.

She shuddered. "I'm scared."

"All will be well." Lucy grabbed Frankie's hand and squeezed. "Whatever we see or whatever happens, at least we will face it together."

Slowly, they opened the door to a crisp white room with the smell of copper and the mechanical sounds of ventilators. A cold draft lingered over Frankie as she stepped further into the sterile tranquility. She gazed over at an intubated Olivia, wires and tubes encircling her bedside. Unlike Scarlet, who'd been covered in bruises, Olivia showed little physical mishandling, yet the machines, lowering and rising, keeping her vitals in constant check, told a different story. The only component that showed any sign of life and vibrancy was a beautiful wall mount of angels singing and dancing across from her bedside. The artwork was a common picture, even Frankie's mother had kept a copy in her home. Taking the piece as a sign of her mother's presence, she looked up to the ceiling and smiled.

Frankie stepped closer to the bed and rested her hand on Olivia's. Her once golden skin radiating from pregnancy glow, now held nothing more than a pale ashen finish. Her dark curls had been matted and tucked tightly to her head, likely from a hair net during surgery. The swelling in Olivia's chubby ankles had partially subsided but puffed from the hospital socks. But it wasn't the pale skin, the swollen ankles, or the multitude of machines hooked up to Olivia's body that both friends noticed the most. *Where was the baby?* Olivia's stomach was no longer round and expectant, yet her stomach was distended, probably from the many incisions and bandages masked by the hospital gown. Lucy, still holding Frankie's hand, gripped tighter.

As they stood staring at Olivia's almost lifeless form, a woman with graying dark brown hair entered holding a laptop.

"Are you relatives?" she asked.

Lucy responded as she wiped her eyes from fresh tears. "Uh, yes. She's my younger sister."

Frankie frowned.

"My much younger sister. We're half siblings," Lucy added, trying to sound convincing. "Are you her doctor? How is she?"

"My name is Dr. Camillus. I searched for a next of kin and couldn't find any," she said as she looked over Olivia's records. "I'm glad to know she has relations. Olivia has had quite an experience."

"What can we expect?" asked Lucy.

"Why don't we step into the waiting room." Dr. Camillus ushered them back outside and directed them to a small, empty room just adjacent to the patient rooms.

Lucy and Frankie sat next to each other in adjoining seats as the doctor took a seat directly across from them.

"I'm sure you have a million questions, and I hope I can answer them as best as possible. Let me start first with the baby and then onto Ms. Mazenod."

Frankie and Lucy waited as the doctor flipped open her laptop and typed a few keys before going over her notes from her laptop. "Around 6:45 p.m. Ms. Mazenod came in with a gunshot wound to the left side of her ribcage. Fortunately, the entry wound caused no direct harm to the child, entering between the ninth and tenth rib. It avoided the amniotic sac and uterine walls, but, given the circumstances, we had to deliver the baby by C-section. At twenty-seven weeks she's barely two pounds. She's being monitored in the NICU."

"She? Olivia had a little girl?" Lucy sat forward on her chair and smiled.

"Yes," said Dr. Camillus. "She's a little fighter, given what she's been through, but her hospital stay will be long on account of her premature delivery."

"Oh, thank God! Thank God!" Lucy fell back into her chair.

Frankie clutched her chest as fresh tears streamed down her face, grateful the baby had survived.

"Ms. Mazenod, on the other hand, had more complications."

Frankie reached for Lucy's hand again, squeezing it tighter.

"We located the entry and exit wounds and confirmed through X-ray the bullet was no longer in her body. Given her pregnancy, we knew the risks were high. The bullet directly penetrated her spleen, causing trauma to the surrounding tissue, which contributed to large amounts of blood loss. Fortunately, the direction of the bullet only grazed her abdominal aorta, the main artery that supplies blood to vital organs. Two millimeters over and the outcome would have been catastrophic."

"So, does that mean she's going to make it?" asked Lucy.

Dr. Camillus looked up from her laptop and scratched her head. "I wish I could give you a direct answer. We transfused four units of blood due to the blood loss. We had to intubate and sedate her to better manage her breathing and blood pressure. She's critical but stable."

"Oh, dear," Lucy said, clinging tighter to Frankie's arm.

"So, what does this mean?" asked Frankie.

"Only time will tell. She's still holding on."

Frankie slumped back in her seat as fresh tears trickled down her cheeks.

"But what I know," said Dr. Camillus with a smile as she stood, "is that miracles occur every day. You can visit with her. It might be good for her to hear your voices."

Lucy and Frankie stood as Dr. Camillus moved toward the doorway.

"Oh, one more thing." She turned to look at both of them. "Social Services will be in later to speak to you. I understand Olivia has another daughter. Given her current state, do you know who will take care of her and the infant?"

Frankie knew that Max had agreed to taking in Cammy until Olivia was better, but would he be open to accepting her baby, and then Olivia when she got out of the hospital? She was about to tell the doctor she'd discuss the matter with her husband, when Lucy spoke.

"They are staying with me, all of them. I'm taking care of them."

Frankie was stunned. What was Lucy saying? She had already lied to the doctor about being her older sister. Was she lying about this too? The doctor thanked them and walked out of the room. Frankie sat back down in her seat.

"Are you sure you can do this, Lucy?" Frankie said with wide eyes. "Why would you want to?"

Lucy sat back down in the chair. "Because I have to. She's me."

Chapter 26

To forgive takes love, to forget takes humility. —St. Theresa of Calcutta

The statement puzzled Frankie. "I'm confused. What do you mean that Olivia is you?"

Lucy began picking at her nails. "I've been debating when I should tell you, but do you remember the day you saw me at the cemetery?"

Frankie arched her brow. "I wondered if you saw me."

Lucy nodded. "I've always been ashamed to tell anyone this story, but I think it's time." She smoothed out her shirt and proceeded. "When I was sixteen years old, I had a boyfriend named Benny. We were in love, crazy in love." Lucy's eyes were wide with expression. "My parents didn't really approve because he didn't fit their idea of what I should settle for, and they thought he would just cause trouble." She sighed. "My parents wanted me to go to college and marry a boy from within our social circle. Benny came from everything that was the opposite of that. But he loved me for me, and I thought he was different from other guys. I didn't care he was poor, and I loved him something fierce. We had promised we would get married when we graduated from high school, except my parents forbade me to see him. So I snuck around despite their request, and we continued to see each other secretly.

"Everything was fine, and we were able to pull it off until the end of my junior year. I got pregnant."

Frankie listened wide-eyed to Lucy's mysterious life story.

"At that point, the dream after high school wasn't just about me and Benny—it included a child, which changed a lot of things. But I knew no matter what, Benny had to be a part of it. What I didn't realize at the time was that while he loved me, he wasn't ready to be a dad."

Lucy briefly closed her eyes and took in a deep breath.

"Still, we gave it a go. We secretly got married and had this dream of happily ever after, but telling my parents would be the hard part. After about a week, I finally drummed up enough courage, and I confessed to them. Naturally, they were furious and demanded I have an abortion. They said if I didn't, they would cut me off, my mother especially. But I refused and told her we had gotten married. That afternoon I moved out, and Benny and I were on our own. We both dropped out of school. Benny got a job in construction, and we got an apartment. We had nothing, but for me it was the happiest time of my life up to that point. I was going to be a mother and I had my guy."

Lucy sighed again.

"Benny, on the other hand, didn't feel the same way. He saw all I had given up and felt he needed to provide the same kind of life to which I was accustomed. I think it was a lot of pressure for him. The first couple of months were a struggle but magical. He would come home each night to kiss my belly while we sat on the ground and ate peanut butter sandwiches. But as time went on, peanut butter sandwiches and no furniture started to affect him. I offered to get a job, but he refused to let me work. His moods would get violent and angry. Eventually, he started to hit me. At first it was a 'misunderstanding,' or I had provoked him. He'd cry and ask for forgiveness and we'd make up, and of course, I'd forgive him."

Lucy took a deep breath and wiped a hand over her cheek. "But one day, when I was about seven months along, he came home drunk. He was rambling on about how I was high maintenance. One thing led to another, and he started to hit me. He finally hit me so hard I lost consciousness. The next thing I remember was being in the hospital, and that afternoon I lost the baby. I fell into the darkest place I had ever been. He came back apologetic and crying, but I knew there was no going back. He was a changed person."

Lucy's shoulders sank as she continued. "I was worried about going back to my parents and admitting they were right. I had no one. I didn't want to admit that getting married had been a mistake. I took my wedding vows seriously. I guess I could have had my marriage annulled, but I was stubborn and didn't want to admit defeat, so we stayed together. Yet a loneliness hung over us, an absence neither of us discussed. I guess the loss of our baby affected us more deeply than we knew, because we were young and unaware of the effects in the moment."

Frankie stared at Lucy, the shock of what she revealed passing over her in a flurry of disparate thoughts. She would have never thought her lively and worldly friend could have experienced such suffering.

Lucy wiped the tears collecting at the tip of her chin before they trickled onto her lap. "Word had also gotten back to my parents that I had lost the baby, and they wanted me back, but still I refused. But then, about six months after the hospital incident, I found out I was pregnant again. I thought this time, things would be different. I thought another baby would fix that void we'd had from the beginning. I was so happy I would get to be a mother again. But Benny didn't take the news very well. I thought the baby would make us closer, a real family like he had always wanted, but he was distant. He was always angry and took up nightly drinking. He repeatedly told me he wasn't good enough, or he would try to make me think I was the cause of his drinking problem. As the months went on, the fighting continued, but I refused to give up. I think deep down I knew it wasn't right to stay, but I wanted my child more than anything. The abuse continued, and he spent so much on drinking we weren't able to pay bills.

"I finally swallowed my pride and called my parents for help. I knew turning to them, living with them, would not be a good resolution, but I was scared and just couldn't let us go homeless. My parents agreed to help me, but they included terms which we had to abide with if we accepted their help. I didn't know how to tell Benny. He was so proud. We were both stubborn in our own way, but I understood our dire circumstances. When I finally admitted I had asked for help, he became enraged and went into frenzy and, well, suffice it to say, I ended up back in the hospital."

Tears trailed down Frankie's cheeks.

Lucy took a few tissues from one of the side tables and handed one to Frankie and kept one for herself to blow her nose. "I was pretty beat up from the outside, and even more from within, but I finally realized he would possibly kill me if I stayed any longer. I realized love shouldn't be so hard, at least not physically. Who would do something like that to someone they loved?

"So, when I see Olivia, I see myself. For a long time, I thought I had to endure it. When the pain and injuries extended beyond me to those I loved, to my babies, and the anguish I caused my parents, I knew I couldn't stay with Benny." She crumpled her tissue into her fist.

"What happened to him?" asked Frankie.

"The police went looking for him, but he was nowhere to be found. Later, they discovered he went on the run and eventually got caught at the other end of the state. What I didn't know was he was doing other stuff too—taking drugs and falsifying checks. Everything on his criminal record depicted a picture of a man I had never known, didn't know existed, or at least that's what I told myself. For a long time, I felt I was partially to blame. I felt sorry for him.

"My parents took me back, even though I was never the same person. I eventually had to testify in court against him, which was one of the hardest things I've ever had to do." Lucy stopped for a second to compose herself.

Frankie handed her another tissue from the box.

"I had to look at him face to face. He had this hardness, this evil in him that I hadn't realized was so strong, almost like something had taken over his soul." She blew her nose again. "What I realized was he was deprived of love. But it wasn't from me—it was from himself, from his past. The courts convicted him of domestic abuse within intent and put him in jail. I found out years later he died in prison because of his bad temper. His evil got the better of him. He never understood love."

Frankie took her friend's hand. "I'm so sorry you had to go through all of that, Lucy. I'm sorry you lost the baby too."

"He didn't kill the baby, Frankie."

"What? But you don't have any children."

"I didn't lose the baby, Frankie. At least not in the way you think. You'd think that was the hardest decision I would have had to make, leaving him." Lucy closed her eyes and lifted her chin to the sky as if she was revisiting a prayer. "Truth be told, that was just the start." She reopened her eyes and took another deep breath. "The doctors had discovered a ruptured disk in my back. They said I would be paralyzed without surgery. But if they operated that meant I might lose the baby. I didn't care and demanded that I stay pregnant, but my mother thought an abortion would help me forget the past and urged me to have one. I was so devastated and scared." Lucy's shoulders shook as she wiped her nose with a crumpled tissue. "I didn't know what to do, and back then, being an unwed mother was shameful, let alone raising a child as a paraplegic. So, my parents, thinking it was the best option, coerced me to sign the papers."

Silence stretched between them for several minutes as Frankie gazed at her friend with bewildered eyes.

"The surgery repaired my spinal cord, but the true damage I experienced was never cured. You see, I never got over that loss or the loss of my first child. I healed from the operation. It took about a year to regain my strength and walk normally, but I was never complete after that."

When she stopped to wipe her nose again, Frankie handed her another tissue.

"I contemplated if living was really better than dying. After the abortion, my mom and I had a strained relationship, an unspoken sadness and distance. I didn't talk about it, and my parents acted like my child had never existed. That's all we could do to survive. Years later, she admitted to regretting the decision, but in that moment, she didn't know the right course of action. She only knew what she thought was the best way. She never forgave herself either."

Frankie reached out and clasped her friend's hand. "Oh, Lucy."

"But we lived like that for a long time. The grief was so strong that finally my parents decided we should move to Tuleberg to get a fresh start. I still think about my child, my children, that could have been. I think about them all the time." She sighed and looked down at the ground. "She would have been about thirty-five, and he would be thirty-six now."

"You knew the sexes of your children?"

Lucy smiled. "I believe with every fiber in me my first was a boy and my second a girl. For a long time, I had dreams of this little girl who came to me in my sleep as she was holding an older boy's hand. In the dreams, she would turn around and look at me. She would cry and ask me why. She had beautiful blonde curls and Benny's blue eyes. It affected me so greatly I avoided relationships because I didn't think that I deserved children."

"But you eventually married Don. That seemed to help, right?"

"I'm almost at that part. There's still a little bit more." Lucy put up her hand to stop Frankie. "As I grew and the pain of the loss was covered up, I buried myself in my career and building up my business. In a way, I became very successful, but not in the way that I truly wanted to be. Well, about ten years after the incident, I had another dream, but this time the little girl came to me with tender and loving blue eyes. She looked into my soul. The words I heard were, 'Momma, I forgive you.'" Tears rolled down Lucy's cheek. "I needed that forgiveness, that approval, so I could move forward with my life.

"I've carried it with me for a long time. I couldn't forgive myself and I couldn't forgive my parents either. I guess the dream intensified those feelings." Lucy looked up at the ceiling as if she was staring at some unseen figure. "But then one day, while I was sitting in a café waiting for a client, I noticed this mother who lost her temper with her young kids. You could tell her patience was thin and, when one of her children knocked over a glass, she lost her cool and exploded. Her yelling frightened her little boy. Realizing she might have overreacted, she picked up the pieces of glass and looked at her child to apologize. The little boy, without any hesitation, looked lovingly at his mother and said, 'It's okay, Momma. I forgive you.'" Lucy snapped her fingers. "Just like that! I don't know why, but it just hit me. I felt like my daughter was speaking to me. She needed me to hear that in the flesh. 'Momma, I forgive you.'"

Tears poured out of Frankie, and she reached for another tissue.

"I realized that our children are so innocent. They don't carry that burden of shame. We do. They just want to love us and forgive us. We put the hardship on ourselves. I had to forgive myself that day. I had to forgive my mom and move forward.

"I went to see my mother that night and told her what happened. We cried and hugged, and I knew she carried this same grief with her. I think my daughter knew I wasn't the only one who needed to heal."

Frankie cocked her head to one side. "What I don't understand is if you forgave each other, why didn't you decide to have children after that?"

"When I was finally open to dating, I met my Don. He made me realize I could have a fresh start, but this time starting a family was much harder. What I didn't know was the procedure had scarred my womb, and I could never have kids. I cried for a long time. I wanted so badly to be a mother, and I had lost that opportunity in the worst way. After a lot of prayer and soul searching, I realized if I couldn't have more children, I could help in other ways."

Lucy turned to Frankie. "When you saw me that day at the cemetery, I was cleaning the tombstones of the forgotten children. Since I was never able to bury my own, I made it a goal to care for others. When I 'go to Napa' for my annual trip," she said, using her fingers to make quotation marks, "I really go to my hometown and take care of the head stones."

Frankie's mouth opened in shock. "I had no idea you carried all this with you, Lucy."

"Taking care of neglected graves makes me feel like I'm taking care of my babies. You know, I named them. My son was Joseph, and my daughter, Hope."

"Is that why you're so close to Monica?"

Lucy smiled. "I envy her for sticking out the tough decisions she had to make at a young age. I see Olivia too, and I know what my life might have been like. They're both such great moms."

"So, is this why you want to help Olivia? Because you weren't able to take care of your own children?"

"I think it's more than that. I want Olivia to know she's loved. And if she doesn't make it, I want her children to know she loved them too."

Chapter 27

Whoever is without love does not know God, for God is love. —1 John 4:8

With the knowledge that Olivia was still in critical condition, Frankie fretted with uncertainty about the future, but Lucy's testimony and her willingness to take Olivia into her home gave some comfort. Cammy and the baby wouldn't be alone. It was agreed that Frankie would keep Cammy until Olivia's situation changed—for the good or the bad. The rest was up to God, and time would indicate how everything played out. Meanwhile, Cammy's gymnastics coach had assisted with the new address of Olivia's apartment so Max and the girls could take Cammy over to collect some of her belongings so she'd feel more at home. Frankie promised to take Cammy to see her mom once she settled in.

The word spread to the rest of the ladies in the book talk, and Frankie started to receive messages from Birdie and the others offering prayers and support. They had decided it would be best to hold off on the last two sessions until Olivia could join them, although she wondered if there would be anymore sessions if Olivia didn't pull through. Finding herself now consumed with Olivia's affairs, Frankie had been negligent in answering the ladies' messages, but promised she would reply once things started to slow down.

Now, two days since the attack, the strain of poor sleep from hospital chairs and the lack of a hot shower was starting to get to Frankie even though she was determined to be there when Scarlet and Olivia woke. Despite her best efforts to continue camping out at the hospital, Frankie needed a shower and some rest. Lucy promised to stay for any updates until Frankie returned.

Frankie returned home and went straight for the bathtub, letting the spray of hot water soak into her skin and muscles aching from exhaustion. The water felt purifying but wouldn't wash away the last two days. What she really wanted was to curl up in bed, sleep off the past, and forget everything that had happened, but she needed to be the strong one for Scarlet, Olivia, Cammy, and her family.

After the shower, she was changing into some comfortable leggings and an oversized jersey shirt when the phone rang. It was Lucy, letting her know Scarlet was finally awake. She clenched her fist in anger. She should have been there when Scarlet woke. Instantly, Frankie's fatigue was replaced with an adrenaline rush, and she was back in the car faster than a dog chasing a rabbit around a race track.

She hastily drove to the hospital after making a quick pit stop at the ice cream store. Frankie wondered what Scarlet's demeanor would be like. She had been the man on the frontline, taking the physical toll, the impact of Travis's attack, but she knew her cousin's overly tough exterior could only mask her internal wounds temporarily. Ice cream wouldn't heal her, but Frankie figured it would be a comforting gesture.

Exiting the elevator on Scarlet's floor, Frankie took in two deep breaths to calm her anxiety. As she drew closer to her cousin's room, she heard spluttering sounds, followed by hefty groans.

Frankie could hear the nurse pleading with Scarlet. "You need to put something in your stomach."

"Blah," said a stubborn Scarlet, followed by a heavy grunt.

"Don't move so quickly. Any sudden moves and you're going to feel more pain. You need to eat something before I can administer your next meds."

Frankie concluded her cousin was now feeling the effects of the heavy sedation wearing off.

"Knock, knock," said Frankie before she entered the room.

"Spttthhhh!" Scarlet strained to dodge the raspberry Jell-O the nurse tried to put in her mouth.

"Aghhhh." Scarlet tried to lift her head to see Frankie out of her partially open left eye.

"Don't strain," Frankie said. "I'm not going anywhere."

Scarlet visibly relaxed when she heard Frankie's voice.

"I don't think I need to ask how you're feeling from that greeting," joked Frankie as she put her bag on the chair next to the nurse. "Here, let me take over."

The nurse nodded and eagerly left the room. Frankie set the Jell-O aside and pulled out a container of cherry-chocolate swirl ice cream.

"It's not your cherry-chocolate chunk. I didn't know if you could chew heavy pieces or not, but I figured this was just as close." She opened the container and scooped a small bite into Scarlet's mouth.

Her cousin gave a soft sigh of relief as the ice cream cooled her lips.

"Doctor says you'll be here for a few more days, but then you'll be home soon, where you can recover with some help."

"Well, I guessth you goth your withs," Scarlet said, trying to speak with the blood-filled pocket on her upper lip. "I'll be on a long-therm vacath-un."

"This is hardly what I meant by taking some time off." Frankie gently scooped another small bite into her mouth. "But if you're worried about the business, I'm happy to step in again for a while to help out. I mean, that's only if you want me to. I don't want to be pushy."

Scarlet half smiled and looked at her with her one good eye. "I'd likth thath."

"Besides, not many people can put up with your demanding butt."

Scarlet took a heavy breath. "How-ths Oliv-ia?"

Frankie wasn't sure how much to tell her. There was so much uncertainty about Olivia's condition and whether she would remain stable. But she knew no matter what she said, Scarlet would feel guilt over the gunshot. Even Frankie felt helpless for the sacrifice Olivia had made for them.

She stirred the ice cream around a few times before answering, then finally mustered up enough courage to fake a confident reply. "She lost a lot of blood, but she made it out of surgery. She has a long road to recovery, so she still needs our prayers."

Tears flowed from Scarlet's eyes as Frankie patted her leg, trying to reassure her. "The good news is she had a healthy baby girl."

Scarlet remained silent. Tears dripped down her bruised cheeks as she gestured to Frankie to grab a tissue. As she gently patted around her puffy eyes, Scarlet tried to turn her head to look at her. "Franthie ... tht-e sth-aved me."

She wiped her other eye gently. "I know."

Frankie replayed the tragedy in her head wondering if any of it could have been avoided.

"Scarlet, I wish … I wish I could rewind what happened to you, to her."

Scarlet teared up once more. "If you hath-nth been there … if you hath-nth stoppth by."

Frankie shrugged. "I want you to know the day at the auxiliary and the studio, neither one of those moments were meant to pry into your life or snoop on you. But I guess if I had to replay it all over again, there was a reason for me to be there."

Scarlet tried to speak, but her breathing became unbalanced. "Aghhh!"

Frankie put a hand on her thigh. "You don't need to say anything just rest."

Scarlet wiggled her fingers as if to tell Frankie she planned to continue. Finally, a few minutes passed, and Scarlet took another slow breath.

"I can'th run," she finally said.

The conversation had taken a new direction that baffled Frankie. "Your legs aren't broken, but running is the last thing you should be thinking about. You just need to take it easy."

"No!" She took another heavy breath. "I mean I can'th run anymore."

"Oh." Frankie gulped as she realized what Scarlet was referring to. She could no longer run from her problems.

"It was-th awful, Frankie." She swallowed in between breaths. "I almost-th … I was-th …" She couldn't finish the sentence. Tears ran down the sides of her swollen face and then turned into heavy sobs that shook her body, which in turn made her moan in pain.

"I know, honey, I know." Frankie tried to comfort her by stroking her hair.

"I don'th like this, Frankie."

"Well, you've just been beat up pretty bad."

"No. I don'th like this feeling … in-sthide."

Frankie knew what she meant. The marks, the bruises, the brokenness, were only half of the scars. Even the bandages on her body couldn't heal her internal sorrow.

Frankie stared at her cousin benevolently. "Scarlet, I know this pain. It wells up inside until you can't breathe."

Puddles of tears poured out her cousin's eyes. "I'd rather get hith a thousanth thimes again."

"But it's a pain you can't escape. It can't be fixed by bandages or body casts. You can run for a while but, if you don't face it, your wounds will never heal."

Frankie stroked her cousin's leg while she wept. Her tears roared like a vortex in the ocean ready to swallow her whole. When Scarlet finally looked as if she could cry no more, Frankie took a tissue and tried to gently pat her face, avoiding the areas of heavy bruising.

Scarlet peered at Frankie through her bulbous eyes. "I guessth … I needtheth that."

She smiled at her. "You'll probably need a few more of those sessions, but I'm guessing that one was long overdue."

"You're really irr-thathing thoo be aroundth, you know."

"I know." Frankie patted her hand. "You're welcome."

They sat in silence for a while, a serenity that was needed for them both.

When they finally did speak, Scarlet took a heavy breath. "Tharles was here earlier."

"I know. The nurse told me he's been here a lot. She says he hasn't really left. You're lucky to have him."

"I know," she whispered, "but I'm sctharth."

Frankie could see the fear in her. Scarlet wasn't used to being vulnerable.

"I don't think you'll ever have to be scared with him."

Scarlet's eyes glided up to Frankie, and then she closed them again. "That's what sctharths me."

"Something tells me he's not going anywhere, so you don't have to admit that to him just yet. I think you've covered enough ground for one day."

Scarlet smiled and closed her eyes.

"On a less serious note, I'm going to swing by your house and pick up some items for you, so you feel a little more comfortable. Any requests?"

She shifted her head slightly, which Frankie took to mean "no."

As Frankie stood up from her chair and moved the blanket from the bottom of the bed to cover her, Scarlet wiggled her fingers again. "Franthie," she muttered.

"Yes, Scarlet?

"Thankths."

Frankie gently kissed her forehead. "Anything for you."

Chapter 28

The bond between friends cannot be broken by chance;
no interval of time or space can destroy it. Not even death
itself can part true friends.—St. John Cassian

"Here you are—one vanilla latte and a wet cappuccino,"
said the perky barista as she handed Frankie her order.

"Great, how much do I owe you?" She took the coffees
and placed them in the car's drink holders.

"It's on the house," said the barista as she winked at
Frankie in full grin.

"Uh, thanks. Just put this toward the next driver."
Frankie averted her eyes away from the barista as she
handed her some extra cash for the next car before
leaving the drive-thru. In the past two weeks, this kind
of thing had happened to her quite frequently as the
news of the "Tuleberg Tragedy"—the nickname given
by media stations—had made national headlines. Olivia
and Scarlet's faces had been spread on every newspaper
and magazine as the prestige of the Perino name
enticed media circles hoping to drag out the story and
sensationalize around-the-clock reels of Olivia, Scarlet,
the Perino family history, and Travis's infidelity. Frankie
had somehow managed to keep her family and Cammy
out of the headlines, but everyone locally knew who they

were, which made it hard, especially keeping Cammy from being approached and prodded.

Frankie took a deep breath as she made a left turn and headed toward St. Dominic's Hospital. The past couple weeks had been nonstop hospital visits and new adjustments to their living situation. Taking a sip of her cappuccino felt like the most normalizing moment of her day these past couple weeks. She stopped at the stoplight, gleeful to sip some froth from her coffee. When her phone rang, she glanced down to see the name Bernadette Dalesandro pop up—Birdie. Frankie had been overdue at getting back to her and the other girls from the group. She just hadn't had time.

She accepted the call and hollered jubilantly into the air as the phone connected to her car speakers. "Birdie!"

"Hi, sweet girl. It's so good to hear your voice."

"Ugh, you have no idea how good it is to hear yours. It's just been crazy. I'm sorry I haven't returned your calls. I promise I haven't tried to avoid you."

"I completely understand. You've been dealing with a lot. It just feels empty since we've postponed the book talk."

"I've missed our Friday nights together, but it doesn't seem right without Olivia."

"I know what you mean," said Birdie. "Even when she missed the last one, the group didn't seem complete."

"I remember," murmured Frankie as she thought back to that tense period of mixed emotions. Even though she and Olivia had been estranged during that time, the group still felt inadequate. Who would have known that would be their last time together? She shook her head and swallowed her thoughts, trying to keep her sorrow out of the conversation. "Anyway, you're probably calling for a reason?"

"Well, I didn't want to bother you much since the—all that was going on—but I figured now was a good time to check in and get some updates. Have they found Travis Perino guilty? The news is only giving us what I figure to be mostly sensationalism."

Birdie was right. The media was mostly playing reels of the family and their wealth and Travis's long history of bad temperedness. They had also tried to paint Scarlet and Olivia as opportunists trying to get at his money. The only real truth was Travis Perino had been treated for his injuries within a day of the calamity then placed in a low detention prison until bail had been made. The bail had been set for an incredibly high price his wife initially refused to pay—even though she could certainly afford it—but after a week, she finally relented. However, her delay created fantastic headlines that the media dramatized.

"Well, what they're reporting is only mostly accurate for Travis's part. He's home now. They're making him wear an ankle bracelet to track his location. Given his temper, his whereabouts are under full scrutiny. Scarlet was initially worried he might come back to retaliate, but since he's on house arrest and all the news reporters are camped around his house, she's been assured there's no way he can bother her."

"That must be hell on earth," Birdie said.

"I don't know much more, other than there'll eventually be a trial, but the evidence is so stacked against him, there's no way around some prison time."

"Everyone knows he's going to try to get off lighter than he deserves by pushing his family's name and connections."

"Well, Charles, Scarlet's boyfriend," Frankie decided to call him the boyfriend although she didn't know if they had officially declared anything, "has just as strong connections in Tuleberg, and he's promised Scarlet and me that he'll do everything in his power to see Perino doesn't go without some kind of consequence."

"Good. I'd hate to see what would happen if that man got off scot-free, given what he did to poor Olivia and your cousin. Speaking of, how is Scarlet?"

"She's doing better. Her face has started to return to its natural color, and she's having an easier time talking, although she's still in a half-body cast. They discharged her a week ago. I'd love to tell you she's back to her old self, but it's definitely been a hard adjustment for her."

"I can't even imagine. Are you taking care of her too?" Birdie asked.

"Oh, heavens no." She laughed. "No, she won't let me, but I'm checking in with her. Charles convinced her, more like demanded, he hire a nurse, although she was adamant she could take care of herself. He's been her caregiver and bodyguard ever since. But I think she kind of likes having someone who can dote on her. She complains about how he makes her lunch and insists on covering her feet with extra blankets, but when he leaves to take care of his own affairs, she's upset that he's not there, so that tells me she's enjoying his company."

"Aww, that's sweet. I'm glad she has some support. It's nice to have people to look out for us. Speaking of ..." Birdie cleared her throat. "I was wondering if I could stop by the hospital today to bring Olivia some gifts. Is she allowed to have any visitors? I know with the hype of the news and all ... well, I wasn't sure if it was possible."

Olivia really hadn't had many visitors. Max had brought the girls, of course, so Cammy could see her mom regularly, but other than that, only Lucy and Frankie had stopped in to see her.

"The doctors have everyone check in before they visit, but they did say it might be good for her to hear some familiar voices, so yes, come by."

"You'll be there today, too, won't you?"

"It's like a second home to me."

"Oh, wonderful," Birdie replied. "I've got some calls, err, I mean I have some things to do before I get there. I've got to go, but I'll see you later this morning."

The call ended then, and Frankie was surprised how quickly her friend had cut the conversation.

As she pulled into the hospital parking lot, she reflected on her own statement to Birdie. *It's like a second home.* She wondered why she'd chosen to use those specific words in referring to the hospital, then she realized the last two weeks had somewhat mimicked her time with her mom. Just like then, she was traveling a lot back and forth and handling calls from the hospital, all the while juggling household tasks.

But this time, managing her family and the hospital duties had extra layers. She had more check-ins with the baby in the NICU, as well as Olivia, all while keeping tabs on Scarlet. The girls, including Cammy, would start school soon and would need back-to-school supplies and fresh clothes. There was more on her plate this time, but her experience with her mother had trained her to handle the heavy load.

She'd been so wrapped up with Scarlet and Olivia she hadn't thought much about the ladies from the book talk. Seeing Birdie would be a nice break—she missed them. Had Monica handled the big send off to college with Regina? Was Judith practicing healthier eating habits now that Sal's health had improved? She missed hearing Maisie's dog stories and Birdie's adventures with her grandchildren. And she wondered about how Johnna was spending the final days with her dying father. She wanted to reconnect, to laugh, to cry, to share in their worlds, but it didn't matter. Frankie felt sure the group would dissolve soon, and that would be the end of their friendships.

Frankie pulled into the hospital parking garage and parked in the west lot. Grabbing her coffee and the one she had picked up for Lucy, she walked to the nearby elevator. The hospital had finally confirmed Lucy wasn't actually Olivia's relative. She had no next of kin other than Cammy, but because the case had been so public, there had been a lot of local support. Charles had helped Lucy and Frankie navigate some legal paths, so Lucy was able to take over Olivia's affairs, although there really wasn't much to take care of.

As Frankie stepped onto the elevator, she wondered what the doctor would say today. Olivia's body was starting to heal, but she was still non-responsive. Her state had puzzled the hospital staff completely. Lucy had been in constant contact with Frankie and the doctors to see what could be done. Today, they would hopefully find some answers.

The elevator opened to the second floor where Frankie was greeted by a mural of baby elephants, kangaroos, and lions all sleeping soundly on the main hallway wall. The NICU unit had lots of paintings dispersed throughout the wing to give the place a serene and homey feel. She walked past a room of incubation machines where baby ducklings danced along the walls, guiding her toward her destination. Frankie could see tiny infants, as small as tea cups, trying to get strong, fighting for their lives as nervous new mothers walked in and out of the area, keeping their constant attention. As Frankie looked for Baby Mazenod, she saw the nurse had taken her out of the incubator to feed her.

Frankie grinned and hurried over. "How's our girl doing?" The baby had started gaining some pink tone to her skin, and her little two-pound form had grown into a vibrant three-and-a-half pounds. Still one of the tiniest of infants, she suckled on the bottle, unaware of her circumstance and the harrowing ordeal she had barely survived.

The nurse smiled up at her. "She's getting stronger every day. She has quite the appetite."

The baby's little eyes closed, and contentment took over as she finished the last drop.

"And how's momma doing?" the nurse asked.

"Getting stronger every day too. Just waiting for her to wake up." It was a sad reality that Olivia hadn't yet met her daughter. In some ways, the baby and Olivia were similar. They both needed constant around-the-clock support.

"Well, I'm going to bring the baby by later. She's strong enough that as long as we transport the incubator, she should be able to have her first visit with Mom."

Frankie's heart did a backflip. It was almost as if the nurse had known what she was thinking. Even if she wasn't fully awake, Olivia would finally be able to be with her daughter. "I think that's a fantastic idea."

She headed back down the hallway toward the elevator to the third floor, sighing with relief to know the baby was doing so well, even though there were still many unknowns lurking in their future. If Olivia didn't make it, these young girls would lose their mother. Frankie understood this in her own way. Even as a grown woman, she had felt like an orphan when her mom died. The feeling of being alone and the loss of so many moments she would never have again just couldn't be shaken.

Everything depended on Olivia waking up. Without Olivia, there seemed only a bleak future, and that's what

Frankie hated the most. Now she had to consider Cammy, and this precious little infant without a name would never know the beauty and wonderfulness of her mother.

She returned down memory lane, thinking about the cause of her own mother's death. Terminal cancer had taught her preparation, a sense of knowing the inevitable, as hard as it may have been. But with Olivia the situation was different. There could be a chance, yet how much of a chance she didn't see. She felt like she was holding her breath underwater every day as she waited for air. How long would she have to hold her breath before she could exhale? She hoped and prayed Dr. Camillus could give her some answers soon. As she exited the elevator, putting aside some thoughts of what-ifs, she spotted Lucy standing at the nurses' station flirting with one of the senior doctors. Lucy threw back her head in laughter as the tall, sixty-something-year-old man with salt-and-pepper hair spoke, revealing a full set of dentures. Her body language read shameless as she overtly pretended to laugh at each word. As Frankie drew closer, she looked at Lucy, who turned a bright reddish hue and reverted back to a more serious tone.

"Here's your coffee."

"Oh, thank you!" Lucy sighed as she took the cup from her hands. "Frankie, this is Dr. Evers. He's a cardiothoracic surgeon." She batted her eyelashes at him. "Did you know he's been a resident doctor here since 1996? I just don't know how we've never crossed paths. I practically know everyone in this town." She beamed at him as his large grill of teeth grinned back at her. "I was telling him about my wines, and he just happens to be an unofficial sommelier, can you believe that?"

Frankie smiled. "Nice to meet you, Dr. Evers." She reached out to shake his hand.

"Gilbert, but just call me Gil." He moved his mouth around as he talked, as if he had difficulty keeping his dentures in.

"Oh, Gil, that's just darling." Lucy lightly patted his shoulder.

Frankie cleared her throat, and Lucy snatched back her hand.

"Dr. Gil, I mean Dr. Evers, I mean, we have to go check on our friend, but maybe I can invite you over to sample some of my vintage wines sometime? Maybe you can give me an assessment of the value?"

"I'd love to. I'll leave my info here at the nurses' station for you, Lucile. Frankie, it was a pleasure." He gestured to her and left Lucy with a smile of sparkling dentures.

Frankie smirked. "Well, you're quite the wine connoisseur, aren't you, Lucile?"

Lucy hooked an arm around Frankie's elbow and guided her toward Olivia's room. "Oh, he just knows a lot about wines, that's all, and that happens to be one of my passions." She twisted her hair like a nervous high school girl. "You know, you got here just in time. The doctor is on her way up to talk to us about Olivia."

"I hope the news is good," Frankie said.

"I hope so too. It just seems so long with nothing changing."

"I know, but we just have to have faith all will work out."

They walked into Olivia's room and Frankie put her coffee and purse on the side table next to the hospital bed.

"You're looking better, girlie," Frankie said to Olivia. She smoothed out the hair near her face. "I just saw 'the little' this morning. She's growing stronger and stronger, waiting for you to hold her. You should see her, Olivia. She's beautiful. She's got your nose. She's such a little blessed beauty."

Olivia lay in her sleep-like state, unresponsive, as Frankie talked and brought her up to speed on the current events. She had gotten into this pattern each time she saw her, talking to her as if she was able to converse back. Olivia's appearance had changed in the course of the last two weeks. Her stitches had been removed from the operations, and her stomach lay flat as if she had never been pregnant.

Frankie adjusted her blankets then strode across the room to open up the curtains and let some light into the room. Olivia's complexion had improved, and Frankie thought she looked like a sleeping beauty waiting for her prince charming to come revive her. The only thing that really made her look sick were the ventilators still attached.

"We've got to get you looking good," she said as she took a brush out to comb Olivia's hair. "I've got a surprise for you. Birdie's coming to visit this morning. We don't want her to see you without you looking your best. Too bad none of the other girls will be here."

Lucy looked at her with gloomy eyes. "It would have been a great treat to see them all. You know, come to think of it, this would have been the final day, if we had actually finished according to our book schedule."

"You're right. It would have been," Frankie said, realizing how quickly time had passed.

Just then, the doctor walked in.

"Hello, ladies," Dr. Camillus greeted them. She had her laptop in hand as she did every time she saw patients. She was very composed but had a gentle face. Frankie wondered if she was married or had a family. The life of a doctor meant long hours and sacrifices. She wondered if Dr. Camillus was the kind who was married to her job or created a balance. One thing was for sure—she loved her patients and took excellent care of them.

Dr. Camillus went over to Olivia and read her notes from the nurse.

"Well, ladies, a lot has improved. The good news is Olivia's healing well from the surgery. Sutures came out yesterday and, so far, no infection or complications, although without her spleen she's likely to become anemic."

Frankie nodded as she took notes.

"And the bad news?" Lucy asked, her eyebrows knit with worry.

"Unfortunately, there are some things that still concern me." Dr. Camillus scratched her head and looked at the two women. "Comatose patients can stay in a sleep state for long periods of time. It's a sleep-like state for the brain, but it still means it's not fully functioning. The problem is the longer the brain stays in that state, the harder it is for the patient to gain full recovery and return to where they were. The longer she sleeps, the chances of her having a healthy recovery diminish."

Lucy asked, "So, you're saying the longer she stays asleep, the less of a chance she has?"

"I wouldn't take it that far yet. Her body has healed incredibly well but given the duration of her sleep-like state, I can only hope she comes out of it soon, or she may have some long-lasting disabilities. We've been monitoring her hands and feet to see whether they curl up. That's usually a sign."

"So, what does this mean?"

"I think you need to have a plan in place, *if* or *when* she wakes up, of how you're going to care for her."

"Well, we've already talked about that. Lucy is going to take care of her," said Frankie.

"I think you need to have a plan in place for long-term care," Dr. Camillus advised. "She may not be the person you knew before this. No one really knows what may happen." Dr. Camillus let her statement hang in the air a moment before she spoke again. "It's something you should both really think about before you make any big decisions."

Chapter 29

No one ever told me that grief felt so like fear. —C.S. Lewis

As the door closed behind her, Lucy and Frankie looked at each other with wide eyes.

"Well, I certainly didn't expect that," Frankie said.

Lucy gripped the chair. "Olivia disabled? So, she 'might' not be able to speak or even walk? I refuse to believe it."

Frankie gripped the rails of the bed. "I don't know what to believe."

Lucy stared at Olivia's unmoving body. "And there's nothing we can do about it?"

"Nothing."

"That's nonsense. I refuse to accept this news."

Frankie turned to Olivia and laid a hand on her still form. She looked like a living doll, beautiful but with no movement. The question of whether her condition "might" or "might not" improve was like a game show contestant choosing between two boxes—one containing the grand prize and the other nothing.

Lucy came up behind Frankie and put her arm around her shoulder. "I think we need some fresh air."

Frankie clung to the bedside until Lucy gave her another nudge.

"Come on, honey, our worrying isn't going to wake her up. There's nothing we can do in this moment."

Reluctantly, Frankie rose and walked with Lucy to the door.

"I should probably call Max and let him know the news."

"Good idea. I, on the other hand, need something less heavy, so I'm going to go find that cute doctor to take my mind off all of this craziness."

They hugged each other and departed. Lucy went down the hallway to the nurses' station while Frankie went outside to call Max. She walked toward a small garden—just a space with a couple of park benches and some pretty flowers—the hospital had created for visitors. Frankie looked at the flower beds filled with asters, mums, and verbenas and thought about the flowers in comparison to Olivia. Even in their shallow flowerbeds, they were durable enough to make it through the late summer. The season would soon change, and so would the flowers. Everything would move forward. Would Olivia change too? Frankie wrinkled her nose as she took out her phone to call Max.

The phone only rang once before he picked it up.

"Hi, babe."

"Hey." Her voice cracked.

"What's wrong, Frankie?"

"I just needed to call and hear your voice."

"Let me move out of the little one's earshot." Frankie heard movement on his end. "Is everything okay?"

"I'm not sure." She sobbed as she proceeded to relay all the information Dr. Camillus had shared about Olivia.

"What does this mean?"

"I don't know. It's so much to think about."

"Listen, we don't have to decide anything right now. I just want you to know that."

"I know ..." she whispered. Frankie didn't want to decide anything. She just wanted Olivia to get better.

"Hold on for a second," he said, as the phone went silent.

"Max?"

A few moments later, a little squeaky voice came on. "Hi, Momma!" said Rena. Frankie knew talking with her daughter was Max's way of cheering her up, and he was right. Frankie instantly felt cheered.

"Rena! Hi, sweetie." Frankie immediately pulled in the sniffles from her voice.

"Cammy is giving me a makeover. She says I need some fashion tips."

"I bet you look beautiful."

"Cammy is the best. Hey, when are you coming home? Can we come see Olivia today?"

The strain of the last two weeks had taken Frankie away more than she cared to admit. "Not today, maybe tomorrow. But I'll be home a little later, I promise."

"Okay, because I promised Cammy you'd want a makeover too, and she said I could help."

Frankie smiled through her sadness at the thought of being made up by a six- and ten-year-old. "That sounds great, sweetie. Listen, is Cammy close by? Can I talk to her?" She knew she had to tell Cammy something about her mother. There was no way she could tell her the news, at least not over the phone, but she felt a calling to reassure her everything would be okay even if it wasn't.

"Sure, Momma. I'll go get her. I just love having her here. I hope she can stay forever."

The reality of the statement made her think about the possibility that it might actually happen.

After a few moments of silence, Cammy's cheerful voice answered the phone. "Hi, Mrs. Waters."

"Honey, I've already told you just call me Frankie."

"Okay, Mrs. Waters," she said anyway. "You know the girls taught me some prayers, and we've been praying them for Momma and my baby sister." Her voice was full of spirit.

Frankie held in her tears, careful to not let them carry through the phone. "Well, that's good, sweetie. Your mom needs all the prayers she can get, so she can get healthy and strong."

"I like praying, especially for Momma. We never really prayed at home."

"You know, when I was a little girl, my mom would tell me it doesn't matter how much money you have, your prayers don't cost a thing. You can give out as many as you want and you'll never go broke."

"That's what Lizzie and Candace told me too."

"That's right, so you just keep on praying, honey."

"Mrs. Waters?"

"Yes, love?"

"Since we don't have a name yet for my little sister, I was thinking, maybe I could give her one, until, of course, Momma decides?"

"What'd you have in mind?"

"Well, Lizzie and I were reading this story today about a mermaid who found this little tiny shell at the bottom of the ocean. No one paid attention to it, but somehow it caught her eye because it sparkled like a gem when only she looked at it, so she knew it was special. Most of the other mermaids thought it was boring 'cause it didn't sparkle for them. They just saw this small ordinary shell, but the mermaid was drawn to it because she knew there was something about it that made it ..." She paused, trying to find the right words. "... unique! So, she kept the shell, but what she hadn't expected was when she rubbed it, it started to change. It grew into a beautiful mermaid named Gemma. Gemma was much smaller than the others, but she was beautiful. She even got blessed with magical powers that none of the other mermaids had, and, well, I got to thinking that's kind of like my baby sister. She's little and she's blessed and she's gonna grow into something special too. Lizzie even pointed out that there's a saint named Gemma, so that's what I wanna call her, at least till Momma wakes up. Little Gemma, 'cause I gotta call her something."

Frankie hesitated on the other end of the phone. Saint Gemma had been the patron saint of her mother. The girls hadn't even known. How coincidental that Cammy would choose that name. Frankie lifted her head up to the sky, smiled, and closed her eyes.

"Mrs. Waters? Are you there?"

"I think it's the perfect name, Cammy," Frankie said in her cracked voice.

"By the way, was there something you wanted to tell me?"

"I … I just wanted to tell you that your mom's still resting, but I know she's going to get stronger."

"My prayers must be working! Thanks, Mrs. Waters," Cammy exclaimed as she hung up the phone.

Fresh tears fell as Frankie ended the call. She sat in silence weeping over Olivia and her children. Was it wrong to give Cammy false hope? Hearing the name Gemma felt like a sign her mother was there and somehow everything would be okay. Maybe it was denial that anything bad would happen, or maybe, just maybe, her faith in God's mercy was so strong that Frankie couldn't deny it.

Chapter 30

God sends us friends to be our firm support in the whirlpool of struggle. In the company of friends, we find the strength to attain our sublime ideal.—St. Maximilian Kolbe

Frankie looked down at her watch. It had been almost two hours since her phone call with Birdie. She wiped her face with a crumpled tissue from her pocket. As she turned over her phone to text Birdie, she noticed a missed message. *Must have come through while I was talking to Cammy*

> LUCY: I'm in the room. Birdie's here, and she's brought a surprise.

Frankie scratched her head wondering what the surprise could be. She pushed the tissue down in her pocket and headed back toward the third floor. The morning had felt trancelike with the update of Olivia's unknown state, and now Cammy's choice of name for her sister. The two pieces of news had Frankie's emotions twisted in knots of sorrow and joy. Who knew what the next knot might be?

As she continued toward the room, she sniffled and pulled her tissue out again to compose herself before seeing Birdie. The last thing anyone needed was a blubbering fool, and Frankie had to be strong for Olivia's sake. If she had to discuss her affairs, she could at least do it without high emotions, even though that was far from what she felt inside.

As she arrived on the third floor, something seemed peculiar. She reached Olivia's room and heard thunderous laughter coming from within—too thunderous for just Birdie and Lucy, and out of sorts for a hospital. As she pushed open the door, she saw Birdie along with Judith, Monica, Maisie, and Johnna sitting with Lucy, all surrounding Olivia's bed. The whole gang was there.

Sobs of tears came rushing down, but this time there was no way to hold back.

"Wh-wh-what are you all doing here?" she stammered between sobs.

"Well," said Birdie as she got up to greet her at the door, "seeing this would have been the last day of the book talk, we decided we couldn't just end. Everyone talked it over and we figured if Olivia couldn't come then we'd bring the book talk to her."

Frankie was confused. "To read the book?"

Judith laughed out loud. "Oh, Frankie!" She shook her head as she got up to join Birdie. "You know darn well half of us stopped reading a long time ago. Even I only did it for good show."

"It's us that everyone misses," said Monica. "We miss us."

"Oh!" Frankie said, taken aback. It hadn't occurred to her everyone needed this group as much as she did. "How did I not see this coming?"

"Well, if someone would answer their phone a little more frequently, I wouldn't have had to make it a surprise," joked Birdie.

"Lucy, did you know about this?" Frankie turned to look at her friend.

Lucy winked at Frankie. "I admit, I'm not as good at returning calls either, but I might have known a little something about this morning."

"We couldn't keep going without Olivia," said Maisie.

"Keep going?" Frankie asked.

"Yes," Johnna replied, "Keep going."

"Remember that first day we all said why we started this group?" Birdie asked. "Do you remember what Judith said? 'There's no such thing as coincidences.' We were meant to be here for each other, and God put us in each other's lives. Somehow he knows we all need each other."

"There's no coincidence here. It just makes more sense this way." Judith smiled.

Frankie gazed at them, her heart pounding. "I guess I didn't think you would all want to continue."

"Well, that's a silly thought," said Monica as she stood up from her chair. "Why wouldn't we? We've all helped each other in some small way, and I'd like to think without this group, we'd be two steps behind. If my mom hadn't pushed me to join, then I wouldn't have met you, and if you hadn't helped me with my daughter and understanding my mom, Regina might not be in college."

Judith nodded in agreement.

Birdie looked over at Frankie. "And if I hadn't switched over to the Friday group, my life would be a little more boring. You girls have definitely kept it entertaining."

Frankie giggled through her tears.

Maisie tilted her head toward Frankie. "She's right, we need each other. I mean, everybody knows new experiences have never been a shortcoming in my life, but this church thing intrigues me. Something tells me there's more in store, so I'm definitely not ready to stop."

Johnna walked toward Frankie and put her hand over hers. "And if someone in this group hadn't encouraged me to be okay with letting others help instead of taking it all on my own, I might not have had those little moments with my dad."

Frankie embraced Johnna as Judith and Birdie pulled back to let her slip in. She held on to her for a long time before letting go. Frankie knew her struggles with her dad had been a harrowing ordeal, and yet, she had still made time for this.

"I know this has to be hard being here. How are you holding up?"

Johnna came up from her hug with warm tears drizzling down her face. "Honestly, I'm awful." She wiped some of the tears from her cheek. "Dad's quickly slipping away, and the doctors say he won't make it to the end of the month."

Frankie caressed her arm.

"He's at home like he wants, and we haven't left his side, but my mom pushed me out today and told me if I didn't attend our little gathering, she wouldn't let me take care of him anymore." Johnna sniffled. "I know she doesn't really mean it, but she said I needed some breathing space, and I think she wanted some time by herself with him too."

Frankie squeezed Johnna's hand.

"Funny how our mothers know just what we need," said Monica as she came forward and locked arms with Judith.

"Funny how they just know." Judith stared back at Frankie with a twinkle in her eye.

She looked around the room and understood no matter the hardship to come, she didn't have to face it alone, and even more important she realized they wouldn't let her.

Birdie spread out her hands. "So, you see, we all need this, Frankie."

Frankie let out a deep sigh and allowed her tears to flow, but this time without hiding them.

There was no way to escape the love in the room, and she didn't want to. She looked at Johnna and Judith and the rest of the ladies. "You know, these past few years in my darkness, I understood the part about giving love. It's what my mom always did, so it's what I did to help me get through the hard parts, but I wasn't really giving love, I was just getting through and coping with the pain."

"What do you mean by not giving love?" asked Johnna.

"I didn't fully understand. I was only doing what I thought needed to be done, like staying busy with my family and joining book talks, but the pain never goes away, because grief is love, and love never goes away." Johnna squeezed her hand. "I was so focused on the love I lost on earth, I couldn't see the love surrounding me." Johnna touched her arm. "Remember the day at the café when you told me, 'When you deny others the opportunity to serve, you deny them the opportunity to serve God.' That's kind of like this, because isn't God love?"

Frankie smiled. "You're right. He is. I guess I need to look a little deeper into my own advice." She chuckled.

Maisie got up from her chair and wrapped her arms around Frankie in an overpowering hug. "Well, we love you, and if you're willing to let us, we're here to help you and each other. Lucy's been telling us what an amazing job you've been doing with everything. I can only imagine how hard it has to be."

Frankie took a deep breath. "It's kind of like being in the twilight zone all over again."

"You mentioned to me earlier that you saw the doctor this morning?" said Birdie. "Did she give a promising update for Olivia?"

Frankie pulled away from Maisie and Johnna as she walked over to Olivia's bed rail where Lucy stood. They looked at each other then turned toward the group. She knew in that moment she needed to accept help from others. If she was going to let them in and put her definition of love to the test, now was as good of time as any.

"There's something we need to tell you that, well—"

"That the doctors suggested," Lucy interrupted. "Dr. Camillus said it's good to speak to Olivia so she can hear familiar voices. It might help her."

Frankie stared at Lucy with disbelief. Lucy shrugged.

"I agree," said Monica.

The ladies moved away from the door and circled around Olivia as Frankie quickly yanked Lucy to the side. "What are you doing? I thought we were going to tell them?" she whispered. "We can't lie to them about her situation."

"We're not lying to them. Dr. Camillus did say we should talk to her. I just don't think it's the right time to divulge everything."

Frankie looked at her with arched brows trying to understand Lucy's logic.

"I'm all for being honest, but this is the first time we've been together in a while, and Olivia needs a little cheer. We all do. Let them talk to her before we spill the beans."

Frankie looked long and hard at Lucy. "Okay, I'll follow your lead, but we need to tell them today, before everyone leaves."

"Deal."

They walked toward the bedside to join the rest.

Birdie stood closest to Olivia stroking her hair. "I wonder what's going on in that brain of hers?" Birdie surveyed Olivia's still form then leaned over and smoothed out Olivia's dark curls. "Oh, our sweet girl." She played with her ringlets. "I didn't know how I'd feel seeing you today, but I knew we needed to. The calendar might say this is our last book talk session, but I promise it won't be the last time." Birdie let out a small tear and pulled back.

Lucy nudged Frankie as if to say she was right in holding off on the news.

"No matter what, we're here for you, honey-girl," Birdie finished in a somber tone.

Johnna came forward in Birdie's place. "Olivia," she softly whispered, "my dad loved the succulents. I wish you could've seen the look on his face." Johnna choked back her tears. "I'm afraid he doesn't have much longer, but we're going to keep up his garden. I promised him. And I'm going to need your help to keep it looking good, so you need to be strong enough to help me." Just like Birdie, a few tears seeped out and Frankie looked back at Lucy as if to say, *Maybe this isn't a good idea after all.* But before she could take an action, Maisie jumped in to lighten the mood.

"Olivia, you know you were smart to miss our last session. My chocolate cake didn't go over too well, and I think Johnna would agree with that." She wrapped her arm around Johnna as they laughed through her tears.

"I'm taking a break on cake and wine for a while," said Johnna as a soft laughter enveloped the room.

"I think I'll stick to dogs instead." Maisie chuckled. "But when all is better, and I know it will be, I want you to come out to the house. There's a new litter of mixed-terrier pups for adoption. Maybe if you're up for it, you and Cammy could pick one out."

Monica joined Maisie on the opposite side of the bed. "I know the doctor said it was good for you to hear our voices, but I so wish we could hear yours." Monica looked down at Olivia. "Both of us being young moms, I know you understand the sacrifice. But I'm learning it's okay to not be everything for your child. You have to let them go sometimes. You'd be proud of me. I only cried a little when Regina left for school."

Judith came up beside Monica, holding her hand as she wrapped her arm around her waist.

"Now that I have more time, Mom suggested I join a dance class, but I'm already good with this group, and James still needs me. Just like your daughters are going to need you."

"Speaking of daughters, Lucy told us the good news that you and your girls will be staying with her," remarked Judith.

"We'll be neighbors, Olivia," exclaimed Monica.

Judith grinned. "That's just an extra reason for me to come over more!"

"Hmmm, maybe we should reconsider this after all." Monica laughed as she jabbed her mother's side playfully.

Judith smiled, ignoring Monica's comments.

Lucy grinned. "I say the more the merrier." She turned to look at Olivia. "Well, honey-girl, you already know how I feel about you. I'm ready to be done with this hospital and have you home."

Frankie hoped for the same, but her pragmatic side seemed to be less convinced of the hopeful. Everyone turned to Frankie and waited for her to speak.

She took a deep breath. "Olivia—"

She was interrupted by a soft voice at the door. "Knock, knock ..."

They all turned to see the nurse from the second floor.

"I thought this would be a good time to bring the baby to meet Olivia but ... oh, you have a lot of company. Perhaps I'll come back in a little while."

"No!" contended Frankie. "I mean, I think right now is the perfect time, if it's safe for the baby."

Judith rubbed her palms together with cries of delight. "Oh, the baby! I'm at a loss of words."

Monica laughed. "Well, that's a first."

The nurse wheeled in the incubator as Maisie, Judith, and Birdie tried to step out of the way, simultaneously peeking through the windows of the tiny incubator.

The nurse gently wheeled the baby next to Olivia's bedside as Lucy stood close by like a mother bird protecting its nest.

"Oh, Frankie this is such a treat to see the baby," exclaimed Birdie.

"This must be the best therapy, having Olivia visit with her. Does she get to visit with her often?" asked Maisie.

Everyone watched as the nurse carefully opened the incubator, then partially pulled down Olivia's hospital gown to reveal her left shoulder so the baby would be able to feel the warmth of her mother's flesh.

"Actually, it's her first time," replied Frankie.

Everyone watched as the baby stayed crunched up with her feet close to her stomach as the nurse gently placed her on Olivia's chest.

Lucy sighed. "Her first time meeting her mother and we're all here. How appropriate since we're all truly her family."

Frankie imagined the baby could hear the familiarity of Olivia's heartbeat, only this time from the outside.

"Her first time?" cried Judith. "And to think she hasn't been able to hold her. Or even give her a name." The faces in the room turned sour at Judith's statement.

"Mom, don't be a downer." Monica nudged her.

"Actually," Frankie put her finger in the air. "The baby has a name, and it's Gemma."

"Gemma?" repeated a surprised Lucy. "But I thought we agreed we'd wait till Olivia woke up. Who named her?"

"Cammy did." Frankie told them about her conversation that morning with Cammy and the story of the mermaid. There was no way she could deny it.

"Then that's what we'll name her unless Olivia has any objections when she wakes up," declared Lucy. She looked down at the baby snuggled on Olivia's chest as she took in the smell and skin of her mother. "Our precious Gemma."

All of a sudden, beeping sounds came from the machines in the room. Frankie felt faint and looked around in distress. "What's happening?"

"I don't think we're going to have to wait long to find out if she objects," whispered Johnna.

Frankie moved closer to the bed.

Olivia's eyes had opened.

Chapter 31

I thank my God every time I remember you.
—Philippians 1:3 (NIV)

Frankie composed herself as she stepped forward to enter Johnna's mother's house. "It was a beautiful ceremony, Mrs. Campos."

Mrs. Campos nodded with a soft smile, looking past Frankie as she mumbled her words of thanks in a daze. Only an hour earlier, she had been seated in the front row of St. Seton's watching as the maple-wood casket of Jonathan Nathaniel Campos was being anointed with frankincense by Father Gabe to commemorate his life, baptism, and now death. His wife's pale face remained in a trance as she greeted the numerous guests who had arrived and those who bypassed St. Anne's cemetery and were already settled in the outside seating of the garden.

Frankie noticed the woman had been so withdrawn that Johnna and her aunts had to carry out the exact requests for the funeral. The ceremony, just like Mr. Campos, had been simple and unassuming. Johnna had organized everything perfectly. The grandchildren had assembled a beautiful slideshow showcasing some of the highlights of his life, while a nephew had spoken of his favorite Uncle Johnnie and how he'd influenced him when making a big career decision. But Frankie was most amazed that Johnna had spoken during the service. She'd recollected her father's entry to the United States from Mexico as a new citizen and the many jobs he'd taken provide for his family. Johnna's stoic composure bewildered her. Frankie knew she would be the one to step up and be the strong one, but it didn't dismiss her dark and heavy eyes as she now laid out trays of food and small bites for the guests in attendance.

Johnna had prepared every detail, from the rosary, to the readings, to the selection of flowers and food. Everything was pristine but simple, down to the last candle and flower arrangement. Frankie and Scarlet left Mrs. Campos and made their way to the backyard where beautiful scenery adorned Mr. Campos's garden, the perfect scenery for his reception. They headed toward the gazebo, which was intertwined with clematis and honeysuckle.

"Wow, this backyard is amazing," said Scarlet, taking in the sights as she plopped onto one of the benches in the gazebo with her arm in a sling. The yard was scattered with beautiful perennials, filling up the flowerbeds and spreading along the fence line with trellises of sweet clematis giving off an aromatic scent.

"Well, I guess Johnna wasn't exaggerating when she said her father had a love for gardening," Frankie said as she admired the extensive landscape and the river rock.

Near the gazebo lay asters, Russian sage, and other flowers Frankie didn't recognize. The plants continued to spread over the flowerbeds as marigolds and petunias wrapped around the walk paths. Frankie noticed statues of singing angels centered near the rock fountain. There was even a small section of cactus rose succulents situated near the gazebo. These must have been the ones Olivia had given to Johnna for her father. They now lay perfectly positioned around the gazebo flowerbed.

"I don't know how she's going to keep up the maintenance of this, but it's beautiful," Scarlet said, snapping a few pictures. The weight of her camera was still too much so she had resorted to using her phone.

"I worry about her. She's got so much on her plate," admitted Frankie.

Scarlet continued snapping pictures. "Just watching her exhausts me."

Frankie watched as Scarlet zoomed in to capture Johnna moving around the backyard, saying hello to guests and family members who offered their cordial sympathies. "My battery would run out if I had to talk to all those people," Scarlet said.

While the ceremony may have been simple, the reception at the house was far from what Mr. Campos might have wanted. Johnna had submitted to receiving help. Even though she had told everyone she would bring in catering, a king's feast resulted when numerous cousins brought oodles of food. Frankie imagined there would be food leftover for weeks. Nevertheless, Johnna scurried around, checking on napkins and plates and anything she noticed missing.

"I think she just wants to make all this perfect for her dad," Frankie said in her defense. "Besides, it probably gives her something to do to stay on autopilot."

"You're probably right, and we don't want a repeat of the coffee shop," Scarlet replied, remembering the day Johnna had her big breakdown.

Frankie nodded. Just as she was about to tell Scarlet to take some candid pictures for Johnna, Lucy and Olivia arrived and greeted them.

"Well, that was definitely a beautiful ceremony. Johnna has exquisite taste—not too grand but just the right amount," Lucy said as she pushed Olivia's wheelchair next to the gazebo.

Frankie greeted them with a smile. "Hi, girls. Here, let me help you."

"I've got it—just hold Gemma for me," Olivia insisted. "I want to get out of this thing and sit on a bench."

Frankie took little Gemma out of her hands. The sweet baby was wrapped tightly in a cotton periwinkle blanket, sound asleep and unaware of everything around her. Frankie breathed in her baby smell and watched patiently as Olivia slowly arched forward, pushing herself out of the chair so she could move toward the gazebo.

"Dr. Camillus says with some physical therapy and rest, I should be back to my old self soon enough."

"You're getting stronger every day," said Frankie. "It doesn't seem like a month has gone by since you left the hospital. You're doing incredibly well and so quickly."

"I know! The doctors are just astonished at how quickly she's improved," said Lucy.

Frankie saw Olivia still seemed weak from the surgeries and giving birth, but her recovery had been quicker than expected.

"Time heals everything," said Olivia with a coy smile as she made her way to the gazebo bench.

Frankie timidly smiled back. They had never really discussed what happened the night of the attack or even their disagreement, but their exchanges over the past month had shown Frankie they'd reconciled.

Frankie joined her in the gazebo and sat next to Scarlet. They looked down at tiny Gemma, savoring her little smells and sleepy coos, as Olivia rested on the bench across from them.

"Well, you look better that I thought. I was expecting you to look worse," Scarlet said as Olivia comfortably positioned herself.

"You too. From what you described over the phone I figured you'd be in a full body cast."

"It finally came off. The itching was so uncomfortable, but now I can move around easier," said Scarlet, cradling her arm.

"I'm sure you're eager to get back to work now."

Scarlet shrugged. "Sergeant Waters over here won't let me work. She says I need to rest."

"Just until your sling comes off. You barely got your body cast off last week and it would do you some good to just enjoy this time. Your clients aren't going anywhere," assured Frankie.

"I guess I enjoy having a little more leisure time, and Charles got me hooked on watching some old Western shows. Black and white TV really makes you appreciate the technology we have now. So, how's everything going for you?"

"Lucy's a great caretaker. I told her it'll only be temporary, so I can get back to work soon."

Lucy stood at the edge of the gazebo, smiling. "You know you're welcome to stay as long as you want, Olivia. Besides, I already told you there's no timeline. And you're making so much progress. There was never a doubt in my mind, isn't that right, Frankie?"

Frankie nodded. "She refused to believe any differently."

Olivia turned the topic back to Scarlet. "Sounds like Charles has been a big help too?"

"Yeah, he's all right." Scarlet tried to play it off as if she didn't enjoy his company, but her blushing cheeks gave her away. "But having him around has been helpful, and I didn't realize how great of a cook he is. I'm so used to ordering out."

Olivia crossed her legs. "Sounds like he's worth keeping around."

"I still wonder why he sticks around, but I can't seem to get rid of him," joked Scarlet.

Olivia laughed. "Well, if he's still around after everything you've been through, I'd say he's not going anywhere."

Frankie watched as Scarlet fidgeted with the settings on her phone's camera. While she had made some progress dealing with feelings, she wasn't a completely changed woman. As she kept shifting in her seat, Frankie stepped in to change the topic.

"So, how's Cammy adjusting without the girls?"

"She really misses seeing them on a daily basis, but we're starting to get into a routine. It's been quite a change, but she likes being with Lucy and helping her around the house. Lucy even bought her one of those mermaid blankets that she could wrap her legs in and some decorations for her room."

Lucy sat next to Olivia. "Every girl needs to be a mermaid now and then." She looked across at Gemma sleeping in Frankie's arms. "These girls are like my very own granddaughters. And with your help, Frankie, to get Cammy off to school, we've made it work."

Olivia smiled as she listened to Lucy. Frankie realized it had been a good arrangement for both of them.

"Well, when you're ready to return to work, Olivia, you just let me know," Scarlet said as she fidgeted with her sling. "Or even if you, uh, just want to come over for a visit."

"Visits would be a nice start." Olivia grinned back at Scarlet as they sat in quiet for a moment, unsure where to take the conversation. The moment felt awkward but not uncomfortable. Asking Olivia to simply visit had been a big step for Scarlet, and Frankie was proud she was working on topics mostly unrelated to work. Frankie broke the quiet again with more small talk.

"Little Gemma is growing every day, isn't she? How much is she up to?"

"She's about seven pounds now. She'll be two months on the fifteenth."

"She seems so small, but I guess for a preemie that's big, right?" wondered Scarlet.

"Yeah, the doctors say she's perfectly fine. That is if you think about her just being born on her original delivery date, she doesn't seem much different than a newborn."

Frankie nodded.

"Well, this little one certainly has an appetite beyond a newborn," commented Lucy. "She's hungry all the time!"

"Whose talking about appetites? I'm starving," mumbled a voice from behind.

Frankie turned to see Judith approaching with Maisie, Birdie, and Monica. She had already snuck over to the appetizers and made a plate for herself and was happily shoveling a stuffed mushroom into her mouth.

"Mom! Where did you get that? They haven't started serving the food yet," Monica said, realizing what her mother had in her hands.

Judith swallowed down the bit of mushroom before responding. "Hey, there's no sign that says I can't have a little snack."

"It's just rude to help yourself until it's been offered," Monica said.

"Well, its rude to just leave it there and not tell anyone if the food is ready. Besides, I've known Julia Campos for a long time and she loves with food. She would want me to help myself and—Wow, look at all these marigolds along the walk path. This garden is really something!" Judith's attention had somehow shifted to the garden. Frankie wondered if the change was intentional.

"It really is," Maisie said, as she pointed to the tall purple flowers swaying in the corner of the yard. "Is that naturally growing lavender?"

Lucy shrugged. "Whatever that purple stuff is, it makes this place look like the cover of a magazine. I wonder what Johnna's going to do with this place? There's no way her mom can maintain all of this."

"Who knows? But I'm sure it's going to need a lot of maintenance," said Maisie.

Judith sighed. "I overheard some of her cousins talk about what they could swindle from her mother. Poor thing. I've been there before with family fighting over possessions. Julia isn't even herself right now, and I'm sure some smug relative will try to take advantage of it."

"Not if Johnna can help it," Frankie said. "I just hope she takes a break after this."

"At the rate she's going, she could run a half-marathon," said Scarlet.

"Scarlet, I didn't see you there." Judith passed her half-eaten plate to Monica and stepped into the gazebo. She leaned in to gently give Scarlet a hug, pushing Frankie over so she could sit between them. "Frankie said you were looking and feeling better, sweet girl. Oh, it's so good to see you. You know I still have someone in mind I want to fix you up with."

Scarlet laughed at Judith's straightforward approach. "I'm actually seeing someone. He's been helping take care of me."

"Well, I hope he's a cute one, but if you ever change your mind, you know where to find me."

Scarlet's face turned beet red.

Monica rolled her eyes and lifted up her hands along with Judith's plate. She knew it was no use trying to contain her mother. Frankie and Olivia smirked. So much for Scarlet trying to get out of the limelight.

Birdie stretched out her hand. "Scarlet, I don't know if we've officially met, but your cousin over here keeps us posted on things, and I'm glad to hear you're doing so well. I'm Birdie."

"Thanks. It's nice to meet you too." Scarlet sighed, a clear indicator she was glad to change the topic.

Birdie cupped her hands and lifted her shoulders. "Since it seems you're pretty acquainted already with everyone, have you thought about joining our little group?"

"I thought it was a book talk. That's what Frankie always calls it."

"Well, technically it is, but then again you'd have to finish the book to actually call it anything, and we never got to that part."

Everyone laughed.

"Didn't you guys read something on heaven or angels or something like that?" Scarlet asked.

"It was on near-death experiences, and it was fascinating," Judith said. "I do intend to finish it. I'm just not very good at sticking to timelines."

"I agree," Maisie said, then turned to Scarlet. "You should join us. We don't really have a title but we're all like sisters."

"More like daughters," said Scarlet.

"Daughters? Why would you say that?" Birdie asked.

"Scarlet has nicknamed us the Grieving Daughters' Club," Frankie said. "But I think that was more for me than the rest of you."

367

Everyone stared at Scarlet. She looked down at the flowerbed, avoiding eyes as she kept crossing and uncrossing her legs.

Maisie laughed. "You know, I kind of like that."

"I do too," said Judith.

Scarlet breathed a sigh of relief.

"But you haven't lost a parent and neither have I," Monica said to Maisie.

"I don't know. It kind of sounds mysterious, and I never know how to refer to us. Besides, we're all daughters to somebody, right?"

Birdie made the sign of the cross. "Amen to that."

"It makes us sound younger anyway, being daughters, doesn't it?" Judith said as she smoothed her hand across her overly hair-sprayed helmet hair.

Frankie laughed. "I'm fine with calling our group 'daughters,' but I didn't realize we needed a name for all of this."

"We don't need a name, but I kind of like having one," said Maisie. "It's nice to feel like we have a special place where we all belong. And while I haven't had as many experiences with grief as the rest of you, I kind of like having that support. One day, I know I'll need it."

"But you just said we're not a grief group," said Lucy.

"No, but I did say we're a group of women who need each other."

"And grief isn't always about death, there's all sorts of loss," added Olivia.

Monica wriggled her eyebrows in thought. "I guess you're right."

Judith grinned. "Well, the Grieving Daughters' Club it is, and Scarlet, you have been officially initiated into the club."

Everyone yelled "hear, hear," although none of them had glasses to toast.

The cheer drew eyes toward the gazebo, and Frankie noticed strange looks from some of Johnna's relatives.

Monica dropped her voice to a whisper. "Hey, we should probably wait on any more cheers or making our club constitution. It doesn't seem right to celebrate at a funeral reception, and besides Johnna's not with us to decide."

"It's kind of ironic that we've formed a grief club while at a funeral reception, don't you think?" Scarlet asked.

"For the last time, we're not a grief club—that's just the name," said Maisie. "Besides, like Birdie said, grief isn't just death. Sometimes we mourn over things in life we've lost, like a job, or relationships, or what could have been. It's not just people."

"I never thought of it that way," said Monica. "Pretty insightful."

"There's still some level of coincidence, though," Scarlet chimed in.

Everyone looked at Judith and then around to each other.

Judith snapped her fingers. "There's no such thing as coincidences!"

Everyone started giggling, but this time they tried to keep their voices down so that Johnna's family wouldn't stare at them. Ironically, Johnna walked in their direction and they quickly straightened up.

"Well, what are all you ladies cackling about? I could hear big cheers from across the yard. I'm guessing it's not to salute my dad," Johnna said as she interrupted the conversation and joined the ladies. Her joke seemed a bit morbid for the occasion, but if she felt comfortable enough to make a death joke, no one was going to correct her.

"We didn't know if you were going make it over here," said Maisie, as she stepped down from the gazebo to give Johnna a big embrace.

"Well, truth be told, I heard you ladies cheering about something, and it was the perfect escape away from my cousins to 'check on other guests.' I can't tell you how glad I am to get out of family conversations right now." She stepped up into the gazebo and took the empty spot next to Olivia.

"How are you doing, honey?" said Lucy, reaching over Olivia to pat her hand.

"To be honest, I think my hair spray is stronger than I am right now. Thank the Lord, I got the extra hold. Most of this is just a blur."

Johnna released a big sigh and stretched her legs out as she slumped back onto the gazebo bench. "Scarlet, Olivia, it's so good to see you," she said as she reached across to squeeze Olivia's hand. "It means a lot to me that you came today."

"I wouldn't have missed it," Olivia said as she squeezed back.

"And everything is so beautiful. You've outdone yourself," said Lucy.

"Honestly, I just want today to be over. All my relatives leave tomorrow, and between my cousin Bernice and Louis thinking they have some kind of input on how to handle the reception and my mother's house, I'm just ready to crawl into bed and stay there for a while."

"You deserve some rest," said Lucy. "From what I've heard, you planned the whole ceremony. I'm impressed at how you keep it all together. I don't think rest is too much to ask."

"Has anyone seen Johnna?" a distant voice said from the steps of the porch.

Frankie turned to see a woman with a large bust, dark curly hair, and a sinister look on her face.

"Hide me! That's Bernice. She keeps asking if she can buy my dad's car. My other cousin, Louise, wants dibs too, and I just don't want to deal with transactions and family inventory. I'm not ready to think about all that. My mom certainly isn't."

"Don't ya love family drama?" Monica said.

"My dad was so clear about what he wanted with his funeral, but he never made a will," Johnna said. "I wish he'd been clearer about that. Now on the day of his funeral I've got vulture-like cousins waiting to pick apart his possessions. It's just overwhelming."

"Does your mom have any input? Wouldn't she want to decide?" asked Birdie.

"She's so out of it right now, she'd sign over the house if someone put a pen in front of her, and that's what scares me. My family will try to take advantage of the situation. I have to stay on guard, so they don't try to corner her. I'd be over there right now, but I just needed a break from my cousin Louise's husband's horrible jokes. Liam has no sense of propriety, and he thinks it's funny to come up behind everyone and grab their love handles. I swear if he comes by me one more time, I'm going to scream!"

Frankie cringed as she spotted cousin Louise in the distance trying to talk Bernice out of the vehicle as her husband wrapped his arm around Bernice's mid-section.

"Someone talk about something else so I can have at least a moment to escape."

"Well, we were just initiating Scarlet into our little club here," said Judith puffing out her chest.

"I didn't know we were an official club," said Johnna, "but I like that idea. What are we going to call ourselves?"

"We were just, uh ..." Monica stumbled.

Frankie could see she was trying to gather her thoughts. Fortunately, Birdie interrupted.

"The Grieving Daughters' Club, but it's not quite what you think."

A silence came over the group as everyone looked at Johnna's reaction, unsure if this had been the right time.

After a moment, Johnna spoke up. "You know, I kind of like that name."

Frankie sighed with relief, followed by Scarlet and Monica.

"I don't care if you call us the Stinking Cheese Club, I just know that I'm blessed by all of you," said Johnna.

Judith relaxed her shoulders. "Well, that's a relief." She got up from the gazebo to get another bite from the plate Monica was still holding.

"Well, when you're ready, honey, and it's okay with Birdie, I'd like to have some of our gatherings at my house," said Lucy. "I know we had all the book meetings at Birdie's, but with the baby and Olivia, it will be easier. Besides, I've been wanting to entertain with my fabulous backyard, and I have yet to throw Olivia an appropriate baby shower."

"I'm fine with that." Birdie smiled.

"Oh, that would be lovely," said Johnna. She stroked the blanket of the baby as Frankie handed her back to Olivia. Suddenly Johnna's attention diverted past the baby and in the direction of Judith.

"Put that down!" Johnna yelled.

Judith spat the meatball onto her plate. "I'm sorry. I didn't think it was that big of a deal."

"Put down those roses right now!" Johnna sailed past Judith, hitting her shoulder as she stormed toward her cousin Louise who was standing on the far side of the yard clipping a Tudor blossom. Louise peered up too late in an attempt to stash the garden shears behind her. "Do you think you can just come in here and snip any flower you want? It's bad enough that you shoved a bunch of cookies in your purse, and I've had to put up with your ungrateful children all day as well as your husband, who thinks he's funny by grabbing all of us uncomfortably, but don't you dare think you can come here and take even one petal of these flowers!"

"Johnna, relax," her cousin said. "They're just flowers. It's just a memory of Uncle Johnnie." She blushed with embarrassment as more eyes focused on them.

"Just flowers?" Johnna screamed. "Just flowers? Don't tell me to relax. My father worked hard on this garden and you're trying to snatch a freebie like you always do!"

"Johnna, stop!" Mrs. Campos feebly yelled to Johnna from across the yard.

Johnna reached her cousin and yanked the shears out of her hand. "If you really wanted a memory of my dad, you should have come and visited him more."

Louise puffed up her chest up as she glared at the stares now directed at her. "You have some nerve, Johnna Christine," Louise said, then spun around and yanked Liam away from her other cousin.

"And don't even think about my dad's car! And take your groping, perverted husband with you!" Johnna added at the last minute as Louise slammed through the side fence to leave.

Johnna looked back at all the guests staring at her with open mouths. Only little Gemma, who Olivia was now trying to console, made any sound. Johnna collapsed on the ground weeping, triggering some of the guests to leave.

Scarlet whispered to Frankie, "Well, at least there's no coffee mugs involved this time."

Lucy ran over to Johnna with Maisie and Monica close behind. They squatted down to the ground, attempting to help her up, but she resisted.

"Honey, you okay?" said Lucy.

"No, no, I'm not okay. That cow doesn't even realize how much hard work my father put into this garden. For her to just pick a rose like it's not a big deal!"

"Just get it all out," said Monica rubbing her back.

"How dare she think she has some kind of claim on this backyard. And don't even think I'm going to let her get her grubby hands on his car."

"Honey, maybe you just need to rest for the day. We'll help your cousins. You need a break." Maisie looked at Monica who nodded.

"He's gone ... he's gone," Johnna's head dropped further as heavy weeping overcame her.

By this time, Birdie, Frankie, Scarlet, and Judith had now walked over to surround their friend and block conspicuous eyes from staring.

"I just can't believe he's gone. One minute he was back here planting flowers and weeding the garden, and the next we're talking about his last request, and now he's not even here."

Lucy looked down at Johnna with soft eyes. "There's nothing easy about losing a loved one. But honey, don't think for one second that these flowers are all that's left of your dad."

Johnna looked up with dark, broken eyes as Lucy continued.

Lucy squatted next to her friend. "These flowers are going to wither away too, but you, your children, your family, and the memories that you created will all continue to live on. You'll keep him alive in all that you do."

Johnna used her sleeve to wipe away a tear. "I just can't believe he won't be here."

"He may not be here in the physical, but he's here, Johnna. Mark my word, he's here," said Judith.

"What do you mean?"

"He's here in you." Lucy lightly touched Johnna's chest.

"But I still want him here. Physically here."

"I know you do. And that's what's hard about death. We don't always get what we want."

Tears continued to pour out of Johnna as Frankie came to squat down beside her and Lucy. "Listen, my friend. This is all new for you and, well, frankly, you're going to feel the loss and emptiness for a while. You're going to be lonely. You're going to be emotional and upset, then angry, then wonder what you did right or didn't do right. And then you might go back and do it all over again in a different order."

Johnna frowned. "You're not very good at making me feel better."

"The point is you're going to feel so many things that your head will spin, but the good news is, we're all here for you. We've all been through it in our own way. We've all grieved, and, believe me, one day when you least expect it, you'll find that the days are a little lighter. They'll never be exactly the same, but they will be a little easier to get through." Frankie extended her hand to help her up.

Johnna pushed her bangs out of her face and rubbed her eyes before grabbing Frankie's hand. "How long will that be?"

"Nobody knows," Judith interrupted. "It's different for everyone. When my mother died, I couldn't do things for almost three years, but I faked it and found that actually made it harder and longer. One day I looked up and saw my daughter looking at me, and I saw my mother's eyes in hers, and that let me know she was okay. So, let yourself feel the sadness. Don't bury it or it'll catch you when you least expect it."

"Like on ungrateful cousins," joked Lucy.

Johnna chuckled through her sniffles.

"But don't try to rush it," added Frankie. "Just know at the end of the day, we're here for you. That's all that matters."

"Thanks." Johnna sniffled as Frankie passed her a second tissue. "I guess the Grieving Daughters' Club is a good name after all." She smiled at the women surrounding her. "I'd better get back to see where my mother is, and I'm sure I have to apologize to some relatives."

"Will your cousin Louise be okay?" asked Maisie.

"I'll have to apologize to her too, but she'll be fine, although I'm not taking back anything I said about her creepy husband."

Judith and Lucy chuckled.

Johnna looked over her shoulder and mouthed the words "I'm sorry" to Olivia, who was still sitting in the gazebo with the baby, finally consoled. Olivia smiled back, indicating all was right.

When Johnna was completely inside, Judith commented, "I'm guessing it's okay now to get some appetizers, although I'll probably bypass the meatballs just to be on the safe side. What do you say, Birdie? Will you join me?"

"Sure, I could use some right now and maybe even a glass of wine."

"I'll join you too." Scarlet stood, holding the sling with her injured arm close to her chest.

"Well, I guess I'll go too," Monica said. "I need to make sure you don't put any mushrooms in your purse, Mom, and I want to help some of Johnna's cousins where I can."

Maisie put her arm out to Lucy. "We'll help too, although I want to check out that purple flower first before I go inside."

"That's what family does!" Lucy said and wrapped her arm in a hook with Maisie's.

Frankie noticed Olivia was now the only one inside the gazebo. "I'll be over here." She walked to Olivia's side, shaking her head. "Well," Frankie said, "that was definitely a heavy moment, wasn't it?"

"Yeah, it was pretty heavy all right."

"But I totally get it," said Frankie. "I know exactly what she's going through."

"Yeah, that moment when you realize they're never coming back is a pretty big shocker, though I was so young I only have small glimpses of it."

"Well, mine wasn't too long ago, and it hits you hard, although it was definitely not as public as this one." Frankie sighed. "But I have to agree with Judith—it's slowly getting easier. It's just getting used to it, that's all."

"Well, isn't that what life is all about? Getting used to things we aren't always prepared for?"

Frankie looked at her and frowned.

"I mean, if things always stayed the same, then we'd never blossom." Olivia looked out over the flowers surrounding them. "Take this garden for instance. You need a lot of fertilizer to keep it going. Even the crappy stuff gets it to bloom regularly."

"Hmm. Funny analogy, but accurate. You seem so at ease about this topic."

"I guess my time in the hospital helped me recognize all my blessings."

"I wish I had understood that concept sooner, but if only we didn't have to go through so much stuff sometimes."

"Not everyone needs to or goes through the same, but I'm kind of glad I did. I mean I don't like it, but I wouldn't be here sitting here with you, holding Gemma, if I hadn't. Johnna will see in her time. Just because we see it doesn't mean she won't. Right now she just needs to feel the sadness."

Frankie looked at Olivia and scratched her head. Something had changed in her.

"Since we're on the topic, I never did thank you, Frankie."

"For what?"

"For butting into my life."

Frankie was a bit taken aback. "But I had ... I thought you saw me as being too intrusive."

"You are," she teased. "But I guess sometimes we don't always know what we need. Your intrusiveness followed me to the warehouse and helped me stand up for myself. It got me a job and helped me prioritize this precious baby that's in my arms—that I might have aborted out of fear. I know you heard me talk the night of the accident, but I never told you personally."

Tears swelled in Frankie's eyes. She took a deep breath. "I had rehearsed in my head so many times what I would say to you once you were awake. I wanted to tell you I was sorry, that I wanted to make things right between us. It never felt like the right time. But what worried me most was what might have happened if you didn't wake up. Would I ever get the chance? I would have taken it so hard if something different had happened. But now that we're sitting here, I don't even know what to say. I wasn't expecting you to thank me."

"Truth be told, I could've easily stayed. I wanted to stay where I was, but 'they' wouldn't let me."

"Stay in the hospital? Why would you want to stay in the hospital longer than you had to?"

Olivia looked to the sky as a smiled crossed her face. "I mean stay with them while I was in the hospital." Olivia pointed to the angel statues in the corner of the garden dancing and singing.

"You saw angels, Olivia?"

She nodded. "And I saw people too. They told me I needed to come back. They said my daughters would be fine, but I had work to do, and I had people who needed me."

"Are you saying you had a near-death experience?"

Olivia laughed and closed her eyes. "It was the most beautiful place. There were colors I can't even describe, and lots of rooms, one reserved just for me. And for the first time in my life, I felt a tremendous amount of love I can't even explain."

"Wow, I can't believe it."

"But they kept saying, 'You need to go back. You haven't finished.' The one that talked to me ... she looked a lot like you, like that picture in your hallway, Frankie."

Frankie's heart skipped a beat. Could it be? Could Olivia have seen her mother?

"Did she say her name ... the one who looked like me?" Tears welled in Frankie's eyes.

Olivia smiled as she reflected on the moment. "No, but I had a sense that I knew her somehow. I told her I didn't want to return, but she said I had some important tasks still ahead. There would still be some tough times, but it would all be worth it. So, you see, while the hard times are certain, the other side is worth the sacrifice. She said God would see me through, and she would be watching me too."

"Why didn't you say anything before?"

Olivia shrugged as she looked down at Gemma. "It never seemed like the right time. Now it's right."

Frankie continued to cry, but with a new lightness. "Did they tell you what you have to do?"

"No, not exactly. They said that when the time came, I would know when to step in and be there. I guess the mystery of life is not knowing. Besides, if I did, I'm sure my stubbornness would try to get the better of me." She laughed.

Frankie smiled through her tears. "Well, I'm just … wow!"

"So, I guess the next step is to give it to God and move forward. But something that I've learned from all of this is that we all have our own journey. We all have to figure it out. And that God also puts some great people in front of us, if we ask him."

Frankie placed a hand on Olivia's shoulder. "Well, if it's any consolation, I'm glad they sent you back. I know I need you, and I should really be the one to thank you."

"You don't need to thank me, Frankie."

"Oh, but I do. These past couple of years haven't been easy, and you taught me about the love that's still here. I'm grateful to you."

"Well, that makes two of us," she said smiling. "By the way, Cammy's been talking a lot about getting baptized. I don't know much about it, but I know she and Gemma will need a godmother. Since I, uh, already know you'll be the intrusive kind and they'll need a good role model in their life, maybe even guide me a little too, what do you say? Will you be their godmother?"

Frankie was still crying, but her tears changed to joy.

She looked down at little Gemma and put her finger out to touch her tiny fingers. "I'd be more than happy to be intrusive."

The End

About the Author

ANDREA BEAR believes that learning life lessons is easier to digest when presented in the form of a story. Feeling the call to write about her grief journey after losing her mother to brain cancer in 2018, she created *Grieving Daughters' Club* to share the experiences some face after loss, tucking a little bit of herself and her lessons into each character. She is already working on the second book of a three-part series. In addition, she is a journalist for *HERLIFE* magazine and contributes articles to online sites such as www.catholicmom.com, and www. queenofpeacemedia.com. She is also a high school history teacher in Stockton, California. When she's not writing or teaching she is shuffling one of her three daughters to volleyball practice or relaxing at a local vineyard with her husband. To read more about her work check out her website at www.andreabearauthor.com

Made in the USA
Monee, IL
15 September 2022

14055459R00216